Mia Merrill

# THE IRON WEB

Larken Rose

*Special thanks to my wife, Tessa,*
*for her extensive help on this book,*
*as a co-author as much as an editor.*

———⊙⊙⊙———

*This book is dedicated to my daughter,*
*Elyssa Layne Rose;*
*may she live to see a better world.*

# PART I

**JESSICA** Carlisle was shocked into consciousness when her radio came on suddenly, her dreams interrupted by a reporter's phony voice in mid-sentence: " ... into its third week, with no apparent progress toward a peaceful resolution." Her hand instinctively swung from under the covers, landing on the snooze button, returning her room to relative silence. For the next few minutes, the tiny hint of consciousness in Jessica's mind struggled to achieve full wakefulness.

"It's your big day, Munchkin," came her father's voice from the hall, followed by a knock on her door. "Get a move on."

That's right, I'm leaving on my trip today, Jessica thought, opening her eyes a crack. "I'm up, I'm up," was her groggy reply, followed by a muttered, "sort of." Her mind reviewed the morning agenda she had planned the night before: finish packing by 8:00, leave for the airport at 8:20, get there by 9:00, and make it through all the checking in and boarding stuff in time for her flight to leave at 11:09. She fully opened her eyes to the familiar sight of her hamster, Brutus, in his cage next to her bed, doing his usual morning mad dash to nowhere on his little wheel. "Good morning, little beastie," she said to him. "I'll miss you. I'll remind the retard again about feeding you." Brutus continued running as if she hadn't spoken.

She managed to throw off her covers, sit up and swing her feet off the bed onto the floor. Her grogginess was falling away as her excitement rose. In a few short hours, she would be on her way to California to meet her cousin—the relatively sane member of a weird family—for their long-awaited camping trip near Sequoia National Park. Jessica had never really been camping before, not what she would consider "real camping," out in the wild without any facilities. But she'd slept outside and cooked outside before, and she didn't squeal in terror at the mere sight of a bug, like some of her school friends. She thought she could probably survive four days and three nights in the wilderness, if a clearing in the woods three miles from a motel could be considered "wilderness." She and her cousin Peggy were going to roam the area, getting lost on purpose, and then find their way back to camp using the GPS that her father had just given her for Christmas. Other than being a little worried about meeting a bear in the wild, she expected the trip to be easy enough. She knew that not many of her friends would think of it as a great way to spend one's nineteenth birthday, but it had sounded like a fun adventure to her.

Her mom bustled in with a tray of breakfast, including toast, egg, and orange juice. "Now hush up," she said immediately, before Jessica could protest. "I know you stayed up too late last night and didn't leave time in your schedule for breakfast. But I want you to eat something. Just sit down for ten minutes and eat. What's left to pack?"

"Just my bathroom stuff, after I use it." Jessica submitted gracefully to her mother's will and picked up the glass of juice. She hated eating breakfast, but she didn't want to argue this morning.

"We'll get everything else into the car, then," said her mom.

Jessica forced down half of the breakfast and put the tray aside. On her way to the bathroom, she stopped at her full-length mirror to survey herself. She'd showered the night before, to save time in the morning, and let her hair dry in bed. What she saw now was a huge, unruly mass of wavy, dark brown hair, with brown eyes barely peeking through, and a twisted tangle of baggy, red-and-white Snoopy pajamas. "Got some room for improvement, I think," she muttered to herself, and hobbled toward the bathroom.

It took Jessica twenty minutes to transform herself into the perfect picture of a young American woman: the dark mass of hair tamed into sleek waves framing her slightly freckled face, and just enough makeup to accentuate her features. The Snoopy pajamas were discarded on the bathroom floor in favor of blue jeans and a pink sweater, which casually displayed the contours of a slender, athletic figure.

"The car's warming up, Munchkin," her father called up the stairs.

Jessica threw on her fur-lined boots, hat, gloves, and coat, kissed her mother, grabbed her bag of bathroom stuff, and ran out to the car. All sleepiness was gone now, swept away by the biting January wind and the excitement of flying to California.

---

**JASON** Reilly peered through the scope, the image gradually becoming more and more steady, until the crosshairs rested solidly on the target: an empty .223 casing sitting atop a cardboard box fifty yards away. Jason felt his heart rate and respiration slow, and steadily increased pressure on the trigger. He always imagined the shot just as it should be, just before the gun fired. The quiet was shattered, and his M16 jumped from the blast. When the scope steadied again, the shell was nowhere to be seen.

"Holy smokes," commented Miguel, a large, muscular man sitting in a folding chair nearby, looking downrange through binoculars. "He actually did it."

"I could do that," said a thinner man standing next to Miguel with his arms crossed, "if I had a few tries." The second man's name was Mark, but he was generally called "Red" because of his curly heap of bright reddish-orange hair. Pale-skinned and freckled, he had the demeanor of a class clown with a streak of arrogance.

"From prone, with a bipod, maybe—if you had all day," answered Miguel, lowering the binoculars. "But Jay here just did it in one shot from kneeling. That's some serious marksmanship."

"Yeah, but could you do that in the heat of battle?" Red asked, walking up to Jason and giving him a thump on the back with a closed fist. "Could you do it when it really counts?"

"Ow," said Jason, flipping the safety on. "I hope I never have to."

Jason came from a long line of police officers, but he was the first in his family to become a federal agent. Although three of his grandparents were Irish, he favored his Italian grandmother with his straight, jet-black hair and olive skin. Some of his fellow agents had taken to calling him "pretty boy" because of his youthful good looks, especially the dark brown eyes framed by long, dark lashes that girls envied. Now even his brothers were calling him that, which annoyed him to no end.

"Aw, where's the fun in that?" Red joked. "What did you join the agency for, anyway, if not to take down some bad guys?"

"Pay no attention to mercenary man here, Jay," Miguel said. "He's a little overly eager when it comes to the idea of gunning people down."

"Yeah, and you should be too, man! Those bastards killed one of our guys—blasted his head clean off, I hear—with no warning! In this business, you hesitate, you die, man!" Red aimed his own rifle downrange and peered through the scope.

"Oh, like you'd know. You've been an agent for what, all of two weeks now?" Miguel joked. "My grandmother has more combat experience than you." Jason cracked a smile.

"Yeah, well, now that we're here in Graveston, all that is about to change," Red said, looking down at his own rifle, and Jason thought he detected a hint of nervousness on Red's face. "Before you know it, we'll be mixin' it up with the terrorists, showin' 'em who's boss." For a moment, seeing the worry Red was trying to hide, Jason considered offering a word of comfort to him, but decided against it, doubting he would react well to it. Red's tough-guy act was a bit overdone and already wasn't very convincing. With badly feigned confidence, Red looked up and added, "I'm ready for whatever those wackos can dish out." He pulled the charging handle on his rifle back for dramatic effect, but let go too soon, causing a round to jam.

"Way to go, Rambo," Miguel snickered, clipping his bipod to his rifle for his turn at the target.

**BETSY** Sharpe—whose real name was Martha, but no one called her that anymore—had been working for Senator Collins for three years now. And even though Grant Collins was no longer merely a senator, but as of two months ago was also the

President-elect, she still had a hard time fully believing it. Betsy had never dared to ask if Senator Collins would continue to employ her when he became president, and considering how much of his life she ran these days, it seemed very strange to her that he had never brought it up either.

She was keenly aware of the fact that Senator Collins was not married, and not even romantically involved with anyone, as far as she knew. And she knew almost everything about Grant Collins. She knew he always wanted a Grande Americano with two sugars first thing in the morning, but after dinner, he would take cream instead of sugar. She knew that his waist was 39 inches, his height was 6 feet, 3 inches, and he was 26 inches across from shoulder to shoulder. She knew that his favorite dessert was crème brûlée. She knew that he had come to Washington to make a difference for the better. About the only thing about him she didn't know, and couldn't figure out, was why this personable, intelligent, cultured, successful, and very handsome man was not romantically involved with anyone, and hadn't been for as long as she had known him. A few times she had caught him watching her as she worked, but he had just looked away and laughed, as if his eyes had settled on her for no reason.

Grant kept the relationship strictly professional, and Betsy had long ago given up hope that their relationship might become romantic. He's still looking for the perfect woman, she thought. And he deserves the perfect woman. To Betsy, the perfect woman was tall, with sleek blond hair, long slender legs, and a face both sophisticated and beautiful. Betsy, on the other hand, was petite and voluptuous. Her face was sweet and childlike. She didn't think she fit the bill at all.

Having worked in Washington for several years now, she had met plenty of politicians and other powerful people, but Senator Collins struck her as different somehow. He was always courteous and kind to her, but never hit on her at all. She wasn't sure if that was a good sign or a bad sign. But mostly, Grant seemed more decent, more real, than most of the people she had met in politics.

"Betsy, can you come in here?" she heard his voice from the other room. "See what you think of my rewrite of this one part." She saved the file she had been working on and went to the door. As usual, there he was, looking like a blond Ken doll in a business suit, a fact the media always had fun with. Betsy was 36, and though he was ten years her senior, he looked as young as she did.

She was partly proud and partly embarrassed that she had somehow acquired the job of being a sounding board for his speeches. She was hired as a secretary, something she was trained in and good at, but no matter how often she told him that she didn't feel at all qualified to judge or critique political speeches, the senator would always coax her into it again, assuring her that the opinions of people who were *not* political junkies were what mattered. So she would give her honest opinions, and he would always thank her.

"Okay, here goes," the senator began, as Betsy took her usual seat in his office. "Blah, blah, blah," he muttered, skimming his handwritten notes, "Where is it? Okay." He stood up straight, and his casual office demeanor instantly transformed into his dignified senatorial persona.

"There is no reason why we cannot, on the one hand, dispense justice fairly and calmly, and on the other hand exhibit the firm resoluteness that this situation requires. Balancing the rights of those accused of wrongdoing with the obligation to protect the public has always been a delicate thing. In many cases, a wait-and-see approach works well. But not here. Those of us who play by the rules, the law-abiding taxpayers of this country, not only have a right to have justice carried out swiftly and surely against those who openly thumb their noses at the rule of law, but we also have the right, especially in these times of economic crisis, to not have our tax dollars wasted, day after day, on a policy that amounts to softness on crime. With no end to this conflict in sight, the do-nothing approach of the present administration is an insult to the American taxpayers in general, and to those in law enforcement in particular. Politicians should not allow political posturing to bind the hands of the men and women in uniform who are out there, putting themselves in harm's way every day, doing their best to protect the public. Every day that goes by without bringing these terrorists to justice is another day for the criminals to plan and prepare for even more acts of violence and lawlessness. Rest assured, when my administration takes office, you will see justice done legally and fairly, but swiftly and surely." Grant stopped and looked at Betsy, waiting for her reaction.

"Sounds a little like you're still campaigning," Betsy said. She didn't like to criticize, but she had learned from experience that the senator could always tell when something was on her mind, and would eventually wheedle it out of her anyway. "You already won the election, remember?"

"Oh, yeah," he kidded, "I forgot." He scribbled down a note on the paper he was holding.

"What's this one for, anyway?" Betsy asked.

"Press conference in an hour," he answered. "Sounds like the Prez fired whoever was in charge of the Graveston operation and brought in someone new—his usual attempt to save face. The new people he brings in will do exactly the same thing anyway, of course, but he likes having a never-ending supply of scapegoats." Grant continued to skim over his notes. "I should include something about the various nasty things the terrorists have done recently."

"Like what?" asked Betsy.

"Nothing new," Grant answered, "but there's been more of it in the last month than ever before. Let's see ... a bank robbery or two, a few assaults, hate crimes, weapons violations, drug-running, counterfeiting." He thought for a moment, scribbled another note, and then added, "threats against public officials."

"That last one might be more likely to win them sympathy," Betsy said with a smile. Grant looked at her without a word, his face expressionless. "Sorry, couldn't help myself," she said, blushing. "Anyway," she went on, trying to change the subject, "how many of those were confirmed to be the work of the Iron Web? Wasn't some of that speculation?"

"Not everything's been confirmed one hundred percent," he commented casually. "But that doesn't matter. The point is: they're nasty and dangerous. People will forget the details anyway, but we need them to get that one point, and not forget it." For a moment he paused, seeming lost in thought. "Nasty and dangerous," he repeated for emphasis. "Oh, and that reminds me, be sure to include the name of David Singh as the powerful and persuasive leader of the nasties. Actually, put it as Dawud Singh, spelled D-A-W-U-D, the non-Americanized version of his name, so he sounds more foreign. Oh, and let's start using the word 'anarchist' more often in what we put out. The 'extremist' label is getting old. We need something fresher, like 'anarchist cult'."

Betsy heard a knock at the door. She got up and walked back into her own office, where she found her friend Sandy standing in the doorway. Somehow Sandy had gotten security clearance, months before, to come into the building whenever she wanted. Betsy had once wondered if it might be the senator's doing, since Sandy was quite the looker, as well as being a hippie throwback who didn't always wear a lot of clothing. But allowing a security breach just to ogle a pretty woman didn't seem like Grant's style— though she could think of several others in the building who would do just that. Maybe instead, Betsy thought, Sandy got security clearance because she was secretly a CIA asset. If so, it was the best cover ever. Sandy was not at all bashful about saying what she thought about anyone who worked for the government, and it was always less than complimentary. Amazingly, Senator Collins never got angry about it; it even seemed to amuse him a bit.

"Hey, Bet," said Sandy. "I just wanted to stop by and make sure the slave-master wasn't going to ruin our lunch plans." She leaned casually in the doorway in tattered blue jeans, her long, straight black hair hanging loose over a low-cut tie-dyed shirt. Betsy glanced at the clock on the wall.

"I think we're still good," said Betsy. "He's got a press conference in an hour, and I think I can come right over from that. He told me I could have a few hours."

"Great," said Sandy. "I'll leave you to labor for this oppressive regime while I pick up Vee from preschool and start cooking." Betsy said nothing, but wished her friend would say such things a bit more quietly.

"Yes, Betsy," came Grant's voice from the other office, "the slave-master says you can go." Betsy cringed.

**JESSICA** Carlisle stood, her arms crossed, looking annoyed as an overweight, pale-faced, red-haired TSA agent clumsily sifted through her belongings. There really ought to be a law against super-dweebs rummaging through girls' stuff, she thought. The kid looked clueless and nervous. Jessica was about to turn nineteen, and she couldn't imagine this guy being much older than she was. So this is who's guarding the world from terrorists? God help us, she thought.

"What's this?" he asked, holding up a small plastic bottle.

"It's shampoo and conditioner," Jessica answered, wishing the guy would get his grubby hands out of her personal things. She was glad she had at least thought to take out the maxi-pads before leaving home. Mother Nature had been nice enough to spare her that necessity for this trip.

"It's not allowed," the boy said flatly, setting the bottle on a table behind him and returning his attention back to the purse.

"Not allowed? It's freaking shampoo," Jessica answered, a little more loudly than she intended.

"It's on the list of items that aren't allowed on flights. You should have read the signs about what you can bring with you," he said, trying to sound authoritative.

"You're scared I might hijack a plane with a bottle of shampoo?"

"We don't know that it *is* shampoo," he answered. Another TSA agent, this one an overweight, middle-aged black woman, had come over to watch, and stood silently, her arms crossed, looking disapprovingly at Jessica.

"Right. It's really anthrax juice," she said sarcastically. "I don't exactly fit the profile of a terrorist, do I?" She stood with hands on hips, dark waves of hair falling over her bright pink turtleneck sweater.

"Look, I know you're kidding, but you'd better be careful what you joke about," the kid said, lowering his voice a bit. "We're supposed to report anyone who makes any sort of inappropriate comments."

"Anyone who makes *what*?" Jessica bit her tongue. "Fine, just do what you have to do, swipe whatever you want, and let me get on the stupid plane." For a moment, Jessica thought she saw a hurt look on the guy's face. It wasn't hard to guess that the uniform was about the only thing that made this loser feel important, and getting barked at by a pretty girl probably didn't help.

"I'm just doing my job," he said in a whiny tone.

"Yeah, I know," she answered more pleasantly. "Well, whoever makes the rules is an idiot." He handed her her bag and her shoes. "Have a nice day," she said, trying to sound sincere as she sat down to put her shoes back on. She glanced at the black woman, who was still watching her with a disgruntled expression. "Nice friendly service," Jessica muttered to herself, and got up and walked away.

As she headed down the corridor she looked out the huge windows of the Philadelphia airport and saw the plane that would be taking her away to California for her big adventure. She couldn't decide which she was more excited about: the trip itself, or getting away from everything and everyone in her predictable life, even if just for a few days.

—⚙️—

**JASON** Reilly's commanding officer, Gerald Bridges, strode into the room, a bunch of papers in his hand. "All right, quiet down," he said. "A lot of this will be old news to most of you, but it doesn't hurt to go over it again." Bridges was around fifty, Jason guessed; a black man with graying hair, but a solid physique and a commanding presence. He pulled down an overhead map over the chalkboard, which showed a few hand-drawn lines superimposed on a satellite photo of the surrounding area.

The Graveston Primary School had let them use the room for the day, after a communication mix-up had delayed the arrival of some of their own trailers. "Here's us," Bridges said, pointing to the right side of the map. "This road we're on pretty neatly cuts off this entire area," he explained, indicating the bulge of land inside the river bend to the west. "The river is wide and fast, and we doubt anyone will be trying to cross it. If they do, we have temporary watchtowers set up here and here," he said, pointing to two points on the far side of the river. "The other side of the river is all open fields, with nowhere to hide. Between us and the river, it's a little unclear just what we're dealing with. There are at least five buildings in the area, mostly log cabins, mostly in the open. There may be a couple more in these wooded areas," he said, pointing to several blotches of green on the map. "We can't tell from the satellite images. Now let's be clear about this. There are several different properties in the area, and not all the owners are members of the Iron Web group. Not everyone in there is necessarily a suspect."

"Do we even know who all is in there?" asked Miguel, casually leaning back in his chair.

"No," said Bridges flatly. "We know a few for sure, and we suspect a few more. Some of these cabins are vacation homes.

**13**

They could be packed with Iron Web people right now, or there could be people in there who have nothing at all to do with them. Some of the buildings might even be empty. We do know that one of the cabins belongs to David Singh, and that he is there now. The major objective is to get him and the other known lawbreakers into custody without hurting any innocent people."

Jason spoke up. "Are there hostages?"

"So far we've seen nothing to indicate that," Bridges replied, "but of course we will approach the situation as if that's a possibility. I wouldn't put it past these people to hide behind their own kids, using them as shields. It wouldn't be the first time."

"Have they said anything about kids?" Jason inquired.

"Not specifically, but even nutcases know how to reproduce," Bridges said, bringing chuckles from several agents, "so it's a definite possibility. Again, we don't know who all is in there. We're not even sure which of the buildings is their headquarters. There may be an underground bunker we can't see, and it could be full of armed people. On the other hand, there could be kids or innocent people who need to be rescued. One of the main things we're trying to find out with the satellite images, the planes with cameras, and the spotters on the ground, is what exactly we're dealing with here. Until we're fairly certain who's who in there and what the situation is, our instructions are mostly to just sit it out."

"What's the overall size of this Iron Web thing?" Red asked. "I mean, it's spread out all over the country now, right?"

"I gotta say, sir," Jason added, before Bridges could answer, "the info I've seen about this group has been pretty sketchy. I know the FBI has been watching them for some time, but even they don't seem to know how many there are."

"It's hard to tell," answered Bridges, "mainly because this isn't like the KKK or something, where being a member is a big deal and there are lists of names—stuff like that. If someone agrees with the teachings of this group, who's to say if he's a member or not? I'll tell you this: based on the internet traffic the FBI has been monitoring, they have a lot more supporters than we'd like. At this point, it's in the tens of thousands. Then again, any kid can go online and say 'the government sucks.' Usually it's just words. The number of people who would do the kinds of things the group talks about, I mean the violence and open lawlessness, is a lot lower than the number of people who might anonymously sympathize with them. And that brings up another important point here. A fair number of the people who live around here, even outside of this area, are somewhat sympathetic to these guys. I don't expect it to be a problem, but keep it in mind. It seems that a bunch of like-minded people were going around buying up properties in this county, one at a time, trying to make their own little wacko kingdom here. And in the last election, the guy they put up for sheriff almost won. If that had happened, this would be a lot harder."

"Don't take this the wrong way, boss," Miguel said, "but what are we even doing here? I mean, this standoff stuff sounds more like FBI business. How is this still ATF jurisdiction?"

Bridges frowned. "I can't seem to get a straight answer to that myself. There's political stuff going on, and I don't pretend to understand it all. For the most part, this is the FBI's game now, though Homeland Security is overseeing a lot of it. They've only got about as many agents here as we do, but at the moment we're just here to assist, and to deal with whatever weapons are found once the situation is under control."

"Well, we still have the search warrant to serve, right?" asked Red.

"Technically, no," answered Bridges. "The original search warrant is now void. The window for serving it ran out a long time ago. Of course, once we think we can get in without getting shot at, we'll get another one." He saw Jason raise his hand, and pointed to him. "Jason?"

"Any hint yet that they might be willing to come out at some point?"

"Negotiations are ongoing, but from what I've heard, it sounds unlikely," said Bridges. "You gotta remember, these people don't believe in law. They make their own rules and they don't care what the rest of the world thinks about it. If they feel like killing someone, like they killed the agent serving the search warrant the first time, then they do it. Government, law and order, civilization—they don't respect any of it. They just do whatever they want—their so-called philosophy isn't any more complicated than that. They're not likely to go along with any deal. Even if they agreed to anything, I wouldn't trust them to do what they promise anyway."

"So, what are we waiting around for?" Red demanded.

"Sorry to disappoint you, Red, but the higher-ups want this solved without a shootout," Bridges replied. "We don't want another Waco here. So we bide our time, keep our eyes and ears open, and wait for further instructions. That's all."

The feeling of a vague menace just out of sight beyond the nearby hills made Jason uneasy. They didn't even know what they were dealing with, who these people were, how many there were, what weapons they might have, and what they might be capable of. And at the moment, Jason didn't think that sitting around waiting was going to make him feel any better about the situation. But for the time being, it seemed there wasn't anything else to be done.

**BETSY** knocked on the door of Sandy's apartment, heard the approach of small footsteps, and the door opened just a crack. "Who goes there?" came a small voice from inside, and a sliver of the angelic little face of Veronica, Sandy's five-year-old daughter, peeked out. "Aunt Betsy!" she exclaimed. The door closed, there was the sound of a chain being undone, and then the door swung wide open.

Betsy stepped in and picked up the child, wondering how much longer she'd be able to do that. Then she looked at her little grinning face with mock surprise. "Who let this rodent in here? Out you go," she said, swinging the child in the direction of the door. The little girl let out an ear-shattering squeal of delight. "I'm not a rodent! I'm Veronica!" she screamed.

"She never gets tired of that one, does she?" came Sandy's voice from the direction of the kitchen. Then she appeared, holding a large spoon. "The slop needs about five more minutes. Take off your coat and wash up."

"Your slop is the best," Betsy commented, putting Veronica down and closing the door behind her. "You're the best cook I know, in fact. I don't know how Carlos ever let you get away."

"Well, he didn't exactly *let* me get away," said Sandy, walking back into the kitchen. "It didn't quite take a restraining order against him, but it was close."

Betsy hung up her coat. "Aw, he wasn't that bad, Sandy. He was nice. And I think he really loved you. You don't give anyone a fighting chance."

"Almost lunchtime, Vee," Sandy said loudly, after her daughter had run off somewhere. "Make sure you quick go find some dirt to roll around in." Then, in a lower voice, she added, "He was too much of a deadbeat. I don't need to be supporting three people. Not nearly as bad as Vee's dad, though."

The approaching pitter-patter of feet ended that discussion. Betsy could hardly remember all of Sandy's long line of boyfriends, stretching back to their teenage years. The abusive one, the drug addict, the womanizer, and then some who were really decent guys. But more often than not, they were obsessed with Sandy, and just wouldn't go away when she was fed up with them. She seemed to attract that type. And it didn't work well, because Sandy didn't work on relationships. She did exactly what she felt like doing.

"What's for lunch?" Veronica asked eagerly.

"Mud and worms," Sandy answered matter-of-factly.

"Spaghetti!" Veronica screeched with glee.

"Hook up a generator to that thing, and the world's energy crisis is solved," Betsy commented as the two women walked back to the kitchen.

"Did you just call my lovely daughter 'that thing'?" asked Sandy with a show of dismay.

"I sure did," answered Betsy, leaning against the doorway, watching Sandy cook. "She's a beautiful thing. Hey, Vee," she said, taking the little girl's hand. "Shall we go wash up together?"

They did, and then Betsy returned to her place in the doorway. "So, how's life?" she asked Sandy.

"Yeah, it's been a whole, what, three days since you've been here?"

"Yeah, it's crazy. I thought campaigning was the worst, but this president-elect stuff is crazy, too. Seems like we're working every day, all day. And sometimes all night."

"Oh, really? Doing what?" Sandy asked facetiously, raising one eyebrow. "Never mind, it's better if I don't know."

"Oh, get your mind out of the gutter. It's not what you're thinking," said Betsy, and then quietly added, "unfortunately."

"Oh, man, Bet," said Sandy. "You've really fallen for Mr. Emperor, haven't you?"

"Well, yeah, I guess," Betsy answered, a bit hesitantly. "But I'm sure nothing's going to come of it."

"That's a good thing, believe me. You don't want to end up married to one of those power-happy slimeballs."

"Sandy!" Betsy protested, but with a small giggle. "Why can't you even consider the possibility that Grant is a good guy?"

"Oh, now it's 'Grant'?" Sandy responded, tasting the bubbling sauce. "Not 'Senator Collins' anymore? But I'll tell you why. It's because of what they do—what they *all* do."

"Who says one of them can't be different?" Betsy objected.

"I'm not talking about personality, I'm talking about the job. What do they do day in and day out? They take money from everyone else, whether we like it or not, and whether we can afford it or not, and then they give it away however they want, whether to lazy people to buy their votes, or to huge corporations to get their campaign contributions. And then they take credit for being compassionate and generous. The whole game is nothing but a fraud. They're just a bunch of con men ripping people off."

"Well, I'm not thrilled with a lot of what they do, but don't you think that some of it is necessary? Some of the programs actually do some good."

"That's debatable, but even if it were true, that doesn't make it okay," Sandy said. "If I steal your purse and give a hundred bucks of your money to some homeless guy, is that a good thing?"

"Well, it's good for the homeless guy, but the stealing isn't good."

"Exactly. That's exactly my point," Sandy said emphatically. She sprinkled in some spices, stirred for a few minutes, and tasted the sauce again. "The government shouldn't be robbing us, even to do good stuff, especially those of us struggling to make ends meet, which is almost everyone these days. Charity has to be voluntary, or it's not charity," she added, "and government is never voluntary. Ergo, no government program or handout can ever be good."

"This coming from the girl who was a devout communist back in college," Betsy remarked. "I agree, charity has to be voluntary, but don't you think that people are entitled to something just because they're people? What about the people who fall through the cracks of private charities? What about people that nobody wants to help?"

"When I was a good little commie, that's exactly how I thought," said Sandy as she poured the sauce over the pasta. "But we didn't really think things through all the way. We used to stay up half the night discussing the greatness of the idea, and trying to figure out why it wasn't working in the real world. But we didn't really *want* to know, because it felt good to be part of a radical movement, and we didn't want to let go of it. We didn't want to look too hard at what we were actually advocating, which happened to be massive authoritarian violence disguised as compassion, and happened to be almost exactly the same as the system we were protesting."

"So now you're Miss Capitalist instead?" Betsy mocked.

Sandy laughed. "Not quite. I guess you'd call me a libertarian, although you know I don't like labels." She was quiet for a moment, thinking and stirring. Then she went on, "You know I gave up on political philosophy for a long time. When I figured out that liberals were just as authoritarian as conservatives, I didn't feel like I fit anywhere in the picture. But you know me. I'm all about 'live and let live.' What I didn't realize back in college was that no party, no administration, no government will ever be for that. Whichever group isn't in power whines about how rotten the one in power is. But if you give the power to the other one, a week later they'll be just as bad." She took her seat at the table. "'Left' and 'right' are completely meaningless to me. There is freedom, or there is tyranny. All the other political garbage you hear, including from your boss, is meaningless bullshit."

Just then Veronica appeared in the doorway. "That's a dollar!" she shouted happily.

"Dang it!" Sandy said. "No fair sneaking up on me."

Betsy cracked up. "You pay her a buck every time you swear? When did that start?"

"Yeah, about a week ago. It's straightening me out a bit, and she's already got her college fund."

"Yeah, I'll bet," Betsy said, tousling the child's golden curls. "Look," she went on, "I agree with a lot of what you say, but if that's all true, we've got to change things somehow. And I still think Grant is a good guy. I think he means well, even if I don't like everything he proposes. I mean, I have to deal with a lot of senators, lobbyists, and the rest of the circus. For most of them, I agree completely that they're nothing but conniving crooks. It's all posturing and persuasion, to see what they can get for themselves. But Grant, he just isn't like that, not really."

"I wonder if you'd still say that if you didn't have the hots for him," Sandy said, beginning to dish out the spaghetti.

Betsy was too exhausted to feign indignation. "Yeah, well, he'll be in the White House soon, and I doubt he'll be taking me with him, much less getting romantically involved with me. I'm just not first lady material."

"Well, let's have some spaghetti and forget about him for a while," suggested Sandy.

**JESSICA** Carlisle woke up, pushed her long hair away from her face, and tried to guess how long she had been asleep. The constant, steady hum of the jet engines droned on, reminding her that she was still on a plane. It had been many years since she had flown. She barely remembered it at all, having been just a kid at the time. That was back before it was a crime to bring shampoo onto an airliner, she thought to herself.

She gazed out the window. What looked like farmland with scattered patches of woods was barely visible through a thin sheet of clouds below her. Still half asleep, her eyes followed what she thought was a soaring bird, until she realized it was another plane, far below hers but still above the wispy clouds. She had almost no depth perception of such huge distances up here. She wondered who might be on that tiny little speck, and where they might be going.

She thought of the days when people had to cross all this with horse and wagon. Now a person could nap for a few hours and wake up a thousand miles away. It sure made things easier, but somehow it also made the world seem less exciting. There weren't enough unknowns anymore; not enough undiscovered wonders.

Some of her friends could not understand her desire to go camping in the wilderness when she could afford a "real vacation." They thought camping was for poor people who couldn't afford Europe or the Bahamas. One of her friends had laughed and said, "but Jess, what if you chip a fingernail?" Jessica chafed under that "pampered rich kid" image they seemed to have of her. But it was true that she'd never had any real hardship in her life, and pretty much got everything she wanted.

Jessica wanted to experience life without all the stuff around her—just her and nature. Her cousins, the weird family, spent a lot of time camping, hiking, horseback riding, and even hunting. Jessica didn't approve of hunting, but aside from that, their family seemed to have something that others didn't. They didn't depend on civilization so much. Maybe that was what she wanted. To know that she could get along without all the trappings. At least this might make her friends stop kidding her so often about being a spoiled rich kid. Her family wasn't all that rich, anyway. Her dad had worked really hard to become a fairly successful businessman. But these days, she pondered, with the economy sinking lower month by month, if you weren't about to lose your house, you were considered rich.

One of her best friends had had to leave the private school they had attended in her senior year, because her parents couldn't afford it anymore. The folks of another friend from her neighborhood had lost their home and moved into a tiny little apartment miles away. It seemed to Jessica that things kept going from bad to worse for most people, and she felt more than a little guilty that she seemed to be one of the few who so far hadn't suffered much because of it.

She gazed out the window, wondering how many of the people she knew could even afford an airline ticket anymore. Still in a daze, Jessica scanned the blue sky, and her eyes rested on the far-off vapor trail of another plane. Her eyes lazily followed it as it drifted slowly closer. Had her dad been there, she thought absent-mindedly, he probably could have already told her the make and model of the plane, even though it was barely more than a dot. She couldn't understand why anyone would want to know that much trivia about one subject, but her dad was the king of airplane buffs.

As her eyes followed the small moving shape, suddenly something about it didn't seem right. In an instant Jessica was fully awake from her daydreaming, her eyes wide. It wasn't an airplane. What before had looked like a distant, slowly drifting airliner was now a gigantic wingless bullet approaching at horrifying speed. Her mind raced to find some non-threatening explanation for what she was seeing, but couldn't. Was that a *missile*?! She found no words, and couldn't even manage a scream, in the time it took to watch the glistening object streak toward the front of the plane.

She was in the second-to-last row, and had a clear view all the way down the fuselage. There was only a split second between when she lost sight of the object from her window and when a ball of blinding yellow light appeared, inside the plane, many rows ahead of her, accompanied by what could only be described as a "thump." It didn't sound like an explosion, because the shock wave had incapacitated her eardrums. She didn't flinch, or duck, or scream. It was too unreal to respond to at all. The orange fireball rolled down the fuselage toward her, engulfing everything in a fraction of a second. It couldn't be real. It wasn't possible. The last thing Jessica saw was the upper half of an elderly woman, eyes and mouth wide open, flying through the air toward her at a hundred miles an hour.

---

**JASON** Reilly was just zipping up his pants, stepping out of the little bathroom in one of the ATF trailers, when he heard the sound: a distant boom that didn't sound like any ordnance he could think of. He ran outside into the bright sunlight, grabbing his rifle which he had left leaning against the front of the trailer, and looked around frantically. It took only a moment to notice four or five other agents looking up into the sky, their hands shielding their eyes from the sun.

Looking almost straight up, he could see a bright light—though he couldn't tell whether it was reflection or fire that he was seeing. He squinted, and several jagged shapes took form, none of them recognizable. After a few seconds he realized, by the increasing size of the objects, that whatever they were, they were not flying, but falling. And they were directly overhead.

Finally he could make out what had to be the fuselage of a large passenger plane. The entire front end of the plane was missing, and half the left side wall was gone. Half of the left wing was also missing, and what was left of it was on fire. The plane rolled as it tumbled, seemingly in slow motion.

Panic suddenly set in as Jason became convinced that the plane was going to land right on top of them. He froze, unsure of which way to run. The vast size of the plane, as damaged as it was, made the thing seem to lumber slowly along. It was directly overhead, but now Jason could see that it was still moving horizontally as well as downward, from the momentum it still had from its former path. As it rolled again, now only a hundred yards above him, Jason watched with horror as he saw three lifeless bodies, one of which seemed to be missing some limbs, fall out of the hole in the fuselage.

Still frozen where he stood, unable to believe that what he was seeing was real, Jason watched what was left of the spinning plane career directly toward the cabins on the other side of the hills. As it dropped out of sight, it must have caught the wind for a moment, because the nose end—though the nose itself was gone—lifted up, as if coming in for a landing. Then the plane rolled onto its back and was gone. Three seconds later, the deep rumble of the impact shook the ground around him.

A business jacket, smoking a bit, fluttered to the ground at Jason's feet. Looking up again, he could see an assortment of papers and effects drifting down from the otherwise clear sky. What on earth had happened? What had he just witnessed?

"Snap out of it," he heard Bridges yelling. "Miguel, get D.C. on the radio, right now. Red! Jason! Find the bodies that fell over there behind that grove of trees. I think there were three. No one crosses the barricade line. I don't know what the hell just happened, but I want you all alert and ready for anything. Johnson, get on the phone and get the local fire and ambulance out here."

Still in a surreal daze, as Bridges continued to bark out orders to others, Jason set off at a jog, Red ahead by a hundred feet or so, toward where he thought the bodies would have landed. He didn't want to imagine what they might look like when they found them.

**BETSY** Sharpe was back in the office after a relaxing visit with Sandy. She sat in her usual chair in Grant's office, legs crossed and hands neatly folded on her knees, ready to listen intently to a draft of Grant's next press release. He was still looking at his notes and thinking, so Betsy gazed out the window at the overcast sky and the lights of Washington twinkling below. His office had a nice view. Thank goodness the days are getting longer now instead of shorter, she thought. She disliked going home from work in the dark.

"Let's see. Okay, let's start here," Grant decided, and cleared his throat. "The criminals today are often better equipped than our brave men and women in law enforcement, and that in itself is a crime. I believe it is the responsibility of those who hold public office, both to make sure our police have the resources and equipment they need to do what they do, and to make sure the criminals do *not* have the resources and equipment they need to do what they do. There is no reason why—"

The door swung open with a slam, and Betsy and Grant both spun around to see a young man at the door, breathless. "Turn on the news," he panted. "Something has happened in Graveston."

Betsy jumped up, almost falling over her chair, and turned on the large television recessed into the wall. The news was already on.

The well-dressed, handsome male reporter was speaking without emotion. "—assume there were no survivors. The flight originated in Philadelphia, with a stop in Chicago, and was on its way to California when the event occurred. White House sources say, based on intelligence gathered so far, that they believe this may be the doing of the group calling itself the Iron Web—a domestic terrorist organization which, until now, has been considered by Homeland Security to be a relatively minor threat." Next to the reporter appeared a high-altitude aerial view of unidentifiable, smoking wreckage. "Authorities say they have been unable to reach the crash site so far, as it is inside the area affected by the ongoing standoff between federal authorities and members of the Iron Web group. But again, there are not expected to be any survivors."

Grant turned off the television. "Get the director of the FBI on the line," he ordered. "I want to know what they know, not just what they're telling the press." Betsy was still in shock. There hadn't been any significant terrorist attacks in the country since 2001, but the image of that demolished plane brought back all of the memories. Had the plane been headed for some other target, like downtown Los Angeles? Had it been shot down? Were there still other planes, heading toward other targets around the country? At that moment, Betsy wanted to be anywhere other than in Washington, D.C. "Betsy!" Grant's voice snapped her out of her trance.

"Director of the FBI, right," she said, hurrying to her desk and reaching for the phone.

# PART II

**JESSICA** was conscious of the pain before she was conscious of anything else. Some delayed survival instinct, combined with the memory of the last thing she had seen, made her tense up, causing an agonizing bolt of pain to shoot up her left leg. She heard a faint whimper, and realized it was her own voice. Her mind raced to determine her situation. Was she still on the plane? Had the plane hit the ground yet? She couldn't see a thing. Was she blind? Was she dead?

A light broke through her frantic thoughts, and the real world slowly came into focus. She was in a dark room, and there, silhouetted in an open doorway, was the outline of a stocky man. "She's awake," the figure said. He started toward her, then halted, as if in indecision. "Don't be afraid," he said. "You're okay. Well, not exactly okay, but you'll live." After a quiet pause, the figure moved cautiously closer. "Can you hear me?" The voice was low and soft. Jessica tried to answer, but couldn't.

Another figure stepped into the doorway: an elderly woman, her gray hair up in a bun, dressed in an old-fashioned green print dress and holding a lantern. As she came closer, Jessica could just make out her wrinkled but smiling, kindly face in the lamplight. "Just relax, dear. You're probably still in shock." The old lady sat down next to the bed and put her hands on Jessica's. "If you can't talk or move yet, don't worry. You're going to be fine. You just relax."

Jessica tried to ask what had happened, but the only word to escape her lips was a raspy, "Plane?" The voice didn't even sound like her own. Her eyes teared up for a moment, suddenly recalling, all too vividly, the horrible sight of that microsecond of carnage just before she had blacked out. How could anyone have survived that?

"Terrible, terrible thing," the man said. She could see his face now. He was old, with gray hair, mustache, and beard. The lines on his face evidenced a lifetime of smiles and laughter, but he wore no smile now. The eyes behind his round glasses were friendly and comforting. He reminded Jessica of some fatherly character from a movie that she couldn't remember. "It just came crashing down all around," he continued, "and—" he stopped short. "Were you alone on the plane?" What an odd question, she thought. "I mean, were you with anyone?" Then she realized what he was getting at, and shook her head. Was she the only survivor? "Well, don't think about it now," he added quickly, attempting a smile. "You're pretty banged up, but my sister here, this is Heather, she's a nurse, and she tells me that the parts that matter came out okay."

Heather laughed softly. "What he means, dear, is that your back is fine, and there's no sign of any serious internal damage. And of course, your lovely face will be just fine in a day or two."

As she spoke, she lit two candles by the bedside, and Jessica could finally see that she was lying in a big, old-fashioned four-poster bed under a huge quilt. "You did a real number on one of your ankles, but I don't think it's broken. You might have some cracked ribs; it's hard to tell. Other than that, and a fair number of scratches and bruises, you seem to be in one piece." Heather shook her head. "I would never have believed anyone

**30**

could live through that. An honest-to-goodness miracle, if you ask me."

Jessica had seen the explosion, but had been unconscious for the fall. How many thousands of feet was it? How could anyone have survived that? Yet here she was. Then Jessica had another thought. Why was she here, in what looked like a log cabin, and not in a hospital?

"If you feel up to it," the old woman continued, "you really should eat something now. We've kept you hydrated pretty well, but you haven't eaten for almost two days." She had been unconscious for that long? Only then did Jessica notice how famished she was. She nodded weakly, and Heather left the room.

"My name is Benjamin Frank—you can call me Ben—and this little cabin is my home," the elderly man said. Then he looked down and furrowed his brow a bit. "You're probably wondering why you're still here, and not in a hospital." He rubbed his short beard. "I'm afraid there's something you need to know."

Jessica just looked at him, too weak to ask a question. "Like I was saying," Ben continued, "you made it through the crash in one piece, but I'm afraid your ordeal isn't quite over. You picked a really bad spot to have a plane crash." He gave her a wry smile. "I suppose you've heard of the whole mess with the Iron Web thing and all, and the standoff with the government?" Jessica nodded. "Well, that whole mess is smack dab between my property and the rest of civilization."

Jessica's eyes widened. She'd never had a clear picture of where exactly the standoff was, and in fact hadn't paid much attention to the story at all. Suddenly it wasn't just a five-second snippet on the news; it was for real. It occurred to her that, had her luck been just a little bit worse, she could have landed right inside the terrorists' compound. What would have happened to her then? She didn't even want to think about it.

"We're on a sort of peninsula, in a wide bend in the river," said Ben, "and the only way out of here is right through the area where all the trouble is. We haven't dared to go out since the thing started."

"Are we safe h-here?" Jessica managed to ask, her voice still raspy. "I mean, how far away are the terrorists?" She looked around the room, as if expecting heavily armed extremists to appear at any moment. Were they miles away, or yards away?

"We're fine here," replied Ben in a soothing voice, patting Jessica's hand. "Nothing has been happening for weeks now. All the same, we've stayed here the whole time. We've got plenty of food stored up, so you don't need to worry about that. Unfortunately, we've lost all communications. The phone lines have been cut, as well as the electric lines. One of my neighbors has a cell phone, but there's no reception in this area."

"My folks," Jessica remembered frantically. "Do they know? Do they know I'm alive?"

"For now, we have no way to communicate anything to the outside world," Ben said, shaking his head sadly. Seeing the anguish on her face, he added, "I'll see what I can do."

How could this be happening? Jessica thought. Ben hadn't really answered her question: exactly where were the terrorists? How far away were they, and were they likely to come this way? They must have been the ones who shot down the plane. Wouldn't they be likely to come and examine the wreckage? Wasn't there some other way for her to get out of here? She wondered if she could even walk. And if they did show up at the cabin, what would happen then? She wondered for a moment if Ben had a gun, but then decided that even if he did, he certainly couldn't hold off an entire group of violent terrorists. And how many of them were there? How could Ben be so sure that they were safe here, or was he just saying that to try to keep her from worrying?

The old lady bustled back into the room with a tray. The smell of chicken soup made Jessica's mouth water. "Here you go," Heather said cheerfully. "It's a little cliché, I know, but chicken soup really is about the best medicine you could get right now." Jessica eagerly tried to sit up, but a jolt of pain from her leg made her gasp. Heather put the tray down on a small table and went to help her. Jessica tried again more slowly, and Heather propped her up with some pillows and set the tray across her lap. Jessica carefully took a spoonful of soup and felt the warmth of it diffuse through her body. At that moment, it seemed like the best thing she'd ever tasted.

⚬⚬⚬

**JASON** Reilly listened quietly as his fellow agents talked. "I can't believe they still won't let us go in," Red barked, practically frothing at the mouth. "We get to go pick up the pieces of the people they killed, but we can't go in and get the guys who did it?" Jason remembered the images of the bodies they had recovered that had fallen out of the plane. Two were intact, but the third was badly mangled, with a face that hardly looked as if it could ever have been human. The image, which he tried in vain to force out of his mind, filled him with horror and anger. He understood Red's frustration.

After the news reports hit, more agents were brought in, both FBI and ATF, and more trailers were set up, but still they were not allowed to go in. Agents paced like caged tigers, enraged at the mass murder that had happened before their very eyes, and at their inability to carry out some righteous retribution. Their hopes rose when two Bradley armored vehicles were brought in, but the Bradleys were just parked alongside the road.

Jason and Red were admiring the Bradleys when Agent Bridges came striding up and said, "Jason, Red, got a job for you."

"What is it?" Red asked.

"Get in the car," said Bridges, "I'll brief you on the way." They followed Bridges to a large black SUV.

"Are we going in?" Red asked with an eager smile on his face.

"Yeah, the three of us are storming the compound, right now," Bridges said, watching Red for a reaction. "No, dumb-ass. We're visiting a neighbor, see if he knows anything." Jason climbed in the back as Bridges and Red got in the front.

"What kind of neighbor: friendly or hostile?" Jason asked.

"The guy is one of those militia nuts," Bridges answered, "so don't expect a warm welcome. But the file says he's all talk. He's got a bunch of guns, but we don't expect any trouble."

"Hey, I'm ready for all the trouble he can dish out," Red said, holding up the MP5 he was carrying.

"Look, Rambo," Bridges said sternly, "he's not gonna like us to begin with, so just shut up and let me do the talking. You two are there for decoration, that's all. Keep your mouth shut, and maybe you'll learn something."

Jason looked out the window at rolling fields of long, dry grass, punctuated by clumps of low, scrubby evergreens. Mountains rose in the distance.

"I pictured this place as nothing but sand and cactuses," Jason commented. He'd never been to Arizona before, and he'd imagined it as one big desert. "I didn't expect there to be any woods here."

"Well, live and learn," Bridges responded.

Jason remembered his mom telling him that if he brought back some pine nuts, she would make him some pesto. He wondered which trees the pine nuts came from, and if they were in season now. Jason held on as the SUV bumped on the unpaved road. No wonder all these people drive pickups, he thought. They turned onto a long driveway which passed through a grove of low pine trees and out into a clearing, in the middle of which stood a cabin. Shingles were sliding off the roof, and a metal pole held up one corner of the front porch.

"Wow, classic redneck pad," commented Red derisively. "Why is it the paranoid kooks always live in these dumps?"

"I'd be pretty pissed at the world if that was my house," Jason said.

Bridges chuckled. "Yeah, well, let's hope he's in a good mood."

The car stopped, and the three got out. There was only the one small cabin in the clearing, and beyond that, a small structure which Jason assumed was an outhouse. A forties-style pickup truck, which seemed to be more rust than metal, stood next to the cabin, sporting a gun rack. As they scanned the area, Red assumed a combat pose.

"Lower your damn gun," Bridges barked at him. "If you walk up there like that, he might just blow your damn head off."

The three of them walked up to the cabin and onto the front porch, which sagged a little under their weight. Bridges knocked on the door. It opened immediately, but only a few inches. Jason guessed that whoever it was had heard them coming and had been waiting by the door, probably armed. He tried to look as relaxed and friendly as possible, so as to avoid being shot.

"Yeah?" came a gruff voice from inside.

"Mr. Samuels?" Bridges inquired, in his deep, official-sounding voice.

"Who wants to know?" responded the voice, in a less-than-friendly tone.

"I'm Special Agent Gerald Bridges, from the ATF, and I'd like to ask you some questions."

"About what?" snapped the voice.

"About some of your neighbors, and the group calling itself the Iron Web."

"Unless you got a warrant, get off my property." The door closed a bit, but not all the way.

"Look, it's just a few questions, and it's not about you," Bridges explained. "If you were a suspect, we'd have to tell you that. And you probably know that already." Jason thought that that was a clever, seemingly offhand way to compliment the guy, to maybe soften him up a little.

"Yeah, I do know my rights," the voice replied belligerently, "and I have the right to tell you to get the hell off my property."

"Look, we only need a few minutes if you'll just talk to us," Bridges said in his best "nice cop" voice. "Otherwise my bosses are going to get a subpoena or a warrant, and that'll be a big headache for all of us."

"A warrant?" the voice laughed. "Based on what? Did you bastards get around to making it illegal to not like the feds?" The door opened enough for Jason to see the man's face. He was an elderly black man, with gray hair and beard, and a wrinkled, angry-looking face.

"All right, then, a subpoena," said Bridges.

"Ya know," the old man said, "if you bastards cared at all about the Constitution—"

"Oh, here we go," Red muttered, rolling his eyes.

The man continued: "—you'd be informing me of my Fifth Amendment rights, not trying to sneak around them. Subpoena or no, I don't have to say a word to you. You and I both know that. Now piss off." He slammed the door, and they could hear his footsteps walking away.

"Well, that went well," Jason remarked.

Bridges turned and walked off the porch, and the others followed. "It's what I expected, but I was told to try anyway."

"So, do we go get the subpoena thing?" Red asked.

"No, that was a bluff, and he knew it," replied Bridges, getting back into the SUV.

"I've never seen a black neo-Nazi before," joked Red.

"He's not a neo-Nazi," responded Bridges. "Did he look like a white supremacist to you?" he asked, shooting a glance at Red.

37

"The guy doesn't even have a criminal record. He is one of those militia types, though. He probably thinks we can't wait to come take his guns and put him in a concentration camp, or something."

"I can't keep all the different kinds of kooks straight," Red commented, looking out the window. Smiling, he added, "They all look the same to me."

"Watch it, Red," said Bridges, starting the engine.

**BETSY** looked up to see Grant Collins striding into the office. "Well," he said, "we got the go-ahead from Langley to say it was Iron Web people who set off that bomb in the Arkansas school last week."

"And was it?" Betsy asked.

"Hey, if the CIA says that's what happened, *we* say that's what happened," Grant answered. "Besides, who else would have done it?" He began rifling through a stack of notes and papers. "Oh, and there are lots of minority students at the school, so let's emphasize the possible racial aspect of it."

"I thought no one was killed. Wasn't the school empty?"

"Yeah, but the angle will still work," Grant said. "Nicely integrated school. Now all those students have to be relocated. It'll set the kids back."

"Press conference or press release?" Betsy asked, wondering which template to bring up on her computer.

"Written," came the answer. "I'm too tired to face the damn press in person right now."

"Want anything about the plane crash in there?"

"Of course. We'll be reminding the public of that every time we say a word in the next month or so, at least. 'The same group responsible for the heinous attack and murder of' blah, blah, blah. You know the wording we want."

"Sure," Betsy said, looking up her special file of catch phrases.

"Speaking of which," Grant went on, "we need a good title for the ring-leader down there. Something easy to remember, simple but distinctive, that we can use over and over again until it sticks in people's minds. Something like, 'Dawud Singh, the guru of mayhem, and his brainwashed followers.' But use something other than 'mayhem.' It makes him sound too much like a comic book villain." He thought for a moment, but then did a backhand wave at Betsy, and said, "Anyway, see what you can come up with."

"Got it," Betsy said.

"Now if only we could find a way to blame the economy on the terrorists," he said, glancing at the front page of the newspaper on his desk. "That would really be something. 'Terrorists hijack Dow Jones, crash it into the ground'." The joke was in bad taste, but it took an effort for Betsy not to snicker at it. "Actually, there might be something there," he added. Betsy gave him a skeptical look. "No, I mean something like, 'at a time when many are feeling the strain on their checkbook, terrorists have no qualms about destroying property and scamming people.' I don't know, play around with that. See if you can make it sound less contrived."

"That's a tall order," Betsy replied.

"Well, to tell the truth," Grant said, "the black market is growing by leaps and bounds, and it's hard to tell how much of that is Iron Web influence, and how much is just people trying to get out of paying taxes while the economy is faltering. But talking about it will only encourage people to jump on the bandwagon, so it may be best to leave that one alone."

Grant stood still for a moment, as if in thought. "If I went down to Graveston, and made an appearance, think it would look presidential, or just seem like grandstanding?"

"Grandstanding," answered Betsy. "Unless you plan on charging in and killing them all yourself, single-handedly."

"Sorry, my schedule's too busy for that, at the moment," he said. "Maybe I could do my own version of Dumb-ass Dukakis in a tank."

"What?"

"Michael Dukakis. I guess you wouldn't remember. He was running for president. He wanted to look tough for a PR picture, but just looked like some sort of moronic bobble-head, peeking out of an M1," Grant said. Seeing Betsy's questioning expression, he added, "never mind, doesn't matter. I won't be going down there."

"Oh," Betsy said, suddenly remembering, "you got another letter from the NRA, asking again for a policy statement on that bill they've proposed."

"Don't they know the election already happened? Now they'll have to live with what they endorsed. Considering the alternative, who else were they going to back? Cops, military, hunters—all of their organizations endorsed me. It's a little late now for them to be complaining."

"Are we just going to ignore it?" she asked.

"Do we have one of those great say-nothing, generic responses, about gun rights?"

"I think so," Betsy said, starting a computer word search, "or at least something I can make into one."

"Run it by me before you send it," he said, and with a smile added, "I want to make sure it doesn't actually say anything substantive that we'd have to defend later."

**JESSICA** Carlisle thought that this was what it must be like to be old. Each slow, painful step took real effort and concentration. Heather had bandaged her ankle tightly, but still she could hardly bear weight on her foot. Ben walked patiently beside her, supporting her weak side as they made their way through the grove of trees beside his cabin. She had been there for three days now, but this was the first time she had ventured outside, having been unable to walk at all until today. She was quite comfortable around Ben and Heather now, and somehow their lack of worry made her feel less concerned with the events going on nearby. Her biggest concern was that Ben still had been unable to find a way to get word to her parents that she was still alive. It pained her to imagine them assuming that she was dead. She tried not to think about it too much.

She was enjoying being outside, in spite of the pain. It was so warm here, compared to Pennsylvania, and the breeze carried the fresh aroma of pine. She felt a little silly in the old-fashioned print house dress Heather had given her. It was pale blue with flowers, and it made her feel about a hundred years old. But the clothes she had been wearing when the crash happened were so torn, and so saturated with dirt and blood—blood which may not have all been hers—that she had asked Heather to throw them away. Aside from her underwear—which had also seen better days, but which she didn't think anyone would be seeing anyway—the gold necklace she wore was the only thing of hers she still had. The thought of going back to the crash site to look for her luggage seemed worse than just giving up everything she had brought along.

Despite the discomfort, Jessica managed to take in the beauty of the place. The bright sunlight slanting through the evergreen twigs and branches as the breeze shook them made the world around her seem to sparkle. Patches of ferns swayed gently in the breeze, and chipmunks jumped from one lichen-covered rock to another. It was like one of those old classic animated movies, only real, and far more beautiful.

"Good, good," she heard Ben's deep voice beside her, after a few minutes of meandering along in peaceful silence. "You're healing just fine. Keep walking and you'll be good as new in no time." Jessica glanced back behind her, and realized with some disappointment what a short distance she had covered. "If you can make it over to the koi pond," Ben said, "you can have a rest."

As they rounded the corner of the cabin, Jessica gasped in wonder at the miniature Garden of Eden that opened up before her. Tucked into the corner formed by the two wings of the log house was a garden of large rocks, splashing waterfalls, and dark little pools. Growing in the spaces between the rocks were more varieties of fern than Jessica had ever seen before, along with spiky swirls of aloes, miniature ones and huge ones, dark striped ones and pale ones. Several Japanese maples covered the garden with a light, twiggy canopy, while their delicate, star-shaped leaves decorated the rocks, plants, and pools below with little splashes of deep red. If it looked this glorious in winter, she thought to herself, it must be truly amazing in the spring.

Jessica saw two stone benches near the largest of the pools, and decided she must make it to them before she could rest. As she limped along the flagstone path in short steps, she was startled by a sharp noise like the plucking of a banjo string. A small frog she hadn't noticed leapt from the path in front of her feet into one of the pools, making a tiny splash. Jessica laughed. This place made the pain seem somehow farther away, and less real. Reaching one of the benches at last, she sat down with a great sigh of relief, as Ben sat down on the other bench, facing her.

"Wow, this place is beautiful," Jessica said. Then she remembered why she was there. "You're sure we're safe out here?" she asked.

"What do you mean?" Ben replied.

"The terrorists," she said, surprised that he couldn't guess what she meant. Then something occurred to her. "Do you know any of them? Like, do they ever come over here?"

"Well, the government has been pretty vague about just who it thinks these terrorists are," he answered, "but a few of my neighbors probably fit the bill." Jessica was puzzled. Why would this nice, kind man put up with living near such people? She had learned from previous conversations that Ben was an ardent pacifist. He had built this house ten years ago to be closer to his sister, who had retired from nursing. But as nice as this place was, she thought to herself, when terrorists moved in next door, she would have moved away as fast as possible.

"Do they ever bother you?" she asked.

"They have a beef with the government. They don't have a beef with me, and they wouldn't have one with you, either," he said with apparent confidence.

"But how can you be so sure? I never paid much attention to the stories on the news," she admitted, "but I know those people have done horrible things to a lot of people, not just the government."

"Like what?" he asked, seeming genuinely curious.

How could he, of all people, not know? Jessica wondered. Maybe he just lived in this beautiful place and never went anywhere or turned on the news. She could hardly blame him for that.

"I don't really remember," she said. "I thought their neighbors all hated them, though. I've heard about schools and other buildings being blown up, and banks being robbed, and—and don't they pick on minority people?"

"They've never given me any trouble," Ben said.

Jessica heard the rustle of leaves, looked up, and jumped at the sight of a figure—little more than a silhouette, with the sun behind it—of a man carrying what Jessica thought was a machine gun. For a split second, she was convinced that it had to be one of the Iron Web crazies; they had come here after all, and who knew what they would do? She clutched the arm of the bench tightly.

Her panic quickly evaporated, however, when the figure stepped into the light, and she had to suppress a giggle of relief. He was just a boy—no more than 16, Jessica guessed—with a slight build and a smiling baby face that reminded her of Elvis, from the silly old movies her mother liked.

It took her a moment to notice that he really was carrying a gun, and it sure looked real. Was it just a paint-ball gun? If not, what was this kid doing carrying a machine gun around? Or was it a hunting rifle? Jessica knew next to nothing about guns, but this one reminded her of war movies. This boy was no terrorist—his face alone convinced her of that—but what was he doing toting a scary-looking rifle like that around? Just being around guns made her uncomfortable. The only gun she'd seen in real life was at a party when a friend of a friend had brought out his dad's handgun to show to some people. Nothing bad had happened, and that kid wasn't a criminal or anything, but it made Jessica uneasy to think of the capacity for destruction that such a small thing could have.

"Uncle Ben," called the boy in a sing-song voice that matched his youthful face. He carefully put the rifle down, leaning it against the corner of the cabin. In his other hand he held a shopping bag.

"Joshua," Ben answered with a smile, and, turning to Jessica, added, "Here's one neighbor of mine you sure don't need to worry about. Everything going okay?" he asked, turning back toward the boy.

**45**

"We're all hangin' in there," he answered, and Jessica wondered who "we" referred to. "And I'm guessing this is Miracle Girl," the boy added, looking at Jessica.

"That's what some people have been calling you," Ben explained, "for surviving that crash. Most of the people around here saw the plane go down. Some still don't believe that anyone could have survived it."

"I hardly believe it myself," Jessica commented.

"That pile of rubble—I can't believe anything could have come out of that alive," Josh said. "And here you are, up and about. Amazing."

"She hasn't been back to the crash site yet," Ben said, "and she was unconscious when we got her out." Turning to Jessica he added, "I and a few of my neighbors, including Josh here, made a sort of temporary cemetery down there, the day after we brought you back here. I expect when things are settled down here, the families will come and exhume the bodies, but in the meantime, we couldn't just leave them there like that."

"It was a mess," Josh said, but Jessica didn't want to think what the rest of the plane, and the rest of the passengers, must have looked like when they had pulled her out. She was also surprised that anyone would ask a kid his age to help deal with such death and destruction like that. She didn't want to picture this happy kid having to sift through smoldering debris and dead bodies. "I can't believe you're alive, but I'm glad you are." He held out his hand, and she shook it.

"Thanks," she responded, straightening her dress, being suddenly conscious of it again. "Now if I can just get home without getting killed by some terrorist, I'll be content."

"No terrorists around here," the boy said, which seemed odd to Jessica.

"Don't forget Halen." The voice came from behind Jessica, and she turned—with just a twinge of pain—to see another man, this one probably around 25 years old, tall and thin, with longish light brown hair, and a face that reminded her of Nicholas Cage, from her favorite movie, "Con Air." "If anyone around here is a terrorist, it's gotta be Halen." He turned to face Jessica. "He killed a U.S. senator with his bare hands, ya know," he said, gritting his teeth and clenching his fists for dramatic effect. Then his face instantly returned to its prior cheerful state. "Hey, pops," he said to Ben.

"Good morning, Douglas," Ben said, with a disapproving look. "I was just telling Jessica here about my neighbors, explaining that she has nothing to fear. And you're not really helping."

"Yeah, these hills are just crawling with diabolical terrorists," said Doug, looking around with mock suspicion. "Can't you tell? Better call in the feds to save us all." He casually flopped down onto one of the empty benches. Jessica wasn't sure what to make of his antics. He seemed to be making fun of the situation as if it wasn't really that serious. But based on what little she had heard, it sounded deadly serious.

"Oh, I almost forgot," Joshua cut in, and held out the bag he was still carrying. "Heather wanted me to bring some stuff over. She said you were about my sister's size. My sister's away right now. Normally she'd kill me if I looked in her drawers, but I think she'd want you to have clothes." Jessica cautiously accepted the bag, and peered in. It was full of clothes—clothes made this century, she thought, and then felt a bit guilty for

**47**

thinking that. Heather had been considerate enough to think of this, in the midst of everything else going on around them.

Jessica rummaged a little, then pulled out a one-piece bathing suit. Doug burst out laughing, and gave Josh a gentle punch in the head. "You think she's going swimming in January, you knuckle-head?"

Josh blushed. "I just grabbed a pile of stuff," he said timidly, looking the other way, "I didn't stop to pick and choose."

"I hope you didn't forget the lingerie," Doug taunted. "But then, Susan isn't really the same size as Miracle Girl here, not everywhere," he continued. Jessica could feel his eyes assessing her, and she kept rummaging without looking up. "I meant that as a compliment," Doug quickly added.

"Mind your manners, Doug," said Ben sharply.

"I wanted to ask, what's the news out there sayin' about all of this?" Josh asked Jessica after a brief, awkward silence. Jessica suspected that he was more eager to change the subject than he was to hear about the news. "How are they reportin' all this outside of here? Like, how did they say it started?" Jessica found Joshua's thick southern accent amusing, and wondered where he was from.

"I didn't really pay much attention," she admitted. "I heard something about a shootout. They said a terrorist killed a police officer or something. I forget, exactly." She pulled a pink knitted top out of the bag that reminded her of her lost pink sweater. She set it aside and kept looking through the bag.

"I was there when it started," said Josh eagerly. "I can tell you exactly how it went down." He glanced over at Ben, as if expecting Ben to stop him. Ben nodded slightly, and Josh continued. "Me and Keith were out shootin'—we have a range set up on the hill. Well, we see Deputy Dog comin' up—"

"Deputy Dog?" Jessica asked, looking up.

"Harold Doggis," answered Ben. "Somewhat unfortunate name for a deputy."

"So he drives up," Josh continued, "and Keith walks to meet him, and I follow a little behind. Keith can be a bit of a wise-ass, ya know. And he's still holdin' his AR. Deputy Dog says old lady Sellers says she saw kids smoking pot in her woods, and said she saw them run across the road and over yonder, into the woods over there on Keith's property." Josh pointed over the hills beyond Ben's cabin. "Well, Dog wants to check it out, but Keith says, 'Where's your warrant?' Dog don't like that, and says he don't need no warrant. Has some legal excuse—I forget what. Anyway, Keith's still standin' there, holding the rifle—not pointing it at Dog or nuthin'—but he says Dog ain't comin' on his property without a warrant. You know how Keith is," he added, turning to Ben.

At this point Jessica stopped looking through the bag of clothes and gave the tale her full attention. She had expected him to tell about some scary group of strangers coming and setting up a terrorist headquarters. But it seemed as if this sweet-faced boy might actually be personally familiar with the terrorists, at least one of them, maybe even sympathetic to them.

Noticing her eyes on him, Josh blushed a little and lost his train of thought. Jessica smiled inwardly. If she could have this effect on a boy with her bruised face, no makeup, and wearing an old lady's house dress, she guessed she wasn't doing too badly.

"Then Dog says he's gonna arrest Keith for obstruction of justice," said Josh, finding his place again. "Keith just says, 'No, you ain't.' Dog says, 'You're under arrest.' Keith says, 'No, I ain't.' Then they both just stand there, not sayin' a word, for maybe five minutes. It looks like Dog is tryin' to decide what to do. After a while he walks to his car and calls Deputy Dawson—we only got three cops for the whole town here. Even when Dawson shows up, they just stand around, like they don't know what to do. It looked to me like Dawson was tryin' to talk Dog into just walkin' away. Dawson's okay. Better than the other two, at least. Dog keeps pointin' at Keith, saying, 'You're under arrest,' but he doesn't do nuthin'. At this point the cops are out on the road, wouldn't even step on the property again. I don't know how long they were there—a long time—but eventually Dog says, 'This ain't over,' and they get in their cars and drive away. I haven't seen the local cops back since then."

"As best I can tell from the folks I've talked to," Ben said, taking up the story, "Mr. Doggis was boiling mad—felt as if Keith had made a fool of him. He called the feds—Doggis has a buddy in the FBI—but they said there was nothing they could do. Not their jurisdiction. I don't know whose idea it was, but apparently some days later they got Mrs. Sellers—elderly lady who lives across the road over the hill, and not the friendliest soul—to say she heard machine guns being fired over here."

"We ain't never had machine guns," Josh cut in. Jessica glanced at the rifle still leaning against the cabin, which she had assumed before was a machine gun. "The cops know what we got, and know it's all legal," Josh went on. "Old Lady Sellers doesn't know what she's talkin' about. Plus, she's as deaf as she is mean."

"Anyway," Ben continued, "based on her word, the ATF showed up a few days later with a search warrant, wanting to look for machine guns. Somehow they got a judge to sign off on a warrant for this whole neighborhood, including all six of the houses inside the river bend. Well, Keith said no way. The road into here goes through his property. So they can't get back here unless he lets them through."

"This part I saw," Josh eagerly cut in again. "I was in Keith's house, lookin' out the window. Keith was out front, and there had to be thirty feds, dressed all in black, all holdin' MP5's and M16's, and a couple things I didn't recognize. They all stood there for the longest time, but Keith wouldn't back down. I could see his hands shakin'. He was either scared to death or mad as hell—maybe both. But he didn't back down, and he didn't make a move. They were talkin' for a while, but I couldn't hear much. I think Keith was sayin' that their warrant was no good. They were arguin' about the right of way or something. But I heard it when the fed up front—the guy in charge, I guess—said that they were comin' in whether Keith liked it or not. Well, Keith pulls out his Glock—doesn't aim it at them, just holds it pointin' down. But man, they didn't like that. They all got their guns up, screamin' at him to put his down. I thought Keith was a goner for sure. Then the guy in charge says he's gonna count to three, and if Keith doesn't drop the gun, the guy'll shoot him. I guess Keith thought he was bluffin', because he just stands there while the guy counts. Well, when he gets to three, he shoots. It was a quick burst, maybe four or five rounds. But it hits Keith in the side and shoulder, and spins him around. I think I saw two other agents fire a round or two, but I don't know who hit him. But as soon as they started shooting, the lead ATF guy, the guy in charge, half his head just explodes—really gross. Then I hear this huge boom coming from way off to the right. The bullet got there before the sound did. I guess that was Halen with his 50 cal, but I don't know where he was. Maybe on his roof. I never saw him. Keith managed to stagger inside, and I ran to help him. We both hit the deck, and I didn't look up again. I thought for sure they'd all be crashin' through the doors any second and kill us both."

The reality of where Jessica was really started to sink in. Despite the pleasant scenery and polite company, she suddenly felt foolish for having been rummaging through clothes a moment before, looking for something fashionable, as if that was of any importance right now. It was one thing to read a story like this in the newspaper. It was another to hear it from someone who had been in the middle of it.

"Halen later told me that he did shoot the ATF agent who had shot Keith, which I wish he hadn't done," said Ben, shaking his head.

"Halen told you it was him?" Josh asked. "I mean, I knew it had to be, but I never came right out and asked him. He must have been hiding somewhere, watching everything through a scope. But he had to, Uncle Ben. Keith would've been a goner."

"He said that after the first shot, the feds were looking around, trying to figure out where the shot had come from," Ben said. "They started to back off, back to their vans, so Halen didn't shoot again. He said he had no choice; it was either kill the guy, or let them kill Keith."

"Did Keith survive?" Jessica cut in, with a tone of surprise.

"Yeah. That freak got hit with three bullets," Josh said, "but they were all flesh wounds. He's still not in the best shape, but he's up and around again now. Man, he never fired a shot at them, never even raised his gun. I saw the whole thing. And they tried to blow him away. I'm glad Halen took out that guy. The bastard deserved it."

"Well, it hasn't exactly helped the situation," Ben replied. "But Halen told me, and I sure do believe it, that he could have killed all thirty of those ATF guys, before they would even have known where he was, and before they could have taken cover. So I'm at least glad he didn't do that."

"I don't want to sound ignorant, here," interjected Jessica timidly, "but what's the ATF?"

"Federal Bureau of Alcohol, Tobacco and Firearms," Ben explained. "A while back they added something else to their name, something about explosives, but most people still call them the ATF. They're the agency that enforces the federal gun laws."

"Yeah, the completely unconstitutional federal gun laws," said Josh. "Bunch of fascists. Ever hear what happened over in Waco?"

"Sort of. I don't know much about it," Jessica said, and realized she had been saying that about a lot of things recently.

"Pretty horrible stuff," Josh commented. "Ask Doug here some time. He knows more about it than anyone I know."

"Basically, the feds murdered almost a hundred men, women and children," Doug said cavalierly. "Called them a cult and said they were dangerous. Then terrorized, tortured and killed almost all of them, and threw the rest in prison. Then they destroyed or covered up all the evidence. Some time I can give you all the details, but you might not want to hear them." The term "conspiracy theory" came into Jessica's mind, but since she knew nothing at all about what Doug was talking about, she kept her mouth shut.

"Anyway," Ben continued, "after the standoff with Keith, the feds backed off, set up their blockade, and brought in more men and equipment. We've all been stuck here ever since."

"Every once in a while one of the feds' helicopters flies over," Josh added, "but that's about all that's been happening around here since then."

"That's it? That's what started all this?" Jessica said, somewhat surprised. She had been waiting for the point in the story when the terrorists got involved, but it sounded as if the story was over. "So who's the Iron Web? Where are they?"

"In the feds' imaginations, mostly," Josh remarked with obvious disdain.

"Isn't there a David somebody?" Jessica asked. "The news kept mentioning him as their leader."

"David wasn't even there," Doug said with a hint of exasperation. "He had nothing to do with it. And he's not the leader of anything. They just don't like his book, so they're using this event to try to paint him as some dastardly villain, even though he had nothing to do with what went down."

"I never heard about any book," said Jessica. "I just kept hearing that he was the leader of this group that's doing bad things all over the country."

"David wouldn't hurt a fly," said Josh indignantly. "And he wouldn't tell anyone else to, either."

"Okay, folks," Ben said, slapping his hands on his knees and standing up. "As Jessica's de facto doctor here, I'm gonna cut this short. She needs her rest, mental and physical." Jessica noticed that she was rubbing her leg, which had been hurting more and more as she sat there, though she had been too absorbed in the conversation to pay much attention to the pain. "Let's get you inside, and get the weight off that leg. There'll be plenty of time to chat later."

"Yeah, probably a good idea," she replied. Ben took her arm to help her up, and Josh, who was closer than Doug, quickly grabbed the bag and took her other arm. "Thanks for the clothes," she said to Josh as she rose painfully to her feet. He smiled, blushed again, and looked away. Josh was quickly endearing himself to her, and she could hardly imagine him firing that scary-looking rifle he carried.

They all walked around to the front of the cabin, and then Josh and Doug said goodbye and headed off into the woods. As Ben opened the front door, the sound of distant, blaring music started up from over the hills. "What on earth is that?" Jessica asked.

———

**JASON** sat in a folding chair in front of his trailer, watching the slowly sloping, grassy hill in front of him, just as he had done the two days prior, without anything happening. "I fight authority, authority always wins." The chorus of the song repeated in a loop, over and over again, from two loudspeakers high atop thirty-foot poles at each end of the line of trailers. Somewhere on the other side of that hill, only a few hundred yards away, were the cabins where the terrorists were hiding out. But with all the agents and trailers now lining the road, the chance of anyone coming out seemed extremely remote. Jason had to fight the urge to doze off in the warm sun.

"I fight authority, authority always wins." The music droned on.

"Man, why do we have to hear this stuff, too?" Jason asked, as Red walked up. "I'm overdosing on John Cougar."

"It's only been on for twenty minutes so far," Red said. "Better get used to it. Besides, we take shifts, so we can get away from it," Red said with a smile. "They can't. It'll wear them down, you'll see. Basic psy-ops stuff. And if you think it's loud from here, step in front of the speakers for a second. They're special speakers designed to focus all the sound in one direction."

"Well they don't work, unless someone decided to aim them at me," Jason said with some annoyance. "What's the point, anyway?"

"To wear the wackos down. They won't be able to sleep, or relax. After a couple days of this, giving up will start looking better and better to them. They did the same thing at Waco, but with some other song. I forget what it was."

"Yeah, and that turned out real well, didn't it?" Jason said flippantly. "If someone did this to me, I think I'd probably shoot them."

"I fight authority—" the music ended with a loud "smack."

"We blow a circuit or something?" Red asked. In the middle of his sentence, a deep boom like the crack and rumble of thunder came echoing over the hills in front of them. In the distance Jason could hear the other loudspeaker blaring on for a few more seconds, until it too fell silent, followed by another distant boom.

"Oh, my God, look at the speaker," Jason said, pointing at what was left of the box atop the nearer pole, about a hundred feet away. Broken plastic and wires were hanging off of it. "They shot it." Red brought his rifle up, and pointed it around in the general direction of the compound. "From the delay, it had to be from really far away," Jason reasoned. "Damn, someone in there has some serious firepower. It had to be 50 cal." He looked over at Red, who was squinting suspiciously toward the hills. "Well, at least we can have some peace and quiet now," Jason said, sitting back in his chair.

"You think this is funny?" Red said with genuine anger. "How do you know they weren't shooting at us?"

"First of all, they can't see us over that hill," Jason answered. "They could only hit the boxes because they're way up on those poles. Second, what are the chances that they'd aim at us, and instead just happen to hit two foot-wide boxes from three hundred yards away? And I can't really say I blame them. It was getting on my nerves, and we're on the quiet side."

"I'm telling Bridges," Red said, and walked off. Jason snickered at how much the statement sounded like a child saying, "I'm telling mom," but he also knew that the incident needed to be reported, and he was glad Red was doing it.

**BETSY** once again found herself sitting uneasily, a forced half smile on her face, as her friend took verbal swings at the next President of the United States.

"What's so extreme and unreasonable about having the cops just go after people who hurt other people, and leave everyone else alone?" asked Sandy.

"It's just too simplistic," Grant answered calmly. "Your ideas sound good in theory, but in the real world, you and I both know that a lot of people make bad choices, and some of those choices hurt other people, as well as themselves."

"So Big Brother gets to decide what all the good choices are, and force them on everyone?"

"No, the people are the ones deciding, through their elected representatives," Grant replied. "The representatives make laws to tell everyone what society will and will not tolerate."

"It's not society who kicks down the doors and drags people off to prison for smoking a joint. It's the pigs who work for the politicians."

Unable to remain silent any longer, Betsy blurted out, "God, Sandy, would you please shut up now?"

Grant burst out laughing, and said, "Don't worry about it. She can say what she thinks. I'm not going to hold what your friends think against you." His voice went back to his official, slightly condescending politician tone, as he continued. "Again, it's fine to believe in ideals like that, but they just don't work on a practical level. If we want society to work smoothly, and for us to all get along, we need a set of rules that everyone has to follow, whether they agree with all of the rules or not. I hope you would at least agree that, while it's fine to try to change laws you don't like through the democratic process, as long as it is the law, we all have an obligation to abide by it."

"Hmm," Sandy hesitated, looking skeptical. "Maybe Betsy's right; I'd better shut up now."

"Well, what do you think the world would be like if everyone decided for himself which laws to follow and which to ignore?" Grant persisted. "Fairly chaotic, don't you think?"

"Actually," Sandy opined, "I'd say that a whole lot of the chaos we have today—death, oppression, and injustice—comes from people making, obeying, and enforcing stupid laws."

"Well, the people have the power to change the law whenever they want," came Grant's retort. "That's what elections are for."

Seeing Sandy roll her eyes, and expecting some less-than-polite statement from her, Betsy cut into the conversation again. "I must admit, it doesn't usually seem like the people have much of a choice. I mean, most of the time it seems like people just vote for the guy they dislike a little bit less than the other guy." Suddenly remembering who she was talking to, she quickly added, "present company excepted," which brought another chuckle from Grant.

"Well, what do you suggest?" Grant asked. His chair was tilted back, and he looked as if he was enjoying himself. "This is how democracy works. It's certainly not perfect, but do you know of any better system? How do they put it? 'It's the worst system of government, except for all the other ones'? Something like that."

"Not to get nit-picky, here, your Highness," Sandy said, making Betsy cringe, "but this isn't supposed to be a democracy. It was supposed to be a constitutional republic, where individuals have unalienable rights, whether the majority likes it or not. Majority rule is not freedom. Majority rule is two wolves and a sheep voting on what to have for dinner."

"Benjamin Franklin. Very good. But I have a controversial question for you, Lady Liberty," Grant said, causing an involuntary snicker to escape from Betsy. "If the Constitution is the law of the land because 'We the People' said so, what if 'We the People' change our minds? What if tomorrow 'We the People' decide that some new system—pure democracy, socialism, a dictatorship, whatever—would better serve the country's needs? Are you going to tell the people that *you* will decide what's best for them, whether they like it or not?" Betsy looked at Sandy, who had no immediate answer. "One way or the other," Grant continued, "someone has to make the rules. And wouldn't it be best if everyone had a say in how that happens, and in what the rules will be?"

"Well, to be fair, the majority has been wrong lots of times," Betsy offered, coming to her friend's defense. "The majority in this country thought slavery was okay for many years. Lots of stupid, unfair things have had majority support in the past." There was a pause, and Betsy suddenly felt self-conscious. She never went head-to-head with Grant like that. "I admit, I don't know what to do about it," she added quickly. "How can there be a system that does the right thing, even if the general public is stupid or malicious? It doesn't seem possible."

"In theory, that's what representative government is supposed to do," Grant responded. "It reflects the values of society, but also serves as a check on mob mentality and a guard against one group oppressing another."

"Except that government is the biggest oppressor of them all," Sandy said. "Power always corrupts. Whoever you put there will be the new biggest problem around. That's why the focus should be on limiting the power itself, to give no one enough power to oppress the people. That's what the Bill of Rights was all about."

"But if the government has no power, how can it protect people?" Grant asked. "Would you disarm the police because you fear government corruption, leaving them unable to do the job of protecting people from the criminals out there? If you take away the military's planes and tanks, for fear of them being used against you, aren't you simply inviting some foreign invader to come here and oppress us far more?"

"This is giving me a headache," Betsy said, in part because she had a lot of work to do and wanted to get back to it. "It sounds like we're doomed, whether we have a huge, all-powerful government, or a puny, weak one."

Sandy spoke up. "Well, if I had to choose, I gotta go with Thomas Jefferson. As he said, 'I would rather be exposed to the inconveniences attending too much liberty—'"

Grant interrupted her to finish the quotation: "—than to those attending too small a degree of it." Sandy and Betsy both stared at him in surprise.

**JESSICA** sat in the recliner in Ben's living room, while the battery-powered radio played in the background. Even during the day, the cabin seemed fairly dark with no electric lights. The events that Joshua had described kept turning over in her mind: the police shooting Keith, and then the agent getting killed. That was pretty bad, but there had to be more to the story than that. She tried in vain to recall what she had heard on the news about it before she had gotten on that plane. If she'd ever dreamed that she would end up in the middle of the Iron Web story, maybe she would have paid some attention to it. She knew there had to be something more going on here than what Josh had described.

At that point, however, Jessica was far less interested in understanding the situation than she was in getting away from it, and back home again. She was thinking of going back to her room for a nap when the words from the radio suddenly caught her attention. "We have an update on the incident on Flight 422. Two members of the group calling itself the Iron Web have been identified as those who—"

Ben walked quickly over to the radio, though seeming as if he was trying to look casual, and switched it off. Looking slightly uneasy, he turned to Jessica and said, "I think it would be best if you weren't constantly reminded of ... that."

"I was just thinking of taking a nap anyway," Jessica said, though Ben's behavior made her, for the first time, a little suspicious. Ben helped her to her feet, and helped her hobble to her room and climb onto the bed.

"When you get up," Ben said, "Heather will probably have some lunch ready for us. Sweet dreams," he said, and closed the door.

Jessica, though tired, lay awake for a while. Her imagination wouldn't let her sleep, wondering just where the terrorists were, how many there were, what they looked like, and so on. Ben didn't seem at all scared of them, but maybe that was only because they knew him. Maybe they wouldn't be so tolerant of a stranger in their midst.

After a while she gave up the attempt to sleep, sat up in bed and looked around the room. Slowly she stood up, holding onto a bed post. Even a few minutes in bed made her muscles feel stiff and sore. She took a few steps to the door, and noticed the sound of whispering on the other side. Putting her ear against the wood, she listened.

Ben's voice was whispering, " ... to explain that?"

"She's going to find out sooner or later," came Heather's quiet reply.

"She won't understand," Ben said, his voice rising a bit. "For now it's best that she doesn't know, for her own sake."

"Don't you think her parents have a right to know that she's alive?" Heather asked.

"For the time being, it's better if they think she's dead. If word gets out what happened here—it's just not safe. You know that."

Hadn't Ben said there were no communications? Now it sounded as if they were keeping her presence here a secret on purpose. Why would they do such a thing? Jessica wondered.

"She's an innocent kid," Heather pleaded. "I wish there was a way to get her away from all this, before things get really bad. Why not use the tunnel that the kids dug?"

Jessica heard Ben sigh. "It's not just a matter of getting her out. You know that. We can't let her leave here, knowing what she knows."

Jessica's mind raced. Couldn't *let* her leave? Why not? She still had a hard time believing that Heather or Ben meant her any harm, but they were obviously keeping something from her, and keeping her from getting home, away from all of this mess. She started to get worried, and a little scared.

**63**

"Well, I have to run now," Ben said in a more natural tone of voice. After a moment of silence, Jessica looked through a crack between the boards of the door, and saw Ben standing there, putting on a black jacket. Then he put something around his neck. It took her a moment to recognize it as a white priest's collar. "I haven't worn this in a while," she heard him say, "but it just might keep things a little more civil." With that, he walked out of the room. Was he off to visit the terrorists? Hearing Heather's footsteps, Jessica suddenly feared that she would come check on her, so she staggered back to her bed, as quickly and quietly as she could.

What could it all mean? Was she being held hostage? Who was Ben going to see? Was he more friendly with the terrorists than he was letting on? Was he one of them? She considered trying to escape, but there was no way, not with her leg the way it was. She made up her mind to confront Ben when he got back. She was getting more and more nervous and suspicious, trying to make sense of it all, but she still couldn't believe that Ben would intentionally do anything to hurt her.

---

**JASON** sat in his uncomfortable metal chair as other agents talked and milled around. "Have a seat, and pay attention," Agent Bridges said, as he walked into the meeting room and tossed his clipboard onto the desk. "Well, we just got word, the guys up top want to up the pressure a bit."

"We're going in?" Red asked with obvious enthusiasm.

"Sort of," Bridges replied. "As things stand now, they're too comfortable in there. I'm sure you've all heard by now what they did to our speakers. So we can add destruction of government property to the list of charges against them. The point is, who knows how long they can stay in there like that? At the same time, we don't want to charge in with guns blazing. Well, maybe Red does," he corrected himself, and several agents snickered. He pointed at the map on the wall. "Here's the deal. On the north end of the area is a single cabin all by itself. It's right on the edge of these woods, which back up to the river. We just got a new search warrant, just for that one cabin. Tonight, if all goes well, we're going to execute the warrant. The plan is to sneak across the river in small boats. The woods aren't that deep, maybe a hundred yards, and we have snipers on that side who can see if anything is moving before we go in. So we cross the river, make our way through the woods, and take control of that one cabin."

"I'm in," answered Red. "How many are going?"

"As best we can tell, the only one who is usually in that cabin is an elderly man. So we won't need an army division for this, and the fewer we use, the less likely we'll be to get noticed before we get there. I'm suggesting just six go in at first, which is the minimum number I like to use for any search. Once we secure the area, we'll bring more across. Volunteers?" A dozen hands shot up.

"Miguel, Sam, Red, Cliff, Jack, you're in," Bridges said, pointing them out. "Jason, think you're ready for your first taste of action?"

"Chomping at the bit, sir," Jason answered, getting a few chuckles in reply. In truth, he was a little nervous about the idea. It was starting to sound more like a military incursion than a normal search and seizure, and he wasn't sure the team really had enough experience at that sort of thing.

"Then you're the sixth," Bridges said. "Again, we don't expect much resistance at that one cabin, but always be ready. You never know what's going to happen, or what might go wrong. Keep alert, and do everything the way you were trained to do it." He looked at his watch. "You six be back here in two hours, and we'll go over the details. We'll go in just after dark. That's all for now." Bridges picked up his papers and walked out of the room, as if he had somewhere important to be. The other agents got up and wandered outside.

"It's about time," Red said to Jason, as they stepped out into the bright sunlight again. "I was getting sick of standing around doing nothing."

Jason didn't say anything as they walked back toward his trailer. As a small town cop, he had been involved in only two raids, both for drugs, and nothing had really happened. But there was always that uncertainty, and it was even worse here. Who knew what they could expect from the people in there?

On the grass in front of Jason's trailer was the box he had put down when Bridges had called them all to the meeting. He sat down cross-legged next to it, and opened it. He took out six empty 30-round magazines and laid them on the grass, brought out the metal ammo box full of .223 rounds and opened it. Then, methodically, he started pushing the rounds into the clips, one by one. He wondered to himself if any of these bullets would ever end up killing a person. He sincerely hoped not. He offered a silent prayer as he loaded the bullets: Please, God, let me make the right decisions.

"You ain't even loaded yet?" Red asked, standing over him, his hands on his hips. "Ya know, they got things that'll do a whole clip in about two seconds."

"I like doing it myself," Jason responded. "Besides, we aren't going in for another few hours."

"Scared?" Red asked in a mocking voice.

"A little nervous," Jason said without shame. "And I suppose you're not?"

"Heck, no. I've got nerves of steel," Red said unconvincingly.

"Yeah, right. Just don't freak out on me if things go bad."

"We're only raiding some old guy's house," Red replied. "Think he'll meet us Rambo-style, a Gatling gun in each hand?"

"It's not him I'm worried about," Jason said, continuing to load the magazines.

"Jay, you got nothing to worry about," came Miguel's voice from behind them. "You're the best shot here." He put his arm around Red's shoulders, shaking him. "Here's the guy I don't want next to me. I'd be more scared of him hitting me by accident than of the damn webbies hitting me on purpose."

"Webbies?" Jason asked.

"The Iron Web knuckle-heads," Miguel explained. "That's what we're calling them now."

"We don't even know how many there are in there," Jason said, looking up. "We have no idea what kind of weapons they have, legal or illegal. For all we know, we could go in there and meet a hundred end-of-the-world crackpots with grenades and sniper rifles. Or we could sneak in and start stepping on land mines and booby-traps. We don't know what's in there."

"Gonna go cryin' home to your mommy, Pretty Boy?" Red teased, in a voice that made Jason want to slug him.

"No, shit-head," Jason said, getting angry, "but it would be nice to live through this."

"Hey, it's not like we're invading the whole compound," said Miguel. "It's one little house, off on the outskirts in the woods. Some old guy isn't likely to have mines and booby-traps in his woods."

"Yeah, you're probably right. I'd just rather be prepared. It beats being captured and tortured to death by a bunch of sadistic, inbred rednecks," Jason said, trying to smile.

"Woah, man," Red said, "you're starting to sound like me."

"Heaven forbid," came Jason's response. After a moment of silence, he added, "Did you hear what they did to the IRS guy over in Idaho? They were doing a search—"

"Yeah," Red interrupted excitedly, "and one of them got captured. The webbies tied him up to a big-ass cross out front of their little hideout, naked."

"That's bullshit," Miguel said. "I think I even know the guy who started that rumor, just to mess with us."

"No, man, it's true," Red said confidently.

"Oh, you were there?" Miguel asked mockingly. "So how come it never made the news?"

"Maybe they didn't want to embarrass the agent by telling everyone what happened," Red suggested.

"Yeah, or maybe it really is all a complete crock," Jason said, hoping he was right.

"Either way, the damn webbies ain't takin' me alive," Red said.

"You're right," responded Miguel. "If I was on their side, you'd be the first one I'd shoot." With that, Miguel walked away toward the trailer where he was stationed.

Having filled a magazine, Jason slid it into one of the pockets on the carrying case of his M16. At that moment he wanted more than anything for this mission to be over and done with. He gazed absent-mindedly toward the rolling hills again. His mind in a peaceful daze, it was almost twenty seconds before his brain noticed what his eyes were looking at. A tiny figure, only the top half visible, was moving over the hill toward him. He jumped up, rifle in hand, which made Red jump, too. Then Red saw the approaching figure, and raised his rifle in its direction.

"What the hell are you doing?" Jason shouted, thinking Red was about to fire.

"I'm just getting a better look through the scope."

"Well, get the binoculars."

"He's got his hands up," Red said, ignoring the instruction. "I think it's a priest."

"So stop pointing a gun at him, and go get Bridges," Jason said.

"He just left. I overheard him saying he was going into town for a minute. We can handle this. Let's go." Red set off at a jog in the direction of the approaching figure, and Jason followed, not feeling as if he had much of a choice.

By that time the figure was easy to make out: a stocky, gray-haired elderly man, dressed like a priest, his hands high, walking at a slow but steady pace. When he was about a hundred feet away, Red yelled out to him, bringing his rifle to the ready. "Keep your hands high, and turn around." The man complied. "Slowly walk backwards, towards us, keeping your hands where we can see them." Red was still shouting, though the man by now wasn't far away at all. "Okay, now down on your knees, and hands behind your head." Again, the man complied, without a word. "Don't move a muscle," Red barked at him. "Check him for weapons," he said to Jason in a loud whisper.

Jason put his own rifle down and walked forward, feeling a little awkward and embarrassed. He patted down the priest, and mumbled, "Sorry about this, Father," in the man's ear, hoping Red wouldn't hear. He stood up again, and said, "He's clean." He walked over and picked up his rifle. He looked at Red, who was starting to tremble a bit, his rifle still aimed at the priest's head. Getting worried, Jason decided he had better take charge. "I'll stay here with him. You go get a call in to Agent Bridges." After a moment's hesitation, Red obeyed, and went running off toward the trailers, though Jason was sure that other agents would have noticed what was happening by now, and would already have Bridges on the line anyway.

For a minute, Jason and the priest didn't move, the priest on his knees with his hands on his head, and Jason holding his rifle pointed at the ground with the safety still on. A gentle breeze made the long grass wave. Jason suddenly felt very foolish, and said, "You can put your hands down." The man did. "And you can stand up, and turn around." When the man did, instead of furious indignation, Jason saw a friendly expression on the man's face.

"I'm Father Benjamin Frank," the man said, and held out his hand. "And I think I can be of some help here."

Still feeling self-conscious, Jason finally shook the man's hand, but all he could think of to say was, "Agent Reilly." The two of them stood there in silence for a while, the priest looking content and comfortable, but Jason feeling more and more silly. "Look," he finally said, "I'm sorry about all that, but we're all a bit on edge here, with everything that's been going on."

"Quite understandable," the man replied.

It seemed like forever that they stood in silence until the old man spoke again. "Well, you picked a good day for working outside." Jason faked a smile, but said nothing.

The center of town was only half a mile away, but it seemed like an hour, during which neither man said anything, before Jason finally saw Red and Bridges approaching. Bridges walked up, his right hand outstretched to the priest. "I'm Agent Gerald Bridges, and I'm in charge here. How can I help you?" he asked as the two shook hands. Jason glanced at Red, whose expression said that he wasn't at all pleased with Bridges' friendly treatment of this man.

"I'm Father Benjamin Frank. As you probably know by now, my house is over by the woods to the right there," he said, turning and pointing over the hill behind him. "I wanted to come out and see if there's any way I can help work this situation out peacefully."

"Well, are they ready to surrender?" Bridges asked with a smile.

"I haven't talked to them yet. I came here first. I was thinking I could be a sort of go-between. These people know who I am, and they trust me. I've never been a negotiator or anything like that, but I'd be happy to take messages back and forth."

"I'm not sure that will work," Bridges responded skeptically, his hands on his hips. "In a situation like this, we don't want a lot of movement back and forth, though maybe we can set up radio communication. Why don't you come inside with me, so I can make a couple calls, and see if we can work something out." As Bridges and the priest walked away, Jason could just hear Bridges saying, "I appreciate your willingness to do this." Jason and Red headed back toward their own trailer.

"You're sure he didn't have any weapons on him?" Red asked suspiciously.

"Look around," Jason said, indicating the numerous trailers, and dozens of armed agents milling about. "If he came out here with a rocket launcher, he still wouldn't have a chance. Besides, Red, not everyone in the world is a bad guy."

"Well, I'd be careful of that guy," Red said, squinting his eyes in the direction Bridges and the man had gone. "Mark my words. He may seem nice, but I bet he just came out to do some spying, to see what we got out here. I bet he's one of them. And I'm not sure he's really a priest."

"We're not exactly hiding what we have out here," Jason replied. "And I doubt Bridges took him in to show him all our tactical plans. Relax." After a moment he added, "Do you think he's the guy who lives in the cabin that the search warrant is for? He said his cabin was over that way." Jason pointed to the right, over the hills.

"Maybe," answered Red. "Maybe they have a spy among us, and knew what we were planning, and he came out to foil the plan."

"Or maybe, if it is his house, we lucked out," Jason suggested. "Maybe Bridges will want to keep him out here, to make it easier while we're in there doing the search."

**BETSY** sat in the audience, watching her boss in action. "Contrary to what some critics have dishonestly claimed," Grant Collins was saying to a group of reporters, "this Act does not make it illegal to criticize the government. Far from it. For obvious reasons, it is already unlawful to specifically encourage people to break the law or to tell people to engage in violent rebellion. No rational person would condemn such just and necessary laws, and this act merely strengthens those already existing laws by closing loopholes that have been exploited by those who seek to undermine our democratic system of government. Whether it be jihadists of the Middle East or domestic terror groups here, extremist radicals have long exploited our freedoms, including our freedom of speech, by hiding what is clearly the advocacy of lawlessness and violence under a thin veil of protected political speech. Well, no more. As the bipartisan committee which proposed this bill has repeatedly explained, this is not about censoring anyone's opinions, or criminalizing dissent. Every American has the right to protest any law or policy, or to criticize the government as often and as loudly as he likes. But what freedom of speech does not guarantee, and what this bill will put an end to, is the open advocacy of lawlessness, murder and mayhem."

"Senator Collins," a young male reporter with curly black hair spoke up, "I have here the actual wording of the proposed bill, and the definition of the types of speech prohibited includes the following: quote, any message, spoken or written, the likely result of which would be the incitement of the violation of any law, by either passive or forceful means, end quote. Isn't that definition a bit overly broad? I mean, who is going to decide what is likely to make people want to break the law?"

"Precise definitions and questions about gray areas are matters which will be decided by the federal courts, not by me," the senator answered. "The point is, it is high time we stopped allowing hate speech, threats of violence, and the open advocacy of lawlessness to tear the fabric of this country apart. This act does not outlaw any opinion, or the expression of any opinion. It only strengthens the already-existing laws which prohibit trouble-makers and scofflaws from intentionally inciting criminal acts and violence."

"I would like to get your opinion on a couple of examples," the young reporter continued quickly. "Do you personally think that uttering the following statements would constitute a crime under the new law? Quote, if the machine of government is of such a nature that it requires you to be the agent of injustice to another, then, I say, break the law, end quote. And one more. Quote, just as it is the duty of all men to obey just laws, so it is the duty of all men to disobey unjust laws, end quote. Would such statements be illegal under the new law?"

"Again, I'm not going to bicker about specifics here, or paint myself as the one who will make such decisions," Grant said dismissively. "I am becoming President, not Emperor. If disputes arise about exactly what the law covers, the courts will have to clarify such matters."

"Do you know who said that?" the reporter asked.

"Excuse me?" Grant replied.

"The quotes I read," the reporter explained, "do you know who said them?"

"Not off hand," said Grant, starting to look annoyed.

The young man smiled mischievously, and said, "The first was Henry David Thoreau; the second was Martin Luther King, Jr."

"Let me say this," Grant said, smiling but clearly irritated. "Clever little verbal stunts and trick questions like that one— however misleading they may be—will be considered legal, protected speech as long as I'm President."

"Mr. President," came the voice of a female reporter, over top of the other questions being shouted.

"I'm only calling on you because you called me that," responded Grant with a smile, pointing at an attractive blonde.

"Would you consider the book, *Weaving an Iron Web*, written by David Singh, to constitute the type of speech that this new law would forbid?" she asked.

"Like I said, that would ultimately be for the courts to decide, but if you ask me personally, yes, I would say so," he answered.

"And just a quick follow-up, sir," the blonde reporter went on. "While we wait to see how the courts will apply this law, as you said they would, how do we know in the meantime what is or isn't against the law to say?" Several other reporters murmured in agreement.

"Let me put it this way," Grant answered with a wry smile. "If there's something that may or may not be interpreted as a threat against the government, or an incitement of people to commit violence or break the law, I advise you not to say it."

"Fair enough," the reporter said with a chuckle.

# PART III

**JESSICA** had dozed off without realizing it. The sound of the front door opening awakened her. Before she had fallen asleep, she had spent an hour lying in bed, psyching herself up to confront Ben about what she had overheard. She got up and, feeling a bit stiff and sore again, walked over to her bedroom door, peering through the crack to make sure it was Ben returning. She saw him take off his priest's collar. Then he reached under his shirt and pulled out some electronic device with wires attached. She didn't know what it was, but this seemed as good a time as any to confront him, so she swung the door open. She suddenly wondered if the device was a pacemaker, and was worried she had startled him. But Ben just raised a finger to his lips to keep her quiet, and proceeded to violently rip the wires out of the device he was holding, which confused Jessica even more.

"I was out visiting the feds," he said. "I volunteered to be a go-between, a mediator, between them and—" he paused, "—and the people they're after. The only way they'd let me come back was if I was wearing a wire." He held up the device he had just destroyed. "I didn't go out there to spy on them, and I didn't come back here to spy *for* them." He threw the bundle in the wastebasket in disgust. "To them, everything is a war game; it's all surveillance, propaganda, manipulation, deception. I was hoping that for once they might be open to some actual communication. I knew it was a long shot, but I wanted to try anyway."

"Ben?" Jessica began, trying to muster her courage. She could feel her heart beating faster, and she almost changed her mind, but she was determined to say it. "What is it that you're not telling me?" Ben just looked at her quizzically. "I heard you and Heather talking. What aren't you telling me? Are you keeping me as a hostage or something? Are you using me to make some deal with the terrorists, or with the government?"

Ben looked down at the floor, shook his head, and gave out a long sigh. "Jessica," he began, "what's going on here is—the world isn't what you think it is."

"You're with them, those Iron Web guys, aren't you?" she blurted out, almost involuntarily. "I heard you say you weren't going to let me leave." She was trying to sound confident and indignant, but she was trembling, and inside just felt scared.

"Relax," Ben said with a sigh, "you're in no danger." After a pause he added, "Well, that's not exactly true. You're in no danger from me, and in no danger from any terrorists."

"How can you say that?" Jessica demanded. "They shot down my plane!" Ben thought for a moment, then said, "Just have a seat, Jessica. Let me see if I can find a newscast."

She sat down on the couch, puzzled. Ben sat down in his armchair, and began to fiddle with the radio on the table next to him. He found a newscast, and they waited a few minutes for the top stories.

"I don't understand what the news is going to tell me about why you're keeping me here," said Jessica.

Ben shushed her. "Listen to this," he said.

The voice on the radio was speaking: " ... now believe there may have been a third hijacker on the plane. Again, as we reported last hour, the Department of Homeland Security has issued a statement saying that they now believe that the crash of Flight 422 was caused, not by a scuffle or shootout on the plane as previously suspected, but by the terrorists taking over and then intentionally destroying the aircraft, perhaps with a bomb. In related news, five members of the same group have been arrested in Idaho, on charges that—" Ben turned the volume down.

"Now they've hijacked a plane?" Jessica asked. "Shooting one down wasn't enough?"

"No, that was your plane they were talking about," said Ben.

"No it wasn't," she contradicted. "The one I was on was shot down. It wasn't hijacked. I saw the missile that hit us."

"I know that," Ben said patiently. "Heather and I saw the missile hit, too. And one of our neighbors saw the plane that fired it."

"It came from a plane?" Jessica asked with surprise. "I saw the missile, but I didn't see where it came from. I was picturing someone on the ground with one of those bazooka things shooting it. What kind of plane was it?"

"He's no plane buff, but my neighbor said it was a fighter jet."

"So the terrorists have jets and missiles now? Where did they get them? Is this an invasion or something?" She thought for a moment, and then pointed at the radio. "Are you sure that that was about the plane I was on?" she asked. "Why would the government think it was hijacked? This might be the middle of nowhere, but how could they just miss a jet flying around shooting missiles? Don't they have radar, or satellites or something, to see that sort of thing?"

"Yes, it was your plane. Flight 422, like the reporter just said. And the fact that they *said* it was hijacked doesn't mean that they *think* it was hijacked," he said.

"What do you mean?"

"I mean, maybe some people in the government would rather the public thought the plane was hijacked, even if the people in government know it wasn't."

"Why would they want that?"

"Because the image of scary terrorists taking over a plane and crashing it fits their agenda. Telling the truth doesn't."

"Well, what is the truth?"

"Good question," Ben muttered, almost as if to himself. For a while the room was quiet. "The truth is that a fighter jet shot down a passenger plane with a missile, and someone in the government is telling the media that the plane was hijacked and blown up from inside by Iron Web terrorists. That's what we know. What we don't know is why."

Then Jessica remembered what she had heard Ben and Heather whispering.

"Why didn't you tell me this before?" she asked then. "And why don't you want me to leave? I heard you say you thought it was better if my parents thought I was dead." Ben's explanation seemed honest so far, but it was only making Jessica more confused.

"I don't know anything for sure," Ben answered, "but we do know this: The news has confidently reported that there were no survivors. Only a handful of people in the world know differently. Whatever motive the government has for lying about this, you're the only one who can—"

Jessica jumped as the front door swung open with a bang. Looking up, she saw a tall man, dressed in ragged, dull greens and browns, a look of angry urgency on his unshaven face, and a rifle in his hands. She jumped at the sight. They had come at last, she thought. The terrorists had come to finish her off!

"They're coming through the woods," the man barked. "Let's go!" Jessica sat stunned, unable to figure out what was going on. Who was this person? By the looks of him, he certainly wasn't police. Was he a neighbor warning them that the terrorists were coming? Or was he one of the terrorists himself? He sure looked the part, but then his words wouldn't make any sense. "Now, right now!" the man yelled. "Drop everything, come on!" The urgency of the command brought Jessica to her feet, despite her uncertainty. Ben rose from his chair, looking, not surprised, but stern and angry. Seeing Jessica's confusion, he took her hand and pushed her firmly but gently toward the frightening stranger. The tall man grabbed her arm, and pulled her out the door, a few steps ahead of Ben. Jessica heard Ben's voice behind her: "My sister, I have to—" His words were cut short by several deafening gunshots. She turned her head to see Ben standing in the middle of his own living room, a look of surprise on his face, one hand on his neck, a heavy stream of blood running between his fingers, and another spot of red spreading through the cloth of his shirt at his lower abdomen. Jessica froze in horror. The stranger dropped her arm, and she wobbled unsteadily in the doorway. The next instant, an even louder blast came from immediately behind her, and the picture window beyond Ben shattered. Jessica screamed and crumpled to the ground, eyes closed and ears covered, as three more explosions burst in rapid succession from the stranger's rifle behind her. Then his strong hands grabbed her again and pulled her away from the house.

He dragged her along at a run for a few yards, then suddenly dropped to the ground with her. "That house, over there," he barked, right in Jessica's ear, pointing off into the darkness. "As fast as you can. Don't stop, don't turn around. Go!" Jessica scrambled to her feet and ran like a hunted deer. Another series of three gun blasts made her cup her hands over her ears. She heard yelling behind her, and more gunshots. Adrenaline coursed through her body and she felt no pain or soreness. She dropped her hands and ran as fast as she ever had before, expecting at any moment to feel the sting of a bullet in her back. It was only about a hundred yards to the lamplight in the window of the other house, and no one seemed to be following her, but it still felt like an eternity. She could hear only her own breath and distant voices, angry and urgent. A silhouette appeared in the doorway ahead of her.

"In here," a voice said, followed by "douse the light." Jessica ran through the door, almost tripped over a chair, and collapsed to the floor exhausted. "What happened?" asked the voice. "What happened?" the voice said again. It took her a moment to realize that the question was directed at her.

"I was—we were just—" she started, but she could hardly speak. She was trembling all over, and she felt completely drained of energy, as if that run had taken everything out of her. She heard two muffled voices talking, but she couldn't hear what they were saying. She felt a blanket being wrapped around her, and someone on each side of her. "Ben was shot," she managed to say. She remembered the last image she had seen of Ben, and began crying silently. "We have to go back. Ben—he's bleeding. Someone shot him." She remembered that awful flow of blood, and knew that no one could survive that, but tried to cling to some hope for Ben. "There was—there was someone else. A man came in. He told us to run. He sent me here. He's still back there." For a moment she hoped that the stranger would somehow be able to save Ben. Everything seemed so unreal. How could this be happening?

———⊷⊶———

**JASON** crouched in the darkness, inside a group of bushes, breathing hard and trying to get his bearings. What had gone wrong? Frantically, he tried to go over everything in his head. It was the old priest's house after all, but they had sent the priest back home wearing a wire, without telling him about the search warrant. He couldn't have known about the raid ahead of time, and Agent Bridges was back at the trailers and could hear what was going on by way of the wire the old man was wearing. How could it have gone wrong?

The six of them had quietly crossed the river in two inflatable boats with trolling motors. They had turned off the motors as they neared the other side, and paddled as quietly as they could to the bank, where they had tied up the boats. Then they had crept quietly through the woods without incident. About thirty feet from the cabin, Jack had quietly checked radio contact. Then they had crept closer, until Jason could see the old man and the girl through the big picture window. He could still picture the girl: a pretty face in a sea of dark hair—hardly a person he'd expect to find in a terrorist stronghold. She and the old man had been talking to each other, and then they had both looked away from him and stood up, and had begun moving across the room away from him. By then the girl was in front of the old man, and all he could see was the old man's back.

He'd heard some yells from around the right side of the building, though he couldn't tell if they had come from his fellow agents or from someone else. Then someone behind him and to his right, maybe Red, had yelled, "He has a gun!" and then the gunfire exploded. For a moment Jason had trained his scope on the old man, but saw that he was unarmed, and that he had already been shot. But where was the shooting coming from? Had the terrorists discovered the wire on the priest, and killed him for it?

After the first gunshots, everything turned to chaos, with windows shattering and gunfire on all sides. After almost a minute of confused pandemonium, Jason had heard screams which convinced him that Miguel and Sam had been hit, and maybe others, as well.

Now he crouched in the shadows of the undergrowth, trying to make sense of it all, and trying to figure out what to do next. How badly wounded were the others? Was anyone dead? Was there still a threat? If so, where was it? He turned in every direction, but couldn't make out much of anything. There were still occasional gunshots, but they were less frequent and farther away. It sounded as if whatever was going on was on the other side of the building. He forced himself to jump to his feet, and, in a low crouch, as quickly and as quietly as he could, made his way through the dark underbrush to the left side of the building, hoping to flank whomever he might find out front.

Once he was out of the field of light coming from the large picture window, he had to go by moonlight. The shadows of the trees and bushes made mysterious shapes everywhere. He saw something move and almost fired a shot before identifying the shape as a cat running through the woods. He got around to the side, his back up against the log cabin, and slid along toward the front. His heart was beating like a sledgehammer as he prepared to look around the corner. Things were quiet for ten seconds, and he made his move, spinning around the corner, rifle at the ready.

For a fraction of a second, he saw only two things in the dim light: an angry sneer on an unshaven face, and the butt of a rifle heading for his own face.

**BETSY** noticed that every few days, another new person was being added to Senator Collins' staff. She walked through the array of cubicles, realizing she didn't know the names of half the people there. But she found comfort in being able to pass through them all, and enter Grant's inner sanctum, where most of the time it was just him and her, as it was back when he was a new senator and she was his entire staff. Walking into the office, she heard Grant talking on the phone.

"Yes, I know that," he was saying with a tone of frustration, "but the penalty provisions are still mush." There was a pause. "That's not what I'm saying. We don't want the wording to sound too punitive, but the penalties have to be clear, and right now they're not." There was another pause. "I don't mind using the word 'fine,' but it would soften the effect if it was phrased as a reduction in the benefit amount, or something like that. It sounds less like we're hitting them on the head." Another pause. "Okay, let me know what you come up with," he said, and hung up the phone.

"What was that all about?" asked Betsy.

"The proposed health care bill," Grant answered. "It's important how these things are worded, even if hardly anyone ever reads the damn things."

"I thought you didn't get involved in the legalese nitpicky details," Betsy said, hanging up her coat and bag. "Isn't that what the lawyers are for?"

"This isn't about the technicalities," he answered, "it's about perception, and perception is everything." He sat down on the front of her desk, as she sat down in her chair. "Think of it this way," he continued, sounding like someone giving an economics lecture. "I can either tell you that I'll give you a dollar if you do what I want, or I can tell you that I'll *take* a dollar from you if you *don't* do what I want. Which sounds nicer?"

"The first one," she answered. "The incentive is a reward instead of a punishment."

"Or so it would seem. But when *we* say it, it's actually a punishment either way, because whatever government gives away, it has to first take via taxes. 'I'll tax you less if you do this' means exactly the same thing as 'I'll tax you more if you don't do this,' but the way people perceive it is drastically different. Giving out tax credits sounds benevolent. Imposing fines sounds malicious. Never mind that when we do it, they're the exact same thing."

"So you want the health care bill to sound like it's rewarding people for doing the right thing instead of punishing them for doing the wrong thing," Betsy said, "even though there's really no reward at all. Just a bigger punishment if they don't do what we want, and a smaller one if they do."

"Exactly. After all, it is *law* we're talking about here. We're not just making a suggestion, or asking nicely. We're using the power of government to make things work the way we want them to work. Even if it's made to look nice, the law always has to coerce people into doing things the way we want them to."

"But it seems so manipulative," Betsy said.

"And it is," Grant replied, standing up again and walking toward his desk. "Law is always manipulation. It's just a question of what it will manipulate, how it will manipulate it, and to what end."

"It sounds pretty shady when you put it that way," Betsy said.

"It's only shady when the *other* guy does it," Grant said with a smile. "When we do it, it's necessary for the common good. When we do it, it's called tax cuts. When they do it, it's giveaways to the rich. When we do it, it's national security. When they do it, it's war-mongering. You know how it works."

Betsy feigned a smile, but this type of talk always made her uncomfortable. She had never had particularly strong political beliefs either way, but she wanted to believe that what she did somehow contributed something good to society. And talk like this only made her feel more like someone involved in a giant scam. She could hear Sandy's voice in her head, saying "Told ya so."

Her thoughts were interrupted by the door to the office swinging open, and a page running in. "Turn on the news," the messenger said. "Something else happened in Graveston."

Wondering what it could be this time, Betsy jumped up and turned on the TV, cutting into the news broadcast in mid-sentence: " ... tells us that a third remains in critical condition. According to Veronica Milton, spokesperson for the ATF, several agents were in the process of serving a search warrant—not at the main compound, but at one of the outlying buildings—when an unknown number of heavily armed members of the group calling itself 'The Iron Web' opened fire on them. Details are sketchy, but sources inside the ATF believe that it was a deliberate ambush, set up in advance by the terrorists. There is already word that the agent in charge on the scene, Gerald Bridges, may be reprimanded, or possibly even dismissed, for failing to predict or properly prepare for such an event, a miscalculation that may have cost three federal agents their lives. We'll have more details as the story unfolds. In other news, the Dow Jones Industrial Average has lost another—"

Betsy turned off the television, and the room went silent. She turned toward Grant, who was gazing out the window, his hands in his pockets. "It's such a shame," she said, which seemed to snap Grant out of a trance. "Is it ever going to be over?"

"It will be when I take office," he said grimly. "That I promise."

"What could make people do that?" Betsy asked, looking back at the blank screen. "Whatever complaints they have, how can they possibly justify this sort of thing, even to themselves?"

"That's the challenge, isn't it?" Grant said, turning toward her. "Getting inside other people's heads. What must the world look like to them, in order for them to behave this way?"

"I'm not sure I even want to know," she replied. "It's like the suicide bombers in the Middle East. Whatever their beef is, how can they possibly think that more killing is going to help anything? How can they possibly think it's a good thing?"

"When people build up enough hatred, and feel their cause is just, there's no telling what lengths they'll go to, what pain and suffering they'll inflict on others in the name of that cause," Grant said. "That's pretty much the story of human history."

"How can it possibly be a just cause to destroy a great country and replace it with chaos? How can anyone think that?" said Betsy.

"I don't know," Grant said. "It looks more like insanity than a political philosophy, doesn't it?"

"Yes, it does," said Betsy. But internet watchers said more people every day were sympathizing with David Singh and his followers—and Iron Web symbols were popping up everywhere. More and more people were being drawn into this dangerous insanity, no doubt driven to it by economic desperation and frustration with the social turmoil plaguing the country. For a moment, Betsy wished that the government would throw aside law and civil rights, just long enough to destroy that nest of vipers.

**JESSICA** and the others—whom she had recognized as Doug and Joshua after her eyes had adjusted to the dark—had huddled just inside the open door on the floor, with Jessica in the middle, lights off, not making a sound, for what seemed to them like an hour—Jessica still shaking, all of their ears trained on the woods outside. There was a scary moment when Jessica rested her hand on her ankle, and felt the warm wetness of blood soaking her pant leg. She was astonished that she could have been hit without noticing it. She pulled up her jeans to look at it, but she couldn't see the wound for the blood, and she looked away again. "We gotta stop this bleeding, now," Josh whispered. "Ya got something clean?" Doug glanced around, thinking. Then he took off the flannel overshirt he was wearing. "Try this," he whispered. For a few minutes, the boys were busy sopping blood and cutting the long sleeves off the shirt with a penknife. Then Josh whispered to Jessica, "Just a shrapnel wound. No bullet in there." They wrapped it as tightly as they could in the shirt sleeves.

Now the three of them sat in silence, eyes and ears straining for any sign of life outside, hostile or friendly. Jessica was surprised by how well she could see with nothing but moonlight for illumination. "Doug, where's that night vision scope you got last Christmas?" Josh whispered.

"It's back at Keith's house, and I ain't going out there to get it," came the nervous response.

All eyes were glued in the direction of Ben's cabin. Jessica kept imagining that she could see things moving out there. "I really should go get the first aid kit," Doug volunteered after a while, gesturing at Jessica's leg, the make-shift bandage already soaked with blood. Doug crept off into the shadows of the house. Only then did Jessica notice the rifle leaning against the wall next to Josh, but it didn't make her feel any more comfortable. How had she ended up in a situation like this? She was a teenage girl from a middle class family, going to a boring school in a boring little town. And now she was in the middle of a gun battle in the wilderness of Arizona. This couldn't really be happening. She suddenly felt completely alone, trapped in a strange world, surrounded by strangers, with no idea what was going on and no idea how to get out. Her last conversation with Ben kept playing over in her mind. "Whatever motive the government has for lying about this, you're the only one who can—" I could go out there and tell everyone the truth, she thought. I can prove that these people didn't hijack my plane. Why don't they want me to tell the world that they didn't do it?

"I see something," Josh whispered, and moved slowly to pick up his rifle. "Someone's coming." Jessica peered into the dark, and she could see it too: an indistinct—but this time very real—dark figure, about a hundred yards away, moving toward them. "Stay down," Josh said, getting into a crouched firing position, "in case I have to shoot." The figure was still approaching, but seemed to be injured, because it was moving slowly and awkwardly. "I think that's Halen, and he's carrying something," Josh said at last. Jessica was suddenly filled with hope. Could it be the stranger bringing Ben to safety? Her hopes waned again as he approached. There was no way that what he was carrying was big enough to be Ben. Josh lowered his rifle, and whistled between his teeth.

"Move it, I'm coming in," said the approaching figure. Josh and Jessica stood up to make way, and for the first time Jessica felt pain in her leg where she had been hit. They backed inside, followed by the figure. It was the tall, scruffy man Jessica had seen back at Ben's cabin—Halen, Josh had called him. And he was carrying a body, but it wasn't Ben's. "They've backed off, I think; I'm going back to make sure," Halen said, gently laying the still body on the floor. "Then I have to get something from my house. Keep your eyes peeled. Don't shoot at anything unless you're sure it's not me. I'll be back." With that, he stepped back out the door and disappeared, without a word about the body he had just left with them. Jessica wondered if it was dead, but didn't dare to move close enough to find out. And who was it? Only she and Ben had been at the cabin when he showed up. Who else was there to rescue?

"It's a damn fed!" said Josh, who had apparently been wondering the same thing. In the moonlight coming through the windows, Jessica thought she could see some sort of government agent's uniform on the body.

"Who the hell is that?" Doug's voice, coming from the darkness beyond the body on the floor, made Jessica and Josh both jump. They hadn't heard him come back with the first aid kit.

"Halen's alive," Josh said, "and he brought us a present."

"Just what I always wanted," Doug responded sarcastically. "Is he dead?"

"No, I don't think so," answered Josh. "I don't see any blood."

"Got any rope?" Doug asked. Jessica and Josh both gave him a suspicious look. "Not to hang him, bonehead," he said to Josh. "To tie him up. If he's not dead, eventually he's going to wake up."

"It's your house," Josh said. "Don't you have any?"

"Oh, wait, I might." With that, Doug disappeared again into the shadows.

"I'll close the door, and then let's get farther inside," Josh said. "Your leg," he suddenly remembered. Jessica looked down. It was throbbing with pain now, but it didn't appear to be bleeding much anymore. Creeping carefully on her knees around the body on the floor, she picked up the first aid kit and took it over to the couch against the far wall. With a grimace, she pulled off the old bandage, afraid of what she might find. She hadn't dared to look when Doug and Josh had first bandaged it. To her surprise, it was just a straight two-inch scratch. From all the blood she had expected something much worse. She started working on bandaging it with what she could find in the first aid kit. Her other ankle, the sprained one, was throbbing, too. She was astonished that she'd felt no pain during her sprint from Ben's house to here; now she wasn't sure she could even stand up.

Josh sat in a chair, his rifle in his hands, pointed in the general direction of the figure on the floor. "Come on, Doug," he murmured to himself, "hurry up."

---

**JASON** thought, just for a moment, that he was in his bed back at his parents' house, until he turned his head and felt the rope scratch against his neck. As he regained consciousness, the pain in his head made him wince. Opening his eyes, he saw four faces looking down at him, barely visible in the dark room, which was lit only by two candles, one on each side of his bed. He tried to sit up, but found that his hands, feet, and neck were all tied.

To his left were the faces of two young men, one of them hardly more than a child, looking almost as scared as he was. At the foot of the bed was the girl he had seen through the window—dirty, disheveled, and frightened, but still very attractive for all that. He still had no idea who she was, but found himself relieved to see her alive. He saw no malice in those three younger faces—only fear and bewilderment.

To his right was another face he recognized: the face he had seen for a split second before everything had gone dark. There was no fear in that face. There was no feeling at all. That face scared him. "Where am I?" Jason asked, his voice hoarse. "I'm a federal agent, you know; you can't keep me here." He was trying to sound authoritative, but his voice sounded thin and weak in his own ears.

"We know who you are," the man said in a gruff voice. "We're still trying to decide what to do with you."

"You don't scare me," Jason responded, but it was a lie. At last he was face to face with a real terrorist.

"That wasn't a threat. If I was going to kill you, it would have been a lot easier to do it hours ago," said the man. There was a light knock at the door. The girl and the two younger men jumped at the sound. "It's Keith," the older man said, standing up to open the door. "I told him to bring some food and water over."

In walked a muscular man in a dirty T-shirt and jeans, carrying some bottles of water and a paper bag. Jason recognized Keith Anderson from the mug shots the local police had shown them. So Anderson was alive and walking around, though Jason thought he could see the bulge of bandages under the T-shirt. Anderson looked about 30, with short, sun-bleached hair and a tanned, angular face. What Jason noticed most were his hard, unforgiving blue eyes— eyes that bespoke a hard life. The taller man took a bottle of water from Anderson, twisted off the cap, and brought it over to Jason.

"How do I know it's not poisoned?" Jason asked. In response, the man calmly pulled out a handgun from his waistband, pulled back and released the action, chambering a round, and then just stood there, looking at Jason, the gun at his side. "Okay, okay, I get it. If you wanted to kill me, you would have already." The man put the gun back in its holster without a word, and held the bottle to Jason's mouth, and he drank.

"Why are we feeding this jackboot anyway, Halen?" Keith asked. "He came here to kill us."

"We came here to arrest you, and let the law deal with you," Jason said, trying not to sound scared. "We didn't come here to kill you."

"Oh, great," Keith said sarcastically. "So you only came here to take us away and throw us in prison. And, of course, to kill us if we resisted. Why?"

"Because you broke the law," Jason said angrily.

"Whose law?" Keith asked. For a moment Jason wasn't sure what he meant by that.

"The laws of the United States, of course," said Jason. "I guess you don't recognize that authority," he added flippantly.

"Not these days, I don't, nor does anyone with half a brain," responded Keith. "But exactly what laws are you talking about?"

"The federal firearms laws," Jason answered.

"In this country, the law of the land is the Constitution," Keith declared, "and not only does it not authorize any federal gun control laws, it specifically prohibits them. And any law contrary to the Constitution is no law at all. Even the Supreme Court has admitted that. On top of all that, we didn't even break any of your stupid gun laws. But tell me this: if the laws of your precious United States of Bullshit said that no one was allowed to have any guns at all, would it be okay for you to kill or lock up anyone who refused to comply?"

"I have to enforce whatever the laws are," Jason answered. "If you don't like them, challenge them in court, or get Congress to change them. You can't just ignore them and expect to get away with it."

"That's not what I asked," Keith said, handing out bottles of water and granola bars to the others. "If all guns were banned outright, would you lock people up, and let them ask some paid-off, politically appointed judge to decide their fate, because they refused to be disarmed?"

"Look, I don't make the laws," said Jason. It felt more than a little weird to be having a political discussion with strangers while tied to a bed. "There's some of them I don't like much myself. But it's not my job to decide what the law should be. I just enforce it."

"Yeah, you and the jackboots of every other tyrannical regime in history," Keith said with disgust. "You're just following orders and doing your job, just like the Nazis did. And you think that that somehow releases you from all responsibility." He turned to Halen. "Why are we even letting this bastard live? Does he deserve pity just because he failed to kill us, and managed to get himself knocked out? How much pity do you think he would have shown us if he still had his gun?"

"I didn't come here to kill anyone!" Jason interjected angrily. To have these people calling *him* a Nazi was too much to bear.

"Doug, Josh, why don't you and the girl go keep watch outside, and send David in here?" Halen said in a low voice. David? Jason thought. David the "King of Chaos," as the media had called him? Jason was sure this meant that he was going to be tortured, or worse. Glancing at the girl's expression as she left the room, he guessed that she was thinking the same thing. He wondered again who she was. She still didn't seem to fit in here at all, but they didn't seem to be treating her like a hostage.

After they left, the room was silent for several minutes. Jason, still unable to move, looked back and forth between Keith and Halen, hoping to find the smallest hint of human feeling, but he got only cold stares from Keith, and no expression at all from Halen. Jason didn't want to imagine what sadistic character these guys were calling in to deal with him. But whatever Jason expected, the man who walked through the door a few minutes later was not it. He was a tall man with a handsome, youthful face, and the dark skin and black hair of someone from India or the Middle East. He was casually dressed in blue jeans and a V-neck sweater over a dress shirt, perfectly clean and well-groomed. He didn't look angry, or even worried. His dark brown eyes were friendly as he greeted Jason cordially.

"I'm David Singh," he said. "Jason—it's 'Jason,' isn't it?—I'm sorry about your present situation, but my friends here had to assume you were dangerous." Despite his looks, he had no accent. He casually took a seat in a chair beside the bed. "You and your fellow agents came here uninvited and armed to my friend's home, and set off this tragic chain of events." His voice was neither angry nor accusatory, but sounded instead as if he was simply reporting a fact. "I wasn't there, at the first encounter or at the recent incident, so I don't know exactly what happened at either," he continued. "I do know that someone, either you or the people you came here with, just shot and killed my good friend, Father Benjamin Frank, a man who was a threat to no one." He paused, but Jason had nothing to say. "What you may not know," David went on, "is that one of you also shot my wife. She was washing dishes at our kitchen sink, in our house, which is a couple hundred yards east of Ben's cabin. A bullet came through the wall and hit her."

"Is she okay?" Jason asked with sincere concern. He was surprised then to see a smile growing on David's face.

"Yes, she's okay," he said softly, "and I was hoping you would ask that first. Many, were they in your position, would think first of justifying their own actions, or at least of denying guilt. She was only hit in the leg. It was nothing serious."

"I don't know what all happened," Jason explained truthfully, "but I never fired a shot." He could see no reason not to tell them that much, though he was reluctant to say much more, for fear of giving them something they could use to their advantage.

"Well, that might be a good sign," David replied, "but you are certainly not blameless. You came to our little enclave here with your fellow mercenaries, and invaded one of our homes. One of you killed Ben, and had that stray bullet been just a couple of feet higher, you would have killed my wife also."

"I tell you, I never fired a shot," Jason insisted. "I never even saw anyone I considered a threat, until this guy," he nodded his head toward Halen, "knocked my lights out."

"This may seem like a strange discussion to be having in these circumstances," David said, "but let me ask you this—and I want you to think hard before you answer. No one here invaded your property, or anyone else's. We leave other people alone. We don't take your money, we don't tell you how to live your life. So why is it that you and your fellow agents couldn't just leave us alone, too? Why did you feel the need to come here like this?"

For a long while, Jason couldn't think of any answer. He'd been told that this was the headquarters of the anarchistic cult that was terrorizing the country. And the man speaking to him was supposed to be the leader of a nationwide terrorist movement. But somehow he couldn't imagine the man he was looking at being involved in any of those heinous things. Had the media gotten it wrong? Could this be the wrong David Singh?

Finally he said, "Well, it started because Anderson over there resisted a search warrant, and an agent was killed."

"Mr. Anderson tried to keep armed invaders off his property."

"Look," Jason said, becoming exasperated, "you talk as if it makes no difference whether it's legal or not. The laws apply to everyone, even if—"

"Why?" David interrupted. For a moment Jason hesitated, at a loss for an answer to the seemingly silly question. "I'm asking you to really think about this," David said, looking very sincere. "Why do I have an obligation to obey whatever the politicians in Washington decide? Are they gods? Who made them my masters?"

"They represent the will of the people," Jason said. "The rules they come up with are what society wants. And everyone has to obey the rules, whether they like them or not—" Jason again struggled for an explanation, and finally settled on, "—or there would be chaos."

"That's what you've been taught to believe," David said softly. "That's the excuse every tyrant uses for what he does: that he's just trying to maintain law and order. But what chaos do you think this little group of people would have caused, had you just left us alone?"

"We had reason to believe that there were illegal weapons on the premises," Jason answered.

"No, you didn't," David responded, though still in a friendly voice. "That was the excuse you put on paper, but the real reason you came here was to make an example out of him," he pointed at Keith, "because he refused to submit to an unjustified invasion of his privacy and property. Isn't that right?"

"I don't know all of the background details, and I didn't do the application for either warrant, this one or the first one," Jason explained. "Someone else did, and a judge approved it. It was just my job to help execute the warrant. That's all."

"And if something is your job, does that mean you don't have to decide whether it's right or not?" David asked calmly. "As long as you get paid to do it, it's not your fault if what you are doing is evil?"

Jason was trying to think of a retort when David stood up and walked over to the bed. He began untying Jason's right hand, as he continued speaking. "Everyone, always, is personally responsible for the choices he makes and the actions he takes. It's just a shame so many people hide behind the excuses of 'authority' and 'rules' to try to evade that responsibility." He walked around to the other side, and started untying Jason's left hand. "You believe so strongly in enforcing whatever your masters tell you to enforce. They call it 'law,' and they tell you that because it's 'law,' disobeying it is automatically evil, and enforcing it is automatically good."

When both of Jason's hands were free, David began untying the rope around his neck. Jason saw Keith and Halen glance at each other, as if they didn't fully approve of David's actions. With Jason's feet still tied, David walked back to the chair and sat down again, crossing his legs and folding his hands in his lap. "Tell me, Jason, can you think of any law, past or present, in this country or any other, which would have been completely immoral to enforce, and completely righteous to resist?"

"Sure," Jason said, thinking of things he had read before about various foreign regimes.

"And the men who enforced those immoral laws, what do you think of them? Did they fully understand what they were doing? Were they all evil?"

"No," said Jason. "I'm sure some were, but I think most people think they're in the right. Some people just don't know when they're on the wrong side."

"Very true, very true," David answered. After that, both men were silent for several minutes.

David stood up and said, "Halen, Keith, can I talk to you for a second?" All three walked out of the room, leaving Jason alone. A moment later, the girl walked in with a bowl of soup. She set it on the table, and frowned at Jason's feet. "I don't know how you can sit up and eat with your feet tied like that," she said. She looked around for something to support his back, and found a few pillows.

"That's fine," he said. "I can sit like this."

He smiled at her as he took the soup, and the girl smiled back.

"You don't exactly seem like you fit in here," Jason said. "What's your name?"

"I don't think I should speak to you," she whispered, somewhat apologetically. "They warned me not to."

"Why would they do that? Surely you haven't done anything wrong?"

"No, but ... " Her brow furrowed again. It looked as if she wanted to tell him something, but she was seriously conflicted. "I just don't know," she hesitated. "I don't think being innocent makes me any safer. I mean, Ben was innocent, wasn't he? That didn't stop you guys from killing him. You would probably have killed me too if Halen hadn't dragged me out of there. Ben was a pacifist priest, for God's sake! How could anyone want to kill him? As kind as he was to me, I'm sure he never hurt anyone. How could you just kill him like that?" As she spoke, her voice rose higher with emotion, and tears began spilling down her face.

"Please!" Jason said, grabbing her hand, wishing he knew her name. "I didn't kill Ben! I don't know who did, but I never would have shot at that man! Or at you, either. I don't know who did. I swear to God it was never meant to happen that way. Please believe me."

She drew her hand away. "I just don't feel safe anywhere," she said.

Their voices had grown louder as they spoke, and suddenly the door opened again. Jason heard Halen say gruffly, "Who the hell sent her in there alone?" as he and David entered the room. David stood at the foot of the bed while Halen threw an unreadable glance at Jason and escorted Jessica out. Jason seethed. He could just imagine those vicious-looking men grilling her about what she had said to him. As if I would do anything to hurt her, he thought.

"Well," David said, "I've persuaded the others here to do for you what you wouldn't do for us. We're going to leave you be." After David untied Jason's feet, Keith walked into the room, holding a rifle. The sight scared Jason, despite David's words, but then he recognized the rifle as his own M16 with the camouflage covers on it. To Jason's amazement, David took his rifle from Keith, and handed it back to him. Jason grabbed the magazine in one hand and pressed the magazine release button. Looking down, he saw that the magazine was full. This guy had just handed him a loaded rifle. Why? Surely these people wouldn't have made a mistake like that. Did they want him holding a loaded gun when they shot him, so they could claim self-defense?

"Now we just have to figure out the best way to get you back out of here," said David.

"Just like that?" Jason replied suspiciously. "You're letting me go? What's the catch?"

"Don't come back," David said. "You only get one warning here."

"And you don't deserve that," said Keith.

The three of them walked down the hall to the living room, where the others were. The lights were still off; Doug and Josh were watching at the windows. The girl was curled up on the couch with a warm blanket and pillow, apparently asleep. Halen sat on the couch next to her, his attention trained on the windows.

"So," David quietly asked Jason, "how do we get you out safely?"

"Simple. Just tell the negotiator that I'm coming back, or I'll talk to him myself," said Jason. "He'll let the team know."

"What negotiator?" asked several voices.

"I know someone in here is negotiating with the feds out there."

The whole group looked around at each other quizzically, and everyone shook their heads. "There were never any negotiations," said David. "They've never said a word to any of us."

Jason was sure he'd heard Bridges talking about negotiations with David Singh.

"I'm going out to keep watch," said Halen, and left. The younger men left, too. Keith seemed reluctant to leave David and the girl alone with Jason.

"I don't want to go until I know what's going on with that girl," said Jason suddenly, nodding toward Jessica. "I don't think she's here by choice, and I want to get her to safety."

"What makes you think she'll be safe out there?" David asked.

"Why wouldn't she be?" said Jason. "Look, this place is about as unsafe as you can get. You guys should get on the radio with that negotiator and surrender right now. I don't know how many of my team died back there, but no matter what I go back and tell them, those guys will be out for blood now. You all need to surrender right now. You may not get another chance."

Jason thought he was probably saying too much, but he didn't care now. "If you all choose to sit here and get exterminated, that's your choice," he went on, with growing passion. "But I don't want to leave anyone here who's not choosing to stay here. Not her, and not those younger guys either. If you've filled their heads with some conspiracy theory to make them think that federal agents are a danger to innocent people, then *you'll* be responsible when they get killed!"

"Hypocritical bastard!" Keith spat out. "Who came onto my property and shot me? Who killed our friend Ben, who only wanted this to work out peacefully? And who is it you're warning us about right now—your goddamned buddies who are 'out for blood'! You said it yourself! We've never shot at anyone who didn't shoot first, and we didn't kill *your* sorry ass, either. So don't tell me you assholes aren't dangerous!"

"Okay, okay!" Jason broke into the tirade. "I get it, man! But listen to me. No one's going to hurt those teenagers if they go out there with me and surrender, right now. I swear to God."

"I know you sincerely believe that, Jason," said David. "And I know that you just want this girl to be safe. So do we. We have reason to believe that she wouldn't be safe out there. But you're right. It's not safe here anymore either."

Everyone was silent for a while. Jason looked at Jessica again. In the heat of argument, the men's voices had risen, and Jessica's dark eyes were wide open now. She sat up on the couch and wrapped the blanket around herself.

"I want to tell him," she said, looking at David, "if he'll promise not to tell them."

"Well, I think that's your choice," said David. He looked at Jason. "I want you to promise—to give us your word of honor—that you won't tell anyone she's here. If it gets out that she's here, she'll be dead."

Jason looked at Jessica, and she seemed less alarmed by the statement than he was.

"What are you talking about?" Jason asked. "Are you saying—"

"It wasn't a threat," David interrupted, looking from Jason to Jessica. "The threat to her life is not from in here, but from out there." Jason had lost all sense of direction, but assumed that David was pointing in the direction of the ATF and FBI trailers.

"What are you talking about?" Jason asked again. "Are you saying that the government would kill this girl? You people are nuts."

"Jessica? Do you understand yet? Do you understand what Ben was hiding from you?" David asked. "Why he couldn't let you leave?"

Jason watched her face intently. She furrowed her brow, as if deep in thought, and said nothing for a while. Then she looked up at Jason.

"My name is Jessica Carlisle," she said. "And I'm the only survivor of that plane crash—the one the news said nobody survived. The plane I was on was shot down by a missile. I saw it with my own eyes. The government lied when it said the plane was hijacked by terrorists. And I'm the only person who can prove that their story is a lie."

"If the people who shot down that plane find out that a witness is still alive," David went on, "they will do anything to silence her and anyone she's talked to. We will all die."

Jason's eyes went from David to Jessica to David in utter consternation. He could see the honesty in Jessica's eyes, but he just couldn't believe what he was hearing. "Is this some sort of mind game you're playing?" he asked suspiciously. "We know who hijacked the plane. We have the cockpit recordings."

David sighed and looked away. Jessica got up from the couch, and stood in front of Jason. She took his face in her hands, and he could see her beautiful brown eyes beginning to tear up. "Look at me," she said. "Do you think I'm some terrorist trying to trick you? I was on that plane. Jessica Carlisle from Abington, Pennsylvania—you can look it up in the airline records. I was flying to California to go camping with my cousin. The plane was shot down by a missile. I saw it. I watched it coming. I watched it hit the plane. I watched it blow people apart like they were made of paper." A tear rolled down her cheek. "By some miracle, I'm still alive. I'm not sure how, and I'm not sure why. But if I die now, the truth will die with me. If you tell anyone I'm here, you'll be killing me, and everyone else here. Promise me you won't do that."

He was still confused, but he saw the honesty in her eyes. "I promise," he said quietly.

**BETSY** sat at a table in the little diner, across from Sandy, watching through the window. In the pools of light from the street lamps, she could see snow falling from the dark sky, leaving a thin layer of white on the cars and sidewalks.

"Earth to Betsy," came Sandy's voice, and Betsy turned to see the waiter standing at the table.

"Oh, sorry," Betsy said, snapping out of her daze. "Just the usual, Tom. House salad and a coffee." The waiter nodded and walked away. She looked in her purse to see how much cash she had. "I keep forgetting to ask," Betsy said to Sandy, "how's your money situation?"

"Oddly, it's pretty good," Sandy answered. "I got a job painting a nursery for a couple that lives a few blocks from me. It's their first kid, and the nursery is bigger than this whole room," she said, indicating the diner. "She wants a garden mural, and we've spent weeks already picking out all the flowers and plants she wants in there. So I'm set for a couple months at least."

"If I ever find out you needed money and didn't tell me, I'm going to kill you," Betsy said in a friendly voice. "You know that, don't you?"

"I know, I know. Well, I have hardly any expenses these days, since lover-boy left, and as—" she cut her words short. "Oh, great," she said in a quieter voice. "My favorite Nazi." Betsy turned to see a familiar police officer walking into the diner. His name was Curtis Walters, and he stood well over six feet tall, as well as being significantly overweight. He had beady, squinting eyes and short, graying hair. Betsy guessed that he was about fifty years old.

Betsy had been present at several confrontations between Curtis and Sandy in the past, and wasn't looking forward to another one. She had never seen Curtis being openly hostile toward Sandy. Instead, he almost always had a smile on his face, but his constant condescending manner and insistence on pestering Sandy every chance he got bugged Betsy almost as much as it did Sandy. For a moment she hoped he wouldn't notice them, but that hope faded in a single second, as he turned toward them, smiled broadly, and started walking over, thumbs hooked in his waistband, looking down his nose at the two women.

"How's my favorite anarchist?" he asked with exaggerated inflection, loud enough for everyone in the diner to hear.

"Constitutionalist, Harold. There's a difference," Sandy answered, sounding bored already. For some reason unknown to Betsy, Sandy always called Curtis "Harold." She assumed it was just to get on his nerves.

"Hey, I believe in the Constitution too," Curtis said, still smiling and speaking loudly. "I just don't think it says what *you* think it says."

"Then maybe you should read it sometime," Sandy said, looking to see if the waiter was coming. Maybe if their food arrived Curtis would go away, Betsy thought. Or maybe not.

"Well, you see, I'm not a know-it-all like you, so I let the judges decide what the Constitution means. That's their job, after all, and I'm pretty sure they have more experience at that than either of us. Wouldn't you agree?"

"Harold, what do you want?" Sandy asked in exasperation. "Shouldn't you be out beating up some black people or something?" The smile on Curtis' face faded just a bit.

"Ya know, one of these days your mouth is going to get you into a lot of trouble," he said, his tone still friendly, but his smile obviously forced.

"Stop threatening me, you fascist pig," Sandy said bluntly but calmly. It took an effort for Betsy to refrain from smiling.

"Well, you ladies enjoy your meal," Curtis said as the waiter walked up with their food. "I'll be nearby, keeping the place safe." With that he swaggered away.

Tom rolled his eyes as he set the plates down in front of the women. "Yeah, if a crook comes in, he'll talk him to death," he remarked quietly. The women smiled at him.

"I know he's an obnoxious jackass," Betsy almost whispered, leaning over toward Sandy, "but do you really think it's a good idea to talk to a cop like that?"

"How *should* I talk to him?" Sandy asked. She dumped a packet of raw sugar into her coffee. "Just because a moron has a badge and a gun doesn't mean he's not a moron, and it doesn't mean I shouldn't treat him like the moron he is."

"True, but I think he bothers you just because he knows he can get a reaction out of you," Betsy suggested. "Maybe if you just ignored him, he'd leave you alone."

"Maybe. But you know, I almost feel obligated to give him a hard time," Sandy said, smiling. "If I don't, who will?" They began digging into their salads.

Some movement at the other end of the diner near the cash register caught Betsy's attention, and she gestured for Sandy to look. There were enough other people in the diner that it was difficult to hear all the words, but Officer Walters was talking to a middle-aged man who was nervously clutching what looked like a backpack. The man had a foreign look—Middle Eastern, or maybe Indian.

"I said, do you mind if I take a look?" Curtis was saying, his hands on his hips, towering head and shoulders above the other man.

"I didn't do anything, sir," said the man with a thick Indian accent.

"Then you won't mind me looking in the bag," Curtis said, reaching for it.

Betsy was surprised to see Sandy suddenly stand up and head across the room at a fast walk. "Sir!" she said loudly. "You don't have to let him search you. You have the right to refuse."

Curtis turned on Sandy, his smile gone, and his face turning a little red. "Go back to your seat, Sandy, and don't make me arrest you for obstruction of justice," he said sternly.

"Justice, my ass," Sandy said. "You're betting that he doesn't know his rights. He's obviously from somewhere else. He probably has no idea what the Fourth Amendment is, and you know it."

"I'm warning you to stay out of this. If you interfere with me doing my duties—"

"It's not your duty to violate people's rights, dumb-ass," Sandy almost yelled, but she stopped a few feet from Curtis. The Indian man was still looking scared, barely visible to Betsy behind Curtis. "Sir?" Sandy said to the nervous man, in a much more friendly voice. "In this country, the police have no right to search you unless—"

"I'm giving you a lawful order, Sandy," Curtis interrupted. "You will step back, go back to your table, and let me deal with this."

"Sir, just ask him," Sandy said in a pleading voice, not moving. "Ask the officer if you have to give him the bag. Ask him what happens if you refuse."

"I don't want any trouble," the man said.

"Just ask him, please," Sandy begged. "Just ask him whether you have a choice." The man looked back and forth between Sandy and Curtis. Curtis was obviously fuming, but seemed reluctant to follow through on his threat to arrest Sandy. Betsy thought that was probably because over a dozen other people in the diner were now watching intently. "Just ask him whether you have to," Sandy pleaded again.

Finally, in a very timid voice, the man said, "Sir, I mean no disrespect, but is she correct? Do I have to give you my bag?"

"I was just asking if I could look at it," Curtis replied feebly. "If you've got nothing to hide, then—"

"Answer his question!" Sandy commanded, looking right at Curtis. Betsy marveled at the sight of her slender little friend standing up to a man who towered over her by more than a foot, and looked to be at least three times her weight—like a sapling challenging a full-grown oak tree. The diner was perfectly quiet now, and all eyes were on Sandy and Curtis.

"If you're not doing anything wrong—" Curtis began again, but after glancing around the room, changed his tone of voice. "No, you don't *have* to give it to me. I was just asking if you would agree to let me look." Betsy watched the Indian man's eyes widen. It was as if he was having a revelation, as if he was witnessing a miracle.

"I apologize, sir," the man said, lowering his head, "but what is in this bag is very personal, and I do not wish to give it to you." Then he looked up timidly, but Curtis just looked away.

"Fine, fine," Curtis said finally, with a dismissive wave of his hand, and turned toward the counter, as if to escape the situation.

There was a long silence, and no one moved. The man looked as if he was ready to leave, but hesitated, still unable to believe what had just happened. Then a young black woman, around twenty, at one of the tables, stood up and started clapping. "Way to go, girl," she shouted to Sandy. After a moment, four others were clapping and smiling too at what they had just witnessed. At the same time, there were a dozen or so looks of confusion or disapproval. By then the man was smiling, and, with his head up, walked out of the diner, giving a nod of thanks to Sandy as he passed.

As Sandy walked back toward Betsy, a dozen or so people started talking, mostly in lowered voices, some obviously objecting to what had happened, some obviously celebrating it, and others trying to figure out what they had just witnessed. Betsy heard someone say, "What if the guy had had a bomb in there?" Sandy sat down, a broad smile on her face, though Betsy could see that her hands were shaking. After a moment, as the sound level continued to rise, Curtis also turned and walked out, without a glance at Betsy or Sandy.

"Ya know, even though you're out of your mind," Betsy said, "that was pretty darn impressive."

"All that is necessary for evil to triumph—" Sandy began.

"—is for crazy hippie chicks to do nothing," Betsy concluded, and gave Sandy a pat on the shoulder.

**JESSICA** and the others sat in patio chairs in the garden area outside the front door of the house, which was closed in on either side by forward extensions of the building. It was a large and relatively new house. Doug had explained to Jessica that his parents had built this recently as a winter getaway home, and he was allowed to live there year round in exchange for looking after the place. Around the house were assorted rock gardens, paths, and short decorative stone walls, including one which closed in the patio where Jessica sat. Beyond the wall was a large rock garden, and beyond that was the lawn, with the grass continuing out of sight over the rolling hills beyond.

David and his wife were talking together quietly in the corner to Jessica's right, and Keith was nearby whittling a piece of wood with a large hunting knife. Halen had been coming and going, and said that the feds were nowhere to be seen in any direction. He had looked everywhere for Heather, but had found no trace of her, and was beginning to think she'd been captured. Dawn was on its way, and the sky was just starting to lighten a bit. She could just see Josh lying at the top of the slope, a hundred yards ahead of her, watching for anyone approaching from that direction.

Jason now sat in a metal patio chair twenty feet in front of Jessica, facing the hills. His elbows were on his knees, his head hung down, as if he was deep in thought. He hadn't said anything for quite a while, and Jessica wondered what he might be thinking. The night before, just after Jason had regained consciousness, when Halen sent her, Josh, and Doug out of the room, she was sure that she'd never see him again—not alive, anyway. When she later found out that they had decided to just let him go, and had even given him his gun back, she was even more confused than before. It seemed to her that the more she saw, the less she understood what was going on.

She sat in her chair, trying to make sense of it all, as the sky in front of her slowly began turning from gray to orange. It had been years since Jessica had seen a sunrise. Except for her short nap on the couch, she hadn't slept for a day and a half. But though she was physically exhausted and in considerable pain, she wasn't sleepy. From the woods and fields all around them, a chorus of frogs and crickets was making a happy racket.

She desperately tried to fit the pieces together in her mind. A part of her had still been waiting to meet the vicious group of hardened criminals calling itself the Iron Web. But she was beginning to think that maybe the people she'd met were all there was. Halen still made her uneasy. She remembered the things Doug had said before about him killing someone—a senator, wasn't it?—and she had no trouble imagining it to be true. And Keith also seemed like a bit of a loose cannon. But though those two made her nervous, she wasn't afraid they would do anything to harm her. Were there scarier members of this elusive terrorist cult lurking around here somewhere, or was this it? She had a hard time reconciling how she had heard the situation reported in the news with what she had seen since being here.

And she kept thinking about David. It hadn't even occurred to her for a while that this could be David Singh, *the* 'David' the media had talked about—the leader of the so-called terrorist group. He didn't seem threatening in the least. In fact, his way of speaking and his demeanor, not to mention his Indian looks, reminded her of Gandhi. He seemed to actually love other people, even strangers—even armed invaders. Furthermore, he didn't seem to be the leader of anything, not in the sense of a commander. A teacher, maybe. But he certainly was no malicious schemer inciting violent actions from a bunch of brainwashed adherents. Then again, maybe his power was in being able to hide malicious motives under a façade of kindness. But she had a hard time believing that.

She looked over at him, sitting on a wooden bench in the corner, holding his wife's hand and speaking in soft whispers to her. Only an hour earlier she had met David's wife, Tasha, for the first time. Tasha was a stunning Filipino beauty with the face of an angel and straight black hair down to her waist. She wore a colorful flowery dress that looked as if it came from a tropical island. When she spoke at all, she spoke softly, and seemed very shy. She had a bandage on one leg, but walked with only a slight limp, and even her limp was graceful.

"If you walk out right past David's garden shed, way over there," Keith was saying to Jason, pointing over the hill Josh was lying on, "you'll still be behind the last rise, so they won't shoot you by accident. Halen can be on his roof with the scope. He'll radio us if the coast is clear. You got this huge white flag, so hopefully they won't shoot you, but if you—"

"I'm not going," Jason said suddenly. Everyone looked at him.

"What?" Jessica heard herself say.

"I was up all night thinking about it," Jason answered. "I'm not exactly thrilled about the situation, but I'm not going back."

"Why not?" asked David, who didn't seem particularly surprised by Jason's declaration.

"Well, what are my choices?" Jason asked. "I go out there, and I have to say what I saw in here. Even if I don't mention Jessica, I have to tell them something: who's in here, how many of you there are, what weapons you have, which buildings you're in. I know the guys out there. Like I said, with agents down already, they'll be out for blood. And if they knew how few of you there are in here, they'd probably come in with guns blazing. If I tell them the truth, you're all dead. And if I lie, my career is over, and they might even prosecute me for it."

He paused for a minute. "And if what you say is true, if Jessica was really on that plane—and I don't want to believe it, but I can't think of a reason not to—and if it was really shot down, then I just—I don't know. Ya know, I don't buy your attitude, thinking you're above the law, and thinking you can do whatever you want, but ... you're not ... ," he hesitated again. "You're not who I imagined would be in here." He looked at Jessica. "And if I go out, and just walk away, and never say anything about it, and then things go badly—I'd feel like a coward."

"Nothing like a pretty girl to bring out a little courage in a guy," Keith laughed, still whittling away at the hunk of wood.

"True," David said, glancing at his wife with a smile. "But I, for one, am quite impressed. You show concern for those you were taught to hate, and told to destroy."

"At least the pretty ones," Keith added snidely.

"Well, even that is a good sign," David responded. After a pause, he added, "Your decision also makes me feel better about something else." He turned to face Jason. "If you leave, and they somehow find out that Jessica was here, even if we're all dead by then, then to them you yourself become an inconvenient witness."

"I don't buy all the conspiracy stuff that you believe," Jason said, "and I'm not so distrustful of everyone in government as you are, but I gotta say, what I've seen and heard here bugs me. I don't pretend to know what all is true and what isn't, but something's not right here."

"Wow, that's the understatement of the year," remarked Keith.

"Bottom line is, I can't in good conscience leave here without Jessica," Jason said, "and I can't leave here with her, either."

Jessica started as Halen appeared next to her from inside the house. She hadn't heard a sound. Though she still found him to be very intimidating, she was beginning to be glad to have someone like him on her side. Then she wondered, when had she decided whose "side" she was on? And based on what? The answer to that was actually quite simple, she realized. At this point, she wasn't at all scared of what the people now sitting around her might do, however misguided or criminal they might be, but she was deathly afraid of what the people

**116**

beyond those hills might do, even if they did it with the best of intentions and a feeling of righteousness.

"Let me guess," she heard Jason saying to Halen. "That was you who took out our speakers." She saw Jason point toward the house, and she turned to see an enormous rifle leaning against the wall, which Halen must have just put down there.

"Try some Metallica next time," Halen said, taking a seat near David and Tasha. What on earth were they talking about? Halen seemed to be joking, but there was no smile on his face. She wondered if he even knew how to smile.

"Got a question for you," Halen said, looking hard at Jason. "If saving Jessica meant ending your career, would you do it?"

"Yes," he answered without hesitation, and Jessica looked at him with surprise. "But I suspect that either way, my career as a fed is over anyway."

"Jessica can't just walk out there," Halen continued. "We all know that. Nor can she just go home, even if we had a way to get her there, which we don't. She can't just turn up alive without anyone noticing. However, there might be another way." By now Jessica was listening intently. "If we can get Jessica to Mexico, and she can get her story on tape, and get it to the media, after that it wouldn't do the feds any good to kill her."

"How exactly are you going to get her to Mexico?" Jason asked with obvious skepticism.

"Well, the hardest part will be getting her out of here without being seen," Halen answered. "The only way I can think of is the tunnel. It won't be easy to get to, and I don't know what we'll find at the other end, but there's an old tunnel the kids dug years ago."

"Yeah, Bernie and I dug it when we were little," explained Doug. "It goes from our old clubhouse to underneath the road bridge. But will that be far enough?"

"I don't know," Halen said flatly. "If we can follow that drainage ditch up into those woods, I think we'd be in the clear. Or rather, *you'd* be in the clear," he said, looking at Jason and Jessica.

"You're not coming?" Jessica asked, her hopefulness dropping several notches.

"No," Halen answered. "I can't walk away from this, but I'll get you as far as the woods, if I can. From there, it's gonna be up to you, Jason, to get her safely to Mexico. If you make it out of here without being seen, no one will be looking for either of you out there. But you'll have to find a way across the border."

"I can do that," Jason said.

"Then we'll go just after dark tonight," Halen said, standing up. "I have some stuff to get ready in the meantime. You two go inside and get some sleep." With that, he walked into the house.

After that the group was quiet, and Jessica sat, deep in thought, wondering if she was up to the challenge of escaping from here, like some fugitive criminal, and traveling to Mexico. She had always talked about wanting to have an adventure, but this was way beyond anything she had ever imagined.

Some movement out in the field in front of the patio suddenly caught her attention. She watched as a doe and two young deer trotted into view just beyond the garden, not a hundred feet away, from around the right corner of the house. The young ones frolicked without a care across the dew-covered grass. The mother froze for a moment, looked toward the people on the patio, twitched her tail a few times, and led her young ones onward, out of sight around the far corner of the house. Jessica looked back at the others, and they had seen, but said nothing, as if that sort of thing was commonplace here. In that moment, she found it hard to believe that her situation was as serious as she knew it was. She thought to herself that if she could have frozen time for the outside world, and stayed here forever, rather than face what lay ahead, she probably would have done it.

---

**JASON** woke up, still sitting in a chair out on the patio. He had nodded off without realizing it. The sun was now setting behind the house, which cast a long shadow that covered the patio and garden. Throughout the day they had discussed their escape plan, and Jason thought it sounded at least somewhat hopeful.

"Who did they tell you was in here?" Doug asked. It took Jason a moment to realize that the question was directed at him.

"What?" said Jason.

"Who did they tell you was in here? What were you expecting?"

Jason thought for a minute. "I don't know what I expected to find here, but this wasn't it," he finally answered. "They told us David Singh was in here, the mastermind behind all the terrorism that's been going on, and some of his followers. No one knew how many."

"God, you don't put much effort into finding out who someone is before you go try to kill them, do you?" Keith asked, admiring the chunk of wood he had whittled down to almost nothing.

"I wasn't trying to kill anyone," Jason said defensively. "But I also don't think I can thumb my nose at the law and get away with it." At that moment he suddenly did not feel at all comfortable about being on such friendly terms with the people he was supposed to be investigating, if not arresting.

"Even if you have a problem with Keith," Doug said, "which almost everyone does," he added with a smile, at which Keith threw a large wood chip at him, "what did the rest of us do? You laid siege to the whole neighborhood. Like, what did Ben ever do? For that matter, what did I ever do? I don't even own a gun."

"Sissy," Josh said to Doug with a smile. Doug picked up the wood chip and threw it at Josh, but missed.

"But you're a member of the group, aren't you?" Jason asked. "Except for Jessica, you're all part of the Iron Web thing, right?"

"The Iron Web is not a group of people." Jason turned around, and saw that it was David who had spoken. Jason hadn't noticed him there, sitting quietly in the corner. "I know it's hard to put aside what you've been told over and over again," David went on, "but it's not some secret club that one gets membership in. It's just a concept."

"Like a religion or something?" Jason asked, puzzled. "Some church that says it's okay to break the law, not pay your taxes, and act like you can do whatever you want?" He was still feeling as if he shouldn't be too friendly with these people.

"Man, open your damn eyes," Keith said calmly. "After all you've seen here, you still believe what your jackboot bosses tell you?"

David continued in a calm voice. "The Iron Web concept isn't nearly that complicated. It's no more complicated than this: I own me, and you own you. I have no right to take your time, your efforts, or your property, unless you voluntarily choose to deal with me. And the reverse is also true. However many people you get together, and whatever you call your club—a gang, a government, or a soccer team—you have no right to take what is mine unless I choose to give it to you. We can make any deal that's agreeable to both of us, but no one has the right to take what I produce, what I earn, and what I have acquired by trade, without my consent."

"Well, so far I agree," Jason said.

"No, you don't," Keith commented with a tone of contempt.

"What do you mean, no I don't?" Jason responded. "Don't tell me what I—"

"Sorry, but he's right," David said softly. "Think about it for a moment. Do you believe in taxation?"

"Well, I'd like there to be less," Jason said, "but as long as—"

"I mean in principle," David continued. "For example, do you believe that the gang that calls itself the IRS has the right to steal a chunk of what I earn, whether I agree to it or not?"

"I've heard about the claims that the tax is unconstitutional," Jason said, "but the courts—"

"I'm not talking about its legality," David cut in. "I'm asking, on a philosophical level, do you believe that government has a right to demand a percentage of what each of us earns?"

Jason thought for a moment, and then said, "Well, yeah, I guess I do. Like I said, I wish they'd take a lot less, and spend it better, but by living in this country you agree to pay the taxes that fund the—"

"Oh, brother." This time it was Doug interrupting with annoyance. "How on earth does standing on this continent somehow count as agreeing to be continually robbed? What if I decided that, by living in this country, you're 'agreeing' to let me slug you in the face?"

"Look, that's how the system works," Jason said, starting to get angry. "If you don't like it, you can try to elect someone who—"

"That's the point," David said, his voice still low and steady. "If I own myself, I don't need anyone else's permission to keep what I earn. I don't need any government, any law, anything or anyone to say it's okay. If I own myself—and I do—I'm the only one who has the right to decide what is done with my efforts, my time and my property. If I need someone else's permission, whether it's one person or the population of an entire country, it means I belong to them, not to me. It means I am their slave. I'm not. I own myself."

"But taxation isn't slavery," Jason argued. "It's the way we all chip in for the things that we can't buy individually, like roads and police."

"Police like you?" Doug asked, and chuckled. "Gosh, why wouldn't I want to pay you for the privilege of having you do an armed invasion of my property?"

"We can get into this later," David said, as if trying to defuse the building tensions. "The point is, the Iron Web symbol gives people who believe that every individual owns himself, and that no one owns anyone else, a way to express that belief, a way to tell others that he believes that. Using this symbol, people who believe in true freedom can create a network, through which they can trade and make deals, without intrusion and interference by all the federal, state and local bureaucrats and thieves."

"In other words, it's a way to do things under the table, so you don't have to pay taxes," Jason commented, still sounding indignant.

"Among other things, yes," David answered. "Now, you view that as some horrible sin, because—like most people—you believe that everyone has a moral obligation to hand over a portion of what he earns to the politicians and bureaucrats. And you think it's a crime—a sin, really—for anyone to try to get around that supposed obligation. In short, you believe we all belong to the politicians—that we are their slaves—and that they have the right to take from us whatever amount they decide, for whatever reason they decide."

"It's the people that decide," Jason objected. "You can run for office if you think you could—"

"I own myself already," David interjected. "I don't need a law that says so. I don't need any election to say so. You see, I'm so extreme that I believe that all men are endowed with the same unalienable rights, including the right to life, liberty and the pursuit of happiness."

"Well, the Founders you're quoting believed in taxes."

"It is true that they gave their new government the power to tax," David replied. "It was one of several fatal departures from the philosophy of the Declaration of Independence. In reality, the government they set up with the Constitution violated the principles of the Declaration almost as much as King George did. Anyway," he continued, shaking his head, "I keep getting off point. I was trying to tell you what the Iron Web is, whether you philosophically agree with it or not." He picked up a stick, and cleared the leaves off of a piece of soil in the garden, and made nine dots, in a three-by-three grid.

"Imagine just nine people who share this belief—who don't think they need anyone's permission to associate and trade with others. They all display the symbol of the Iron Web, so people who share the belief can find each other. Any of them can make deals with each other. This guy might hire that guy to mow his lawn. This guy sells a car to that guy." David began drawing lines in the dirt, from one point to another, as he spoke. "It makes a giant network—a black market, really—that is just about impossible to break. If you do the math, just nine people make thirty-six different ways for people to trade. The government can eliminate an individual, by locking him up or killing him," he explained, crossing out one of the points, "but it does nothing to the rest of the web. As the number of people involved rises, the number of combinations rises exponentially. If you had a million people doing this, there is nothing in the world that any government could do to stop it, or to control it, or tax it, no matter how intrusive or vicious government became. The system can't be infiltrated, because there is no system. The organizers can't be discovered and shut down, because there are no organizers. It's not some gang or club. It's an idea. The idea that people—each person owning himself, and each *knowing* that he owns himself—can circumvent and defeat any parasite class that tries to control and exploit them." David dropped the stick on the ground and sat back in his chair. "That's what the Iron Web means."

"It still just sounds like a way to break the law, and to get out of paying taxes," Jason remarked.

"And it is. Again, you view that as a horrible thing, because you view obedience to authority as a virtue, because you think the politicians have a legitimate right to rule the rest of us. As a result, you think that it's inherently evil to disobey their commands, their 'laws,' including the ones that say that you and I aren't allowed to trade without telling the politicians about it and giving them a cut. Some of us think that's insane. And by using this symbol to find each other, we can try to avoid all the regulators, inspectors, licensing bureaucrats, tax collectors, and all the other busybodies who stick their noses into other people's business," David said. "In other words, it's a way to try to live free, even in a world of slaves and masters."

"So you don't believe in licenses, either? Anyone should be allowed to do brain surgery in his spare time?" Jason asked sarcastically.

"Yes, if the doctor and patient both agree," David answered. "The other side of owning one's self is being responsible for one's own actions and choices. If I'm stupid enough to let some average Joe cut my head open, then it's my own fault if I die from it. If I decide to build my own house out of one-by-two pieces of balsa wood, and it falls over, it's my fault, and my loss. No one has the right to tell me that I can trade only with whomever *they* think I should trade with."

"I still don't buy it," Jason said, shaking his head. "You want America to be full of substandard housing that falls over, and back-alley brain surgeons? You'd never know who was for real. It would be chaos."

"In nature and in human society, from uncontrolled chaos an amazing order naturally flows," David explained. "From controlled and managed order, destruction and disaster flow. We're all trained to think that civilization comes from the institutions of authority and government controlling everyone and everything. Not even close. Civilization comes from individuals recognizing the rights of other individuals. It comes from mutually voluntary interaction, where we all treat each other like equals. If you want to see what comes from the institutions of authority and government, try visiting a war zone, or a public housing project."

"The guy is a mercenary for the parasites," Keith cut in. "He's never going to understand."

Jason was beginning to hate that man. He ignored the insult and spoke up again. "I don't buy this whole philosophy, but what I really don't understand is how you get from this to advocating violence. Why all the guns? Don't the people you shoot at own themselves, too? How does that work?" It came out sounding more sarcastic and bitter than he had intended.

"If I own myself, and what I acquire by work or trade," explained David, "then I have the right to protect that property, just as I have the right to protect my life. In fact, whatever I work for or produce *is* a part of my life, because I used up a piece of my life acquiring it. And if someone tries to take it from me by force, I have the right to use force to stop him. Would you tell someone who is being carjacked, 'Yes, it's your car, but you have no right to stop anyone from taking it from you'? Of course not. That makes no sense. The right of ownership has to include the right to *defend* what you own from any and all intruders and thieves, or the right is meaningless."

"Okay, I see your point, but I think you're making things simpler than they are," Jason said. "The utopia you're describing sounds nice, but it wouldn't work in the real world. In the real world, there has to be a set of rules, and someone has to enforce them."

"Incidentally," David said, "what I'm describing here is just what I personally believe. Even the others *here* don't agree with me on everything. Keith here is a Constitutionalist. He wants the country to have a government the way the Founders envisioned it, whereas I don't think even that small amount of authority is legitimate. And Ben was a pacifist. He understood the right of self-defense, but for himself, he refused to resort to violence for any reason. How ironic that he was the first to die: probably the only one here who wouldn't have resisted. The point is, this isn't some monolithic cult of people who have all memorized some set of religious teachings. Even in this small group right here, we've got some major differences of opinion. But we get along with each other because we all agree that people should be left in freedom so long as they're not attacking or defrauding anyone else."

"And what if someone does rob or murder someone? What if some guy claims to be a certified brain surgeon and kills someone who believed him?" Jason asked. "Your principles sound good, but if there's no government to enforce them, what good are they?"

"We all have the right to defend ourselves, and others, from violence and fraud," said David. "We don't need government or any special authority for that."

Jason had never heard such an idea, and didn't know what to say. After a period of silence, Doug asked Jason, "Can I ask you a question?"

"Yeah," said Jason.

"Why did you come to our homes with guns drawn?"

"To serve a search warrant. You know that," Jason replied.

"Yeah, I know that," Doug retorted. "I'm asking what the moral justification was, not the legal excuse. Personally, I'd need a really damn good reason before I'd go invade someone else's property and aim a gun at him. Someone showed you a piece of paper and told you to do it. *That* was your justification?"

"A judge decided that there was probable cause to think that we would find illegal weapons here," Jason said, starting to feel defensive again.

"What kind of illegal weapons?" Doug asked.

"Machine guns."

"You mean like the one you brought with you?" Doug asked, pointing at the rifle leaning against Jason's chair. The question caught Jason off guard, and he said nothing for a moment. "Do you see anything odd about that?" Doug asked. "I don't even own a gun, but I've been shooting a few times. I've never aimed a gun at a human being. I don't even like to hunt. But let's pretend we actually had machine guns here. Let's pretend I had an M16, just like the one you have. Let's see if I have this straight. You came to my property, carrying a machine gun, when I hadn't hurt or threatened anyone, based on the rumor—the false rumor, by the way—that I might have my own M16 here, the same kind of gun you brought here. Doesn't that seem just a bit hypocritical to you?"

All Jason could think of to say was, "I'm authorized to have a machine gun." In the midst of the debate, it again struck him as curious that these people dared to let him have his loaded rifle with him all this time.

"All that means is that some politicians said you can have one, and said we can't," David said calmly. "Would you accept that double standard with other rights, too? If they said you could speak your mind, but we aren't allowed to, would you come in here to arrest us for saying what we think? What other rights do you have that we don't? Aside from it not even being true, all your bosses alleged was that we were doing something that you do every day: possessing machine guns. And for that you invaded our property with guns drawn, and some of you even shot at us, and one of you killed Ben. And then you wonder how we can possibly justify having guns to defend ourselves. If we showed up at your ATF offices, guns drawn, demanding for you to surrender your guns and let us take you away and put you in cages, would you feel justified in defending yourself? If we started shooting at you, wouldn't you return fire?"

"It wasn't supposed to be a shootout!" Jason said, almost shouting. "It was just supposed to be a search."

"A few days ago I had to search for my car keys," David said. "I didn't think to have a machine gun with me. You brought guns here because you intended to trespass on our properties and rummage through our houses and belongings, whether we wanted you to or not. Isn't that right?"

When Jason didn't speak, Doug broke in. "When you come onto my property, armed and with the intent to do something against my will, when I haven't done a damn thing to anyone, don't pretend that I'm the bad guy and you're the noble hero. You're not."

"I didn't say I was a hero," Jason replied, feeling more and more uneasy. He didn't want to admit it, but he knew they had a point. If anyone ever tried to disarm him, he wasn't just going to go along with it quietly.

After a moment of silence, David spoke up again. "If your friends came charging over that hill right now, would you use that rifle on us?" He pointed to the rifle leaning against Jason's chair.

Jason immediately said "No," and meant it. After a moment, he added, "But now that you mention it, it's probably better if you take it. If they did show up right now, it would look better if I'm unarmed."

"Instead of them finding you sitting around chatting with known terrorists," Doug said with a smile, "with a rifle handy, and doing nothing about it?"

"Something like that," Jason responded, and had to chuckle. "God, this is so messed up." The group got quiet again.

Doug stood up. "I'm going in to see what the news is saying," he said, and walked into the house.

Jason thought of his parents, and wondered how they were handling this. What would the news be reporting about him? Would they say he was likely dead, or assume that he was being held as a hostage? For his parents' sake, he hoped for the latter.

He jumped at a loud thud right next to him, and looked up to see Halen standing there, looking even less cheerful than usual. Looking down at the table beside him, Jason saw some sort of handheld electronic device, next to a tiny black object with a wire sticking out of it.

"Was this your doing?" Halen asked bluntly. Jason looked at Halen, and back at the objects on the table. It took a moment before he figured it out.

"A bug?" Jason asked. Then he shook his head. "No way. I didn't bring that here."

"Then how the hell did it get in here?" Halen asked, leaning over, his face inches from Jason's. "Did you stay here because of your conscience, or did you stay to be a spy?"

"I don't know how it got here," said Jason, trying to think. "Sometimes they can shoot them in with a dart gun, but it would be inside a little missile-looking thing."

"It wasn't," Halen said flatly, still inches from Jason's face.

"They might have snuck it up here on foot," Jason suggested, starting to feel nervous. "I don't know." He knew he hadn't done it, but he also knew that, to everyone else, he was the obvious suspect.

"I have enough motion sensors and infrared cameras set up around here now that I seriously doubt they brought it in on foot," Halen answered.

"Has anyone come here in the last few days that you didn't know really well? Or maybe they snuck it in weeks ago," Jason said, trying to come up with some explanation that might get him off the hook.

"I do regular sweeps of the place," Halen said, "and this was not here yesterday."

"Where exactly was it? Was it inside or out?" Jason asked, but Halen just stared at him. "Look, I can see why you suspect me, and why you don't believe me when I say I didn't do it. But I didn't." He pointed at Jessica. "If nothing else, I wouldn't put her at risk that way."

"The bug was out at the side porch, where we hardly ever go, so I doubt the feds could hear anything through it," Halen said, finally standing up straight, which gave Jason a feeling of relief. "And that is the only thing that makes me think that you didn't do it," Halen added. "You would have put it in a more useful location." Jason glanced over at Jessica, who had a hand over her mouth and a look of shock on her face. He thought he could guess what she was thinking: did the bug mean that the feds now knew she was here?

"No, it's disabled now," Halen said to Jessica, as if he were thinking the same thing. "And I doubt they heard anything out where it was."

"Oh, man," Jason said, remembering something from many months earlier. "Halen, how small a thing will your motion detectors detect?"

"Anything bigger than a rabbit, they'll pick up," Halen said.

"I think I know how they did it. Can you show me where it was?" Somewhat reluctantly, Halen agreed.

Jason followed Halen into the house, down the stairs to the basement, out the back door and around to the left, to a small side porch that he hadn't seen before. Halen pointed to where he had found the bug, in the corner on top of the concrete slab of the porch.

"Yeah," Jason said, thinking to himself. "They would have gone for the front porch, but there's that little wall and the garden. Here they have a straight shot," he said, pointing to the grass which came up level to the porch. "Months ago," he began explaining, "I saw them playing around with a tiny little remote-control car, I mean like this." He put his hands about four inches apart. "It even had a camera on board, infrared, so they could see what it saw. They probably snuck it in at night." He thought about the perimeter of the house. "Yeah, I think this was the only place they could get it to. There are walls and gardens everywhere else. It can't go over anything that rough. It could just barely handle the grass here, I think." Halen seemed satisfied with the theory, and went in through the porch door, Jason following. "It wasn't even an agency thing," Jason said. "It was one guy I know, electronics geek, who had made it himself out of various parts."

"Well, they actually did us a favor," Halen said. "It tells us they probably don't have any other bugs in here, or they wouldn't have bothered going to all that trouble just to put another one in a useless location. But also," he added, as the two of them walked through the living room and out onto the patio again, "it gives us a way to send them a message. I didn't destroy the thing, I only disconnected the battery. If we need a way to give them information, or a little misinformation, now we have it. I'll have to think of the best—"

"Jessica, come quick!" they could hear Doug's urgent voice calling behind them. Halen and Jason turned and stepped back into the living room, where Doug was fiddling with the radio. "I think you should hear this," he was saying to Jessica, as she rushed into the room from the patio. He turned up the volume on the radio.

The voice on the radio sounded exhausted and depressed: "Nothing will bring her back. I can't even describe the pain we feel— a huge emptiness, like everything good has gone out of our lives."

Jason watched Jessica's face as it took on a look of profound anguish. "It's my dad," she choked out, beginning to tear up.

"She was so beautiful, gifted, and just ... good," her father's voice continued, with some difficulty. "What kind of monsters cut short a life like that?" There was a short pause. "To think of all the other families who are having to go through this is just incomprehensible." His voice took on a grim, angry tone: "All we can do now is whatever it takes to make sure no one else ever has to go through this."

A male reporter's voice then spoke up. "Again, that was the father of Jessica Carlisle, a young woman just out of high school, just one of the hundred and seventy-eight people whose lives ended as a result of the hijacking of Flight 422. Comments from the relatives of other passengers on that flight have ranged from fury at the terrorists to pity for them. But one thing they all share is the conviction that, whatever it takes, we cannot ever allow this to happen again. This is Brian Folden, reporting for KTC News just outside—" The radio shut off with a loud click. Jason watched with a feeling of helplessness as Jessica broke down and wept.

"Doug, come with me," Halen said, and walked out of the room with him. Jason knew it had been for Jessica's sake, and thought better of Halen because of it.

Jason went to Jessica and put his arm around her shoulders, gingerly, not sure whether she wanted comfort from the likes of him. "We're going to get you out of here," he said. "You'll get back home. You'll see your folks again. I'll get you out of here alive," he said. "I promise."

After a few minutes of silence, during which Jessica regained her composure, Halen walked into the room and said, "Time to go." Jason turned to see Halen standing there, dressed in his ragged greens and browns, holding a crossbow with a scope on it.

Halen turned to Jessica and held up a small backpack. "This is for you," he said. "Granola bars, beef jerky, and all the money we could find. I want you to have it in case we get separated. I couldn't pack much more or it would hamper you." Jessica nodded and snapped the straps together. "This one's for you, Jason," Halen said. "Yours is just food." Then he handed Jessica a ragged, dark green flannel shirt. "Wear this over your clothes until you get to the woods," he instructed. "Then throw it away. Jason, you'll blend in well enough at night as you are. Besides, if we're spotted, the uniform might keep you from getting shot. Are we ready?"

Jason nodded, trying to look confident and hopeful for Jessica's sake. "It's been nice visiting," he said with a smile, "but I'm ready to get the hell out of here." There were quick, awkward goodbyes all around, and then Halen led Jason and Jessica down the stairs to the basement and out the back of the house through the glass sliding door. Jason felt an unseasonally warm breeze on his face.

"Stay close on my tail," Halen said quietly. "Move when I move, stop when I stop." He flipped a switch on the scope on his crossbow, and only then did it occur to Jason that it was a night vision scope. "Let's go." He set off at a quick walk around the house, and Jason and Jessica hurried to keep up.

The sky was almost black, but there was enough light to see a little. They walked right out into the open field, bearing a bit to the right. They crept single file, Halen in front, Jessica in the middle, and Jason bringing up the rear. Suddenly Halen stopped. "I can see people over the hill, just the tops of their heads," he said in a low voice, scanning the horizon through the scope. "Keep going, but crouch down."

They were approaching a house, which Jason believed to be Halen's. It was lit on the far side with floodlights, but the side facing them remained dark. As they got closer, Jason could hear a couple of voices over the rise. He didn't recognize either of them. The lights were on inside the house, and he could see shadows moving around inside. Looking around, Jason noticed a small square structure, about a hundred feet closer to them than the house.

By now Halen had the crossbow hung across his back by its strap, and was cat-crawling, smoothly and steadily, toward the little shed, which Jason assumed to be the clubhouse Doug had mentioned. Suddenly, when they were only about thirty feet from the clubhouse, Halen dropped down flat on the ground and lay motionless. Jason saw Jessica do the same, and he followed suit. It was a moment before he heard voices approaching, and two agents came around the corner of the house.

"The guy just gets on my nerves," one of the agents was saying casually, as they strolled around the house. "He's such a brown-noser, even worse with the new guy than he was with Bridges." Jason's head was on its side, but he could see the light from a flashlight dancing around the area. He prayed the light wouldn't land on him.

"It's not gonna get him anywhere, anyway," the other agent was saying, as they walked closer. "Reynolds is just as disgusted with him as you are." By now the voices sounded right on top of them, less than ten feet away, but Jason didn't dare to look up. He closed his eyes and tried to relax, desperately hoping the agents would keep going.

"I doubt the guy will last long," said the first agent. "I don't know anyone who actually trusts him." It sounded to Jason, to his great relief, as if the agents had gone past and were heading around the far side of the house. After the voices faded, he looked up and saw that the coast was clear.

Halen was up and crawling again, and quickly disappeared into the darkness of the clubhouse, followed closely by Jessica. Jason scrambled in as quickly as he could. It was nothing more than a kids' fort, about six feet square, with one door, facing the way they had come, and windows cut in the other three walls. The three of them barely fit inside it, and Halen motioned for Jason and Jessica to back up against the wall.

After scratching around in the dirt, Halen pulled up the corner of an old, dirt-encrusted piece of carpet. From beneath that he lifted a two-foot-by-two-foot square of plywood. Then he disappeared down into the ground, quickly and silently. Jason felt for Jessica's hand, and she went in next, as he helped lower her into the hole. When she disappeared from sight, he followed, carefully arranging the board and carpet so they would close over top of the hole just the way they had been.

Except for the dim green glow the night vision scope cast on Halen's face, the three of them were now in complete darkness. "It's a long tunnel," Halen whispered, "and it wasn't made for grown-ups. It'll be a few hundred yards of crawling. Just take your time, and feel your way along. Take rests when you need to. There's no hurry at this point."

With that, the three of them set off, crawling slowly through the darkness, feeling their way across the cool soil and rock of the tunnel. The tunnel had many twists and turns, which Jason assumed was from the kids having to dig their way around various rock formations.

"You doing okay?" he asked Jessica in a whisper, after several minutes of crawling in silence.

"Yeah, I'm fine," she answered.

It seemed to Jason as if they kept going for half an hour, through the seemingly endless weaving tunnel, far beyond the distance he had expected it to be. But then, he realized, judging distance in a situation like this was nearly impossible.

"Almost there," he heard Halen whisper. "Don't say a word until the end." Every breath and every brushing against the walls sounded incredibly loud in the tight space. Jason just hoped no one on the outside could hear any of it. After another twenty feet or so of crawling, they all stopped. Jason could see a thin sliver of dim light ahead, with Halen's and Jessica's silhouettes in front of it.

After a moment of complete silence, Halen said, "I don't hear anyone. I have to break the boards loose to get out." Jason didn't like the sound of that, but just crouched patiently. He heard the creak of rusty nails being pulled through old wood, and wondered how Halen was doing it. After the first board came free, light poured in, seeming a lot brighter to their straining eyes than it really was. Halen carefully drew the board into the tunnel and laid it alongside the wall.

Looking through the hole as Halen worked on the next board, Jason could see what looked like the underside of a small bridge, going over a drainage culvert. The road was just above them, and it was about a four-foot drop into the ditch below. To the left, he could just see the river. Much of the area outside seemed to be lit by artificial lights, though under the bridge was still relatively dark.

The second board came free, allowing enough space for them to pass through. After sliding the board into the tunnel, Halen leaned through the hole and hung his head down, looking both ways. He sat up again, nodded at Jason, and noiselessly dropped into the gully, bringing his crossbow to the ready and scanning from side to side.

Jason held both of Jessica's hands as she backed out of the hole and down into the gully. Jason followed, and the three of them sat under the bridge for a few minutes. Compared to the tunnel, it felt brightly lit and completely exposed, but they didn't hear any voices nearby. Uphill, the drainage ditch continued, slowly curving out of sight to the right. It was just a swale, only two or three feet deep and about ten feet wide. The floodlights from the nearby trailers lit the ground on both sides of it, but the bottom of the ditch was in shadow.

"It's about a hundred yards up that ditch to the woods," Halen said in a low voice. "Stay low, out of the light." He suddenly stopped talking, and the three of them froze. There was the sound of an approaching car, and then something that sounded big rumbled over the bridge above them. Halen looked at Jessica. "Are you ready for this?" She nodded, but Jason thought she looked scared to death. "I can't cover you from in front of you, so Jason, you're going first. Jessica, you're second. When we get close to the woods, as soon as I know you'll make it, I'm turning back. Good luck."

Jason got on his stomach and started doing an army crawl, pulling himself along with his elbows, his legs dragging behind. Once he was out from under the bridge, he felt even more exposed than before. He felt better if he looked only at the ground in front of him, crawling inch by inch.

After ten feet or so, he rolled onto his side and twisted his head to look back and see how Jessica was doing. She was only a few feet behind, but then Jason noticed with horror that someone was walking over the bridge, rifle in hand. He tried to think of some way to signal Halen without drawing the man's attention. Before he could do anything, the man turned straight toward him, and was squinting into the ditch straight at him. Jason didn't feel hidden at all, but for a moment the man didn't seem to notice him. Jason thought he recognized the face, and tried desperately to put a name to it. The man reached behind his back and pulled out a flashlight. Turning it on, he aimed it directly at Jason, blinding him.

"It's me," Jason whispered loudly, putting his hands up. "It's Jason. Don't shoot."

"What the hell are you doing down there?" the man asked from the bridge. "Aren't you the guy they captured?" His voice also dropped to a whisper. "Did you escape?" Jason's mind raced, trying to decide what to say. He glanced down and saw Jessica lying face down in the ditch, not moving.

"Turn off the light," Jason whispered, "and I'll tell you what's going on." It sounded silly after he had said it, but the other agent still seemed more curious than alarmed.

"Look, just come on up here, man," the agent began, but then the light from his flashlight landed on Jessica and he stopped. "Who the hell is that?" he asked, his voice rising. For a moment Jason thought of saying she was a hostage he had rescued, but he knew he couldn't let them get Jessica into custody. His mind raced, trying to think of a way out of this.

"I got her out, too," Jason said. "But listen, you can't tell anyone." He struggled for the right words to say. "I can't explain why right now. Please, turn off the light."

But the agent walked to the edge of the bridge, leaned over, and shone his flashlight at the area below him, where Halen was lying on his back, his crossbow raised and pointed at the agent.

"Nick, wait!" Jason said, suddenly remembering the agent's name. "Don't move! Don't make a sound!" For a moment the agent obeyed, frozen in indecision, an expression of panic on his face.

"Don't do it," Halen said, as the agent began reaching for his weapon. "Drop it!" he yelled, as Nick brought his rifle up.

"Over here!" the agent yelled, bringing his rifle up to his shoulder. There was a loud click and a sound like a hammer hitting wood, and the agent toppled off the bridge with a crossbow dart stuck into his forehead. As he fell, his last reflex squeezed the trigger and a rifle blast shattered the stillness.

"Shit!" Halen shouted, standing up. "Back into the tunnel, right now!" Jason jumped to his feet as Jessica did the same, and now he could see the line of trailers along the brightly lit road, and a half-dozen armed agents now running toward them. "Jessica first!" Halen shouted, and, grabbing her by the waist, all but threw her up into the opening of the tunnel. "Use this to see," he said, handing her the spent crossbow. "Fast as you can, don't wait for us."

By then Jason was under the bridge, and after picking up the dead agent's rifle, Halen gave Jason a leg up into the hole. Jason blindly crawled as fast as he could into the pitch blackness, not sure how far ahead Jessica was. He heard gunfire far behind him, but kept going. He scrambled and crawled, his knees and hands scraping painfully against the rocks. He was still hearing occasional gunshots, but now they sounded a hundred miles away.

Ignoring the pain, Jason crawled on as fast as he could, until he crashed right into Jessica, who sat motionless in the tunnel.

"What is it?" Jason asked in a whisper.

"We're here," came the answer. "Now what?"

It amazed him how much shorter the tunnel had seemed on the way back. Jason stood up and felt the board above him. Carefully lifting it a bit, he heard far-off talking and shooting, but nothing that sounded nearby. He pushed as hard as he could, and the carpet and board flew back out of the way. He scrambled out, looked around, saw no one, and put his hand down to help Jessica up.

"I think Halen's coming," she said as she crawled out of the hole. "Or *someone* is coming," she added. Jason and Jessica peered into the blackness. They could hear a scuffling sound coming closer. "Halen?" Jessica whispered into the tunnel, but got no response. Looking terrified, Jessica raised the crossbow at the hole.

When Halen's head suddenly appeared out of the hole, Jessica was aiming the crossbow right at his face. Halen cracked a smile. "Good girl," he said, climbing out, "but crossbows aren't semi-automatic." She seemed puzzled for a moment, before apparently realizing that the crossbow, having been fired, had no dart in it.

"Our cover is blown anyway, so just run," Halen said, pointing downhill into the darkness. "Go!" Jason and Jessica jumped out of the clubhouse and started running. At first Jason held back, not wanting to leave Jessica behind, but was soon amazed to find that he could barely keep up with her. He glanced back once and saw Halen following a hundred feet behind. Rounding the corner of the house at last, Jason could just see Doug and David standing on the patio. As they reached them, they collapsed to their knees, panting.

"You okay?" David asked anxiously. "We heard gunshots. What happened?" Keith stepped out of a nearby bush, lowering his rifle.

"We're okay," Jason answered breathlessly. "Halen's right behind us." The words were just out of his mouth when Halen walked around the corner, seeming perfectly relaxed, and not even out of breath. "Well, it almost worked," Jason said with a sigh.

"You did good," Halen said to Jason, slapping him on the shoulder. "We didn't get out, but we all got back alive, at least."

"I hate that Nick had to die," Jason said, trying not to make it sound like a criticism.

"I waited as long as I could," Halen said. "It was him or me. I'm sorry it had to be either. Even one casualty is always one too many," he said, and dropped the rifle he was holding onto the ground.

"Only one?" Jason asked. "What about the gunfight?"

"I was shooting the ground," Halen said. "It was just to buy you guys some time. They weren't about to charge across an open field, thinking someone was shooting at them."

"Well, they know about the tunnel now," said Jason.

"Yeah," Halen said. "It won't help them much, since both ends are in their territory. But it's useless to us now, too. Goddamn it. If that one guy hadn't been there, you'd be long gone by now." Halen looked up at Jason. "Do you think they recognized you?"

"Well, from the quick look I got, I recognized two of them," Jason answered. "So yeah, they probably recognized me, too."

"Well, I guess that makes you one of us now," Halen said grimly. "I have to say, though, I'm pretty impressed with you. You could have gotten away yourself, but you stayed and did the right thing."

"Fat lot of good it did," Jason remarked.

**BETSY** looked up to see Sandy in the office doorway, and her eyes widened with surprise. Sandy wore an elegant ankle-length, deep blue dress with a sweetheart neckline and black high-heeled shoes. "Where are you going, all dressed up like that?" Betsy asked.

"I can't do lunch today," Sandy said. "I'm off to prison."

"It's about time, you radical," Betsy kidded.

"No, really," Sandy said, "I'm visiting a guy in prison."

"Your choice of men out here isn't bad enough?" Betsy joked. "Now you're trying the prisons?"

"It's a guy I know from way back," Sandy replied. "He's not a boyfriend. I knew his sister for years. He's at a state pen in New Jersey. I have an hour until my train leaves," she added, sitting down in the nearest seat.

"What's he there for?" Betsy asked.

"He got caught with a bunch of weed, and got five years. He's just over halfway done there. Thought I'd go cheer him up a bit."

"That dress ought to do it," Betsy said. "Really, Sand, are you sure it's a good idea? Is it safe and all?"

"It's low security there," she assured Betsy. "The murderers and psychos they keep somewhere else. Most of the people there are just there on drug charges."

"Oh, so you'll just be hanging out with drug dealers," Betsy said skeptically. "Well, in *that* case—"

"No offense, Bet, but I think selling drugs is a lot more respectable than working for the government."

For once, Betsy was actually offended. "And pushing drugs to kids in the playground," she retorted, "is that more respectable than what I do?"

"Oh, you know that stereotype is a crock," Sandy said with disgust. "Just propaganda to vilify people who sell or use drugs, and to justify using violence in the fascists' glorious crusade against them. Try living in a poor neighborhood, with no education, no jobs around, with a wife and kid to feed, and see what you'll do for money." Sandy sat down in the chair opposite Betsy's desk.

"Okay, I'm sorry," said Betsy, who didn't like arguing with people she cared about. "But it's still not exactly a respectable profession. You know that drugs ruin a lot of people's lives."

"Not nearly as many as the *war* on drugs does," came the retort from Sandy. "We've got over a million guys in prison in this country, just for getting caught with drugs. A lot of them have wives, kids, people depending on them. And they're doing ten or twenty years locked up for selling a little dope or something. How much does that help society?"

"I know, I know. You already convinced me that drug laws don't really help, but are we supposed to just ignore the problem?"

"Ignoring it would be better than this!" said Sandy vehemently. "Carlton, the guy I'm visiting today, he tells me that guys in prison are still getting drugs, I mean on the inside. You got these guys in a locked box, under constant surveillance, with no privacy, getting searched constantly, and they *still* manage to get drugs. If they can't keep drugs out of their own damn prisons, why would anyone imagine they could keep them out of an entire country? It's just idiotic, and they know it. They don't do it because they hate drugs, or because they care about addicts; they do it for the power it gives them. The shredding of the Fourth and Fifth Amendments, and so much of the other illegal garbage the government does today evolved out of the war on drugs. Drugs were just the excuse for increasing their power."

"I'm still not so sure that legalizing it wouldn't just give us a few million addicts instead," Betsy remarked.

"Well, I know it's politically incorrect to say this, but people have a right to be addicts. If they steal to buy drugs, or endanger others by driving drunk, that's another story. But if they sit at home frying their own brains, nobody has a right to stop them. And anyway, the drug abuse epidemic that the politicians say would happen is pure bunk. Did ending alcohol prohibition make everyone into a drunk? No. What did it do? It immediately ended all of the Mafia's involvement in rum-running and moonshining. As libertarians like to ask, when's the last time two liquor stores had a shootout? All of the drug-related violence occurs because it's *illegal*. Repeal those laws, and the price will drop, the danger of overdose will all but disappear, and the shootouts and gang activity will end overnight. And don't think the bastards in office don't know that. They love the crime, and the violence, and the rest of it. It gives them something to point at and say, 'This is why we need more power and money, to fight against this.' They make sure things keep going just the way they are, knowing it can never be solved, and not wanting it to be solved. Then they go home and have a drink, or a snort of cocaine. Hypocritical bastards."

"Wow, you're really on a soapbox today," said Betsy, laughing. "Maybe you're right, but I don't know how you can be so sure about their motives. You just assume that everyone here is an evil schemer. What if some of them just think it's the right thing to do? What if they really think that trying to stamp out drugs is good for society?"

Sandy sighed. "I know I rant and rave a lot. It's just, being here, in Washington, I can't just ignore it the way I used to. It's in my face every day." She sighed as she smoothed the soft blue fabric of her dress. "But to answer your question," she said, "I think these guys might have some good motives when they're running for office, but once they're in, once they get an insider's view of how it all works, they really can't miss the truth. Inside the machine, people learn fast what the game is really about, and it's not about good intentions and helping people." Just then Grant walked through the door. Sandy looked at Betsy with a big smile, and added in a cheerful voice, obviously meant for Grant to hear, "It's about ruling the world." She stood up to leave.

"Are you trying to corrupt my loyal subjects again, Sandy?" Grant asked, countering her insolent gaze with a friendly smile.

"Would I do such a thing?" she answered with feigned surprise. Then she sashayed out the door in a swirl of deep blue silk and sleek black hair.

"Wow," Grant said. "She's a vision today. What happened to the ripped blue jeans?"

"She's going to prison to cheer up a friend," said Betsy.

# PART IV

**JESSICA** sat on the living room couch, feeling restless and nervous, wondering if she'd ever get back home again. Her sprained ankle was throbbing, and she had scratches and bruises all over herself from crawling through the tunnel.

Halen had told everyone that he had decided not to reactivate the bug the government had sent in. He explained that whatever false message they might send, pretending to have more people and more weapons than they really had, or pretending to have fewer than they really had, there was no telling how the feds would react. And he didn't want the feds hearing anything about Jason or Jessica, or himself, for that matter, and didn't think it would help to make up any fictional hostages or civilians. In the end, he explained to the group, he had decided that the best message to send would be to tie the bug to an arrow and use his compound bow to launch it out toward the trailers, as a way of saying, "You can't spy on us that easily." So that's what he had done.

Now they were spread out through the house again. Tasha came into the living room with a pot and placed it on top of the wood stove. "Would you be good enough to watch this for me, Jess?" she asked. "It's just some frozen vegetables." She made a face that told Jessica she didn't think much of boiled frozen vegetables, but it was the best she could do.

"Of course," said Jessica. She got off the couch and sat next to the wood stove. "Something smells good."

"I'm cooking steaks on the camp stove in the kitchen," Tasha said, smiling. "Doug has a whole deep-freeze full of food downstairs, which has kept frozen so far, despite the lack of power. But there's not a fresh vegetable or a fresh bottle of milk in this whole neighborhood, not since about a week ago." Then she laughed softly. "We're probably the only ones who care, anyway," she said. "I think these men could live happily on cold Dinty Moore beef stew, right out of the can." Her laughter was like silver bells, Jessica thought. Tasha was the most graceful person she had ever seen.

Jessica smiled. "I'm sure David appreciates good food, doesn't he?" she asked.

"Oh, yes," Tasha answered. "We do our own special blend of Indian, Filipino, and American cuisine at home. But there's not much I can do with what Doug has here."

"I'm sure you're doing better than I would," said Jessica.

Tasha smiled and went back to the steaks.

From the next room came the sound of Doug playing an acoustic guitar. David came in and took a seat across from Jessica.

"How are you feeling?" he asked.

"Kind of sore all over," she admitted, "but still breathing."

"All of this must seem awfully strange to you," David said sympathetically.

"Yeah, it still doesn't seem real. It's like I landed in a completely different world. All this legal and political stuff—it's just way over my head." She thought for a moment, and then smiled. "There was this guy in my class at school who insisted that the government has some supercomputer somewhere that always knows where everyone is, and knows everything about everybody. He was always going on and on about the government secretly implanting computer chips in our heads, monitoring and controlling our thoughts." She looked at David, and for a moment wondered whether he was going to tell her it was all true.

David just smiled. "Those of us who want freedom in the world are a minority, and every minority movement will have its share of those people," he said. "People who think outside the box are, by definition, not normal, and the truth is, most people will accept almost anything as true, if it fits what they want to think. But let me ask you this: What do you think happens when an overwhelming majority of the people believe something utterly ridiculous?"

Jessica frowned in thought for a minute, then said, "Well, it wouldn't be seen as ridiculous. Like when almost everyone believed the world was flat. Back then, everyone thought the ones saying it was round were the crazy ones."

"Yes," said David. "So in most people's minds, the truth-tellers would be put in the wrong-and-crazy category right along with the people who really are wrong and crazy."

"Yeah," said Jessica. "I guess the majority can get away with believing anything, as long as they all believe it together. It's so easy to think what everyone else thinks, whether it's right or not. I'm sure I do plenty of that myself, without noticing."

"You have a good mind, Jessica," said David, smiling again. "Did you go to public school?"

"Private," she answered. "A school founded by the Quakers."

"I see," said David. "A very intelligent man once said, 'When you find yourself agreeing with the majority, it's time to stop and reflect'."

"That was Mark Twain!" said Jessica, proud of having actually known that bit of trivia.

"Indeed it was," said David. "So, back on the subject of conspiracy theories, some people are a little too willing to think outside the box, to the point where they begin to think *everything* outside the box is true. And of course it's not, any more than everything *inside* the box is true. This gives rise to the stereotypical conspiracy nut. But many of those bizarre conspiracy theories begin with a grain of truth. You see, even those hard-core wackos don't overestimate how heartless, devious, and power-happy people in government can be; it's just that sometimes they overestimate the *competence* of tyrants. If the people in power could directly monitor and control us all, they would be doing it already, without a doubt. They're always trying to come up with new ways to spy on us and control our actions, but they simply don't have the manpower or technology to pull off some of the conspiracies that some people believe in. Ironically, I think those wackos may actually be helping the tyrants by giving everyone the impression that they can do such things, which keeps all the nonconformists scared and paranoid."

"I guess I always just believed what I saw on TV and read in magazines," said Jessica. "I thought people who said the media was lying were crazy. But now I know for a fact that they lie, at least sometimes, because they lied about the airplane I was on." She lifted the pot lid a little and looked in. The water was on the brink of boiling.

"Well, yes, of course they lie when they have to," David said. "But lying can be complicated and hard to control. So most of their mind control is just good old-fashioned propaganda, and that, all by itself, is amazingly powerful. The way people's thoughts and minds can be controlled with mere words is astounding. It's a field of thought I've accidentally learned a lot about recently." He looked at Jessica, as if considering something, and then said, "Can I do a little test on you?"

"Sure, I guess," she answered.

"I just want to ask you some simple questions, and I want you to answer as quickly as you can. Don't stop to think. Just tell me the first thing that comes to mind. Okay?"

"Okay." Jessica nodded, with just a hint of apprehension.

"Is it bad to commit murder?" David asked.

"Yes."

"Is it bad to eat fish?"

"No."

"Is it bad to steal?"

"Yes."

"Is it bad to drive a Corvette?"

"No."

"Is it bad to break the law?"

"Yes."

"Okay, we're halfway there. Now, *why* is it bad to commit murder?"

"Well," Jessica said, hesitating for a moment, "because it's wrong to take someone else's life from them. Life is precious."

"Good. Next question. Why is it bad to steal?"

Jessica thought for a moment, trying to quickly spit out whatever came into her head. "It just is. If something belongs to someone else, you can't just take it. I can't really describe why."

"Good enough. Last one. Why is it bad to break the law?"

"Because," she began, but hesitated. "We all have to obey the law. If everyone went around stealing and killing—"

"Wait, wait," David interrupted. "I didn't say *which* laws I meant. I didn't say the laws against murder and theft. I just asked if it's bad to break the law. So I ask again, why is it bad to break the law, regardless of what law we're talking about?"

"Well," she began. "Well, there have to be rules, and we all have to follow the rules, sort of like Jason was saying." After a moment, she added, "It's the only way we can all get along and live together in peace."

"Okay, now we get to the important part," David said. "What should those rules be?"

She thought for a moment. "Well, no killing and no stealing, for starters. Respect each other's property. Basically, live and let live, and don't hurt other people."

"Excellent answer," David said. "Now for the most important question anyone will ever ask you: Are those what the rules should be because some politicians said so, or because the universe says so?"

"The universe? I don't quite know what you're asking," Jessica said.

"I'm asking whether murder is bad, whether stealing is bad, and whether we should all treat each other with respect—live and let live, as you said—because someone in *government* told us to, or because that's just how people should behave?"

"The second one. That's just how people should behave. It's what works well for everyone."

"Agreed. Now, who writes the law?"

"What do you mean?"

"I mean, who makes what everyone calls the law? Who makes up those rules?"

"The politicians and lawyers, I guess. The government."

"Not God? Not the universe?"

"No."

"And if they wrote a law saying that murder is a *good* thing, would it *become* a good thing?"

"Of course not."

"If the law said that stealing was okay, would it be okay?"

"No."

"If the law said that instead of your live-and-let-live idea, we should attack and rob each other, would that be good?"

"Of course not," she said with a slight smile.

"Okay, this time you're allowed to think before you answer." He spoke in a slow, steady tone as he asked the question again: "Is it bad to break the law?"

She considered the question, which didn't feel like the same question as before. "It depends what the law is," she answered.

David's serious expression morphed into a smile. "And, last but not least, *who* decides whether a law is a good law or a bad law, and whether or not you should obey it?"

"Well, if it protects good people from bad people, it's a good law—if it makes society more peaceful and happy—" Jessica was quiet for a long time.

"And who decides whether or not a law does that?" David asked. Jessica just looked puzzled. "Congress decides whether to enact a law, the courts decide whether to uphold it, and the police decide whether to enforce it, but who actually decides whether it's a good law or a bad one?" Jessica was still thinking, and after another minute, David added, "In other words, who ultimately decides whether or not *you* should obey that law or break it?" He waited for a moment in silence as she pondered the question. "I know you know the answer," he said with a smile. "You're just afraid to say it."

"I guess," said Jessica slowly, "I guess that's a decision that each of us makes for ourselves. So I guess ... *I* decide."

"Welcome to humanity," David said with a smile, giving her a pat on the shoulder.

"But what about the people who think—" began Jessica, but she was interrupted by Josh bursting through the front door.

"They're coming!" he said, out of breath. "They're coming straight at us!"

"Two Bradleys heading this way," came Halen's voice from upstairs. "Stay out of sight."

Jessica was shocked out of the comfortable conversation, and found herself desperately looking around, wondering where to go and what to do. Then she heard Halen shout from upstairs, "Wait, they stopped." After a pause, he added, "They've parked the Bradleys sideways, one on each side of the road coming in, just this side of David's house. I think they were just moving the front line up. I don't think they're coming here yet." Despite his words, it was a long time before anyone dared to move. Finally, Halen came walking down the stairs. "They shut the engines down," Halen said in a low voice. "They just wanted to up our stress levels a bit."

"It's working," said Jessica, and she looked down at her trembling hands. Then she smelled something burning. "Darn it!" she said, "I scorched the vegetables."

"Just so we're clear," Halen went on, as the others all came into the living room, "when they try to come in—and they will, sooner or later—who here is fighting, who's hiding, and who's running?" Jessica knew that "wait and see" would only last so long, and then they'd all have to make a decision, but Halen's bluntness made her uncomfortable. She wasn't about to pick up a gun and start shooting, but what else was she going to do? Hide? Where? Run? To where? Some of the others seemed unsure as well. "Tactically speaking," Halen said, after a moment of silence, "it's best if we stick pretty much together, but without bunching up." Halen looked from face to face. "Okay, next question: who here is ready to pick up a gun?"

"Got mine," Josh said, holding up his rifle. He looked nervous but determined.

"If I have to," Doug said, self-consciously folding his arms.

"I'm just a spectator," Jason said. "I won't be shooting at anyone."

"Really not looking forward to it," said David, "but willing and able if absolutely necessary."

"You know me," Keith said, the grin on his face not quite concealing his concern.

"Two lookouts at all times," Halen said. "Combined, the two upstairs corner rooms have a view of almost everything."

"What about the back?" asked Doug.

"They're not that creative, or that competent," Halen said, "though I'll keep an eye out that way. They'd have to come across the river and through the woods."

"To grandmother's house we go," Doug added flippantly.

"When they come," Halen went on, "it will be from the front, inside or hiding behind the armor."

"What are we supposed to do against Bradleys?" Josh asked in a slightly quavering tone.

"Nothing," Halen said bluntly, "but they'll have to get out of them at some point. You can't do a room-to-room search with a Bradley."

"No, but I bet you can flatten a house with one," Doug said, "if you have enough time."

"What about the rest of us?" Jessica asked, and looked at Tasha for support. "Is there a bomb shelter or anything?"

"Not in here," Halen answered. "I have one, but they've taken over my house already. Just do what you can to keep your heads down. If bullets start flying, stay close, but don't get in the way."

This discussion was too much for Jessica. They were standing around talking about what to do once a full-scale shootout with the government began. How could they be so matter-of-fact about it? This was unbelievable, and terrifying.

"What's the point of this?" she demanded suddenly, trying desperately to sound less frightened than she was. "Are you guys really going to hold off the federal government by yourselves? Won't they just send in more until they crush you? We can't escape, we can't talk to them, and we can't win—isn't surrender our best chance?"

"It may be our best chance to live a bit longer," said Halen. "But some of us would rather resist to the bitter end than ever beg those bastards for mercy. There is always a chance that some help is on the way, and I will hold onto that hope as long as I'm alive. If no help is coming, then I just want to take out as many of those thugs as I can before I die."

"I have to tell you," Jessica said timidly, reluctant to say it, "that I'm thinking of going out there and surrendering myself, and taking my chances out there, before it's too late."

"Josh, Keith, can you take first watch?" Halen asked, as if he hadn't heard Jessica. I'm so pathetic to him, he doesn't even want to acknowledge me, she thought. "We'll do two-hour shifts," said Halen. "Doug, Jason, David, and Tasha, stay on the first floor, but out of sight. Jessica." She jumped as Halen said her name. "Come downstairs with me."

———⁂———

**JASON** sat on the living room floor next to Doug. They'd pulled the cushions off the couches and chairs and put them on the floor to sit on. The lights were off, but the curtains were open. They were all quietly alert. After about half an hour, Tasha crept to the kitchen and brought back the steaks on a platter with knives and forks.

"Here's meat, anyway," she said. "We should probably eat if we can. The vegetables got burnt, but that was no great loss; they were just frozen ones."

"Are you dissin' the awesome cuisine I got here?" said Doug with mock indignation. Tasha managed a weak smile. Jason could see that she was quite shaken, but hiding it well.

The steak was good and everyone ate as much as they could, but the stress dampened all their appetites.

Jason considered how strange it felt to be awaiting something like this without a gun at his side, but he knew it was better this way. At this point there wasn't anyone on either side he was willing to shoot at. So he waited nervously in the living room, hoping that somehow this thing could be resolved without everyone in there dying, but unable to imagine how that could come about. Several times he had considered going out by himself, and if not for Jessica, he would have done so. He considered taking her out there and lying about who she was, but he knew they wouldn't get away with it long enough to escape. Even though he couldn't imagine what good he could do from where he was, he wasn't willing to just walk away from her.

He knew full well what was going to happen now: "scorched earth" policy all the way. The feds had lost five agents now: the one who was killed after shooting Keith, the three who died as a result of the raid on Ben's place (the third had eventually died at the hospital), and then Nick, whom Halen had killed with the crossbow. Jason wished he knew exactly which agents had died from the raid on Ben's house, but the media hadn't mentioned their names. Now those who remained out beyond the barricades, if unleashed, would show no mercy. The only thing left that might make them show a little restraint was if they thought there might be innocent hostages inside. They probably still didn't know about Jessica being there. Only Nick had seen her, and he was dead. Jason, on the other hand, had probably been recognized by at least a couple of other agents, who now probably considered him a traitor. He couldn't very well now claim that he was being held prisoner, nor did he have a good explanation, without mentioning Jessica, for why he hadn't come out when the supposed "terrorists" had released him. And though he was still skeptical about what David and the others were claiming, he was no longer sure he'd be safe out there himself if they ever found out about Jessica being there. None of the options felt good.

"I'm surprised they haven't sent in a radio or something," David was saying. "I would have expected them to be trying to persuade us to come out and beg their forgiveness."

"Maybe they don't want us coming out," Doug said. "Or maybe they just don't want their thugs talking to us and finding out who's really in here."

"You may be right," David replied. "They've had to tell quite a few whoppers to demonize us enough to get away with what they're doing. That's just a basic military tactic: you've got to make your army despise the enemy, or they might not shoot at him."

Jason said nothing, but felt a twinge of shame, knowing that the tactic David was describing had worked perfectly on him. Though it was vague, he could still recall the general image he'd had of the people in here before meeting them: malicious, violent people with no respect for other people or their property. But that description was sounding less and less like the people in here, and more and more like the people out there. He assumed that his fellow agents meant well, as he did, and that they thought they were doing the right thing, but someone somewhere in the chain of command wasn't being straight with them. Bridges, for instance, had struck him as a straight-up guy, but someone had been feeding him false information through those nonexistent "negotiations." The agents out there were facing a fictional enemy, he thought.

"And while they tell everyone that we're the scum of the earth," Doug said, "they tell each other that they're the righteous heroes saving the day. It's pathetic." Jason wondered if Doug intended that as a personal attack. It felt like one. But thinking back to the discussions that he and his fellow agents had had, the way they had talked about the "webbies" and their cult leader, and the way they portrayed themselves as the enforcers of justice and order, he realized that Doug was right. How willing he had been to believe what he was told.

"If we had a way to send a message to all the people with guns out there," David said, waving in the direction of the government trailers, "what would you want to tell them?"

Without hesitation, Doug snapped, "Burn in hell, you Nazi pigs."

"I'm sure that would win them over," David said with a smile.

"Well, really," Doug said, "as I've said a million times before, if we treat them with respect and act all civilized, all it does is legitimize what they're doing, and make it seem okay. You've said it yourself,

David: if we don't identify evil as evil, and show it for what it is, we're basically giving our blessing to their thuggery. Those bastards don't deserve to be treated with any respect. Calling them 'sir,' and treating their control-freak plans as if they deserve polite, reasoned rebuttal instead of vicious condemnation, only gives their crap respect it doesn't deserve. They should be treated like the crooks they are."

"You may be right, Doug," said Tasha, "but it doesn't help to use that kind of language. It's not the way to win allies."

"Nothing will win over the stupid American people at this point," Doug replied. "Unless we scare the hell out of the tyrants, nothing is going to change. Having a nice rational debate is never going to do it. No offense, David."

"It only makes us look bad, and makes it easier for people to hate us and think we're a bunch of scary extremists, when they hear talk like that," Tasha responded, her voice low and soft, as it always was. "We should be above that, so anyone paying attention can see that we're the ones with reason on our side."

Because of Tasha's stunning looks, and how little he had heard her speak, Jason had imagined Tasha to be some sort of obedient, submissive "mail order bride." But, though she spoke softly, Tasha had no accent, and her words conveyed a level of education and intelligence that Jason had not expected.

"It's already hard enough to get people to want freedom," David added. "We shouldn't be turning people off by sounding bitter and uneducated, even if the anger is completely justified, which it is, in this case."

"Winning over the masses is a lost cause," Doug replied, throwing his hands in the air. "It doesn't matter how politely and logically it's explained to them; the American people don't *want* real freedom, and they hate anyone who does. Forget trying to convince them. The majority will never be on our side, and we don't need them."

"Well, it sure would help to have more of them, like right now, for instance," David remarked. "And we are seeing more and more people paying attention."

"Too little, too late," Doug retorted. "The only way we'll stop the beast is to scare the hell out of its pawns. They don't care what's right, or what's true. They never even think about that stuff. They will do what they're told, no matter who it hurts, unless it hurts *them*. It's like that guy said about the Nazis: if occasionally one of them didn't make it home, it might have made a difference. It might have made the thugs think twice about what they were doing, and whether it was worth it. As long as being a fascist is a comfortable and safe occupation, the beast will have a never-ending supply of unthinking thugs." Doug suddenly looked over at Jason, as if just remembering he was there. "No offense," Doug said with a smile.

"None taken," said Jason, which wasn't quite true. Of course he cared about what was right, and what was true. Of course he didn't want to hurt innocent people. The whole reason he was in law enforcement was to catch the bad guys so they couldn't hurt people. Jason saw the world differently, but that didn't make him a heartless bastard. Then Jason remembered when he'd first seen David. David's eyes seemed to look right through everything superficial and see the goodness of his heart. He felt safe with David, and wanted to listen to him. Doug and Keith just made him feel defensive.

"If you think anyone who disagrees with you is a heartless, evil bastard," said Jason, "how are you different from the guys out there who think you're a bunch of terrorists?"

"Good point, Jason," said Tasha. Then, addressing Doug again, she said, "I think if we give up on trying to win the rational debate, we've lost already. If we can't win the hearts and minds of people, hopefully including the people who work for the government, then what's the point?"

"The point is to achieve freedom for the few people who actually want it," Doug answered. "How much has sitting around talking actually accomplished? People have been teaching about freedom for hundreds of years. Most people never listen. Yeah, this extremist here," he said, pointing at David, "has gotten a lot of people thinking about stuff they had never thought about before, but in the end, what good will that do? When has polite talk ever reduced tyranny?"

"Not very often, unfortunately," David admitted.

"Not *ever*," Doug replied emphatically.

"Not by itself, maybe," David continued, "but even when it comes down to a revolution, it matters how many people are on the side of freedom, and that depends on words. As I've said before, I think it was more Thomas Paine than George Washington who won the American Revolution. He didn't convince a majority, but he did convince a lot of people, enough to win their freedom—for a while anyway."

"You see how clueless Americans are today," Doug said, his voice rising a bit. "How many do you think could even begin to comprehend Paine's *Common Sense* pamphlet? If Paine were alive today, the public would hate him; he'd either be in prison, or dead."

A smile appeared on David's face. "If he were alive today, he'd be dead?"

"Oh, shut up," said Doug, trying not to smile himself. "You know what I mean."

Tasha spoke up again. "But if Thomas Paine just called the king vulgar names, what good do you think that would have done? If he had cursed and used more vicious language, would that have won over more people, or fewer? All the angry rhetoric, even if justified, is counterproductive."

"I just think it's too late in the game to be trying to win over any more of the sheep," Doug said.

"Well, I hate to make your point for you," David commented, "but alcohol prohibition is a pretty good example of a few hostile, impolite people managing to do what no amount of reason and talk could."

"Exactly!" Doug exclaimed. "Tarring and feathering a few damn revenuers, and lynching a few, forced the monster to give up the prohibition racket. When have words ever done that? It worked because no one dared to be a revenuer. It became unenforceable, and the feds had to repeal it and pretend it was their idea. It's no different now. Unless being a federal thug becomes a lot more dangerous, they'll keep right on doing whatever they want. When we see a few IRS crooks, or ATF, or DEA, or whoever, hanging from the trees in D.C., then we might see freedom coming back. Not before."

"It's just not good," Tasha responded, shaking her head as if the words hurt her. "Lowering ourselves to their level isn't the answer. Sometimes revolution *can* be accomplished by non-violent means. Gandhi did it that way."

"Oh, come on," Doug said. "Using force in self-defense isn't putting ourselves on their level."

"You don't hang people from trees in self-defense," Tasha answered, with a flash of fire in her eyes that startled Jason. "When you talk like that, people see us as the aggressors. It just feeds the claim that we're nasty terrorists."

"It doesn't matter what the sheep think of us," Doug insisted. "It only matters whether we let freedom completely die here, because we're so concerned with what other people think about it."

"Well, as one who still wants to see this settled without violence," David cut in, "I must admit, our current situation doesn't give me a lot of hope that we're going to win the battle of ideas."

"And we shouldn't have to," Doug said. "You said yourself, the rights we have don't depend upon any law, any election, or popular opinion. We have the right to defend our freedom, whether the sheep out there understand that or not."

"True," David agreed. "It would just be a lot easier if more people wanted to be free."

"Yeah, well, they don't," said Doug flatly.

"No, they don't," Tasha said with a sigh.

After that the room fell silent, and Jason was left wondering what his fellow agents would think if they could have heard this. What would Agent Bridges think? Jason wasn't even sure what to think of it himself.

**BETSY** hung up her coat and sat down at her desk to see if she could get a thing or two finished before Grant arrived. She was supposed to be off today, but Grant had just called her and said that something had just happened that he wanted to respond to. "Don't bother with office clothes," he said, "the place should be pretty empty. You know I'd just come to your apartment if I could," he added apologetically. Betsy understood. They didn't want any rumors going around about the President-elect and his voluptuous little secretary. She looked up as Grant walked in, whistling a tune. "You're in a good mood today," she commented.

"Did you read the Sunday paper yet?" he asked, plopping the one he was holding onto her desk. Betsy picked it up, but Grant gave her the report without waiting for her to read it. "Halford just got indicted on all sorts of juicy stuff."

"Well, at least you're being a good sport about it," Betsy said wryly, scanning the story. The words "bribery," "extortion," and "fraud" popped off the page at her.

"Good thing he didn't beat me in that last senatorial election. Imagine how much more exciting it would have been if this had come out right after he was elected," Grant said, opening his briefcase and arranging his papers.

"If it had come out during that election, it might have made things a lot easier for you," Betsy commented.

"Hey, he spent double what I did on that campaign," Grant remarked, "and I got double the votes he did. It was easy enough. I guess the people knew the guy was a crook before the FBI figured it out."

"Well, it says here they've been investigating him for quite a while," Betsy said. She put the paper down and looked at Grant. "Do you ever wonder if they're investigating you?" Grant looked up from his papers, his eyebrows raised, but didn't say anything. "I don't mean you did anything that needs investigating," she added quickly. "I mean, don't you think they snoop on all congressmen, at least a little?"

"I'm sure they do, and that's just fine with me," Grant declared. "It makes me look good—Mr. Squeaky Clean."

"Sure you don't have even one little skeleton in your closet?" she asked.

"If I did, don't you think my opponents would have found it before now?" he replied.

"A non-denial denial," she responded.

"Very observant," he said with a smile, "but ultimately what matters isn't whether I did anything or not, but only whether the public *believes* I did. It's a slight advantage to actually not *be* a crook, but not as much as you might expect. Public image has very little to do with reality. It's easy to make an honest guy look like a crook, and vice versa. It's a question of who has the best spin doctors."

"You don't think Americans are savvy enough to see the spin for what it is?" Betsy ventured. "You just said they figured out Halford before the FBI did."

"That doesn't mean they're savvy," said Grant. "It just means they're willing to believe bad stuff about politicians. And Halford wasn't a very good liar."

Grant glanced at some papers, and put them aside. "Case in point," he said. "The election of 2008. Half the country was convinced that Barack Obama was the Second Coming. Based on what? What did they know about him, or about what he believed? Not a damn thing. It was all emotion, all packaging, all spin. And yet you had millions of honest people working their fingers to the bone to give that man an enormous amount of power. Same thing with Bill Clinton. The charm and charisma trump everything else.

He seemed like a swell guy, so the public gave him the White House. Twice, even. And look at Reagan. Even people who hated his policies loved the guy. Conservatives have been desperately looking for another one like him ever since. Those who run for public office learned a long time ago that if you give the people substance, you only confuse them and scare them away. If you give them empty, feel-good fluff, they will flock to you in droves."

"And is that what you gave them?" she asked, half teasing.

"Absolutely. I would have lost by a landslide if I had spent time trying to explain the details of the policies I was proposing. The real stuff goes in one ear and out the other. Only very general concepts will remain in most people's minds: tough on crime, cares about the poor, will fix the economy. And I could have created that image no matter what policies I was actually proposing."

"That's a pretty sad statement about the country, isn't it?" Betsy asked. "It sounds as if the people are just falling for whatever sales pitch sounds better."

"That's exactly what they're doing. It's what they've done for hundreds of years, and will probably keep right on doing forever. Every time there's a poll about economics, or political philosophy, or anything like that, the American people demonstrate that they don't know anything about anything. They don't *think* anything because they don't *know* anything. But you can still *feel* things, no matter how ignorant you are, so that's what they do, and that's what everyone running for office panders to: the emotions and feelings of the electorate."

"So what's to stop a complete tyrant from gaining power here, if he has a slick enough PR team and knows the right buttons to push to play on people's emotions?"

"Nothing," Grant said. "Absolutely nothing." Betsy hoped he was going to say something else, something a bit more comforting, but he didn't.

**JESSICA** sat in a chair in the corner of the basement, waiting for Halen to speak. Halen sat on the couch that faced the back window and sliding glass door of the basement, and he seemed deep in thought. She had nervous flutters in her stomach as she waited for him to chew her out for being such a stupid coward. Then she thought how silly it was to feel nervous about this man's disapproval when she might not live another day. But she did want his approval, she realized, very much.

Halen was still a little intimidating, yet she felt safest when she was near him. The things he did seemed like magic to her: always in the right place at the right time, never missing a shot, like some invincible movie hero. Surely if she just stayed near him, he would never let her come to harm. But she knew that she was thinking with her feelings, not her brain. She felt a visceral attraction to this man who had saved her life, to his raw power and amazing skill. But her conscience recoiled in horror at his ability to kill people with no apparent feeling at all. Even if it was necessary and justified, how could a really good human being remain so unaffected?

"You don't really know someone until they have complete control over you, until you're completely at their mercy," Halen began, startling her out of her thoughts. "When they can do whatever they want and get away with it, that's when you can see who they really are."

For a moment Jessica felt nervous, wondering if he was talking about their current situation, just the two of them alone in the basement, but then Halen went on: "I've spent a total of eight months in someone else's custody—one month as a prisoner of war in Bosnia, before I escaped; two months in a military prison, until it was decided that I was *justified* in knocking out my commanding officer; and five months in a Texas state prison, about a thousand years ago, for getting caught with some weed."

That's not so bad, Jessica thought, having expected to hear about a murder or two.

"And I learned more when I had hardly any freedom at all than I did during all the times when I could do pretty much whatever I wanted. Mostly what I learned was not about the criminals. They were pretty predictable, whether it was the sadistic psychos or the pathetic dope dealers. No, the fascinating ones were the ones who had been given power, power to control other human beings—the sort of people you would be surrendering yourself to if you go out there."

She had already been trying to imagine what would happen if she did go out. Even if they didn't know she had been on the plane, would she be thrown in prison just for being there, as a suspected terrorist? Even if it all got sorted out in the end, she dreaded the thought of even a day in prison; scenes from all the prison movies she'd ever seen raced through her head.

"Some of the guards I knew were pretty normal, just doing a job without thinking about it, not really caring one way or the other what happened—callous, but also relatively harmless, ambivalent morons doing what they were trained to do. But a lot of them weren't there by accident. A lot of people gravitate toward those jobs, not because of the pay or the prestige, since there isn't much of either, but for the power trip it gives them. They get to rule over their little land of make-believe, where they are the kings with lots of subjects to push around."

"Now, in this country they can't get away with as much as the movies would lead you to believe, at least not anymore. They can't usually get away with torture, rape, murder, that sort of thing." Hearing him say that made her feel a little better. "No, it's not usually that blatant, but the essence of it is the same: what they love the most, what they live for, is the feeling of being above someone else. And the only thing that makes them feel high is making someone else feel low."

"But the people who want that, there is no one lower than them. And I think somewhere inside, they know it. Every prison guard on a power trip, every cop who likes pushing people around, every husband who beats his wife—they do it because deep down inside, they know they're worthless piles of shit. But instead of trying to make themselves better, they focus all their energies on trying to make sure that someone else is beneath them, under their control, subservient and inferior to them. And any job that pretends to give someone authority, even just a little or even just in certain ways, is the perfect excuse for these people to let their inner sadistic scumbags come out and play."

"Something I learned very quickly after being captured in Bosnia, which I should have noticed even in state prison, is that the fastest, surest way to make someone into a tyrant is to bow before him, grovel in front of him, and beg for his kindness. Ironically, the POWs where I was did a lot better if we were a bit confrontational, even verbally abusive to the guards. Yeah, they'd put us in the can, or starve us for a while, or do a little torture, but as long as we didn't treat them like our superiors, they couldn't break us. More often than not, they'd be scared of us. Someone who acts like a slave will be treated like a slave. Someone who acts like a bulldog, well, the best a tyrant can do is kill him. Ayn Rand called it 'the sanction of the victim.' If you give the impression to your oppressor that you accept, or even *approve* of, his oppression of you, things will only get worse. Whatever else happens, never tell someone that you accept that he has the right to rule you. Never. You will make him into a monster, and you will make yourself into a slave."

After a long silence, Halen suddenly turned and looked right into Jessica's eyes, startling her. He continued in a low but firm voice. "If you go out there and beg mercy from them, what you will find, with very few exceptions, is that the entire system—the politicians, the judges, the government lawyers, the cops, down to the lowest bureaucrat—is nothing but a giant club for those people, the people whose only desire is to have others beneath them." Had he stopped speaking right then, Jessica already would have given up any thought of surrender, but she didn't want to say anything yet. She was fascinated by his words, wondering what horrific experiences lay behind them. So she continued to listen quietly.

"Those are not good people," he continued. "If you plead for mercy from a good person, he'll want to help you. He'll feel empathy, relate to your humanity, and want to minimize your suffering. Not people in government. Most of them are fundamentally different beings. If you plead to them for mercy, that is what they live for. What they want is to have others groveling beneath them. Rather than wanting to help, they will prolong your fear and suffering just as long as they can, because it is your helplessness, and the power they can hold over you, that gives them their jollies."

Jessica found the thought disturbing, and had a hard time believing that everyone inside the system was like that. "I know some people like that myself," she said, "and I'm sure there are lots of them in the government. But isn't there anyone in the system who can be trusted, any way to get to someone who might do the right thing?"

"You mean the good guy in the system, who at the end of the movie arrests all the corrupt guys? That guy?" Halen asked, one eyebrow raised.

"Yeah, that guy," Jessica replied with a sigh, hanging her head in hopelessness. "No such thing?"

"Not anymore," he answered. "Not for a very long time now. One of their best tricks is to have all those courts, all those agencies, all those checks and balances, to give the impression that people can go to them for justice. But in the end, it's no more helpful than if the Mafia had an I.A. unit."

"I.A.?"

"Internal Affairs," Halen responded. "The cops who are supposed to investigate cops. Once in a blue moon they'll put on a show of hanging some jackboot out to dry, when they can't find a way to cover up what he's done."

"Like when they get caught on video, like the clips of police brutality all over YouTube?"

"Yep, like that. It's a lot harder to get away with lying about something when it's on tape. But when it comes right down to it, every government is in the business of controlling and extorting the peasants. If you work for the system and get in the way of that agenda, you won't be there for long."

"But what's the alternative?" Suddenly Jessica shivered, missing the warmth of the wood stove upstairs. Halen looked suddenly concerned. He went to a shelf and took down a thick, dark gray blanket, motioned her onto the couch, and wrapped it around her. She laughed a little. "Everyone here treats me like a princess."

"Your injuries were pretty serious," Halen said gruffly, sitting down on the other end of the couch. "We need you to get your full strength back. Now, what were you just saying?"

Jessica was suddenly so happy in the warmth of the blanket, with Halen close beside her, that she lost her train of thought. She resisted the urge to snuggle up against him. "Oh, yeah, I was saying, maybe they're all corrupt, maybe they're all on a power trip, but what are we supposed to do about it? You can't just shoot any cop who does something you don't like."

"Well, shooting a few might make them think twice before being so obnoxious," he said. "But no, I'm not suggesting that everyone just gun down cops and bureaucrats on a whim. But what people don't understand is that government only gives us two choices: unquestioning obedience or mortal combat. They're the ones who will escalate everything to violence to get their way. Every law is a threat of force. Whatever the law is, if they catch you disobeying, they'll take your stuff or throw you in jail, or both. They don't negotiate, and they can't be reasoned with. They worship legislation, as if their laws are divine commands from the gods, no matter how stupid those laws may be. 'Hey, I don't make the law, I just enforce it.' Sound familiar? You either do as you're told or they hurt you. And if you resist at all, then things get really nasty, really fast, like you see here."

"But don't some courts still limit what the cops can do?" Jessica asked. "I mean, I heard about what started this, the search warrant. I'm no lawyer, but it sounds pretty lame to me. They talked some grouchy, confused old lady into saying she thought she heard a machine gun, and they all come storming in? That's not right. Don't you think there's a chance a court would agree? I mean, instead of having a shootout over it?"

"I doubt any court would do the right thing in this case," Halen said. "They have too much at stake. But even if they did, so what? Are we supposed to just let them do an illegal search, in the hopes that later some court will say it was wrong?"

"Well, the outcome might have been better. I'm not saying it's okay for them to do it, but it seems like resisting just makes everything worse."

"In the short term, it does," he explained, "but in the long term, things will get a thousand times worse if no one resists. If they have no right to do something to begin with, then we have the right to stop them from doing it. If some night you're out walking and someone attacks you, and you have a gun, do you let him rob you, let him beat you up, let him rape you, and then go to court the next day and sue him? Or do you stop him from doing it in the first place, if you have the means to do so?"

"You're right," she replied. "It's just that scaring off a mugger is a lot different than having a shootout with the cops."

"Resisting rotten cops is a lot more dangerous," he said, "but in principle, it's exactly the same. The Fourth Amendment doesn't say that we have the right to sue cops if they invade our homes without a good reason. It says we have the right to have them *not do it in the first place*. And that means we have the right to stop them from doing it if we can. Of course the control freaks won't approve, and will paint us as the scum of the earth for daring to decide for ourselves what our rights are, and what government is allowed to do to us. And these days most Americans will agree with them. We're taught that it's a virtue to bow to authority, and even taught that if authority does us wrong, our only civilized recourse is to beg some *other* authority to protect us from the first one. But if you're not allowed to defend your rights, by force if necessary, then they aren't rights at all. If it's up to government to decide what rights we have, then we have no rights at all. You might as well ask a carjacker whether you have the right to keep your own car."

"But don't the courts sometimes limit what the cops can get away with, at least to some extent?" Jessica asked. "I mean, I'm not saying they do a good job of it all the time, but isn't there sometimes some justice there? I've heard on the news things about how the Supreme Court rules on what cops are allowed to do and what they're not allowed to do. Years ago a friend of my brother's got busted for having pot, and the court said that the cops broke the law somehow, and so they couldn't prosecute him for it. I forget the details, but don't the courts still rule against the cops sometimes?"

"Sometimes," Halen said. "But even when a court slaps their hands, what difference does it make? The cops don't get prosecuted. They always get away with it, or even get promoted. Even when some judge says, 'You shouldn't have done that,' who cares? They already did it, and they'll do it again. If every once in a while they lose a drug case or something, they don't care. Because the power they get from breaking the rules far outweighs any adverse consequences they will ever face."

"Can't they get fined or something, or maybe fired?" Jessica asked, still trying to cling to the hope that the justice system really might provide justice once in a while.

Halen's expression suddenly turned angry. "Lon Horiuchi shot Vicky Weaver in the head and killed her while she was standing in the front doorway of her own home, holding her baby." He spoke through clenched teeth, nearly spitting the words out, and Jessica shrank away in fear. She had no idea what he was talking about. "The damn feds did their pretend investigation. That murdering bastard Horiuchi didn't get prosecuted. He didn't get fined. He got promoted, and gunned down more innocents at Waco. And the few who survived the killing fields in Waco, including the little old ladies, were arrested and thrown in prison. And even after they were all acquitted of the bogus murder charges against them, that piece-of-shit federal judge—Smith, I think it was—had most of them locked up for years and years, just for living in a place that the feds decided to invade for a publicity stunt."

Jessica had never seen Halen angry, and it made him a whole lot scarier than he already was. Halen seemed to sense her alarm. At least he stopped talking for a minute, took a few deep breaths, and calmed himself down. "Sorry, but there's so much that most people never hear, never know about. For every example of police abuse or political corruption that makes the news, there are a hundred that you never hear about. The number of lives ruined, the number of people harassed, robbed, locked up—if you knew just the cases I've seen first hand, it would make you sick. There are a whole lot of people who have learned the hard way just how little our justice system cares about justice. The system cares about one thing, and one thing only: its own power. It would be nice if all that stuff we learned in school about checks and balances, separation of powers, due process, rule of law—it would be nice if all that stuff was real, but it's not. The only language tyrants understand is violence. It's the only way they know how to communicate, and unfortunately, it's the only response they pay any attention to."

"I wish I could say that you're wrong about that," Jessica said, "but I know a few stories myself, just from people I know, that pretty much prove what you're saying. I'm sure they're nothing like the ones you know about, but they're bad enough."

Despite the raw, intimidating power, both physical and emotional, that this man exuded, Jessica suddenly felt safe enough to say what she truly felt. "I don't *want* you to be right. I want you to be some nasty criminal that I can dismiss as a dangerous wacko. I want to be able to say that what you do is unjustifiable, and that you should be locked up. Because if what you say is true—and I wish I could prove you wrong, but I can't—then I don't know what to think. If things are really that bad, if the system is completely corrupt and broken and it's really time for another American Revolution or something, well, that idea just scares the hell out of me." She took a deep breath. "I guess what I'm saying is, I wish you didn't make this much sense, because I'm starting to agree with you, and it's freaking me out." She made a feeble attempt to smile.

Halen's face slowly morphed into a real smile, and he said, "I like you. You're a good kid." Somehow hearing him say that made her feel a little better, though she wasn't thrilled about the "kid" part. "And I think you're now officially a terrorist," he added.

"Bummer," she replied. Both of them were quiet for a while, as Jessica tried to process a new image of Halen in her mind. As blunt as he usually was, she hadn't expected him to be nearly so articulate or sophisticated. This was not just some unthinking angry thug, killing anyone he didn't like. In a way, it would have been easier for her if he had been.

"I think there was food upstairs before I asked you down here," said Halen, getting up suddenly. "Let's get you some food and warmth."

Back upstairs, Doug and David made a place for Jessica closest to the wood stove, and Tasha brought her a plate of steak. Halen settled in a chair by the window, watching. "Keith's coming," he said.

Keith's expression was grim and sad, and his clothes were covered with fresh dirt. He squatted next to Halen and they spoke quietly.

―――❦❦❦―――

**JASON** sat looking out the upstairs window toward the rolling hills out front, feeling a bit uneasy about taking a turn keeping watch. What was the point of watching? So he could warn the people here when his fellow agents were coming in? If he saw them coming, he wasn't even sure whether he'd say anything or not. If the agents could take everyone by surprise, they might be able to bring them all in without any bloodshed. That's what he would have wanted when this all started. To bring them in with no one hurt, and let them have their day in court. But he knew now that that wouldn't be good enough, not for the people in here, who weren't about to accept any government court's decision about their fate, or for the people out there, who, because of the agents they had lost already, now most likely intended to slaughter everyone in here.

David sat next to Jason in another chair, staring out the same window. Jason wondered whether he had come along to keep him company, or to keep an eye on him.

He found it really strange that these people would so easily trust him, even enough to hand him a loaded gun. He didn't feel like a prisoner; he was now here by choice. But the complete contempt for the law shown by these people made him uneasy. They seemed to believe in no rules at all, as if every person could just make up his own rules. What if someone decided to go on a killing spree, or rob all his neighbors? A world without rules brought to mind a *Mad Max* type of existence. And yet these people, in many ways, seemed perfectly kind and reasonable otherwise. No, these people weren't the problem, but if their philosophy were adopted by people with bad intentions, people with no regard for human life, then what?

"Can I ask you something?" David's voice brought Jason out of his thoughts. "Every chance I get, I ask cops this question. Of course, you don't have to answer, and even if you do, I'd never tell anyone what you said without your permission." David looked directly at Jason. "Do you believe that?"

"Yeah, I guess. What's the question?"

"What's the worst thing you've ever seen a fellow police officer do?" David asked.

Jason didn't have to ponder that one for long. The question alone instantly brought back the images of a night about two years before. But he wondered whether he should tell David about it. It wasn't exactly a shining example of "law and order" at work.

"You can leave out names and details, if that makes it any easier," David suggested.

"It was a couple years ago," Jason began, and paused. Other than a few fellow cops, he had never spoken of this to anyone. He had tried not to think about it either, because the memory made him feel so dirty and ashamed. He felt as if he was making a confession. It occurred to him that he had not been to confession in three years, and there was a good chance he wouldn't be alive much longer. Suddenly he felt compelled to make this confession, at least to another human being. "I wasn't a fed yet, and I had only been a cop for six months. It was night, and my partner and I were cruising around." As he told the story, the images came back to him as vividly as if it had happened yesterday. He was glad that both he and David were supposed to be staring out the window, so he didn't have to look at him as he spoke.

"There was a little house over on the edge of town, the poorest part of it. I'm driving through there with my partner and we see a cruiser sitting in front of a house. We thought we'd just see what was going on and if the officer needed assistance. The front door's open, so we come into the house. It's mostly dark, but we hear noises and find the other cop in a corner room, and there's this kid on the floor, maybe fourteen or fifteen years old, bleeding from his face. The other cop tells us we can go, that he has it under control. We're about to leave when the kid says, 'Don't leave me,' or something like that. I turn around and see the cop hit the kid right in the face, backhanded, with his gun in his hand. The kid is just lying there on his back, hardly moving at all, but he's still conscious. The cop says something like, 'You still haven't told me what I want to hear.' I was just standing there, not knowing what to do. My partner was trying to pull me away. I asked what the kid had done. The cop just says, 'Get lost, rookie,' or something like that. The kid tries to say something again, and the cop hits him again. Both eyes are swelling up, he's bleeding from his nose and his forehead and around his eyes. He's not fighting back at all, not even trying to block the guy's punches. He's just a scrawny little kid, and he knew it would be pointless to resist. I just stood there, and every ten or fifteen seconds the cop hits him, right in the face, closed fist and all. The cop wasn't even mad. That's what really bugged me. I mean, I could understand if he just had a fight with a guy, or a chase or something. But he's just calmly squatting there over this young black kid, every once in a while hitting him like that. I didn't know what else to do, so I asked if we should just take the kid in. And a few times I asked what the kid had done, but he wouldn't say."

Jason paused for a long time, the images of that night clear as day in his mind. "And I was just a cop in a little town. This wasn't some big city or something. Even after being there just a few months, I knew maybe half of the people who lived there. I didn't know this kid, but I knew other people on the street. After a while, my partner convinced me to go out of the room, but we stayed at the front door until the other cop came out. I didn't know what he would do if we just left, so I at least stayed there for a while. Then the other cop comes out and we all leave."

"Did you ever find out what it was all about?" David asked.

"Yeah. The thing bugged me for a long time, and finally I brought it up again to my partner. And he just says, 'Didn't you know? The kid filed a complaint against that cop.' I thought he meant he filed a complaint after getting beat up, but my partner said no, he'd filed a complaint with the department earlier because the cop had been going after his older sister, basically stalking her. That's why he beat the kid up, for reporting that to the department."

"Did anything ever come of it?"

"A while later the chief interviewed my partner and me, and we told him what happened, though we tried to make it not sound quite as bad as it was. The chief talked to the cop, I guess, but nothing happened to him. And the cop must have known what we told the chief, but he didn't seem to care. He wasn't mad at us or anything. He just treated it like it was no big deal."

Jason paused for a moment and let out a long sigh. "But the image of that kid," he said, shaking his head, "so completely helpless, and so completely hopeless, not even trying to fight back, like he knew that he had to just let it happen, even if it meant dying. There was nothing he could do, and you could see it in his face. I mean, I've seen plenty of fights and injuries worse than that, but there was something about that kid, and that situation. You just don't treat other human beings like that. You shouldn't even treat an animal like that, just hurting it for fun. That's messed up. And that look of helplessness, like he was waiting for me to save him."

"Maybe in a way, you did," David said gently. "If you hadn't stayed, it might have been worse."

"It's funny you say that," Jason said, "because a year or so later, I met the kid again. I didn't even recognize him at first, but he comes up to me, a big smile on his face, and thanks me. I asked, For what? He says, for saving him, for not leaving him there alone with that cop. Man, that made it hurt even more. I didn't even lift a finger to stop the guy. All I did was stand around like a damn coward, and here this kid was thanking me for it, as if I was some great hero. I didn't even know what to say. I don't remember what I said to him, but it was probably something stupid, and then I just walked away."

"After the department let it slide, did you do anything else about it?" David asked.

"Nope. Never brought it up again, until now."

"If you came on a scene like that, but the guy doing the hitting wasn't a cop, would you have stopped him?"

"Of course. I'd have his sorry ass in handcuffs in half a second for assault and battery," Jason answered without hesitation. David said nothing, and he didn't have to. Jason silently asked himself the obvious question: Why would he let a cop do that, but no one else? Shouldn't cops be better than that? Aren't they supposed to be the good guys, protecting everyone else from things like that? "It's a cop thing, you know," Jason said at last. "It's just, we're together day in and day out, feeling like it's us against the world. It's like being on a football team or something. You gotta look out for the guys on your team, no matter what." He gazed out the window at the rolling hills. "So that's what we do, even when we shouldn't."

"Thank you for honestly answering my question," David said. Then, after a long silence, he asked, "Any chance of a career change for you if you ever make it out of here? There's a lot you could do for justice without a badge, you know."

"I don't know," Jason answered. "Being a cop is what I know, but I also know a few guys who quit because of what it was doing to them. One guy used to tell me all the time, the more you fight the criminals, the more you become like them. I don't quite buy that completely, but he has a point. How far do we stretch the rules to go after the rule-breakers?"

"Ever consider being a private security guard?" David asked.

"Nah. I'd feel like a complete loser," Jason said. "It's a running joke among cops that security guards are just the losers who couldn't hack it being real cops, or couldn't make it through the police academy." He looked up at David. "Besides, wouldn't that still make me a fascist pig?"

"If all you do is protect people, their rights and their property, and if you do it because they agreed to hire you for that, there's nothing wrong with that," David said.

"How is that different from being a cop?" Jason asked.

"Because," David explained, "being a cop is about acting as the enforcement arm of something else, something called government, that pretends to have the right to do things that normal people have no right to do: tax, regulate, and otherwise mess with people who haven't hurt anyone. Everyone has the right to protect himself and his property against thieves and attackers. If someone chooses to hire someone else to do it for him—to do what he himself has a right to do—that's perfectly fine. No one imagines the private security guard to have more rights than his employer, or more rights than anyone else, or even more rights than he had before he got the job. Like everyone else, he has the right to use force to protect people from violence and fraud; he does *not* have the right to *commit* violence or fraud. In the case of a private security guard, everyone can see that. In the case of government agents, people imagine them to have some rights and powers the rest of us don't have, as if they are something higher than normal human beings."

"These days, I don't think many people think cops are better than everyone else," Jason commented.

"I don't mean that they think you're actually better people. I mean they believe, however good or bad a person you are, that by being employed by people calling themselves government, you somehow acquire the right to do things that you didn't have the right to do before, and that most other people still don't have the right to do.

For example, if I made someone pull over and demanded a hundred bucks from him because his tail light was broken, he'd probably slug me, and rightfully so. But when someone with a badge and a uniform does it, people perceive it to be legitimate, even necessary. If I told my neighbor he had to give me a thousand dollars a year for the privilege of living in his own house, he'd call the cops on me. But when people claiming to be authority do it, and call it 'property taxes,' it's accepted by almost everyone as perfectly legitimate, and the one who resists it is seen as the crook. Most of the laws cops enforce aren't about protecting individuals, they're about robbing and controlling individuals who haven't attacked or robbed anyone. And cops are not paid by willing customers. They are paid by taxpayers, who have no choice in the matter. Yes, sometimes cops actually stop people from committing real crimes—the kind that have victims. But most of the time, you get paid with stolen money to oppress the very people you helped to rob."

"Well," Jason chuckled, "at least you're honest about what you think. I just feel like you're missing something, but I can't quite put my finger on it. Like, what if some private person or some gang wanted to hire me to go rob people for them, and we both agreed to it voluntarily? You wouldn't think that was okay, would you?"

"No, because I don't think that anyone has the right to rob people. Not you, not the Mafia, not the government. And if they have no right to do it, they have no right to hire you to do it for them. The point is, *you* make an exception for government. What you do in the name of government, I don't believe you would do for any civilian, no matter how much money he offered you, and I believe that's true of most cops. If you didn't also believe that being a cop gives you extra rights, you wouldn't do it. For example, if some millionaire said to you, 'I don't like my neighbors having guns, and I'll pay you $100,000 to go disarm them,' would you?"

**186**

"No. That would be illegal, not to mention unjustified."

"How about if they said, 'I want to hire you to go take money from my neighbors to pay for my kid's schooling'? Would you?"

"No," Jason replied. "Again, that would be illegal and immoral."

"But all 'legal' means is that the government told you to do it. The way people view law these days, whether something is 'legal' or not depends only on who gave the order. If the people who call themselves 'government' do it, it's legal. If anyone else does, it's not. But whether the order itself is good or evil, and whether anyone should obey it, has nothing to do with who gave the order. If you pay someone to commit murder or armed robbery, that's a bad thing, even if you call it 'law' when you do it. Wouldn't you agree?"

Halen's voice from downstairs interrupted them. David stood up and said, "Well, our watch is over. I've got something I have to do, but I hope we can continue this discussion later." He paused for a moment and smiled. "Wouldn't it be fun if we could include the guys out there in this conversation?" he asked, pointing toward the hills.

"Yeah, that would be interesting," Jason admitted.

**BETSY** was approaching the senatorial office building, on her way back from another lunch at Sandy's, when she noticed a crowd of a few dozen people milling around out front, though it was below freezing outside. As she got nearer, she recognized a few other people who worked in the building.

"Margaret," she called to someone she recognized, "what's going on? Fire drill?"

"No one seems to know for sure, but it's some security thing they're doing," the woman responded, huddled tight inside her hooded coat. "It's been going on for half an hour already. They take two or three people at a time, and that's only every ten minutes or so. At this rate, we'll be out here forever."

"Was there a bomb threat or something?" Betsy inquired. "Is anyone hurt?" As she glanced around, she saw many disgruntled faces, but no one looked frightened.

"I'm not sure," answered the woman. "Some people are saying it's just some emergency exercise or something. I'm sure glad I wore my heavy coat today. They didn't tell us a thing about this."

For the next twenty minutes, Betsy stood around with the others, wondering what was going on. She asked a few other people if they knew anything about the situation, but they didn't.

"Martha Sharpe?" It was so rare that anyone called Betsy by her true name that it took her a moment to even notice. "Martha Sharpe?" A tall, dark-skinned man in a police uniform was calling her name and looking around at the crowd.

"Over here, officer," Betsy said, raising her hand. "I'm Martha Sharpe," she said, and wondered what he wanted. No one else was being called by name.

"Come with me, Ms. Sharpe," the man said, now close enough that he didn't have to shout. With some difficulty, Betsy followed him through the crowd, as he led her into the lobby, which was also full of people, and past the security checkpoint into the wide hall beyond. "Senator Collins asked that we get you through this as quickly as possible," the man said, his voice much lower now, the roar and bustle of the crowd behind them.

"Get me through what?" Betsy asked. "I don't even know what's going on."

The man stopped at an unmarked door, and opened it. "You'll need to leave your bag out here," he said, indicating a chair sitting in the hall next to the door, "and any cell phones or other electronic devices." Betsy complied, and the man gestured for her to go inside. Instead of following her in, he stayed outside and closed the door, and she heard the door lock. It was a small room, with two folding metal chairs and an old metal desk. Betsy was the only one in the room, but there was another door on the far wall. She sat down and waited for someone else to come in, still wondering what this was all about.

She sat there quietly for at least ten minutes, feeling a little nervous, though she couldn't say why. Finally she stood up and checked the door she had come in. It was locked. She walked to the other door, and knocked on it lightly. "Hello? Anyone there?" Maybe they had just forgotten her, or didn't know that she was still in there. She cautiously tried the door knob, and it too was locked.

She wasn't scared, but she was beginning to be quite annoyed. She knew that people who worked in a building like this had to expect a fair amount of inconvenience due to security measures, but she didn't like being locked in a room alone with no means of communication. What if there had been a fire, or some other real emergency? What if she had to use the bathroom? She was pretty sure this violated some building code or personnel code, and it just felt insulting.

The door in front of her swung open, making her jump a little, and two men in Department of Homeland Security uniforms walked in. "Sit down, ma'am," one of them said, and Betsy thought his tone none too polite. She took a seat in the chair again, and looked at the two men. The one who sat down at the desk, the one who had spoken to her, looked about forty, with short black hair, almost in a crew cut, and glasses. He was carrying a folder, which he opened up and laid on the desk, and started looking through. The other man was a bald, stocky black man, probably about thirty, who stood with his back to the wall and his arms crossed, a grouchy expression seemingly permanently imprinted on his face. Neither of the men seemed happy to be there.

"Name and Social Security number," the man at the desk said. It took Betsy a moment to realize that it was meant as a question.

"Martha Sharpe, but I usually go by 'Betsy.' My Social Security number is 218-77-5523." The man wrote something down, and didn't say anything else for a few minutes as he read something. Betsy was beginning to feel as if her time was being wasted.

"When's the last time you traveled outside the country?" the man asked, not looking up.

Betsy had to think for a moment. "I went to Canada, it must have been about ten years ago. And a few years before that, I went to Mexico with my family, but only for—"

"You've never been to Egypt?" the man asked, interrupting.

"No," answered Betsy, wondering what the reason for the question was. The man jotted down some notes.

"In case you're not aware of this," the man said casually, "it's a crime to lie to a federal agent."

"I am aware of that, and I didn't lie," Betsy said, a little irritated and a little suspicious. Did they have her confused with someone else? Why would they think she had ever been to Egypt?

"I didn't say you did," the man said. "I was just putting you on notice." He looked through his papers some more. "Do you own a gun?"

"No," she answered truthfully. The man scribbled something down. "Can I ask what this is about?" she asked, after a long pause.

"Just answer the questions," the man said curtly. Betsy was getting more and more annoyed with this rude treatment. "Have you ever advocated that someone break the law?"

"I don't think so," she answered, trying to think back to something she might have said, or even written, back in her college days. "Not that I remember."

"Think carefully, ma'am, because it's a very broad question," the man said, looking up at her for the first time. "It might have been something minor. For example, did you ever joke to someone that they should cheat on their taxes a little? Or did you ever help someone get some pot? Or did you ever say you wished someone would kill some politician or cop, even if you were just kidding?"

"I don't know," Betsy said, her voice giving away her growing exasperation. "How am I supposed to remember everything I've ever said or joked about?"

"So, you may have advocated that someone break the law at some point in the past?" the man asked, his pen poised to write down her response.

"Probably. I don't know." The more her mind raced, trying to guess what this might be about, the more on edge she became. "I might have told someone to hurry up when they were already driving the speed limit. I might have told someone to creep through a red light at an empty intersection at three in the morning. Heck,

I might even have told someone to cut the label off a mattress, that label that says 'not to be removed under penalty of law'."

"This is not a joke, ma'am," the man said, his face still dead serious. "Your answers are being recorded."

"Well, then, my official answer is, How the hell should I know?" She suddenly thought of Sandy. Boy, would she have a few things to say about this. "Look," she said, trying to calm herself, "I understand why you have to make sure people are who they say they are, and do background checks and things like that, but I already went through all this. Everyone who works here already did. They had to, to get jobs here. You must know that."

"This is not an employee screening test. We're conducting an investigation regarding a matter of national security," the man said with added emphasis. "That's all you need to know."

**JESSICA** sat in the basement with Halen, remembering back to when she had first seen him, in the doorway of Ben's cabin, barking out orders. He had seemed so wild, dangerous, and scary at the time. But now, despite having heard him talk so openly about killing people, both as a soldier in war and on his own, he was her biggest comfort. For his part, he tolerated her presence and seemed to enjoy showing her things and conversing with her. But she searched in vain for any glimmer of affection in his eyes, or any trace of the warm approval she was used to seeing in the eyes of boys and men.

He sat cross-legged on the floor, with a few small boxes and other things in front of him, doing something with bullets. It seemed to Jessica that he was unloading and then reloading what she assumed were gun cartridges. He looked up and, as if sensing her curiosity, tossed something shiny to her, which she barely caught. "Just trading out ball ammo for hollow point," he said. She wasn't sure what that meant, but she looked at the bullet she was holding, and it had a hole in the front of it, with what looked like a star design inside. "Ball ammo makes a little hole; hollow point makes a big hole," Halen explained casually. Jessica wasn't eager to learn more on the subject. "While we're down here," Halen said, as if remembering something, "Doug's folks used to have a satellite phone, which he thinks might still be around somewhere, if you want to do a little rummaging."

She stood up and looked around. "What does it look like?"

"A big handset, made of yellow plastic," he answered. "He says it'll be hard to miss if it's still here."

Jessica walked over to a dresser and started going through drawers one by one.

"In case you're wondering," Halen suddenly said, continuing to load bullets into magazines, "I didn't learn how to kill because I think it's fun. I hate it. It's like having the job of killing rabid dogs, only a thousand times worse." Jessica was uncomfortable just thinking about such things. "Real life isn't like the movies," Halen continued. "In the movies, the bad guy is always so obviously evil that when he dies, in some spectacular finale, everyone stands up and cheers. That's not how it works in real life. In real life, the people who have to be fought or even killed to protect the innocent are hardly ever truly evil themselves. Instead, their sin is usually just being stupid, and doing what they're told. Guys like Jason. He's a nice guy, right? His heart's in the right place. But it's only by a twist of fate that he's here with us, and not on the other side of those hills waiting for an order to attack us. There's no glory in killing someone like him. But sometimes it's him or you. Sometimes it's him or some other innocent person. Authority changes many good people into agents of evil, and sometimes they have to be destroyed. Whether this country is headed for absolute tyranny or freedom, the road there won't be pretty."

Jessica glanced up from the drawer she was going through, and saw an expression on Halen's face that looked both powerful and profoundly sad at the same time. "Imagine this," he continued. "You're standing in a nice living room, and a handsome young man walks in—blond hair, blue eyes—and kisses his pretty wife and cute kid goodbye as he heads off to work." He paused for a moment. "It's 1942 Germany, and the young man works for the Nazis. He's going off to work, ready to herd the masses of soon-to-be-dead Jews into the cattle cars on the trains. He probably won't actually kill anyone himself. He's just one cog on one wheel of the machine." He looked down at the floor, and stopped loading magazines for a moment, as if remembering something. "And there you are, with a gun in your hand," he said. Then he looked up, straight into Jessica's eyes. "Would you kill him? Could you?"

"Just shoot him, right there?" she asked. "No, I couldn't." She didn't hesitate, because it was the honest answer. But was it an answer she should be proud of, or ashamed of? She wasn't sure. She closed the last dresser drawer and went to the closet.

"What if you could be there, a couple hours later, when he's helping to herd a few hundred more innocents off to their deaths, would you wish you had? If you could watch the people dying in the gas chambers, or being lined up beside the ditch and shot. The people who did that—if you could have gone back to the day before and killed them, killed them all, would you?"

The thought terrified Jessica. "I don't know," she said, looking for a light switch in the closet. "Maybe I should, but I really don't think I could."

"That's because you're a decent person," Halen said, which surprised her. "But this is where the belief in 'authority' leads. Good people don't want to use violence. They want to get along, and treat others with respect. But not the state. The state uses violence for everything it does. Every law is a command, and if people disobey, force is used to make them comply. And good people don't want to resist, especially not with violence. Even if they don't like the law, even if they think it's unjust, the last thing they want to do is kill some poor pawn who is just doing what he was told."

Halen tossed a full magazine aside and picked up the next one. "It would be so much easier if only bad people did bad things, but through the belief in 'authority,' otherwise good people routinely become agents of evil. Even the atrocities of Hitler's regime, Stalin's regime, and all the others, were the result of a few truly evil people, and thousands upon thousands of merely obedient people. The real villains aren't stupid enough to go to the front lines themselves. That's what compliant subjects are for. But the result is that the good people of the world are left with a horrible choice to make: either let the bad stuff happen, or kill people who are merely misguided or ignorant. Most people choose the first option, and mankind has suffered unspeakable horrors because of it."

"You don't make the future sound very bright," Jessica remarked, rummaging through the boxes on the closet floor.

"Because of the belief in authority, it won't be. Whether in the end tyranny wins or freedom wins, either way, a lot of good people will suffer and a lot will die in the process. Basically good people will be killing basically good people. That's what every war is. The average soldier who fought for Hitler was no different from the average American soldier. He loved his country. He valued law and order, and took pride in following his orders, doing what he was told to do, and doing it well. But his nationalism and pack mentality—and most of all, his unshakable faith in authority—rendered him blind to the evil he was committing. It's the same with every army, and every cop. Above all else, they take pride in their ability to obey without question, as if it's a *virtue* instead of the most heinous sin a person can commit." He tossed another magazine aside.

"Most people who commit evil are not guilty of hatred or malice," he continued, "they're just morally negligent. They don't take the time to question what they are told. They hurt other people—rob them, harass them, imprison them, even kill them—just because they were told to. And not only don't the obedient take responsibility for their own actions, they don't even see what they do as *being* their own actions. They pretend they are just tools of something called 'law,' and they judge themselves based only on how well they obey orders, never questioning whether they should obey those orders at all."

The image of the fat kid at the airport, trying to look authoritative in his TSA outfit, popped into Jessica's head. It hadn't been his idea to inconvenience her, but he did anyway, because that's what the rules told him to do.

"Tell me this," Halen continued. "If you hadn't hurt anyone, but someone believed it was his duty to capture you and put you in a cage for the rest of your life, and kill you if you resisted, what would you do?"

"Defend myself, or try to get away, I guess," she said. The question didn't really seem hypothetical: she had done nothing wrong, yet her life was now in danger.

"And what if you were trapped? What if your only choices were to kill the guy or to let him lock you up forever? Could you kill him?"

"I don't know. I hope I never have to make a decision like that." She paused for a moment, finding the discussion more uncomfortable than ever. "I agree with what you're saying—the innocent should be protected, even if it takes violence to do it. I just don't really know if I could do it myself."

"Well, the way things are going now, you may soon have to decide between killing one of those order-obeying drones out there, or letting him kill you." Having found nothing of interest in the closet, Jessica walked out into the room again. Halen paused for a moment, looking right into her eyes. "Let me put it this way. Would you rather let your mother and father lose their daughter, or would you rather kill another human being in order to save their kid?"

Jessica suddenly remembered her father's voice on the radio, and had to fight back tears. Her family's grief was like a knife in her heart. "Well, I don't know how to shoot, even if I wanted to," she said, knowing it was a cop-out. "And I'm not sure if I could do it anyway."

"Well, I can help with the first part," Halen said, perfectly seriously. "But making the choice is something only you can do."

"God, I can't believe I'm talking about killing cops—killing anyone," she said, throwing her hands in the air. "I just want my nice easy life back." She forced herself not to cry. Of all the people she could think of, Halen was the last person she wanted to break down into tears in front of. "How did I get into all this? This all seems unreal."

"You're learning first hand that people don't just decide to make themselves into revolutionaries," he replied. "They are made into revolutionaries by others. They're usually just people who wanted to mind their own business and be left alone, but came to the point where they realized that things were bad enough that someone had to do something, and that 'someone' was them. And because most good people dislike conflict and violence, they usually wait until it's too late before they decide to do anything."

Halen stood up, and in one smooth movement picked up a rifle off the couch next to him, hit a button to drop the magazine out and caught it with his other hand, and then pulled back the action to make sure the chamber was empty. Then with both hands he held the rifle out toward Jessica, the barrel pointing to her left. "Time for a crash course," he said. She stood still for a moment, before reluctantly walking toward him. When she started timidly reaching for the rifle, he pulled it back a bit. "First of all, don't ever point it at anything or anyone you don't intend to kill." He paused for a moment, as if to let that message sink in. "Safety's on the left. Try looking through the scope. Aim it out the window." She cautiously accepted the rifle, scared that it might go off at any moment. She held it up the way she had seen people do it in the movies. It felt awkward and heavy.

"I can't see anything," she said, the scope showing nothing but blackness. "Oh, wait," she added, adjusting the gun a bit. "Okay, I was too far back."

"Keep the butt of it snug against your shoulder," Halen said, standing behind her and bringing the rifle up a bit. "Keep your finger off the trigger until you're ready to fire." Jessica jerked her finger away from the trigger. "It's not loaded," he said patiently, "but always treat a gun as if it is."

"Would this thing flatten me if I fired it?" she asked.

"It's only .223," he responded, but she had no idea what that meant. "It gives a little kick, but it won't knock you over. Just hold it snug, but not too tight against your shoulder." Halen adjusted the rifle a bit, and repositioned Jessica's left hand farther forward. "The most important thing for accuracy is not to jerk the trigger. When you're ready to fire, give the trigger a steady squeeze, not a sudden yank." Jessica was already feeling the fatigue of holding the rifle up, and lowered it. "It's a shame you don't have time for some real practice," Halen added, "but somehow I don't think it would be a good idea to go outside and start shooting at cans right now."

"Is this, like, a machine gun?" she asked, feeling self-conscious about her ignorance. She had never held any sort of gun before, and knew nothing about them, but thought this one looked like a pretty serious weapon. She felt only slightly less scared holding it than she would have if someone else had been pointing it at her.

"No. Only one bullet comes out when you pull the trigger. But it is semi-automatic, so as soon as you fire, it's ready to fire again, but you have to let go and pull the trigger again."

"If my dad could see me now," Jessica muttered, as if to herself, as she scanned the fields outside through the scope.

"Well, whether he ever sees you again might depend on whether you know how to use this thing," Halen commented, which didn't really comfort Jessica.

Suddenly feeling silly, she carefully put the rifle down on the back of the couch. "I don't know," she protested. "I don't think I could do it. I don't think I could fire at a person."

"I hope you never have to find out," he said, picking up the gun himself, "but I'm afraid that, considering where you are right now, it's something you'd better think about."

How about if I just stay near you? she thought, but didn't say it out loud. Despite her growing attachment to him, Jessica still wasn't sure what to think of Halen. When he spoke to her, he seemed perfectly reasonable and kind. But the things he had done, even the fact that he knew how to do them, still disturbed her. Could someone be that good at mortal combat and still be a good person? It seemed to her like an unsolvable paradox: sometimes good people have to use violence to stop bad people, but how can someone become so proficient at killing and still be a good person?

She remembered having a similar thought before, when an issue came up in a civics class at school. Assuming there were some people in the world who were so bad and dangerous that they should be put to death—and Jessica believed there were— was it even possible for a good person to have the job of executioner? Would a good person ever agree to do such a job? And if not, should the job be given to some sadistic monster who might enjoy it? Which would be worse, to have a good person suffer the anguish of taking human lives, or to have an evil person take joy in it? She didn't really want to think about it, but one thing she knew was that, just then, she was glad to have someone like Halen around.

---

**JASON** stood in the open doorway, looking out past the patio to the hills beyond. Somewhere over there, just out of sight, was the trailer he had sat in front of for so many hours, watching those same hills from the other side. And here he was, still watching and waiting, feeling the same nervous uncertainty. Whatever malicious presence his mind had previously imagined on this side of the hills, that was no longer what he feared. Nor did he fear any particular person out beyond those hills. He feared only being caught in the middle of a conflict that he no longer wanted any part of.

"Coming through," came a gruff voice behind him. He turned to see Keith carrying a large wooden box, and stepped out of the doorway to let him through. Keith walked over to a patio table and set the box down. He started taking out its contents and arranging them on the table: glass bottles, wires, rags, 9-volt batteries, and some other odds and ends. He sat down and started working at assembling something out of the pieces. Jason watched for a while, reluctant to ask what he was doing. Keith seemed to him the most hostile person there. Even Halen, who was so cold and callous, but not openly malicious, now bothered Jason less than Keith did. Then again, all of them, including Keith, had agreed to set Jason free, and even let him have his rifle back, still loaded.

"What are you making?" Jason finally asked, trying to sound civil.

"Some presents for your buddies," Keith said, not looking up from his work. Jason would have guessed they were Molotov cocktails, but the wires and batteries hinted at something more sophisticated. Saying nothing more, he watched quietly as Keith assembled a total of five devices, each having a bottle full of liquid—something flammable, Jason assumed—with some sort of trigger mechanism attached. Then Keith put them back into the box and walked out beyond the garden, into the field. He knelt down, took out one of the devices, and put it on the ground, carefully covering it with the dry grass.

It was clear to Jason that they were some type of explosives or fire bombs, and that Keith was setting up a mine field, with the five devices equally spaced across the front lawn, about a hundred feet from the house. For some reason, this bothered him a lot more than the guns that Halen and Keith perpetually carried. Obviously these people meant to forcibly resist any assault on the place, but the image of a fellow agent being engulfed in a ball of flame after stepping on one of these things was too much for him to quietly accept.

"Is that really necessary?" he asked Keith as he came back, carrying the empty box.

"That depends on whether your Nazi friends out there decide to come goose-stepping in here," Keith said with obvious disdain. "If so, then yes, it's necessary to cook those bastards alive."

The harshness of the comment snapped Jason out of his assumed role of neutral spectator. Trying to remain calm, he said, "I think your image of those guys is more messed up than their image of you. They have families, you know. Wives and kids."

Keith walked right up to Jason, until his face was just inches away. "Then maybe they should have stayed home with them," he growled, "instead of coming onto my property with their Gestapo bullshit."

"If you had nothing to hide here, maybe you should have just let them do their job," Jason said, his voice beginning to rise, his fear turning to anger. "If you had just let them do the search, and they found nothing, none of this would have happened."

"If we all just cowered before fascists like you," Keith snarled, "and let you do whatever the hell you want, you might be nice to us. Is that it?" He leaned in even closer and, hammering his index finger into Jason's chest for emphasis, added in a harsh whisper, "If not for David and Halen, I would have blown your damn head off long ago, so feel free to shut the hell up."

At that, Jason reached to push Keith's hand away, but Keith blocked the swing with one hand, and with his other hand grabbed Jason by the throat. It felt like a vise around his neck, instantly cutting off breath and blood. In desperation, he swung with his free left hand at Keith's face and caught him hard on the jaw, but Keith barely flinched. His adrenaline rising, Jason swung again, and this time Keith ducked, but let go at the same time. Jason was so focused on being able to breathe again that he didn't notice the left uppercut from Keith, which felt like a baseball bat as it slammed into the side of his jaw. He reeled backward, almost falling over, his balance and sense of direction gone haywire. The world seemed to be spinning, but he could just make out the image of Keith lunging toward him, both hands outstretched. Jason swung his foot up, and mostly by luck, planted his boot firmly in Keith's stomach, which stopped his forward progress, but also sent Jason toppling over backward, crashing into two aluminum patio chairs in the process. He quickly struggled to his feet and turned, expecting another charge from Keith.

Instead, he saw David standing in front of him, with Keith behind him, red-faced and breathing hard, his hands clenched into fists. "Is this really necessary?" David asked in a calm voice. Neither Jason nor Keith said anything. "I don't know what this is about, but I was under the impression that, whatever you think of each other, we had achieved a state of peaceful coexistence here." Still, neither responded. "Any reason we can't go back to that?" At last Keith seemed to calm down a little. Without a word, he picked up the empty box and walked into the house.

"Are you okay?" David asked Jason.

"Yeah," came the reply, "I think so. That guy is a freaking maniac. He needs to be put on a damn leash." David held his hand out toward a chair, and Jason sat down, his heart still pounding and his hands shaking a bit.

"I don't know what that was about," David said again, taking a seat next to Jason, "but just so you know, Keith has plenty of reasons for not liking the police, and I don't just mean philosophical reasons. So try not to take it personally."

"Yeah, and I'm sure the cops around here love him, too," Jason remarked, his breathing starting to slow down to normal.

"If you knew his story, you might be a little more sympathetic to his confrontational demeanor." David gazed out over the hills. When Jason said nothing, he went on. "Keith's father was a cop, as well as a generally rotten person. He bullied Keith and his mother for years, while the other cops looked the other way. Eventually Keith left home, and he's been in trouble with the law ever since. He was never exactly a *good* kid. He's always been a hothead—getting into fights as long as I can remember. It's not too hard to figure out that he sees his dad in every bully he encounters, and takes it on himself to punish them. He's got this rage inside him; it's as if he's on a one-man crusade to wipe out the abuse of power, and he's frustrated that he can't get all of it. Mind you, I'm not telling you anything he's trying to keep secret," David continued. "In fact, he seems to be quite proud of his run-ins with the authorities." Jason said nothing, but listened with interest.

"The first time he went to prison, it was for beating an older kid, almost to death," David said. "The older kid was the leader of a gang, a gang that had been terrorizing a black family—the first one to move into their white neighborhood. When the gang decided to pick on the youngest kid in the family, Keith took on three of them and almost killed the biggest; he put that boy in the hospital for a month." A sad sort of smile appeared on David's face as he gazed at the ground. "Keith said the gang never bothered those people again." Then David leaned back in his chair, folded his hands on his stomach, and turned his eyes to the sky. "On another occasion, he went to prison for destroying a police car with a sledgehammer while the cop was inside a local housing project running his own little extortion ring. The cop ended up getting fired, but Keith went to prison again. After that, you can bet that the local cops weren't exactly friendly with Keith, and he wasn't very friendly with them."

"He's been to prison twice?" Jason asked.

"Three times. He was also convicted of shooting his father."

"He killed his own father?" Jason asked incredulously.

"Didn't kill him," said David. "Didn't even shoot him, in fact. He was just *convicted* of shooting him. When Keith's mom finally got the courage to divorce his dad, the guy just wouldn't leave her alone. She got a restraining order, but he still came around, and the other cops wouldn't do anything about it, of course. It was getting really ugly, and she began to fear for her life. She bought a gun, and when he came after her again, she shot him. He didn't die. He was only hit in the leg. But since he was a cop, the local DA didn't want to let it slide as an act of self-defense. To make a long story short, Keith refused to let his mom go to prison for defending herself, so he said he did it. His mom kept insisting that she'd done it, and his dad refused to testify against either one of them. In the end, the jury still believed that Keith was guilty. Go figure. They believed his lie, and he spent years in prison for it." There was a long pause.

"Wait a second," said Jason, frowning. "With that criminal history, he's not allowed to have guns at all."

"Well, he was seventeen, still a juvenile, when he was convicted of the shooting," David explained. "And he was even younger when he fought that gang. The only one that happened when he wasn't a minor was the incident with the police car. And the cops were so embarrassed by the events surrounding that one that he got it bargained down to misdemeanor disorderly conduct. So after all that, he's got no felonies on his record, and isn't even on parole anymore. So under state and federal law, he's still allowed to have guns. Of course," he added with a smile, "he'd probably have them whether the government said he could or not."

David suddenly stood up, as if he had somewhere to go. "So now you know. I realize that knowing all that may not make dealing with him any easier," he said, "but it may make his behavior a little more understandable. And on a practical level," he added, "I expect that if you decide to avoid him from now on, he'll probably avoid you, too." Having said that, David walked away, leaving Jason sitting alone, thinking about Keith. Maybe under that unattractive blanket of hostility and anger lurked a heart more noble than most. Jason had always felt it was his calling to defend the innocent from the bad guys. It seemed that Keith felt the same calling, but it had taken him down a very different road. Jason wondered what he would have done if his life had been like Keith's.

**BETSY** stood in her office, arms folded and brow furrowed. "I mean, it was just so stupid," she was saying to Grant. "It must have been half an hour of all these stupid questions."

"I didn't realize they were making it such a big deal," Grant said sympathetically, "or I would have seen if I could have gotten you out of it somehow."

"Well, it wasn't really a big deal. But why do they have to have such rude jerks doing the interviews? And why couldn't they give us some warning that they'd be doing it? Worst of all, by the time I got out, the crowd was gone. I think they let everyone after me skip the thing altogether."

"Yeah, I later heard they were just going through the procedures for a certain number of employees. It was just a practice." Then he laughed. "I had them move you to the front of the line, to get you through faster. If I'd just done nothing, you would have gotten here sooner, and without going through all that. Big help I was, huh?"

"Well, thanks for the attempt, anyway," she said.

He glanced at his watch, and stood up. "Oops, late again. I'll be right back," he said, and strode out of the office.

Only a moment later, before Betsy could even sit down at her desk and re-open the file she had been working on, Sandy came barging through the door, without knocking, looking furious. "Unbelievable!" she said, "un-freaking-believable! Wanna hear what just happened to me?" she demanded rhetorically. She sat down hard in the chair facing Betsy's desk. Betsy didn't have time to answer before Sandy continued. "I was at home, just me and Vee, when there's a knock on the door. I open the door and it's two feds! It's the damn Secret Service!"

"What? Why?" Betsy couldn't imagine that Grant would have suggested such a thing, and wondered if it had anything to do with what she had gone through earlier today, with the security procedures.

"A couple days ago I was in one of those online political chat rooms, arguing with the fascists and the socialists. Well, it turns out the feds were monitoring it, and didn't like what I had to say."

"What did you say?" Betsy asked, trying to imagine all of the controversial things her friend might be capable of uttering.

"I said the world would be a better place if the President got hit by a bus and died," Sandy answered.

"That's all?"

"Well, that was the worst, and that's the part they asked me about. They had a printout of the whole discussion. What's worse," Sandy said, leaning forward and lowering her voice, "the whole chat system is supposed to be anonymous. No one uses their real names. But they knew it was me. Snooping bastards. They showed up at my house and started grilling me in front of my kid, like I'm some dangerous criminal. And they kept trying to get inside, even pushed me a little once, but I said that unless they had a warrant, they could bloody well stand in the hallway. I should have just slammed the door in their faces and not said a word, but I was so surprised by the whole thing, I didn't have time to think."

"So, what happened? I mean, they didn't arrest you, did they?"

"No, but they threatened to if I didn't answer their questions. They asked me all sorts of stupid stuff. Vee was there the whole time. I thought of sending her away, but then I thought they might behave better with a little kid watching. Man, I was shaking for an hour afterwards, ready to strangle someone."

"Well, what did they ask about?"

"Who I voted for, what I thought of the President, what I thought of Senator Collins, whether I had been a member of a bunch of different political groups, most of which I've never even heard of—they might have been making them up. And they asked what I knew about the Iron Web." Sandy jumped to her feet and walked to the window. "Man, this pisses me off! What is *wrong* with this country?! You can't say what you think now without having feds show up at your door?"

"Did you get their names?"

"No," said Sandy, looking down. "I was so caught off guard, I didn't even think of it until after they left. And they were there almost half an hour. I should have been taping it." She threw her arms up in disgust. "This is how they do it! They don't come right out and say, 'You can't criticize us,' but if you do, they investigate you, harass you—I feel like strangling someone!"

"Not me, I hope," came Grant's voice as he walked back into the office.

Sandy turned toward the window, folded her arms, and went dead silent.

"Sandy, why don't you tell him?" Betsy suggested in her most soothing voice.

"Why?" Sandy barked, spinning around, her expression as angry as ever. "They work for him already. Don't you get it?" After that she clammed up.

"Who works for me?" Grant asked, still pleasant and calm.

"If you won't tell him, can I?" Betsy asked. Sandy said nothing, and Betsy continued. "She got a visit from the Secret Service because of things she said in an internet chat room."

"What kind of things?" he asked casually, putting his briefcase down beside his desk.

"Saying I wished the President would get hit by a bus," Sandy said, still facing the window.

"I wouldn't mind that either," Grant said in an offhand way, sitting down at his desk. "I hope they don't visit me next."

"It's not funny!" Sandy almost screamed, spinning around toward Grant, and Betsy could see she was on the verge of tears. "Those fascists came to my house and treated me like a criminal in front of my kid! And it was all because I said what I think. I didn't threaten anyone. I didn't tell anyone to do anything illegal."

"Well, what do you intend to do about it?" Grant asked, still calm and friendly, which only seemed to annoy Sandy even more. "File a complaint? Maybe a lawsuit? Sounds like something the ACLU might be interested in."

"It doesn't matter what I do," Sandy said, sounding exhausted. "They already did it, and they'll do it again—if not to me then to somebody else. I just can't believe the country has come to this."

"Well, times change," Grant said. "People in government are pretty on-edge these days. They know there are a lot of people angry about the economy, our military policy, and so on. And some of those angry people mean them harm."

"So that makes it okay to spy on everyone," Sandy snapped, "and harass anyone who happens to criticize the government?"

"It doesn't make it okay, but it's to be expected," Grant replied.

"To be expected? What does that mean? We're supposed to put up with it?"

"Well, I'll ask again: What are you going to do about it?"

Sandy fumed silently for a moment, and then barked, "Nothing. Not a damn thing. They know I don't have the time and money to do a thing about it, and they know that nothing would happen to them even if I did. So they'll get away with it."

"Well, then, it's probably best if you put it out of your mind as soon as possible, instead of letting it stress you out like this," Grant said kindly.

"Just pretend it didn't happen?" Sandy asked, incredulous.

"Well, what good will it do to dwell on it?" Grant asked.

"Isn't there anything you can do?" asked Betsy.

"Like what?" Grant replied. "I could ask them to leave you alone, and I will if you want, but chances are they would anyway from now on. Tomorrow they'll have their eyes on someone else. They do a little intel, make their presence known, and move on to someone else. That's how they operate."

"Make their presence known?" Betsy said, somewhat surprised. "That sounds creepy. Sounds a little like the Mafia."

"These are dangerous times," Grant replied. "They're doing whatever they think they have to do to protect the President. It's their job."

"So we throw the First Amendment out the window, because these are dangerous times?" Sandy asked sarcastically. "That sounds a whole lot more dangerous to me than folks mouthing off in chat rooms."

"Well, the focus of the Secret Service is the security of the President," he responded. "If you want someone to focus on freedom of speech, try the ACLU. Sorry, but that's life."

Sandy stood there fuming for a minute, her arms crossed, and then said to Betsy, between her clenched teeth, "I'll see you after work," and walked out.

Betsy looked at Grant, who was calmly going through his morning stack of mail and articles to review. His cavalier attitude about what Sandy had been through bothered Betsy, but she couldn't think of anything else to say, so she quietly went back to organizing files.

**JESSICA** had decided to try her hand at whittling. She'd seen Doug and Keith doing it a lot, and some of Doug's carvings were really good. She sat on the back step with a small knife and a chunk of wood, attempting to make the chunk resemble a duck. It took a lot of concentration, and made the time pass.

Halen was nearby, looking into the woods with a scope, checking and adjusting things.

"Halen, can I ask you something?" Jessica asked.

"You can ask me anything you want," he said curtly. "And I'll decide whether to answer or not."

She shaved off a few more bits of wood while she gathered her courage. "I heard something about you killing a senator," she said.

"That was a statement," said Halen. "I thought you had a question."

"You don't like to talk about it?" she asked.

"No, I don't like to talk about it," Halen replied. "But if you want to know why I did it, I'll tell you."

"I do want to know," she said. "At least I think I do."

Halen adjusted things for a while, until Jessica thought maybe he wasn't going to tell her after all. But after a few minutes, he sat down next to her on the step, with something like a metal box, and began taking it apart.

"I'd rather just tell you than have you imagining all kinds of things," he said. "It happened four years ago. Seems like forever, though. It all started at one of those fancy parties where politicians kiss each other's asses and tell each other how important they are. A few of us Marines, including a buddy of mine and me, were there in full-dress uniform—decorations to please the politicians." Jessica found it hard to imagine the man in front of her as a well-kempt, disciplined Marine. "Chuck brought along his wife, Cleo—gorgeous girl. Well, it wasn't long before the senator's son, Andrew, was hitting on her. However it happened, later on in the evening, when he was pretty sloshed, Andrew managed to get Cleo alone, and when he couldn't seduce her, he attacked her. She managed to get away before much happened—she was a strong girl, and he was really drunk—but when she found Chuck and me, she was in tears. When Chuck heard what happened, I only barely managed to hold him back from tearing Andrew to pieces. I told him it would be better to do things the legal way." He stopped talking for a few minutes, concentrating on taking apart the device. Jessica wondered if she really wanted him to go on.

"I was wrong," he said finally. "Cleo filed charges against the bastard, but a judge who was a drinking buddy of the senator dismissed the case. Meanwhile, we found out that she wasn't the first woman Andrew had attacked. The guy made Bill Clinton look like a monk. There were accusations of sexual harassment, rape, assault and battery—lots of them—all in D.C., and all dismissed without trial. The senator apparently had friends in all the right places."

"Chuck kept talking about killing the bastard, since the law was obviously never going to touch him. I talked him out of it. It was my idea for them to go public with the story, to tell the world just what kind of people the senator and his son really were. Cleo did a couple of interviews with reporters, and Chuck did one too, telling their story and the stories of Andrew's other victims—at least the ones who dared to talk about it. And they were told that the story was all set to run. But it didn't."

"The night before the story was supposed to come out, the DEA raided Chuck and Cleo's house." Halen went silent again, for a long time. "They were both killed," he finally said. "At least Chuck took out four of those bastards before they got him. The government's version of the story was predictable: they said

Chuck was a drug dealer—which I know was an absolute lie—claimed that they announced who they were and why they were there, and that Chuck fired first. I suspect that's pure bullshit, but of course we'll never get the truth, because as usual, the victims of the government thugs are dead. So they killed him, dragged his name through the mud, and called it a day." Jessica had stopped whittling and was now listening intently, her eyes wide.

"After that, I pulled whatever strings I could find, inside the military and out, to try to get some justice. But the feds did just what they did at Waco and Ruby Ridge: the crooks investigated themselves, and exonerated themselves of any wrongdoing. What a joke. I tried going to the media, but they wouldn't run the story in any way other than the government version."

"The last straw was another story," Halen continued in his emotionless voice. "At about the same time, a young girl in Maryland pressed charges against Andrew for rape. It was outside of D.C. and the senator couldn't pull strings so easily. So a preliminary hearing date was set, and it looked like someone was actually going to get Andrew into court."

He paused for a long time again. "Someone killed her, a few days before the hearing. Sweet little girl, still in high school. Quiet, shy, good student. They found her at home with her throat slit." Jessica gasped involuntarily. "No signs of forced entry, the house was locked, nothing was stolen," Halen went on. "She was murdered to protect darling little Andrew, Son of Satan, from having to face any consequences for his actions."

Halen took a deep breath. "I didn't sleep for three days. That little girl haunted me. Chuck and Cleo haunted me. I was desperately trying to figure out who to go to—who in the system I could trust—who might provide a little justice. And then—and I remember this clear as day—it suddenly hit me, how utterly insane it was for me to try to find anyone inside their little club of narcissists who might give a damn. That's the beauty of their game: they do whatever they want, and then they tell their victims that if they want justice, they have to go beg for it from someone else inside their club—someone appointed and paid for by the crooks themselves. It was like trying to find someone inside the Mafia to tell the heavies to please be nice. What could be more absurd?"

"Anyway, a week after the girl was killed, the senator had another fundraising party at his house. I showed up with the knife Chuck used to carry—a big, Rambo-looking thing the rest of us would always kid him about. The security at the party was pathetic. I walked right in, in full-dress uniform again, the knife worn in open view on my belt. I guess they figured anyone dressed like that was a government thug, and no threat to the masters. Anyway, I walked right up to the senator and asked to speak to him in private. He led me into an empty room, and I jammed the knife up under his jaw, straight up to the top of his skull." Jessica jumped at the words. There was no drama or emotion in Halen's reporting of the event. He described it just as he might describe swatting a mosquito. Somehow it would have been less disturbing for her if he had sounded angry. But he described the event without a hint of feeling.

"He never had time to make a sound," Halen continued, "and died with a look of surprise on his face. I left the room, locked the door behind me, and went to find Andrew. It wasn't long before I found him trying to coax a couple of power groupies out of their dresses. I politely asked them to step outside for a moment. I didn't have the knife then. I'd left it stuck in the Honorable Senator's head, as a message. So I had to kill Andrew with my bare hands, not that it was very hard. It seems beating up petite young women was the extent of his manly abilities. I snapped his neck, walked downstairs and right out the front door. I've been in hiding ever since." After a moment, he added, "The feds out there don't know I'm here. If they did, they would have leveled this place long ago."

Jessica just sat and stared at her carving. She was sitting right next to a fugitive murderer. Those hands right beside her, working on that box, had snapped a man's neck and shoved a knife into another man's head.

"After that," Halen continued, "I monitored the newspapers and the radio, thinking it wouldn't take long before somebody recognized the knife and put the pieces together. Then the story would finally break: vigilante justice carried out against overprivileged rapist and his corrupt father. It took a couple days before anything hit the papers, and the story was that the senator and his son had died in a boating accident. And every paper cried about what a tragedy it was for us to lose a great man like the senator. They all made him out to be some great statesman, and a crusader for the little guy."

If this had been a movie, Jessica thought, she would have cheered for the guy who had taken the law into his own hands. But knowing it was real, and hearing the killer himself describe the event, she couldn't decide whether he was a hero or a monster. She wondered if it was possible for someone to be both at the same time.

"I never realized until that moment just how big, and how well-orchestrated, the government's lie-machine really is," said

Halen. "Sure, they can expose a little scandal here and there, and leave a sacrificial lamb hanging out to dry now and then, but when it comes to the big game, you will never hear or read a word that might threaten the power system itself. Every word, down to the last detail, even in the stories which pretend to be critical of the government, is a carefully planned message, designed to keep the people stupid and enslaved. They can get away with any lie, however patently untrue, however ridiculous, because all of their little puppet mouths in the media will say it in unison, over and over again, until the masses accept it as the gospel truth."

"Like how Iron Web hijackers crashed the plane I was on," Jessica interjected.

"Yeah, just like that," Halen answered. After a short pause, he stated, "So now you know."

Jessica whittled for a while, trying to collect her thoughts. Halen went on working on his device, as if he didn't care what she thought of him. But Jessica felt she had to say something. She had to have some response to that story.

"I think what you did was right," she said finally. "The justice system is supposed to take those predatory people out of society. But when it doesn't—well, somewhere out there is the next girl Andrew would have gone after. You saved her, though she'll never know it. She'll never even know who you are."

"It's enough for me to know that she'll never know who Andrew is, either," he replied. "That alone makes it worth it."

"Does it bother you? I mean, if I killed someone, even if it was the right thing to do, I think it would haunt me forever."

"It would," he said. "Killing is sometimes a necessary evil, but it's always an evil. Every time you do it, you kill part of yourself as well. The guys who like to brag about what they did in war, they're either lying, or they're monsters. Good people don't want to think about that stuff."

"I'm sorry I made you talk about it," Jessica said.

"Don't be," said Halen. "I'd rather you heard it straight from me." He was putting the metal box back together now. "I want you to know how to handle a gun, but I hope to God you never have to use one. No matter how necessary or justified it is, taking a life will always take some humanity away from the one who does it. No one comes back from war unharmed."

She carefully carved off a few shavings from her duck before she looked at Halen again. "Do you think you could ever go back to a normal life?" she asked. "Have a wife and kids?"

"No, it's too late for me," he answered without hesitation. "I'm damaged goods. I've managed to keep myself relatively sane, and I still know the difference between right and wrong— I still know there *is* a difference—but the world out there—" He stopped talking for a minute. "Every once in a while, I go into town, and I realize how different the world looks to everyone else. They're chatting about what to have for dinner, or what happened on some stupid TV show. They'll never know. I can't just forget what I've seen, and what I've had to do. I can't ever go back."

"Sort of like Frodo, in *Lord of the Rings*," Jessica blurted out. "He said that the Shire was saved, but not for him." She suddenly felt silly, comparing Halen's life to a fantasy story. "Sorry, I know it's just fiction," she said quickly, "but I love those books. And Tolkien, the author, drew a lot from his own experiences in World War I. He was—"

"Hey, Jess!" Josh's voice came from the top of the stairs. "Wanna play cards with me and Jason?"

———◈◈◈———

**JASON** sat cross-legged on the floor, happy to be in Jessica's company, even if Josh was there too. He'd been trying to read a book he'd picked from the bookshelf in the master bedroom, a bookshelf covering an entire wall and packed with interesting titles, from classic novels to current events. And this is just their summer home, Jason thought. He had learned from Doug that his mother was a college professor and his father a defense attorney, both extremely well-read.

But, interesting as the book was, he couldn't distract himself from his thoughts. He was relieved when Joshua came down the stairs, having finished his turn watching out the window, and suggested a game of cards with Jessica.

"Where's your family, Josh?" Jason asked.

"My parents' place is up the road a bit, about a mile," Josh said. "I come down here and hang out as much as they let me."

"Don't you go to school?" Jason asked.

"Nah, I left school last year," Josh replied, dealing out cards. "I thought it was stupid and talked my parents into lettin' me do the whole homeschooling thing. It's no trouble for them. I'm doing this online program that gives me a high school diploma, and when I'm not doing that, I learn real stuff."

Jason vaguely knew that homeschooling was a divisive political issue right now, with some groups determined to outlaw it and others just as determined to defend it. He had never really thought about it much himself.

"So, what's 'real stuff'?" he asked Josh.

"Well, lots of books you won't find in the school library, for starters," Josh replied with a chuckle. "And real-life stuff. Like, I have an online business. And I come here to learn to shoot and hunt, and generally how to survive in the wild."

Jessica looked up from her cards and made a wry face. "I was going on my first real camping trip when the plane crashed," she said. Then she went quiet, as if she didn't want to express her next thought. That's happening a lot around here, Jason thought. It seemed as if everyone was trying to keep the conversation light.

"How long have you been shooting?" she asked Josh.

"About two years," he said. "Since Keith got out of prison. Halen's taught me a lot since he's been here, too." He stopped talking and took his turn. "Halen's tough, though," he said when he was done. "I used to laser myself sometimes—and sometimes other people, with the Glock. Only when it wasn't loaded, of course."

"What's lasering?" asked Jessica.

"Oh, just when you point the gun the wrong way as you're moving around. Picture a laser always pointing out the end of the barrel; you're supposed to make sure that line never points at anyone. Like when you're drawing, you can laser yourself if you're not careful. Go, Jason."

Jason took his turn in the game while Josh went on. "Anyway, the first time Halen saw that, he smacked me so hard on the shoulder I almost fell over. He wasn't even mad. You know how he is. He just said a sure consequence trains you better than a hypothetical one. I only did it one more time, and got another whack."

Jessica's eyes were wide. "You don't think he'd do that to me, do you?" she asked.

Josh shrugged, and with a mischievous grin said, "Don't see why not. He's serious about gun safety. But he's also spent hours with me, teaching me to slow my breath down and Zen out, you know, so there's nothing in the world except me and the target. I'm pretty good now. My groupings on the target keep getting smaller."

"I wish I could actually shoot at a target," said Jessica.

Jason thought wistfully that it would be fun to go shooting with these people, and even more fun to teach Jessica to shoot. "What are your hobbies, Jess?" he asked.

"In school I was on the track and field team, and the swimming team," Jessica replied. "I took dance lessons since I was little, and I ride horses in the summertime."

"You must have won a lot of races," said Jason, with a rueful smile. "You're faster than me with your ankle sprained."

Jessica rubbed her wrapped ankle. "And I couldn't walk the next day, remember?" she said. "It's finally getting better now, I think."

Jessica carefully put some cards down. "What are you into, Jason," she asked, "besides being a fed?"

"Well, I've been shooting since I was about five, Dad being a cop and all. I've been in a lot of competitions."

"Really?" Josh said. "Have you won any?"

"A few," said Jason modestly. Then he put down his cards and won the game.

**BETSY** finished the file she was working on and put her computer to sleep. She got up and walked to Grant's doorway. Grant was intently studying a yellow legal pad, his feet up on the desk, chewing on a pencil and scrunching his hair thoughtfully.

"Senator Collins?" Betsy asked politely.

"What?" Grant looked up, and Betsy suppressed a giggle at the state of his hair. "Don't 'Senator Collins' me," said Grant. "You asking me for a raise or something?"

"Nope, just going to lunch. Need anything first?"

"No," said Grant. "But I was thinking. I have a lot to do on this piece I'm working on, and I'd like your help with it after I get all my thoughts down. What would you think of taking this afternoon off and coming in tomorrow? Would that mess you up too much?"

"Of course not," said Betsy. "You know I have no life." She said it jokingly, but unfortunately, it was true.

"Well, go have a life tonight," suggested Grant magnanimously. "Go out with the girls or something. It's Friday night."

He's missing the whole point of Friday night, Betsy thought. It's special because you *don't* have to work the next day. But she could see that he was feeling good about it, and she didn't want to burst his bubble.

"All right," said Betsy. "I'll see you in the morning." She turned to go, then turned back again. "Oh, one more thing, Senator," she said.

"What?"

"You might want to comb your hair." She turned away with a giggle.

As she shrugged into her coat, a scrunched-up sheet of yellow legal paper sailed through Grant's doorway and almost hit her.

As she walked down the hallway, Betsy's mood sank a few notches. She knew Grant meant well, but frankly, the thought of the whole Friday evening ahead of her was somehow depressing. I guess I'm a workaholic, she thought. And then, Why am I lying to myself? It's not the work I want so much, it's Grant. I would love the evening off if I could spend it with him.

She pulled her winter coat tighter around her body against the biting wind, and hurried home to her empty apartment.

# PART V

**JESSICA** sat across from Halen in front of the wood stove, losing yet another game of chess. She'd thought she was pretty good at the game until she played with Halen; he was always two steps ahead of her, and always seemed to know what she was planning.

Jessica marveled at the way this life had begun to feel normal. It felt a bit like a summer camp, with eight people packed into one house. Two people kept watch at all times. Long before she had arrived, Halen had set up battery-powered motion sensors and infrared cameras around the house. And Keith's mine field was still out there. There wasn't much more they could do to prepare themselves. They listened to the outside world on their radios; every day it seemed that another crime was being attributed to the Iron Web. They all hoped that help would come to them before it was too late. At least, Jessica was sure that everyone there hoped for that, though that hope was seldom actually mentioned.

They played cards and board games. They had done a little laundry in the kitchen sink, since they still had running water but no electricity, and had hung the clothes on racks next to the wood stove to dry. The luxury of the clean clothes was somewhat mitigated by their board-like stiffness.

Before Jessica had arrived, Tasha and David had brought some supplies from their own home over to Doug's. Tasha still had to cook on the camp stove and wood stove, but with what she had, she created exotic Indian and Indonesian dishes, in addition to good old American steak and potatoes. Jessica was not the only one who had commented on the irony of eating gourmet food while hiding out from the feds.

"I give up," said Jessica, knocking over her king.

"You weren't quite doomed yet," said Halen.

"Why not? What could I have done?"

"Let me be you," said Halen. He stood the fallen king back up, and turned the board around. "You see the attack coming over here, but if you go like this," he said, moving her bishop, "you pin my rook to my king, so it can't move down there to check you."

"Halen," Josh said, walking up to them. "Do you have any cleaning patches?"

"There might be a few in the butt of my AR," he answered, casually picking up the rifle lying next to him. Jessica noticed that, no matter how casually Halen seemed to be handling the gun, the barrel never pointed at anyone. He opened a little door in the back end of the gun, tipped the barrel up, and out fell various rods, metal brushes and pieces of cloth, a few of which he handed to Josh. Josh thanked him and walked away.

It occurred to Jessica that she had become accustomed to seeing guns lying around all the time, and they no longer made her feel so uneasy.

"Want a lesson?" Halen asked. She looked up and met his eyes, having been absent-mindedly staring at the rifle he was holding. "Charging handle," Halen said, pointing at a tab on the top of the gun behind the carrying handle. "Pull it back and let go to put a bullet in the chamber, so it's ready to fire." With two fingers he pulled it back and released it, his other hand catching a round that came flying out. "There was already a round in there, but that's how you get the first one in."

"And you don't do that every time; when it fires, it loads the next bullet itself, right?" Jessica asked. Halen nodded.

"Safety," he said, pointing to a small handle on the side of the rifle, just behind the trigger. He turned it toward "fire" and then back to "safe." "I usually keep a round chambered, but with the safety on." He held the rifle out toward her. "Now you do it, but keep your finger off the trigger."

Though she still doubted she would ever be able to shoot anyone, no matter what the situation, she decided she should at least be brave enough to hold the thing again. She started to stretch out her arms, as if to ask for the rifle, but pulled back. "Halen?" she asked timidly.

"What?"

"If I put a gun down the wrong way, will you whale on me?"

For the first time ever, Jessica saw Halen really laugh. Ten years dropped away from his face, and she caught a glimpse of the young man he had once been, before all the bad stuff happened. "Did Josh tell you that I beat my students?" He laughed again as she nodded. "Luckily for you, I'm a sexist; I only beat my male students. But you should see your face right now," he said, grinning. "Priceless."

She looked into his eyes. Was he really that far gone? For a moment he seemed less wounded, as if maybe someday he could rejoin the rest of humanity. She impulsively reached out and put her hands on his.

For a moment neither of them moved. Finally, Halen looked up at her. He looked tired and worn again. She looked intently into his eyes, desperately trying to communicate her feelings without speech.

Halen's face slowly faded into a sad expression. He looked down and shook his head. Then he leaned backed a bit, pulling his hands away from hers.

"No, Jess," he said quietly. "I'm sorry. I have no way to make you understand," he said with a pained expression, "but I can't ever go back. Real happiness, relationships, love—those aren't a part of my life anymore. They can't be, ever again. I'm broken inside, Jess, to a degree and in a way I can't explain, a way I wouldn't even want you to understand. It's always in there, even if it doesn't always show." He looked up at her again. A sad, forced smile appeared on his face. "Even if the Shire is saved, it will never be, for me," he said.

The sound of shattering glass startled them out of their thoughts. Someone outside was shouting something over a loudspeaker, but the words were incomprehensible. Halen jumped up and said, "Well, they're here." He picked up his rifle from the couch, paused for a moment, and handed it to Jessica. "Go to the basement," he said shortly, "and keep that with you. A round is chambered, safety's on."

Halen pulled a handgun from his waistband, and gestured for Jessica to head down into the basement. As she hurried down the stairs, she heard more breaking glass from behind her, followed by gunfire and shouting. She quickly decided to hide in one of the big storage cupboards. She put down the rifle, opened a sliding door and pulled out a large bin of camping gear, intending to take its place. Something was stinging her eyes. It took her a moment to realize that it must be tear gas coming down from upstairs. So she couldn't just hide out in the basement after all. Squinting her eyes against the burning gas, she grabbed the rifle and staggered, almost blind, to the sliding glass door facing the backyard. She got through, and found herself in bright sunlight.

No one was in sight, and the sounds were all coming from behind her. Far away to her right she recognized Ben's cabin. Down the long, gradual slope in front of her was another house, and there was a third far off to her left. Behind all of the houses was one long wall of woods, though she had no idea how far in the edge of the river was. She decided that running to the house dead ahead would be the most likely way to stay out of everyone's view. She was just about to make a run for it when she heard a voice yelling off to her left. "I'm hit! I'm hit!" She recognized Joshua's southern drawl, but she couldn't see him. She stood frozen for a moment, not knowing what to do. Then she saw Josh stagger into view around the corner of the house to her left, his right hand dragging his rifle, his left hand on his upper chest, a black stain covering his front. His expression was one of bewilderment and terror. Jessica ran to him, dropping her rifle and embracing him as he fell to his knees. She sank to the ground, still holding him. Her mind was screaming, "No! Not Joshua! Please, God, not Joshua!" But she had no idea what to do. She looked around in all directions, not even knowing what she was looking for. "Help! Somebody help!" she screamed out, but there was no response. Shouting and gunfire continued on the other side of the house. Still frantically looking around, she felt Josh's body go limp in her arms.

"Hold on, Josh, just hold on, I'll—" But as she looked desperately into his eyes, the life went out of them. She clapped her hand over her mouth and wept.

---

**JASON** was jolted awake by the sound of gunfire overhead. It was a moment before he got his bearings, and then things started coming back to him. He had lain down on the bed in the corner room to rest for a moment, not intending to fall asleep. He got up and didn't see or hear anyone near. Looking out the side window, he saw only fields and trees. But something was definitely happening out front.

He was still unarmed, and thought it better to stay that way. But he needed to know what was happening, and hoped he could find out without getting shot. Stepping out of the room into the hall, he smelled tear gas. He turned to his left, ran out the side door, and peered around the corner. He saw a parked Bradley in front of the house, facing to his right, not a hundred feet away. Crouching down behind it was an agent he quickly recognized as Miguel.

The familiar face in the midst of all this mayhem made Jason forget his decision to remain hidden. "Miguel!" he shouted out, stepping out into the open, his hands open and arms wide. "Miguel, don't shoot! It's me!" An expression of recognition was just forming on Miguel's face when he suddenly let out a grunt of pain and bent over forward. At the same time he involuntarily squeezed the submachine gun he was holding and let half a dozen rounds fly.

Jason felt something like a hard punch in his left shoulder, and something hit the side of his right ankle. He watched helplessly as Miguel fell to the ground, clutching at his stomach and yelling something. Suddenly two more agents came into view from behind the Bradley. These Jason didn't recognize, and they started firing in his direction. It occurred to him that they must have assumed that he was the one who had just shot Miguel. He ducked back inside and looked for somewhere to run, expecting the agents to follow him in.

Out of desperation, he ran straight through the living room, squinting his eyes and holding his breath against the cloud of tear gas filling the room. Barely able to see, he managed to find his way to the room at the far side, hoping to exit by the side door. A strange rumbling sound made him pull up short. He then watched in amazement as a giant metal tank tread came tearing through the front wall of the room. The front of an enormous steel monster came rumbling about five feet in, stopped for a moment, and then backed out, leaving a ten-foot-wide hole in the wall. Jason turned and headed back toward the living room.

What was left of the picture window shattered as two more tear gas canisters came flying in, one missing his head by inches. Through the smoke and gas, he could make out the silhouette of a giant Bradley vehicle lumbering past. They were coming in, Jason guessed, and knew he had to get out quick. He ducked around the corner to the stairs leading to the rec room downstairs. He jumped down three steps at once, and a bolt of pain reminded him that he had been shot in the ankle.

As he arrived downstairs, the whole house trembled, and he wondered if the top floor had collapsed. He was looking out the back window, trying to persuade himself to make a run for the woods, when he heard a loud cracking sound above him. What felt like a ten-ton weight hit him on the head, and he lost consciousness.

"**BETSY**?" It was Grant's voice from the other room. She got up and walked into his private office. "Thanks for coming in today. This shouldn't take long. I want to read this to you and get your reactions. Then you can type it up."

"What is it?" said Betsy, taking a seat in her usual chair.

"A press release, but also an addition to the web site, explaining what the new bill will do. I'll have you proofread it too, but even for the written stuff, it's important to see what it sounds like when it's spoken out loud." He scanned the page, scribbled a last-minute note to himself, and began reading.

"This Act, nicknamed the 'Peace of Mind Act,' will help the men and women of law enforcement—those who put themselves in harm's way in order to keep the rest of us secure and free—by providing them with several new tools to be used in their constant battle against crime and terrorism, as well as closing existing loopholes in the law which are being exploited by those who seek to use terror and violence to disrupt our great society. To do this, the Act will do all of the following:"

"Number one. This Act will close a legal loophole allowing cop-killers to escape justice. There is a gray area under existing law regarding the use of force against law enforcement agents who are in the process of making arrests which may be legally flawed. In short, there is case law which has been exploited by criminals who attempt to justify their use of violence, sometimes even deadly force, against police officers, because the criminals didn't believe that the arrest was justified. Even in the rare case where an arrest is done improperly or without legal justification, the proper venue in which to resolve such disputes is within our court systems. This Act therefore includes legislation making it a crime to forcibly resist any arrest, while also providing legal remedies to those who have been subjected to improper arrest."

Throughout her several-year process of learning how Grant liked to word things, Betsy also had acquired the ability to spot the things he was intentionally *not* mentioning. She knew, for example, that the new law would make it a crime to resist even a completely illegal, unwarranted arrest, which an astute reader might infer from the wording, but which Grant's description carefully avoided specifically saying. She chose not to mention it.

"Number two. This Act will end a legal loophole that allows criminals to, in effect, spy on federal law enforcement agencies to determine their game plan ahead of time. Under the Freedom Of Information Act, or 'FOIA' for short, federal agencies must provide the general public access to many types of government records. There are already exemptions in the law regarding documents relating to matters of national security and ongoing criminal investigations, among other things. Nonetheless, some criminals continue to use FOIA requests as a means to find out about ongoing investigations or actions being taken against themselves or others. This makes it easier for the criminals to cover up their crimes, and allows them to escape capture and prosecution more easily. The Act will therefore add a new exception to the FOIA, to keep secret any documents which the directors of the FBI and CIA, or the Secretary of the Treasury, believe could jeopardize their efforts to combat crime, particularly terrorism, both here and abroad."

"Number three. This Act will allow for more effective law enforcement actions in areas that are plagued by overt violence or lawlessness. When one person is accused of a crime, it is a very different scenario from when a mob becomes unruly, or when violence or crime on a large scale is being perpetrated. In the one case, it is often a simple matter to determine the identity of the accused, to obtain search warrants or arrest warrants, and so on. However, when faced with many unruly individuals at once, of unknown identities and unknown intentions, the police simply cannot function under the same set of rules they must use for dealing with a single suspect. The Act therefore allows for the temporary designation of 'Heightened Conflict Areas,' or HCAs, in which some police procedures and policies will differ from their usual methods. This part of the Act does not create any new crimes, nor does it allow for long-term confinement of anyone without formal charges being filed, or without going through the usual legal channels. But it does allow the police to do their job, without unnecessary risk to themselves or to the public, by providing them with extra powers in situations involving crowd control or any forcible conflict involving six or more possible suspects. These powers include:"

"Item A: the authority to temporarily detain any unidentified individuals found in the HCA, but only as long as necessary to establish their identity and to run a background check for any outstanding arrest warrants. After that, any individual not being charged with a crime is to be released immediately.

"Item B: the authority to temporarily prohibit the private possession of firearms or other weapons within the HCA, until the conflict is resolved and the legality of the weapons is established, at which time they will be returned to their rightful owners.

"Item C: the authority to perform warrantless searches, of individuals and vehicles, but only to the extent necessary to locate and confiscate any weapons within the HCA. (If the weapons were possessed legally and promptly surrendered to the police, the individual will not be charged, and the weapons will be returned to their rightful owners once the conflict is resolved.)"

"Item D: the authority to monitor all communications—whether sent through the air, wire, or other means—between areas inside the HCA and areas outside the HCA, until the conflict is resolved. (Because such monitoring constitutes a search without a warrant, information thus gathered is not to be used as evidence in any court of law, but will be used only to prevent the prolongation or escalation of the conflict.)"

Betsy put her hand up. "Can I interrupt for a second?" Grant looked up from the page. "There's an issue I've heard talked about on the radio. I don't know whether you'd want to address it in the press release or not. Some people are claiming that the law would allow the government to designate an area as one of these HCAs without making that public. They're afraid the government can just declare an area to be an HCA, listen in on any conversations they want to in the area, and then remove the HCA designation again without ever telling the public they did it. Is that true?"

"More or less," Grant admitted, "though there are time limits on how long an HCA can be kept secret. As the bill stands now, after two weeks, a secretly designated HCA would either have to be made public or the designation would have to be removed."

"Okay, sorry for interrupting," Betsy said. "Go on." So the government could secretly designate and undesignate HCAs, as long as the designation lasted for less than two weeks at a time. She tried not to show her surprise at Grant's confirmation of what she'd been sure was just another bogus, conspiracy-nut rumor.

"This provision of the Act does nothing to the long-term legal rights of anyone accused of a crime," Grant continued, "but merely allows for the safe, prompt and effective resolution of large-scale violent or dangerous situations. Once the police have the situation under control, have determined which individuals, if any, have engaged in criminal activity, and have taken those individuals into custody, the rules revert back to normal, and the HCA designation for the area will be removed."

Betsy raised her hand again. "Sorry, but I forgot to ask before, is there a time limit on how long an area can have an HCA designation?"

"Not really," Grant replied, "though to keep the designation in place, the agency handling the conflict has to issue weekly reports explaining why the designation should be continued for a certain area."

"Okay, thanks," she said. "That might be worth including in the release, to help reduce the concerns some people have." She didn't mention that her own concerns about the Act had just increased significantly. After all, determining national policy wasn't her job.

"Good idea," he said, and went back to his notes. "Number Four. This Act will close a legal loophole which now allows the use of threats of violence and lawlessness when those threats are disguised as freedom of expression. This is another area where case law has been somewhat vague, and where criminals have exploited the law to suit their purposes, by disguising acts of terror as freedom of speech. For example, the image of a burning cross has the obvious intention of intimidating or terrorizing minorities. Likewise, other images and symbols have been used, in place of openly threatening words, to intimidate or coerce either members of the general public or government agencies into doing what the criminals want. To put an end to this, the Act includes new legislation which will prohibit the displaying of logos, symbols, slogans, or other images deemed to serve no other purpose than the advocacy of violence or other lawlessness. All of the various federal agencies will then promulgate regulations specifically listing the images which are to be prohibited."

"Can I interrupt again?" Betsy asked timidly.

"Sure. Think the word 'promulgate' is too much for a press release?" Grant asked with a smile.

"No. I was going to ask, is this what I heard about before: the law that was going to ban the symbol of the Iron Web?"

"Well, it doesn't really ban any image outright," he answered. "But if someone displays an image in such a place and in such a manner that it falls within one of the categories deemed to constitute a threat of violence or an incitement to lawlessness, then yes."

"Including the Iron Web symbol?"

"Very possibly," he answered.

Betsy thought for a moment, but then just said, "Okay, go on." She was surprised that Grant wasn't getting annoyed at her questions, which at this point felt even to her a little like heckling, but he just took them in stride.

"Actually, that's all; that's the end of the list," Grant said, putting down on his desk the bunch of papers he was reading.

"Wasn't there something else about guns?" Betsy asked. "I thought the gun registration plan was going to be part of this bill."

"It was going to be, but we're not sure we could get it passed this time around, with all the stink the gun rights groups are raising about it, and we don't want to tie up the whole bill over that one issue. After all, my inauguration is only days away," Grant added with a smile.

"Speaking of which," said Betsy, glad to be finished with the press release, "how often does this happen, having legislation introduced by a senator, passing just in time for him to become president and sign the bill?"

"Not very often, I suspect," Grant said, and went back to scribbling down notes and going through papers.

Trying to make it sound casual and off-hand, Betsy spoke up. "Just this morning I saw that Iron Web design on a T-shirt." She paused, looking at Grant's face for a reaction, but he didn't look up from his papers, and said nothing. "You'd think a group that wants to strike fear into people's hearts wouldn't use a symbol that looks like the combination of a rainbow and a flower. I guess I've seen the design in black and white a couple times too, but the colorful version doesn't exactly convey the bad-ass gang image," she added.

"I'm sure that's on purpose," he said, still not looking up but rummaging through the pile on his desk, as if in search of something in particular. "They probably still hope to win some more people over to their way of thinking. That wouldn't work very well if they used a skull and crossbones for their logo."

"Grant," she said, feeling uneasy and nervous, but feeling compelled to speak up. "Don't you ever worry that someday the police might be as big a threat to our freedom as the criminals are?" With that, he stopped what he was doing and looked up at her, but she could read nothing in his expression. "I mean, that's a lot of power you're talking about, and not every cop is what we wish they all were." She stopped again, somewhat puzzled, as a smile slowly appeared on Grant's face.

"People are only concerned with what they're afraid of," he said, going back to rummaging through his pile of papers. "If they start being more afraid of the police than they are of terrorists and criminals, then things will swing the other way. Until then, we do what the people want." Just then Grant's phone rang, and Betsy saw the light for his private number blinking. He picked it up and listened, without saying a word. He face turned very solemn. "Something big is happening down in Graveston," he said, as he jumped up and walked out of the room.

**JESSICA** stood in the smoke-filled room, in shock from what she was hearing around her. It sounded to her like the end of the world. There was gunfire and shouting, the sound of breaking glass and explosions, though most of it sounded far away. After she had left Josh's lifeless body, she had come back into the basement, hoping she would find Halen somewhere in the house. He was the one thing in the world she could think of just then that felt like security. If she could just find him, he would keep her safe. Finding him was her only goal.

She grabbed a winter hat to hold over her face as a breathing mask, but by then most of the tear gas had escaped through the shattered windows and the gaping holes in the walls. She tried to run, but debris and wreckage lay everywhere, hindering her progress. She looked into all the rooms on the first floor, and finding no one, ran up the stairs to the second floor. The house shook again, nearly knocking her off her feet. She ran across a clear space into an end room, and quickly surveyed the scene.

The room was pulverized, with plaster dust everywhere, and chips of wood and glass all over. But at last, underneath the front window, half covered in some fallen curtains, Jessica recognized Halen's jacket. He was crouched down in the rubble, and she could see the barrel of his rifle pointing toward the front window. She felt an immense wave of relief, and, dropping down low to stay out of sight, started crawling toward him, calling his name over the noise. Within five feet of him, she stopped dead. Something was wrong. Halen wasn't moving, and the position of his body didn't look right. A wave of panic swept over her. "Halen?" Her voice sounded like a faint little squeak. She moved closer, not daring to breathe. Please be alive, Halen. Please be alive, she begged silently. Please don't leave me alone here. His face was turned away from her, and one hand stretched out awkwardly back toward her. As soon as she touched his hand, she knew that he had left her forever. The man she had feared, admired, maybe even loved, was gone. Her invincible movie hero had been felled by some lucky shot. She could see no blood, and she didn't want to look. She lost all hope, and all her strength, mental and physical, vanished in an instant. She sat on the floor in the dust, cross-legged, holding Halen's hand in hers, her mind refusing to accept that this was now no more than an empty shell.

Slowly, her awareness of her surroundings came back to her, and her instinct to survive flickered back to life. She could hear a gunshot now and then, but the fighting was becoming more and more sporadic and distant. She looked at Halen again. He had done what he could to prepare her for this, to train her to survive. She couldn't let him down by giving up.

"You weren't a monster," she said softly, a tear rolling down her cheek. "You weren't." A Bible verse came into her mind: "Greater love hath no man than this, that a man lay down his life for his friends." Halen had made that ultimate sacrifice, yet he had died feeling that he was incapable of love. He could not see that his love for the innocent had been honed into a deadly blade that felt like hatred. He had given up more than his life for that love. He had given up glory and honor, and the luxury of human feeling, to protect not only his friends, but also innocent strangers, from harm. And he would be remembered with scorn and hatred, as a vicious criminal. Religion had never been a big part of Jessica's life, but now she fervently hoped that Halen's spirit was still somewhere close to her. She kissed his lifeless hand one last time. "Go with God, Halen," she said. "Thank you." After a moment, she added, "I love you."

And what would he say to her, if his spirit could speak to her now? Probably, "Pick up that rifle and get the hell out of here! Now!" At that thought, she felt some of his strength flow into her. She had to live to tell the world who Halen really was.

Cautiously, Jessica stood up straight, still holding the rifle Halen had given her. Through the large front window, which was a mass of cracks and bullet holes, she saw someone she didn't recognize, not dressed like an agent, running past. She decided she had better try to find the others, if any were still alive, so she headed back down the stairs and ran to the side door. Stepping out into the sunlight, she saw wreckage everywhere. It looked as if a tornado had come through. In the distance she saw smoke rising from what was left of Ben's cabin. Not sure what else to do, she started walking in that direction. Despite the occasional gunfire far behind her, she suddenly noticed that she could hear birds singing in the trees. The human race could exterminate itself altogether, she thought, and the birds would go right on singing.

She saw no one as she wandered through the wreckage, and she was at a loss for what to do. She stopped at what was left of an old tool shed, about a hundred feet from the house, and crawled inside. By now she was too numb to cry, and too overwhelmed to pay much attention to what was going on around her. But if she was going to survive, as she was determined to do, she had to think. She had to come up with some sort of plan. It took a moment for the sound of crunching footsteps in the debris to make it to her brain. Someone or something was moving around amid the wreckage. Maybe it was someone who could help her.

She glanced out around the corner of the shed and saw a lone agent, looking exhausted and lost, less than two hundred feet away. He looked almost like a kid, with his mop of bright red curly hair. She looked just a second too long; he turned and saw her. Instead of hiding, she didn't move. Maybe he wouldn't shoot a girl. Maybe she could surrender. But did she dare to be taken captive? When they found out who she was, might they really kill her? Maybe she could surrender now, pretending she had been a hostage, and escape later.

Her thoughts of surrender vanished when she saw the look on the agent's face. "I found one!" he screamed hysterically. But there didn't seem to be anyone else around. He raised his rifle in Jessica's direction, and without taking time to aim, let loose two volleys of bullets, which missed her and pierced the walls on either side of her. She held up her hands, hoping that would make him stop shooting. Instead, to her horror, his face contorted into an image of pure hatred and he charged toward her, stumbling over boards and rubble, firing aimlessly as he came. Time slowed down as Jessica's senses took in every detail around her. She inexplicably noticed a cranberry-colored glass vase that had been thrown clear of the house and lay unbroken on the lawn.

She ducked back inside the shed, picked up the rifle lying next to her, and steadied herself on one knee. She couldn't do it. Could she? "Stop thinking and do it," she told herself. "This psycho is not going to kill my daddy's girl." Still kneeling, she leaned out from behind the wall and brought the rifle up to her shoulder. It felt awkward as she tried to take aim. The image in the scope was half-obscured, blurry, and shaking wildly. When she saw the crosshairs meet the image of the man, she squeezed the trigger. Nothing happened. She pulled again, as hard as she could. Nothing.

The screaming agent was closing the distance as her mind raced. Then she remembered: the safety! She frantically looked for it, found it, pushed the pointer to the "fire" position, and brought the rifle back up to her shoulder. Through the shaking scope, the man now seemed to be right on top of her. She winced, involuntarily closing her eyes for a moment as she squeezed the trigger, expecting the man to fall on top of her at any second.

It was the piercing sharpness of the sound, more than the kick of the rifle, that made her jump. The gun slipped from her hands and the small blue smoke cloud quickly cleared, but the man wasn't there. Raising herself a little, she saw a figure lying face down in the grass, not thirty feet from her, not moving at all. Her ears were ringing from the shot, and the other shouting and gunfire seemed miles away. Around her, all was still.

She sat and stared at the man she had killed. She, Jessica, had snuffed out a human life. Twenty-some years of living, breathing, learning, playing, working—whatever this man did with his life, it was all over now, and there was no way to undo what she had done. Was this man nice, and funny, and friendly when he wasn't following orders? Did he have a mom and dad, or a sister who would cry as he went into the ground? Jessica felt sick to her stomach. She was a killer now. That fleeting moment had made her a different person, had changed her, perhaps, as much as it had changed him.

Then she felt anger welling up inside her. She had felt terror as he bore down on her; then her mind had pushed all feeling aside to focus on the task of survival. Now a blinding rage set in. Why was this bastard trying to kill her? What did he know about her? What had she ever done to him—ever done to anyone? He had forced her to kill him, and at that moment, that angered her much more than the fact that he'd tried to kill her. "You asshole!" she screamed at the corpse, "you stupid asshole!" Then she hugged her knees, put her head down, and started sobbing uncontrollably. A tiny beetle crawled across the toe of Jessica's boot, and crept down into the grass.

---

**JASON** woke up, covered in dust and debris, his head aching even worse than it had after being knocked out by Halen. He felt his head, which had been bleeding a bit, but the cut had crusted over. It took a moment to remember that he was in the basement of Doug's house, which was barely recognizable, with half of the ceiling having caved in. He tried to move, and pain in his shoulder and ankle again reminded him that he had been shot. He clenched his teeth and sat up. He could hear distant gunfire, but the immediate area sounded quiet. The Bradleys must have gone somewhere else. He struggled to his feet and staggered to the sliding door that led out to the backyard. Limping outside, he couldn't see anyone. The fighting sounded as if it was far off to his left, on the other side of the house. If there was still fighting, someone must still be alive.

As he scanned the devastation everywhere, the image of Jessica's face popped into his mind. He suspected that by now she was probably dead somewhere, but he swore to himself that he would search until he found her, even if he found only her dead body. He had been just a spectator, not a participant in the battle, unable to do anything other than wishing it would stop. He had stopped trying to figure out which side he was on, or who was in the right. The only certainty he clung to was that Jessica didn't deserve to be there, and if he could just save her, that would be enough, no matter what else happened.

Because of the dust and debris covering everything, at first he didn't recognize the shape lying on the ground to his left. When he realized that it was a body, he walked toward it. He didn't have to get very close before he knew that it was Josh, and knew that he was dead. Beside him lay an AK-47-style rifle. For a moment Jason considered picking it up, but decided against it. Even now, there was no one here he was willing to shoot at, and his being armed would only make both sides more likely to shoot at him.

He wandered back inside, deciding to search what was left of the house systematically, room by room. He didn't dare call out for fear of drawing unwanted attention. He checked every closet, under every bed, and behind all the furniture. He went room by room through what was left of Doug's beautiful house. Walking into the room on the north end of the house, he recognized the crumpled form of Halen by a picture window. He didn't need to go any closer to know that he was dead. He stood in that room, trying to guess where Jessica might be, when he glanced out the window and saw something in the doorway of the tool shed outside. There could be a body in the shadows, he thought, with blue jeans and boots just catching the sun.

He ran downstairs and down the hall, scrambling as quickly as he could over the broken wood, glass, and plasterboard on the floor. Now his shoulder and ankle were really starting to throb with pain. Running out the door and over the stretch of grass to the shed, he was more and more certain that this would be Jessica's body. His heart pounding with trepidation, he looked in. Jessica was curled up in the shadows, her eyes closed. A lump rose in Jason's throat as he crouched down and cautiously shook one of her feet.

"Jessica?" he whispered desperately. "God, please be alive," he said to himself. She started to move, almost as if she had been asleep, and Jason was so relieved he almost laughed. "Jessica? We have to go. Can you walk?" For a moment she just stared back at him, looking dazed and confused.

"I—I think I can walk," she said listlessly.

"Listen. The feds have backed off again, but we can't stay here." He quickly scanned the area. "They might not be back for days, or they may be back any minute. We have to go." It suddenly occurred to him that he was calling his former comrades "the feds." He no longer felt like one of them. The only one whose "side" he was sure he was on was Jessica.

"Go where?" Jessica asked, and Jason suddenly realized he had no idea how to answer that. "You're bleeding," Jessica said, pointing to his shoulder, but Jason just shrugged it off.

"It's okay," he said. "The bullet went all the way through." At least it was functional at the moment. He helped Jessica to her feet, and looked around. Ben's cabin was still smoking. To reach the house on the far side, they would have to cross a wide open space, visible from almost everywhere.

"That house," Jason decided, pointing to the house directly behind Doug's at the edge of the woods. The two of them started hobbling across the field as fast as they could, looking right and left for any sign of friend or foe. The walk across the open field seemed to last forever, and Jason kept urging Jessica to hurry, imagining a sniper's bullet hitting at any moment. Jessica seemed distant, as if she didn't care what happened. The house they were approaching was much smaller than Doug's, with only one story, and hardly enough space for more than two or three rooms. But it was better than being out in a field.

As they reached the front door, Jessica pulled back on Jason's hand. He hadn't noticed until then that he was holding her hand. "Look," she said, pointing down at the doorstep. The last stepping stone of the path leading to the house had been moved aside, and in the smooth soil beneath had been scratched an arrow pointing diagonally to the left, with roughly drawn characters spelling out "200M."

Jason quickly brushed out the markings with his boot and kicked the stone back into its place. "Let's go," he said, and started leading Jessica into the woods, in the direction the arrow had been pointing. "Just go as fast as you can. By what that said, it's only a couple hundred yards away."

"What is?" Jessica asked.

"Wherever they're hiding, I guess."

"Wherever *who* is hiding?" Jessica asked.

"Guess we'll find out when we get there," Jason said, wondering the same thing. Who might still be alive? He suddenly wondered if Jessica knew that Halen was dead. He didn't dare tell her just then.

They had to force their way through some patches of thick undergrowth, but mostly the woods were fairly open. Even after Jason thought they had covered two hundred meters, he still saw nothing but woods in all directions, and wondered if he had misunderstood the markings. Then he noticed a structure, so obscured by vines and weeds that it almost looked like a small hill. There wasn't really enough left of it to call a cabin. Most of the roof was gone, and the front wall had fallen outward. This wouldn't offer much shelter, from the elements or from attackers, he thought. "Over here," he heard a whisper, and saw a hand waving from around the corner of the ruins. Still supporting Jessica as much as he could, despite the throbbing pain of his own injuries, he hobbled around behind the cabin.

He had expected to find half a dozen people or more hiding out there. But there were only David, Tasha, and Doug. "Where are the others?" he asked.

"What others?" Doug asked, his face long and wearied.

**BETSY** suddenly remembered the time, and jumped up to turn on the radio on the counter next to her. "What are you looking for?"

Sandy asked from the kitchen as Betsy scanned through the various stations. "Grant is doing an interview," Betsy said.

"God, you're like a groupie or something," Sandy remarked. "Is it really that important, that you have to listen to his BS in my house?"

"He likes to ask me afterwards how he did," she said, still looking for the right station. "I think I already missed half of this one."

Finally she recognized Grant's voice coming from the speakers: " ... the sort of message we should be sending out. But I promise you, once I take office, this matter will be resolved immediately, fairly, and without any more wasting of taxpayer dollars. My administration will make it clear that in this country, compliance with the law is not optional. Coddling criminals is only going to encourage further criminal acts, as we have seen all too well this week. To the members of this so-called Iron Web group, I say this: This will end as soon as I take office. Lay down your weapons, give yourselves up, and each of you will have your day in court and will have your chance to argue your case. But it will be within *our* legal system. No longer will you be permitted to act as a law unto yourselves. Your time is running out, and your best option is to surrender now."

"Resistance is futile," Sandy muttered sarcastically. "You will be assimilated."

"I find your contempt and disregard for the laws of this country ironic," Grant's voice continued, referring to the terrorists but sounding as if he was responding to Sandy, "as it is only this nation's respect for the law and due process which has allowed you to continue to waste the government's resources day after day the way you have. In many other countries, you would have been dealt with swiftly and severely long ago. Here, you have a right to have your say, present your case, have your day in court, and let a jury of your peers decide your guilt or innocence. Instead, you have continually thumbed your noses at the greatest legal system in history. Well, mark my words: even in this land of constitutional rights—the assumption of innocence until guilt is proved, the right to a fair trial—there are limits to the patience of those whose job it is to protect honest law-abiding citizens by seeing to it that everyone—*everyone* either complies with the rules that keep our society orderly and safe, or is held accountable and subjected to the full punishment of the law."

As the radio show host commended Grant for his monologue and began to ask him something else, Sandy snorted in obvious contempt. "What's wrong with that?" Betsy asked. "He's not saying they don't get a trial, or that they'll be shot on sight—although at this point, I'm not sure that would be a bad thing. What's wrong with what he said?"

"It's not so much what he said," Sandy replied, bringing two lunch plates out to where Betsy was seated, "but the way it's all carefully designed to manipulate the emotions of the listener."

"Well, let me listen," Betsy said, picking up the sandwich on her plate, "and afterwards tell me why he's the root of all evil."

"Oh, he's not the root of all evil," said Sandy, smiling. "He's just a tiny twig on the enormous tree of evil." But she stopped talking then as Grant began to answer the interviewer's next question.

"Right, right," came Grant's voice from the radio. "During the campaign, some people actually complained that the President and

I agreed on too many things, as if that must be a bad thing. But I think most people are tired of silly partisan bickering. I'm not going to disagree with someone's position on an issue solely because he's a member of the other party. That's ridiculous. So yes, the President and I agreed on a lot, and at the same time we have significant differences of opinion on some fundamental issues."

"What would you say was the issue you disagreed about most?" the host asked.

"Well, there were several. For example, though he would never put it this way, the President's comments, and the legislation he has supported, suggest to me that he doesn't think average Americans should be allowed to own firearms, while I'm a firm believer in the Second Amendment."

"If I could interrupt for a second," the host cut in, "one friend of mine is a big gun rights guy, and he was pretty upset when the NRA endorsed your candidacy."

"Right, right. Well, some people think the Second Amendment means anyone can have any kind of gun, whenever and wherever they want, with no restrictions. Not surprisingly, those people weren't very happy with some of the bills I've proposed, which make it easier for law enforcement to trace where a gun used in a crime came from, making sure that people with psychological problems or criminal histories aren't walking the streets with machine guns, and so on. These are perfectly reasonable, necessary restrictions, and they don't at all infringe upon the rights of law-abiding citizens to own firearms in this country."

"Okay, moving on, because we don't have much time left," the host continued, "you've also criticized the President's stand on universal health care."

"Well, we need to be clear in our terminology here. I want everyone who needs health care to receive it. That's what universal health care should be. What I don't want is a giant federal bureaucracy telling doctors and patients what care they need, and how it should be administered."

"We're running low on time here, and there was a lot more I wanted to cover," the host said, sounding hurried. "Could I just throw out a series of issues and get maybe a ten- or fifteen-second comment from you on each?"

"Sure, go for it."

"Education."

"Again, the federal government shouldn't be running everything, micromanaging everything from Washington. At the same time, with all the prosperity this country enjoys, even during the current economic slump, we should certainly be able to see to it that no child in this country should miss out on a good education due to a lack of funding and resources."

"Social Security."

"This is a complex issue, and this is one thing on which the President and I pretty much agree. There are ways to make the system sustainable, to protect our seniors and give them what they were promised, without bankrupting the younger generations. But that discussion takes more than a few seconds."

"Crime."

"The way to reduce crime is through deterrents, and deterrents don't work if those who put their lives on the line to protect us, law enforcement at all levels, have their hands tied by policies that reward the criminals and punish the good guys. When someone is found guilty of a crime, the punishment has to be fair but sufficient, swift and unavoidable. No more having dope dealers tying up our court systems for years because they got a stubbed toe while they were being arrested. You do the crime, you do the time."

"Last, but not least, terrorism."

"Well, we could talk for hours about that, but what it boils down to is this: people who use violence, or the threat of violence, to try to achieve some political agenda—and this is whether we're talking about some anarchist cult in this country or Muslim extremists over in the Middle East—they should be dealt with swiftly and severely. No deals, no compromises. As I said, when I take office, such criminals and their intimidation and fear tactics will be stopped by whatever means necessary."

"And that's all the time we have today," the host said as the background music began fading in, signaling the end of the show. "Thank you very much, Senator Collins—soon to be President Collins—for being on the show."

"You're quite welcome, and thank you for having me on," Grant responded.

"Well, that about wraps up—" The host's voice was cut off by Sandy turning off the radio.

"What a freaking hypocrite," she said. "Man, why do people still fall for this crap?"

"What was wrong with what he said?" Betsy asked, putting down what was left of her sandwich.

"The brave men and women of law enforcement," Sandy said in an exaggerated, mocking imitation of Senator Collins. "Yeah, the brave, jackbooted Nazi thugs of law enforcement. Give me a break. How bad do things have to get before the stupid American people stop pretending that the cops are the good guys?"

"Okay," replied Betsy, "I admit that with all those videos of police abuse you keep e-mailing me, and all the other stories about it, I'm starting to see why you distrust the police so much. But they do occasionally catch some bad guys, you know. There really are terrorists in the world, and even the cops like your buddy, Curtis Walters, might help to stop them."

"What terrorists do you think I need Dumb-ass Walters to save me from?" Sandy asked. "You mean the Iron Web, right?" She paused, but Betsy didn't say anything. "Ya know," Sandy continued, "I've been resisting the urge to say this, considering who you work for and all—"

"What?" interrupted Betsy. "Tell me you're not siding with the terrorists now."

"Hey," Sandy replied indignantly, "you work for the biggest terrorist organization on the planet: the damn U.S. government." Then she leaned forward in her chair, looking down at the floor, and got very quiet. "Seriously, though," she added at last, looking up at Betsy again, "I want to ask you a favor."

"Uh oh, the wacko is getting serious," Betsy joked, but Sandy didn't smile.

"Shut up," Sandy said. "I mean it." She sighed again, as if gathering the courage to say something. "You've never read the book, have you?"

"What book?" Betsy asked. "You mean that book about the Iron Web, by David what's-his-face? The terrorist manifesto?" Sandy just looked at her and didn't say a word. "I've seen excerpts from it," Betsy said.

"Betsy, you know me," Sandy said softly, looking directly into Betsy's eyes. "I'm a throwback, a pot-smoking, live-and-let-live hippie, only with an attitude and a gun. I'm no terrorist—though I can't say the same for your boss. Do me this favor. Read the book." She turned to her right, pulled open the drawer of the end table next to her, and pulled out a well-worn copy of a book, the cover of which said "Weaving an Iron Web," above the image of the familiar, colorful geometric pattern.

"Sandy," Betsy began, getting a little concerned.

"I'm not asking you to agree with it, or even to tell me what you think," Sandy said, holding the book out toward Betsy. "But you know as well as I do how often people get dehumanized, demonized and prejudged, right before they get murdered." Only once or twice in the many years she had known Sandy had Betsy seen her like this. "All I'm asking," Sandy went on, "is that you find out who it is that your boss intends to exterminate. That's all. I've bitten my tongue on this for too long. Read it!" she said firmly, pushing the book toward Betsy.

"Grant isn't trying to exterminate anyone," Betsy said defensively, and hoped it was true, but she took the book from Sandy.

"Don't skim it, *read* it," said Sandy in a softer voice. "And don't assume you already know what it says. Trust me, you don't. Promise me you'll read it. All of it, Bet. Please."

"I promise," Betsy said, Sandy's uncharacteristic seriousness making her feel slightly uncomfortable. "I'll read it tomorrow."

**JESSICA** watched as a chipmunk skittered from log to log and rock to rock, occasionally twitching his tail and chirping. It was a beautiful day, with a bright blue Arizona sky and a warm breeze. The group now sat behind the remains of the old cabin, in a loose circle in a clearing carpeted with pine needles. Doug was relating yesterday's events to David and Tasha.

"So Keith got word to Carl and Tarzan, and they somehow got across the river and came up from over there," Doug said, pointing off into the woods. By then Jessica had lost all sense of direction. "Then all hell broke loose. I don't know what Carl had, but feds were dropping like flies, and I know Tarzan can't shoot like that. But then they must have made a run for the house, over where Keith still was, but the feds must have had a sniper somewhere. Carl went down. Tarzan stopped to help, and they got him, too." Jessica didn't want to interrupt to ask who Carl and "Tarzan" were. "Then it looked like the feds were backing off. I ran back around inside the house to find Keith. When I got to him, he'd been hit, three times I think. And he was still shooting at 'em." He stopped talking for a while, and when he spoke again, his voice was very low. "After a while, things got quiet. I thought Keith was just resting, but when I shook him, he was gone."

Last night, after she and Jason arrived, they had huddled in the poor shelter of the ruined cabin as darkness fell, trying to assess their situation. The only real unknown at that point was Heather, and it was a safe bet that by now she had been captured, if she was still even alive. They had confirmed that everyone else missing from the group was dead, so there was no one else to search for or wait for. They had no food, no water, and no weapons. More likely than not, the feds by now had taken control of all of the buildings in the area, so there was nowhere else to go.

They spent the night huddled together for warmth on the floor of the cabin—hungry, thirsty, cold, and overwhelmed with grief and despair—until sheer exhaustion took them off to sleep, one by one. Jessica dreamed of the red-headed agent running at her, screaming. She heard the sharp crack of rifle fire, and her eyes flew open. Had she dreamed that, or was it real? She lay trembling for a while, but heard no more noises.

Of course they all woke at the crack of dawn, cold, stiff and hungry, and moved out into the clearing. Jessica had spoken very little to anyone. Jason had told the others about Halen and Joshua, so she didn't have to. The grief had simply overwhelmed her, and she felt an empty stillness inside, as if she would never want to do anything again. She grieved for Joshua and Halen. And she grieved for the red-headed agent, and for the innocent girl who had boarded that plane to California. She grieved for her parents and her brother, who all thought she was dead.

She'd told no one about her killing of the agent. It felt as if talking about it would give it another layer of reality. If she never spoke of it, maybe it wouldn't be real. But she couldn't stop the incident from playing over and over in her mind. The gunfire coming at her, the screaming man, the crack of the rifle. The body lying still.

"We need food and water, first of all," she heard Jason saying. "You all should stay here, and I'll go back to Heather's. I've got the best chance of surviving if I'm seen."

The others agreed. "Doug," Jason said, "can you give me a leg up into that tree so I can get my bearings?" But when Jason lifted his arm to grab the lowest branch, a cry of pain escaped him, and he clutched at his shoulder. David was beside him in an instant.

"Let me see the wound," he said. Under Jason's jacket, his shirt was stiff with dried blood. David's face looked serious as he pulled back the shirt and assessed the wound. "You're not going anywhere, Jason," he announced. "And we need first aid and medicines as soon as possible."

"It's gotta be me, then," said Doug. "I know these woods like the back of my hand. I've got a good chance of getting there without being seen."

Jessica watched anxiously as Doug quietly walked off into the woods. There seemed to be nothing to say. She looked over at Jason. He was sitting against a fallen log, looking pale. She could tell that he was in a lot of pain and trying not to show it. David and Tasha sat on the ground, holding hands. Jessica got up and sat down again next to Jason, as close as she could without touching him. No one spoke.

---

**JASON** watched Jessica as she sat cross-legged on the ground, her head down, playing with twigs and leaves. David and Tasha were leaning against each other and talking in quiet whispers. It seemed like at least an hour since anyone had said anything aloud.

Jason kept mulling over the facts in his mind, trying to think of some way for them all to survive this. Maybe the feds were calming down with the passage of time, he thought. Maybe if they could hold out for a while, they'd at least have a chance of being captured instead of shot.

But then what? The government would make sure that David went to prison for the rest of his life, one way or another, and maybe Tasha, too. Doug might get off, but what would happen to Jessica? If the government was hiding something, as it must have been based upon what Jessica had told him, was there any limit to what they might do to keep her quiet once she was identified? And if they might kill Jessica, now they were all at risk, because they had all met her, which made each of them a threat to the government's official story. He tried to tell himself that the U.S. government wouldn't just assassinate people over something like that, that it was all just conspiracy theory paranoia. But try as he might, he couldn't convince himself. He had heard enough stories, just during his short time as a federal agent, to know that there were some pretty powerful, ruthless people in the system, and that they played by their own set of rules. What if Jessica went along with the government's story? She could say that she had been asleep the whole time, and had no memory of what happened on the plane.

Maybe if they were found by someone Jason knew, someone he could trust, they could get the story out to the media. Maybe getting the truth out there quickly enough could protect Jessica. Once the world knew she was alive, and heard what she had to say, killing her would only make people suspicious. Maybe publicity was their only hope. Then again, Jason knew how strictly controlled all evidence and information was in a situation like this. No, if they were found, they'd be as good as dead. Jason didn't want to admit it, even to himself, but deep down he knew it was true.

He looked around, wondering if it was possible to remain hidden out here for a few days. Maybe then they could find a way to get out, after the world had decided that everyone in here was dead. But the woods, though they followed the river a long way, were never more than a couple hundred yards deep. It wouldn't take long for the whole area to be thoroughly searched. Building a fort or digging a hole wouldn't keep them hidden for long. Eventually they'd be found.

Overhead, clouds had been racking up until the blue sky was all but hidden. "Doug's back," said David, pointing into the woods. Doug was walking back slowly and quietly through the trees, carrying a plastic watering can.

He walked into the clearing, shaking his head. "A couple of feds are camped out at Heather's," he said. "Damn them. But I got us some water." He set the watering can down on the ground. "Might be a little hard to drink from," he said apologetically. "I got into the back of Heather's tool shed, and came back by way of the spring."

The water was most welcome, and for the next half hour, they took turns, one person holding the can while another drank from the spout, until everyone's thirst was quenched.

"I was thinking on the way back here," Doug said. "Wasn't the guy who lived here before, old man Hargroves, kind of a survivalist? I never knew the guy, but Keith used to talk about him a lot."

"Yes!" said David, standing up suddenly and looking around on the ground along the cabin wall. "I just remembered, this cabin had a cellar. I remember it. I was in it once. Kind of a secret basement, almost like a bomb shelter. Old Hargroves built it himself. And knowing him, it wouldn't be empty. It has to still be down there. But I don't remember how to get in."

Jason stood up, felt a stabbing pain in his leg, and limped over to the cabin. Doug was already on the cabin floor. He stamped on it a few times, and it made a hollow sound. His eyes met Jason's.

Jason started working around the front of the cabin, kicking the leaves away from the wall, looking for any way to get in. Even if the place was empty, he thought, it might at least give them a place to hide a bit longer. He was looking around out front, where the wall had caved in, when he heard David say, "Over here!" Hurrying around to the side, he saw David on his hands and knees, brushing aside leaves and dirt, exposing a small hole under the wall, leading down to complete darkness. He painfully got on his knees and helped to dig. This obviously wasn't supposed to be an entrance; it was just a place where a portion of the old floor had rotted and fallen through. Then Doug pushed Jason aside, and David and Doug slowly widened the hole enough for someone to fit through it. "I don't suppose anyone has a flashlight?" Jason asked, without much hope.

"Wait, I do," Doug answered, seeming surprised himself. He pulled out a keychain with a tiny LED light on it. "Better than nothing." He crouched down at the hole, aiming the little light into it. "I can't see squat," he said, squinting into the blackness. "Let me go in." Jason watched as Doug got on his stomach, feet toward the hole, and wiggled through it backwards. "I hope the floor isn't too far down there," he said. When he was almost through, David helped lower him down.

David stepped away from the opening as the first raindrops came splashing down. "Good timing," he said. "If nothing else, we might be able to stay dry down there."

Doug's voice sounded again, distant and echoing. "It's not exactly the Ritz. The floor is just dirt, but the ceiling—the cabin floor, I mean—actually looks like it's in pretty good shape. Some of the cinderblock wall is falling apart." There was a brief pause, followed by the sound of stone grinding against stone. "Wait," came Doug's voice again. "I think I can make some half-ass stairs so the rest of you can come down."

"Assuming we plan to hide here for a while, we should make something to cover the hole," Jason suggested, "something that the last one in can pull into place."

"Good idea," said David, beginning to gather up sticks and leaves. "Though I sure hope we're not just crawling into our own graves," he added.

**BETSY** opened a folder on her computer and dialed Sandy's number on her cell phone. "Hey, Sandy, it's me," she said when her friend answered. She sighed, and said with some effort, "You were right."

"About what?"

"The book. And Grant. I started reading the book last night, and I couldn't stop. I got like two seconds of sleep, and now I'm here at work again."

"It's Sunday," said Sandy.

"I just have some things to wrap up and I want to talk to Grant today, before I lose my nerve."

"So, what did you think of the book?"

"Well, I think that what we've heard about these Iron Web people isn't at all true. And the spin that everyone's putting on this thing is completely wrong. They're putting a lot of words into David Singh's mouth that aren't at all what he's saying. They're making this man look dangerous when he's not. And I just can't believe it's a mistake, Sandy. They have to know it's wrong. *Grant* has to know it's wrong. I'm sure he's read the book; he reads everything."

She stopped for a moment to breathe. "You know, Sandy," she went on sadly, "I just kept telling myself that he wasn't like the others, that he was really a good guy, playing the game as much as he had to, you know, because you don't last if you don't play the game. But I really believed that he was different inside, and that some day he would do something different." Sandy said nothing. "But this goes beyond spin. The way these people are being portrayed is probably going to get them all killed, while he's making political hay with this." She was silent for a minute, collecting herself. The disillusionment was too much for her. "Maybe I just wanted him to be different. But what he's doing, and what he's saying, it just doesn't match the man I thought he was."

Betsy appreciated Sandy not saying "Told ya so," but wished she would at least say *something* now. "I know this is hard for you, Bet," said Sandy. "I know how much you like him, and I totally understand why. If I didn't hate politicians so much, I'd have a crush on him, too. I really am sorry that he's not what you hoped he'd be. Love isn't just blind, you know, it's also stupid. God knows I'm living proof of that. And I won't say I told you so, because everyone told me so every time I started going out with some hot new jerk, and I never listened." She paused and continued in a softer tone. "So, what will you do now?"

"I'm quitting," Betsy said flatly. "Right now. Today. I just can't be here a minute longer. I know it's unprofessional as hell, but I just don't care right now. I've never gone off half-cocked in my whole life, and I think it's about time I did." She heard a suppressed giggle from Sandy.

"Grant should be back any minute now," she said, looking at the clock on the wall, "and then I'm telling him that I have to resign. We never talked about me going to the White House with him anyway, but I want this to be my choice, my doing."

"Way to go, girl," said Sandy. Betsy could just picture a broad grin on her friend's face. "Listen," Sandy continued, "when you're done there, come on over. I'll help you decompress, okay?"

"Okay, thanks. I think Grant's coming. I'll see you soon," said Betsy, closing her phone.

Before Grant was even through the door, he was talking. "I have a meeting in an hour and a half, and before I go I wanted to—"

"Grant," interrupted Betsy, in a tone serious enough that he stopped talking and looked at her. She took a deep breath. "I can't in good conscience work here anymore." She was looking at the floor as she said it. Grant said nothing, and she didn't dare look at him to see his expression. She was seriously afraid that if she looked at him, she would forget the whole thing. "What we do here, this—this whole game we play here—Sandy's right. It's all about power and control. It's all a lie, and it's making me sick. I can't be part of it anymore." Of course she was as upset about leaving Grant as she was about the principle of the thing, but she wasn't about to say so. She was on the brink of tears, hoping that it didn't show, and she finally looked up at Grant. His face showed no anger and no shock.

He sat down in the chair facing Betsy, and said soothingly, "What brought this on? Tell me what this is about."

Betsy steeled herself against his disarming tone. It would be so much easier if he got angry, she thought. "It's been a lot of things," she said. After casting about for a way to say it nicely, she finally gave up. She'd dared to open her mouth, and now she might as well say what she really thought. "When I came to Washington, I thought I could do some good," she began. "I thought government was about helping people. I've spent five years learning how wrong I was. Everything here is a sales pitch. It's all spin, and backroom deals, and compromises. We support this bill if that guy will support ours. We'll change our position on this issue if that guy will endorse this candidate. It's all about trading favors, and sweet-talking contributors. This building is full of people who spend day after day throwing around other people's money, buying votes here, selling out to this or that lobby."

Now her words were tumbling out effortlessly. "Does anyone here actually believe in anything other than money and power? Even the programs and things that sound good, that sound like they're designed to help people—around here they're just tools for getting votes, and looking compassionate, and getting attention." She pointed out the window. "All the *good* people I know are out there in the real world, trying to make ends meet, trying to pay all their bills, not to mention their taxes. And all the people in here are throwing away billions here and billions there, wherever they think it might buy them loyalty or recognition. We put on the act of being compassionate and caring, of wanting to make the world a better place, but it's all a show. It's all a lie. It sickens me, and I can't be a part of it anymore." She stopped talking, partly because she felt as if she were about to cry.

After a pause, she heard Grant say, as if to himself, "The urge to save humanity is almost always a false front for the urge to rule."

Betsy was prepared for some sort of excuse or spin, and was confused by his response. "What?"

Grant seemed to snap out of a daydream. "What? Oh, sorry. It's a quote from H.L. Mencken. Smart guy. He also said that every election is a sort of advance auction on stolen goods."

"Well, that's what I mean," she replied, wondering why he wasn't trying to contradict her. She wished again that he would argue and snap at her. "That's what it feels like. It's a power game, and whether it actually does anyone outside this city any good, no one seems to care, as long as they get the PR image they want, and the votes they want. Money and power, that's all it's about. All of it. And it's not what I want my life to be about. It's not what I came here to do." She paused for a moment to control the tremble in her voice. "And it's not what I thought *you* were about, either."

Grant leaned forward and put his hand on hers—something she never remembered him doing before—and she became aware that she was nervously gripping the arms of her chair. She loosened her grip a bit, and he walked away from her to the window again. She knew the power that Grant had to persuade almost anyone of anything, but he wasn't doing a thing to dissuade her from her decision. Was that a good sign, or a bad one?

"Grant," she asked in as steady a voice as she could manage, "have you ever read the book, *Weaving an Iron Web*?"

"Let me guess. Sandy talked you into reading it," he said, not turning around.

"Well, yes," she answered, "but you didn't answer my question."

Still gazing out the window, he answered, "Yes, I've read it."

"And?"

"And what?" he asked, turning toward her with a faintly derisive smile. "Shall I write you a book report on it?"

"No." His levity annoyed her. "They're not what you say they are—those people in Graveston. If you've read the book, you know that." For years she had quietly listened to all sorts of political spin from him, and even helped him fashion some of it, but had never directly confronted him about any of it. Now she was essentially calling him a liar right to his face, and her stomach was doing somersaults.

Grant walked up to her, leaned over, put his hands on her shoulders, and looked straight into her eyes. "Betsy, let's discuss this later. For now, I ask only one thing of you. Stay here today and tomorrow, just until the inaugural address. After that, do whatever you feel is right."

"I guess I can stay on that long," she said, surprised at his response. She expected some spin, or maybe even a confession of sorts, but not this. "I don't want to leave you hanging or anything," she added lamely, wondering if he was just concerned with the practical matter of running his office.

"It's not that," he said softly, dropping his eyes but not moving away from her. He opened his mouth as if to add something, but then closed it. After a moment he looked up at her again and said, in a low voice, "Just promise me you'll stay until then. After that, I won't lift a finger to stop you, and I'll give you whatever glowing references you want." He stayed in that position, looking into her eyes. She felt as if he was trying to hypnotize her, and it felt as if it was working.

"I don't know what difference that will make, but I'll promise that much," she said, looking away from him. Then, to her surprise, he leaned over and kissed her gently on the forehead. He stood up and turned toward the window. As if to himself, he muttered, "A lot can happen in a day." Then he turned and walked out of the room.

# PART VI

**JESSICA** sat in a dry corner of the dark cellar, watching rainwater drip through the boards of the floor above and collect in puddles at the other end of the room. Tasha had gone outside and positioned the watering can to collect rainwater as it ran off the corrugated aluminum roof. But now that her thirst was quenched at last, Jessica's body was persistently demanding food.

"We should probably save the battery in that light," David said as Doug wandered around the room, examining the floor and walls.

"No need," Doug responded. "It's one of those LED things. It'll burn a zillion hours on one puny little battery." He picked up some boards on the floor and looked under them. "Chances are, it'll be alive long after we are."

"Thanks for that bit of optimism," Jason said. "What are you even looking for?"

"I don't know," Doug answered, "but the guy who lived here built this place as his own little survivalist retreat, expecting civilization to come to an end. You'd think he would have had some useful stuff down here."

"Where is he now?" Jessica asked.

"Died of cancer, right in this house," David said. "It was about fifteen years ago. He's buried out in the woods, not two hundred yards from here. That was what he asked for. Didn't have any kids. He didn't have much at all, but he never complained about that."

"Oh, man," Doug said. "Check this out. There's a section of cinderblocks here with no mortar between them. This is it! I know it!"

"How about we see if there's anything there before we call Geraldo?" Jason said mockingly, but he stood up and limped over to where Doug was standing. "Yeah, it does look like some of these have been taken out before."

Jessica watched for a while as Jason and Doug, in the dim glow of the little keychain light, tried to get one of the blocks to move. They used sticks, keys, anything they could find, to try to pry it out. Finally they got one to move out an inch, enough to get a grip on it. Each grabbing a side, they wiggled it back and forth. Finally it came loose, and they both stepped back as it loudly crashed onto the boards lying on the floor below.

"It might be good if we didn't advertise our whereabouts so much," David said.

"Sorry," Doug said, picking up the light and shining it in. "Oh, yeah. Jackpot."

"Time to call Geraldo?" Jason joked.

"There are shelves of boxes and plastic bags," Doug said, as he put his face into the hole. His voice sounded distant and muffled. "There's a radio, too. Oh, man, there's even a rifle in the corner."

"Let me see," Jason said, and Doug handed him the light and stepped back. Jason peered in. "Yep, looks like an M1 Garand.

Not bad, if there are any bullets. I don't know what good it will do, though. I don't think Doug with one rifle is going to hold off the entire federal government—including the army, for all we know. But what's all that other stuff? Let's get this wall down."

In only a minute or two Jason and Doug had the rest of the loose blocks removed, making an opening about four feet tall by three feet wide. "Okay, Indiana, you first," Jason said to Doug, who climbed right in.

"How do you know it's not booby-trapped or something?" Jessica asked anxiously.

"They're using the method of trial and error," David remarked. "But I don't think old man Hargroves would have done that. Any batteries for the radio?" he asked.

"Aw, cool," came Doug's muffled voice from the hole in the wall. "No batteries. It's the kind that you charge up by cranking it." A whizzing sound came from the hole, and then the scratchy static of a badly tuned-in radio broadcast. "No way, it works! Dang it, where's the volume?" After a moment the noise faded to almost nothing. "That's better."

"Look for a first aid kit," David said.

After a brief pause, Doug's voice could be heard again. "Got it. Sending it out." Jason brought out a green metal box with the familiar emblem of a red cross on it.

"Are those MREs?" Jason asked, peering in. "It looks like he's got a million of them."

"What, these?" came Doug's voice from the hole. A dark green package came flying out of the hole, and Jason caught it with his left hand. "What are they?"

"MRE, meals ready to eat," Jason answered. "They keep almost forever." Suddenly he stopped and looked into the hole. "Wait a second. You're the survivalist, militia-type guy. How did you not know that? Aren't you guys always supposed to be prepared for the end of the world?"

Doug's face came out of the hole. "I missed that lesson. I was busy reading *The Anarchist Cookbook* for the hundredth time. If you're done stereotyping me, it's your turn to go in, jackboot. It's getting tough to breathe in there." He stepped out, and Jason stepped in.

It occurred to Jessica that, in a very real sense, Jason now fit in with this group as well as anybody. Philosophically, he and Doug might be worlds apart, but circumstance had made them allies. When survival itself was the goal, everything else seemed trivial.

"Man, look at all this stuff," came Jason's voice from inside. "Ammo box for the M1, blankets, propane, matches. What's this?" There was the sound of a metal tin opening. "Holy smokes. One, two, three." There was silence for a moment. "Eighteen gold coins, and maybe twice that many silver ones."

"Not bad," said Doug. "At least, it wouldn't be bad if we ever get out of here alive. Are they one ounce, or half ounce?"

"I have no idea," came Jason's voice. "They're a little bigger than a quarter."

"One ounce," David said. "Worth around two thousand FRNs each, last time I checked, which was a while ago."

"FRNs?" Jessica asked.

"Federal Reserve Notes," David answered.

"What you call dollars," Doug added.

"What I *call* dollars?" Jessica asked curiously. "What do *you* call dollars?"

"Man, don't get him started on monetary policy," David said.

"The short version is this: paper currency used to represent something, like silver or gold," Doug explained. "You could trade it in for the real thing whenever you wanted. It used to *say* that right on the front: 'payable to the bearer on demand.' But after people got used to using the paper, a bunch of crooks figured out that they could just print more paper, without it representing anything, and then loan it to us at interest."

"You mean counterfeiters?" Jessica asked.

"Well, yes, it is counterfeiting, but not the way you mean it," Doug answered. "I'm talking about the Federal Reserve. It makes up money out of nothing, and loans it out to people and governments. And once all the people and all the governments are perpetually indebted to the international bankers, the bankers pretty much own the world. It's a brilliant, relatively simple way to control everything."

"This conspiracy stuff is all way over my head," Jessica said, not sure how much of it to believe.

"It's actually a very simple concept. It's just that you never heard it in school, or in the mainstream media," David said.

"More conspiracy?" Jessica asked, sounding dubious.

"Shhh!" The sound came from Doug. Everyone went silent, except for Jason, who was still in the hole, talking to himself. "Jason, shut up," whispered Doug. All went quiet. All ears strained to hear something. After a moment, there was the unmistakable sound of voices outside, and they were getting closer.

"Clear here," came a voice just overhead. There was the sound of footsteps above them, and dust fell from the rafters. Doug quickly shut off the light. "The captain said we're supposed to burn any structure we find." Jessica felt panic setting in. "This ain't much of a structure," came another voice, "and good luck getting this soggy heap of crap to burn." There were now more footsteps coming from above. "Yeah, forget it. The bulldozers can take it down tomorrow. Do the guys in nest D have a view of this place?" There was an unintelligible response. "Good enough. Another couple hundred yards of these woods, and that's it. Eyes open. Let's go."

The sound of footsteps and voices gradually faded, but it was a long time before anyone in the basement dared to say a word.

———

**JASON** felt as if time had slowed down. Each minute seemed to drag on for an hour as he sat in that wet, dark basement. While Doug and Tasha prepared a dinner of MREs, David had insisted on doctoring Jason's shoulder and ankle with the first aid kit. The ankle had received an open wound that had bled freely and was healing well. But although David didn't say much, Jason could see that he was deeply concerned about the shoulder wound, which had closed without being sterilized. He muttered something about antibiotics, but the only medication in the kit was aspirin. David gave him some with a drink of water. "I don't know how old it is," David said. "It might be ineffective. But it's all we have."

Jessica had assisted David over Jason's objections. "Shut up and lie down, Jason," she said. "I've seen injuries before."

Jason was impressed with the girl's courage and fortitude. By her own admission, she had lived a fairly pampered, privileged life. She'd then been thrust without warning into a war zone, and had turned out to be remarkably strong. Time and again he'd seen an irrepressible spirit bubble up through her fear and grief. But something had changed since yesterday. Her sparkle was gone, and even her own survival did not seem to interest her that much. His heart ached for her. He wanted to hold her, and let her cry out her grief. The group avoided speaking of Halen, as if no one wanted to acknowledge how much hope had died along with him. But Jason knew, more keenly and painfully than anyone else, that Halen had been much more than hope to Jessica.

Now the rain suddenly came down harder, like gunfire on what was left of the old aluminum roof. The wind blustered, bringing cascades of leaves and twigs down on the cabin floor over their heads. The noises outside kept playing tricks on Jason's ears. It would sound as if someone were walking around up there, and sometimes he thought he could even hear voices. He kept telling himself that the other agents wouldn't bother searching in this weather; they would wait until it cleared; it was just his imagination. Time continued to crawl by.

"I think I should go out there and surrender." Though he spoke quietly, Jason jumped at the sound of David's voice; no one had spoken for so long. "They won't stop looking until they find me. But the rest of you, I doubt they even know you're here. They probably think Jason's dead by now, they don't know Jessica is here at all, and I doubt Doug is really on their radar." Jessica saw him squeeze his wife's hand. "I can't see this ending well either way, but if I go out, they might stop searching, and the rest of you might have a chance to sneak away."

"I'm going with you," Tasha said.

"No," David said firmly, shaking his head. "Whatever horrible crimes they make up about me, they'll just lock you up as an accomplice. Maybe even an enemy combatant. You're the main reason I have to go. I won't let them get you. Not ever. No matter what."

"Don't go at all," Jason said. "You heard them. They'll bulldoze this whole area anyway, like they did in Waco. You'll be killing yourself, and you won't be saving anyone."

"I'd rather die with you than lose you," Tasha said to David, in a voice almost too soft for Jason to hear.

"Were you at Waco?" Doug suddenly asked Jason.

"No," Jason answered, grateful for the change of topic. "I've only been an agent for a few weeks now. But I know a couple guys who were there. One of them is like super-macho man, brags about stuff he probably never did. The other one, he doesn't really like to talk about it." Jason leaned back against the cool wall, remembering the look of sadness on the other agent's face whenever he spoke of Waco. "After work one day we were hanging out, just the two of us. After a few beers, he starts talking about Waco. He says when it was happening, he was all juiced up, like they all were, you know: the righteous cavalry bringing evildoers to justice. He was in on the raid that started it all, before the FBI took over. When the shooting started, they were outside, just shooting at anything that moved. He said it was like one of those old carnival games, where the metal ducks pop up and you shoot them. He saw movement in a window, turned and fired. He was pretty far away, but he swears he saw it clear as day, and said the image won't ever leave him. It was a middle-aged woman, he still doesn't know who it was, and he got a perfect head shot. Saw the splatter on the far wall as she dropped out of sight." The room was dead silent for a moment. "Says he hasn't fired a gun since then," Jason continued. "He tried to quit the agency, but they gave him some office job instead. They told us he got some injury that kept him from doing operations. It was a lie. He told me that flat out. Killing that lady messed him up bad. He started drinking a lot. His wife left him." Jason didn't want to talk about it anymore, and the room was quiet for a long time.

"There's someone up there," Doug suddenly whispered.

"It's your ears playing tricks on you," said Jason. "It's just the rain."

"No, not this time," Doug said. "Someone is calling." They all sat quietly, and then Jason heard it too.

"Oh my God, I think it's Heather!" Jessica choked out. Doug scrambled up the makeshift cinderblock stairs to the covered opening, and pushed the debris out of the way. A dim light flooded in, bright to Jason's eyes, which had adjusted to the dark. Doug disappeared out of the hole, and everyone in the basement sat still. For a moment, Jason considered making a run for the rifle, which now leaned against the far wall, but decided against it. In a minute or two, there was movement outside the hole again. Someone was coming in, and with the light blocked, the room went dark again, except for the keychain light in the corner.

When light came in again through the outside hole, Jessica could just make out the form of Ben's sister, Heather. "I thought I might find someone here," she said. She turned toward David, and the light from outside revealed a huge dark brown patch on her dress, from her stomach down the front of her skirt.

"Oh, no!" David said, jumping to his feet.

"It's okay," Heather said. Her voice was weak, but she sounded almost as cheerful as ever. "It's stopped bleeding now. It went across sideways," she said, drawing a line across her stomach with her finger. "That was a close call, but it didn't hit anything important." Jason was amazed. This little old lady, completely drenched from the rain, wounded, after having staggered around in the woods alone for who knew how long, seemed perfectly cheerful.

But as Heather glanced around the room, her smile faded. "I was hoping I would find more people here," she said.

David shook his head sadly. "This is it," he said. "They got Ben first. And then Josh, and Halen, and Keith. Carl and Tarzan, too."

"And who might this be?" Heather asked, indicating Jason.

"This is Jason," Doug answered. "He's a fed—or at least used to be, though he's pretty much one of us now."

"How do you do?" she said politely, not seeming very surprised. "I've been looking for survivors," she added. "I found Ben's grave."

"Keith went over and did that last week. We thought you got captured long ago," David said. "Halen looked everywhere for you. We'd have kept looking, but we were so sure ... "

"How did you not get caught?" Doug asked her in amazement.

"I'm a little old, and a little slow, but I still have a few tricks up my sleeve," she answered cryptically, with a wink at David.

Jessica walked over to Heather and put an arm around her. "You're wounded, and soaked," she said.

"If you gentlemen could look the other way for a bit," said Tasha, "we should get Heather into some blankets and look at that wound."

The men obliged, but Jason worried about the old lady. It was likely to get cold at night, and there was no way to dry her clothes down here. They couldn't make a fire in the basement, and they didn't dare make one outside, even if they could get something to burn.

The best Tasha and Jessica could come up with was to help Heather out of her wet clothes and zip her snugly into a sleeping bag, with a blanket over her wet hair.

"We've got a fine menu of MREs here," David said. "Let's see ... black bean and rice burrito, spaghetti with meat sauce, grilled chicken breast, chicken and rice pilaf, beef enchilada ... "

"You can even have it hot," said Doug. "They come with these magic heater pouches."

"Best of all, there's hot coffee," said Tasha.

"It's like a five-star hotel here," said Heather.

After Heather had chosen her meal and watched the magic heater pouch at work, Doug heated coffee for everyone, and they all focused on enjoying this simple pleasure.

"So this is the dastardly terrorist organization the whole country is so frightened of?" Heather said facetiously. "It's a shame. It's a shame we couldn't have done more good."

The statement surprised Jason. After all this woman had just been through, her main concern was that she hadn't helped the rest of the world enough. "Those people out there," Heather continued, "they've all been whipped up into a frenzy. They're all scared to death of things that aren't a danger at all, and pay no attention to the things they should be afraid of."

"Have you been here before, Heather?" David asked. "I mean, down here, while Hargroves was still alive?"

"I've been to his cabin, but I didn't know he even had a basement," she answered.

"Well, thanks to Willard, we have lots of food, a first aid kit, and a radio," David said. "He had a secret stash hidden behind the wall over there."

"That, I didn't know about," Heather said, "but with Willard, it doesn't surprise me in the slightest. I was only over here a few times. We tried to be good neighbors, but Willard and I didn't get along very well. He seemed so angry all the time. I understood what he was angry about. Still, it makes life unbearable if all you ever think about is what's wrong with the world. He would always talk about how stupid people are, and how bad things were going to get. I know he was frustrated that he could see these things and couldn't do anything about them, couldn't make people listen." Heather looked up at David. "I'm proud of you, dear," she suddenly said with a smile. "That book of yours, that's making some people sit up and take notice. That's why they're working so hard to paint you as the devil. You know what they say: if no one hates you, you're not making a difference."

"Speaking of which," Doug cut in, looking as if he had bad news to report, "I almost forgot. Before all hell broke loose yesterday, I heard a news broadcast. I tried to remember it exactly. They said a group up in Idaho, claiming they were acting on behalf of the Iron Web, has been terrorizing blacks, and even killed a black couple up there. Said it was something about having a new Aryan Nation rise out of the ashes of the failing United States, blah blah blah."

"Well, that's really going to help the Iron Web image," Jason said. "Anyone you know?" he asked David.

"You tell me," said David, in his usual patient way. "I told you what the concept of the Iron Web is. Do you think that concept is compatible with racial violence, or with building any sort of nation? Maybe some people were uninformed enough to assume—without reading it—that my book advocates that sort of thing. There are some groups latching onto the Iron Web's popularity without the slightest understanding of what it means. Or it could be just another false flag operation by the government. There's so much ignorance and so much corruption out there, sometimes it's hard to tell where one ends and the other begins."

"What's a false flag operation?" Jessica asked.

"Ever heard of the burning of the Reichstag?" Doug asked.

"What? I don't think so," Jessica answered.

"Hitler had his own guys burn down the German parliament building, and then blamed it on the opposition," Doug said. "The technique is nothing new. It's called a 'false flag' operation—you do something really bad in such a way that it looks as if your enemies did it. It's a simple way to get public opinion on your side, and governments around the world have been doing it for millennia."

"The name comes from the trick of sending in a ship, bearing the flag of your enemy, and having it do something horrible that you can blame on your enemy," David explained. "After my book became an underground best seller a couple of years ago, the government's been trying to link the Iron Web concept to racism and crime and violence of every kind. Of course, it's idiotic to claim that terrorizing and murdering people is compatible with the idea of people owning themselves, yet most people will blindly accept the connection without a second thought."

"I must admit," Jessica said, "I sort of expected you guys to be a bunch of white separatists or something, though I'm not really sure what gave me that impression."

"Well," said David, "I'm sure you heard the media making those connections every day, and especially if you weren't really paying attention to the story yourself, those connections just stay in your mind by default." He smiled, putting his arm around Tasha. "Yeah, we're secretly KKK members," he joked. "They've started accepting Indians and Filipinos as part of their new diversity program."

Jessica looked slightly embarrassed. "Well, I didn't know what color you were," she said. "I never saw a picture of you or anything."

"That probably wasn't by accident, either," Doug said. "They calculate all these things very carefully. The last thing they want is a picture of Tasha circulating around, as an example of the despicable terrorists who are trying to destroy the world. David, on the other hand," he added in a kidding tone, "he's a pretty shady-looking character; they could plaster his ugly mug all over the place and scare almost everyone."

"And half the country would assume I'm Iraqi," David added.

"I hate to say it," Jason cut in, "but you're right about that vilification stuff. All the agency's press releases are scripted and fine-tuned by special PR guys. We're the good guys, and whoever we're investigating is the scum of the earth. Every word and every image that makes it to the media has to fit that message, though it can't be so blatant that people see through it. The amount of spin they put on stuff has made me uneasy more than once. Don't get me wrong," he added quickly, "I believe in a lot of what the agency does—or at least I used to—but I have to cringe sometimes at how much they spin and twist things to always make the agency look like a bunch of heroic angels."

"What is this, confessions-of-recovering-fascists day on Oprah, or what?" Doug joked.

"Something like that," said Jason ruefully.

"There's just so much that people don't understand, and never even think about," David said. "Trying to clear things up, when people in power are constantly trying to confuse matters, is a tough job. There are so many levels of misunderstanding in most people's minds, that it's hard to even know where to begin. Even the term 'white separatist'—tell me, Jessica, what stereotype does that term bring to mind?"

"I don't know," she said, but after a moment's thought she came up with, "cross-burnings, those white pointy hoods and KKK outfits, mobs lynching black guys."

"Yes. And that's the image that some people want to push, as inaccurate as it may be. The number of cross-burnings and lynchings has been almost zero for decades, but the stereotype remains. Most white separatists just want to hang around with people who are culturally similar to them. When any other group does that—the Chinese, the Japanese, Koreans, Hispanics, blacks, Italians, Irish, Indians—everyone accepts it as perfectly natural. But when whites do it, people think they're evil."

"You're defending the KKK?" Jessica asked.

"Well, I'm not defending everything the KKK might do," David answered. "What I'm saying is that, if people want to hang around only with other people of the same religion, or the same skin color, I think they absolutely have that right. Personally, I wouldn't want to limit my acquaintances that way, but I don't think I have any right to foist my own preferences onto others. If all the black people in some neighborhood want to limit their patronage to only black-owned businesses, that too is their right, even if it seems silly to me, or puts me out of business. In fact, if some group wants to go around saying that they're the best Sneetches on the beaches, they can go right ahead. If they want to say that they're a super race and everyone else is inferior, I have no right to stop them. The only time they become my enemies—the only time it's justified for anyone, inside or outside of government, to use force against them—is when they decide to try to forcibly rule, or assault, or rob, or kill someone else."

"The leftists claim to be tolerant," Doug whispered to Jessica, but in a voice loud enough for all to hear, "but this guy is even tolerant of the goddamn KKK."

"But he's not defending lynching or anything else violent," said Jessica. "Just their right to hang out with each other and express their ideas. So I guess I'd have to agree."

"I own myself, and they own themselves," David responded unapologetically. "As far as I'm concerned, they can say or do whatever they please. As long as they leave others in peace, I'll leave them in peace."

"Man, he's not kidding," Doug said. "Remember that guy at the lumberyard who called you a 'nigger'?" he asked David, who chuckled.

"Yes, he didn't seem very well informed about which insults go with which ethnic backgrounds," David joked. "Didn't know a nigger from a dothead. But why should I care if someone wants to call me names? I'm a little more concerned about the people trying to rob and control me."

"Doesn't the KKK share a lot of your complaints about the government?" Jason asked. "And maybe that common ground makes people associate you with them."

"To a point," David answered, "but like a lot of groups that object to the current regime, if you put them into power, they'd just establish their own flavor of tyranny. Nobody likes being beat up on, so it's no great virtue to oppose your *own* oppression. If you don't value freedom *in principle*, liberty for your friends and enemies alike, then there's nothing noble about you. People don't understand that, which is how you get people like Fidel Castro and Che Guevara. They start out by using the flag of freedom to resist the old tyranny, only to turn around and support a new tyrannical regime. They love their *own* freedom—who doesn't? But they couldn't care less about freedom in principle. That's why history is just a long string of oppressions, toppled by resistance movements, and then replaced with new oppressions. The American Revolution came close to being an exception to the rule, but even that eventually led to an empire that was worse than the one before. Whenever someone claims to be a freedom fighter, you have to ask yourself, is the guy fighting for *everyone's* liberty, or just for his own? If it's only the latter, then he's just another tyrant waiting to happen."

It suddenly occurred to Jason how much David's words also applied to law enforcement. It felt good taking down the bullies who hurt other people. But when cops were the ones doing the bullying and the hurting, what then? How often had he looked the other way? How often did *all* cops look the other way? Was being a cop about fighting injustice, or just about being the biggest kid on the block? Jason thought he now knew the answer to that question, and he didn't like it.

"Back to your question," David went on, "the KKK, if given the reins of power, would do just what the government is doing now, with a different flavor of oppression. However, they're still right regarding a lot of things that they complain about, like taxes, gun control, and one of their favorites, legislative coercion being used to benefit one race over another, even though they just want the chance to do the same thing in the other direction."

"You mean stuff like affirmative action?" Jessica asked.

"Yes. I'm not a fan of coercion, even when it's given a nice-sounding name," David responded. "I don't know if you know this, but I was a dentist for many years, and a good one, too. When I went to school to learn dentistry, I wrote down on my registration that I was Caucasian. The lady there, trying to be nice and helpful, told me to change it to Indian. It's an advantage to be a minority, she said, not a disadvantage. But I told her, that's exactly why I won't put that down. Either my accomplishments alone qualify me, or I don't want to be there. Hell will freeze over before I ever stand by while someone is forced to employ me, or forced to let me into a school, because of my ancestry. I'd rather they said, 'We don't want your kind around here.' It would be less insulting than getting so-called 'help' via government coercion. If anything should offend a minority, that's it: a bunch of elitists telling them, 'You can't possibly succeed unless we give you a head start.' And yet the politicians who say that always get the bulk of the minority vote."

"I never thought of it that way," Jessica said. "I guess what the whole thing implies is pretty insulting. But what do you do about the white guy who won't hire someone just because he's black?"

"Why do anything?" David asked. "No one has a right to a job, and no one has the right to force an employer to hire anyone. How would you like it if one day the government told you that it would be deciding, based upon racial and religious diversity, what restaurants *you* were allowed to go to, what convenience stores you could visit, and so on? You would have to make sure that thirteen percent of the mall stores you go to are black-owned, or the government will fine you or imprison you. Sound justified?"

"Of course not," answered Jessica.

"Well, it's the same thing. However short-sighted, bigoted, or just plain stupid I think someone is, how he spends his money, and who he chooses to associate with, is entirely up to him. I own me, he owns him." David paused for a moment. "I wish you could have met Carl. He wrote an amazing piece about the exploitation and victimization of subcultures by government."

"The what and what of what?" Jessica asked.

"Sorry," David said, laughing. "I'm talking about how tyrants target groups that really do have legitimate complaints, feed whatever bitterness and resentment they have, and use it to increase the government's power over those very same people, and everyone else. It's a fascinating topic, and Carl was a true scholar. I think he even surpassed Walter Williams and Thomas Sowell."

"Never heard of them," said Jessica apologetically.

"A couple of uppity niggers who left the plantation," Doug said bluntly. Doug's politically incorrect language bothered Jason, and looking over at Jessica, he could see that she was also a bit shocked.

"What he means is that they're two very intelligent black gentlemen," David said, shooting Doug a disapproving glance, "who've been writing for a very long time about how politicians who pretend to care about minorities are the biggest threat to them. What Doug here meant by his somewhat less than tactful choice of words is that those who pretend to want to help minorities, mostly the leftist politicians of the last few decades, are the biggest racists and bigots around—modern-day plantation owners, if you will, who are using the black race to serve their own power and greed. When a black person sees through the bill of goods the leftists have been selling

**287**

them for decades, the socialists and their media pawns will demonize that person and try to take him down. In the old days, the plantation owners called them 'uppity niggers.' Today they're accused of self-hatred, or being 'too white'."

Jason still remembered the euphoria of the Obama campaign, followed by depression, food shortages and civil unrest. As a child, he'd gone to school with black kids, played with them, and felt comfortable with them. Now a word like "nigger" could lead to fighting in the streets. The word made him shudder, even as a joke.

"I wish Carl were here to explain it," David went on. "And Carl— he was black as can be, I mean physically. He was born in Ghana, and came to this country when he was a few years old, and was discriminated against by blacks and whites alike. He scoffed at the so-called 'African-American' agenda, which teaches that equality can come only from begging the government for goodies and favors, and from using the force of law to make things fair. Carl wrote about how the supposed solutions to racism and poverty offered by the collectivists had done more damage to minority communities than even overt slavery had. The welfare state, the war on drugs, gun control, the education system, and all the other supposedly benevolent government programs have been the driving force behind the illiteracy, illegitimacy, crime, violence, and drug addiction that are so high among black Americans. And yet the people who made all that happen, knowing full well in advance what the results would be, still get the great majority of the black vote. People who live in ignorance and poverty, whose parents lived in ignorance and poverty, and whose kids are living in ignorance and poverty today, are still more worried that someone somewhere might be calling them the 'n' word than they are about the conniving criminals, both black and white, whose lust for power has all but destroyed the self-reliance and self-respect of millions of American blacks."

"Ya know, I once heard a black girl at my school say something like that," Jessica said. "I wasn't really sure what she meant at the time, but she said something like: the best way to keep someone down is to keep giving him things that he hasn't earned."

"Smart girl. And I bet she got her share of grief for saying that, too," David suggested. "Anyway, the point is, if people are to be free and happy, then everyone—black and white, male and female, old and young, rich and poor, ignorant and educated—has to accept the fact that every individual owns himself, and that no one owns anyone else. Only when we understand that truth, and stop trying to use the beast called 'government' to try to coerce others into making the choices *we* think they should make, will true civilization ever survive."

"You make it sound so simple," Jessica said.

"It *is* so simple," David responded. "The only thing that makes it complicated is the constant collectivist indoctrination cranked out by the media and the schools. True freedom and self-ownership is the simplest, most self-evident thing in the world. It's so obvious that people have to be constantly trained to *not* see it. It's the belief in authority that depends upon mental gymnastics, ignoring obvious contradictions, and engaging in ridiculously complex and convoluted rationalizations, to try to justify one group of people ruling another."

The room fell silent again, and Jason pondered what David had said. Yes, there was some truth to it, but the real world couldn't really be that simple. What would a world look like where no one was in charge, where each person just made up his own rules? Surely that would just lead to chaos, and even more violence and crime than ever. It was hard for him to imagine any other type of society without government.

**BETSY** sat on Sandy's couch, nursing a hot cup of tea and trying to "decompress," as Sandy called it. She felt as if she'd chickened out. Grant had hypnotized her and spoiled her grand exit. Now she would be leaving on his terms instead of her own.

"So, after all we talked about," Sandy said, "he still sweet-talked you into staying. Gotta give it to that guy—he's a master."

"No, it's not like that at all," Betsy protested. "I'm still leaving, just not until after tomorrow. He just wants me to see him into office, for old times' sake, I guess."

"Yeah, unless he begs and pleads for another week, or a month." Sandy sighed, looking exasperated. "He thinks once he's president, you won't be able to resist working for him. Bet, that's what these people do. They're masters of manipulation and control. Power freaks, every last one of them. If you don't break this off now, Mr. Charm will drag you along forever."

"But you weren't there," Betsy objected. "This was different. *He* was different. He was—" she hesitated, not wanting to say the word, "—sincere."

"Oh, please. A sincere politician?"

"It was just weird," Betsy said, unable to find adequate words. "He didn't even try to disagree with me or argue about it." After a pause, she added, "He kissed me on the forehead, which isn't like him at all."

"He did what? If only he were married, you'd have some good blackmail ammo," Sandy commented. "Sounds like a scandal to me."

"Look, I'm serious," Betsy said, cracking a smile. "It wasn't like that. Look, I just can't leave now. I promised I'd stay until tomorrow, and I will. But I promise, I'm outta there the day after that. Deal?"

"Cross your heart?" Sandy asked, sounding skeptical.

"Hope to die," Betsy answered cheerfully, drawing the sign of an "X" across her heart with one finger.

Sandy poured more tea through a strainer into Betsy's cup. Sandy was a connoisseur of exotic teas and coffees, and she scoffed at tea bags.

"Wonderful tea, Sandy," said Betsy. "Totally decompressing."

Sandy smiled. "So tell me more about what you thought of the book," she said.

"Well, it wasn't at all what I expected. I just kept waiting for the author to start sounding like an angry terrorist, and advocating violence, and he never did. The truth is, it's all about *non*violence."

Sandy smiled. "I know. He makes it all so obvious, you wonder how you didn't see it before. Hey, maybe you should tie up Senator Slick and make him read it."

"He already has," Betsy said.

"Are you sure?" Sandy asked. "How do you know that?"

"He told me, just yesterday."

"And he still keeps throwing out all those lies? What a scumbag."

"I guess. It was really weird, though. He mumbled this quote, something I think I've heard you say before—something about when people say they want to save the world, they really just want to be the one in charge."

"Mencken?" Sandy asked.

"Yeah, that's it," Betsy said, recognizing the name. "That's what he said."

"Mein Führer is quoting H.L. Mencken now?" Sandy asked in wonder. "Wow. That *is* weird. When he starts spouting Albert Jay Nock, let me know."

"Who?"

"Never mind."

"Anyway," Betsy said with a sigh, "the day after tomorrow, I pack up my things, and I'm gone for good. I've had enough."

"Shrug, Dagny, shrug," Sandy said with a smile.

"What?"

"Forget it," Sandy said. "While you're unemployed, I'll give you some more good stuff to read—there're some other authors I'd like you to meet: Ayn Rand, Nock, Lysander Spooner, and a few others."

Betsy laughed as she sipped her tea. "You're expecting me to be out of work for a while, aren't you?"

**JESSICA** woke up and looked around the dark room. There was the sound of someone snoring, but no other movement or sound. She decided the others must all be asleep. There hadn't been enough blankets to go around from the stash they had found, but the men had insisted on making the three women fairly comfortable at their own expense. Heather seemed very tired, and hadn't even finished the ration they gave her. Jessica thought the MREs were surprisingly good, despite being down there for who knew how many years. She had to wonder whether Heather wasn't doing worse than she let on.

For a long while Jessica lay in the darkness, wondering what time it was. It was always fairly dark in this windowless hole, but she could see some light between the boards above, telling her that it was morning. It seemed like ages since anyone had been outside, and she thought that someone should at least take a peek, to see if anything was happening they should know about. They hadn't done a very good job of covering the opening again after Heather showed up. Luckily, they'd had no unwelcome visitors.

Sitting up, she suddenly felt something on her leg. Looking down, squinting in the dim light, she saw a large wolf spider, the spread of its legs well over two inches, perched on her thigh. On any other day, in any other place, she would have been terrified. She would have tried to kill it. But the world had changed a lot for her in the last few days. She just sat there calmly watching it. What would have been a source of terror before was now just an irrelevant little distraction. She knew that wolf spiders were relatively harmless. This creature had probably lived down here all its life, and this group of giants, thousands of times its size, had invaded its environment. The thought of killing it was suddenly distasteful to her.

Eventually the spider crawled off of her and wandered into the shadows. When survival itself was uncertain, she now realized, little else mattered very much. She tried to think of anything in her previous life that really mattered. Her family and her friends, they mattered. Everything else—grades, clothes, hair styles, winning races and getting blue ribbons—all seemed so unimportant now. Thinking back, she couldn't imagine how she'd ever thought that any of those things mattered so much.

She slowly got to her feet, careful not to bump her sleeping companions as she disentangled herself and her blanket from those next to her. The air in the basement was cold. She gently placed her blanket over Jason, who didn't have one. If she was going to die here when the men with guns and bulldozers showed up, she wanted to at least see the outside world again first. It was probably too early for anything to be happening outside. Without thinking too much about it—because she knew it was not really a good idea—she decided to sneak outside for a moment. They had rigged up a makeshift bathroom in the basement the night before, hanging an old tarp as a screen, so she couldn't use that as her excuse for going outside. But she had to go out, she had to go see the world again, maybe for the last time.

She crept over to the cinderblock stairs. When she put her foot on the first step, it made a crunching, grinding sound. She winced and froze. But there was still no sign of any other sound or movement, so she continued. An inch at a time, feeling like a tiger stalking its prey, she crept up the stairs until her face was at the mass of sticks and leaves that served as a door. Looking through a tiny hole in the debris, she could see woods, dimly lit, as if the sun was about to come up.

She carefully moved the debris, one leaf or twig at a time, widening the opening until she could stick her head out. The sound of birds was everywhere, and the ground looked like silver velvet, with a thin sheet of dew covering everything. Gathering her determination, she climbed all the way out as quietly as she could.

The morning was still and peaceful, except for the chattering birds. For a long time, she just stood, looking around. Finally, pushing all thoughts of danger from her mind, she started to walk, with no particular destination in mind. Distracted by the beauty of the woods at dawn, she hardly noticed the chill. Something off to her left caught her eye, and she looked over to see a striped skunk calmly waddling along, not twenty feet from her. She watched the creature for a while as it rummaged through the leaves for food. Then she kept walking.

None of this area was familiar, and she wasn't really paying attention to where she was going or how to get back. She was taking a break from worrying and thinking, and just enjoying being alive. She could see the edge of the woods ahead, and the golden light of the rising sun to the east was just starting to illuminate the tops of the trees in the woods across from her. She didn't see anyone around, and strolled out into the open. Her eye caught movement again, and far off to her left she saw the mother deer and her two young ones, which she assumed were the same ones she had seen before, from Doug's house.

She wondered if the doe was pregnant with her next fawn, and what the youngsters would think when they were displaced by a tiny new baby. She remembered when her own mother brought her baby brother home.

She wondered how anyone could justify bringing hatred and bloodshed into such a place. Scanning the area, she could see the wreckage of Doug's once-beautiful home, and in the distance, the blackened ruins of Ben's cabin. Off to her right she could just make out two other houses in the distance, though she didn't know whose they were. Despite the signs of yesterday's chaos, Mother Nature's beauty shone through. Jessica wished she could stay in this paradise forever, and have the rest of the world just leave her alone.

And then it hit her: wasn't that exactly what all of these people had wanted? The people she had met—Ben and Heather, David and Tasha, Doug and Josh, even Keith and Halen—they hadn't come here to cook up some scheme of destruction, or to plan terrorist acts. They came here hoping for one thing: to be left alone. At that moment, it seemed to Jessica that the supreme right above all others was the right to be left alone. Keith and Halen were like the skunk, she thought. Their defenses were formidable, but if you didn't threaten them, you had nothing to fear from them. And the rest of us, she thought, are like the deer: all we can do is run and hide.

And why hadn't this little neighborhood been left in peace? Because some kids were supposedly smoking some pot. That's what led to all of this? That was why all the men with guns and the armored vehicles had come here? "They needed to show everyone who's boss," Jessica said quietly, but aloud. "They needed to show that *everything* is their business, that everything and everyone belongs to them, and that any who resist them will be destroyed." It was no different from a gang staking out its territory. You hurt a few people and scare the rest, and every once in a while make a show of force to let people know who's in charge.

"I own myself." She pronounced it slowly and carefully, as if understanding the words for the first time. It really was that simple. Whom had she harmed? Whom had she ever robbed or hurt? No one, except for the red-headed agent who had tried to kill her. What possible excuse could there be for anyone to have tried to harm her? Laws and badges didn't make it okay. She had the absolute right to be left alone. "Everyone has the right to be left alone," she said out loud.

"Jessica!" The sound of her name being urgently whispered snapped her out of her train of thought, and she turned to see Jason at the edge of the woods behind her. "What are you doing? Come back," he said. His voice sounded urgent and frightened. She turned and walked slowly back in his direction. Seeing Jason in the daylight made her wonder what she looked like herself. His face and clothes were muddy, and his hair disheveled. His brown eyes were full of anxiety.

"You had no right to come to this place," she said when she was close enough.

"What do you mean? I woke up and didn't know where you were," he said, looking confused and a little angry about the scare she'd given him.

"I don't mean now, I mean at all," she said. "You, and all the other agents, you had no right to come to this place. You brought death and destruction here," she added, pointing to the ruined houses in the distance.

Jason was breathing hard, making clouds of mist, as if he had been running around looking for her. He said nothing for a while, as he got his breath back. "I know," he said at last. "I know that now. I didn't understand when I came here." He looked up and scanned the horizon, looking nervous again. "And the ones who have this place surrounded still don't understand it, so please come back to the cabin." She nodded, and the two of them walked back through the woods, Jason nervously jumping at every snap of a twig, and Jessica calmly taking in the scenery.

Jason had always meant well. Jessica was sure of that. Even back when he came here with the rest of the feds, he must have thought he was doing the right thing, she thought. There was no malice or hatred in him, even at the beginning when he didn't know what was going on. He was obviously attracted to her, but there was more to it than that. He wasn't the kind of person that Halen had warned her about, the kind who wanted other people under their feet. He treated people with respect and sympathy, even when he disagreed with their beliefs. He'd really believed there were violent criminals back here, she thought, or he wouldn't have come. He just didn't know it was all a big lie. And how many lies had she herself believed before falling into this place?

He's a good man, Jessica thought, and she felt a little bad for chastising him for believing the wrong thing. Hadn't he changed his mind in the face of evidence, when a lesser man would have clung stubbornly to being right? Maybe this is what Halen would have been like, what he *had* been like, before prison, and war, and Andrew. He had gone from government enforcer to freedom fighter. Now Jason seemed to be headed down the same path, for whatever it was worth at this point.

When she and Jason finally reached the hole leading down into the basement, Jessica could hear voices inside. She hoped that she hadn't caused too much concern, but she was still glad she had come out to greet the world again. Jason held her hand to steady her as she climbed down the steps into the darkness.

"You gave us quite a scare," Heather said, her smile looking more strained than usual.

"I'm sorry," Jessica answered. "I just had to—" She couldn't put into words what had compelled her to do it, so she didn't finish the sentence.

"While you were gone, we got some more news," Doug said, and his expression told her that the news wasn't good. "It was on the radio just now. Last night, around sunset, about thirty or forty guys who were on their way here to help us were intercepted. It sounds like there was a massive gun battle."

"I didn't hear a thing," Jessica said, amazed at the news.

"It was almost ten miles down the road. I'm not sure where they were coming from. Anyway, a bunch of feds went to stop them, and things got really bad really quick. I think only seven or eight of the guys survived, and I'm sure they'll be in prison for the rest of their lives. But the media is talking about between forty and fifty federal agents dying in the fight. Of course, who knows whether they're telling the truth?"

"If the story is true," Jason said, "by now agents will be swarming the whole area for miles around, with itchy trigger fingers. Maybe the National Guard, too, if not the Army. Now that the sun is up, they'll bring in everything they have. They won't leave a blade of grass standing."

"Well, if anyone was waiting for the cavalry to arrive," David said, "I think you can stop waiting." With that, the room went silent.

⸺⸰⸺

**JASON** had gotten an old kerosene lantern to work, after some tinkering, to supply a little more light than Doug's keychain. It sat on a cinderblock in the middle of the room. By that time enough rainwater had seeped through the ground that there were several large puddles along two of the walls of the basement. Jason had the radio on, with the volume very low so that only he could hear, in case anything of importance came on. The mood in the room was one of defeat and hopelessness.

"No one's ever gonna know what happened here, are they?" Jessica asked in a quiet, tired voice. Jason wished he had some words that could comfort her, but he didn't. He remembered all too well his promise to get her out of this alive, but he couldn't bring himself to repeat that empty promise now. "My folks will never know that I wasn't killed in the plane crash," Jessica continued. "The world will forever think that Iron Web terrorists killed me." Jason watched Jessica as she spoke. As dirty and bedraggled and sad as she was, her face still enchanted him. "My dad voted for Collins," she said. "The big law-and-order guy. He'll be cheering the loudest when the government comes in here and kills us all." Jason felt a physical pain in his heart as he watched Jessica break down and cry. "He'll never know," she sobbed.

Tasha and Heather went to sit on either side of Jessica, and put their arms around her. Jessica's case was the most tragic, Jason

**300**

thought, and he imagined the others thought so too. She'd been thrown into this situation completely against her will, and snatched from the jaws of death only to die a couple of weeks later. And she was so young.

"The victors write the history books," said David, sounding resigned and hopeless at last. "Soon little boys and girls across the country will be told the story of how the courageous and noble federal law enforcers defeated that band of violent terrorists. Barring a miracle, we'll just be one more lie in the history books."

"Cheery thought," Jason said, wishing David had something more hopeful and inspiring to say, at least for Jessica's sake. He motioned to David and Doug to come sit with him, farther away from the women. If they had to talk like this, he reasoned, he could at least try to keep Jessica from hearing it.

"Well, that's how it's always been," David said softly as he sat down. "Kids are taught to praise and adore tyrants, and taught to hate any who resist them. We make fun of it when other countries put their own spin on history. We're stunned that anyone could still think that Josef Stalin or Chairman Mao was a good guy. But this country does the same thing, teaching our kids to adore tyrants like FDR and Lincoln."

"Lincoln?" Jason asked. Was nothing sacred to this man?

"Yeah, that deified crusader for freedom and justice," David commented in an offhand way. "Just another tyrant with a good PR program."

"You're not gonna tell me he didn't really free the slaves now, are you?" Jason asked. He was happy to talk about anything that would distract him for a while.

"Well, since you asked, he didn't," David replied. "The great Emancipation Proclamation, which I assume you've heard of, only declared slaves free in areas *not* controlled by the Union. It wasn't a great victory for freedom; it was a military tactic, one used by lots of tyrants before Lincoln, including King George: tell your enemy's slaves that if you win, they'll be free. It's a fine way to cause havoc on the other side, but it has nothing to do with principles."

Jason sighed. "Is there anything I learned about this country that you aren't going to tell me was a lie?"

After a short pause, and an attempted smile, David said, "If I can think of anything, I'll let you know."

"Whatever you do, don't get him started on FDR," Doug said.

The voice of the news reporter coming from the radio, even at that low volume, suddenly caught Jason's attention. After a moment, he said, "Uh, David, you'd better hear this," and turned up the volume so that the others could hear it.

The reception was clearer than it had been before, and the words easy to understand: " ... released by the Justice Department show that he was convicted of corrupting a minor and statutory rape, and was investigated but not charged regarding another allegation of soliciting sex from young boys."

"Why exactly do I want to hear this garbage?" David asked. "Who are they talking about?"

"You," Jason answered. He turned down the volume as the reporter moved on to some other story. "Before I could turn it up, they said your name, and mentioned your book." After that, the room fell silent again.

"You wonder if it's true, but you don't want to ask," David said at last. It was a statement, not a question. "It's brilliant, really," he went on. "Totally evil, but brilliant. You hardly know me, so it's perfectly reasonable for you to wonder if it's true. It's not, of course. Pure fabrication, start to finish. But accusations like that, however baseless, are very powerful propaganda tools. How many people out there will doubt for a second what the media is feeding them? How many borderline sympathizers will distance themselves from the concept of the Iron Web after hearing this? The media could announce that I single-handedly exterminated a small, non-existent country, and most Americans would eagerly believe it, and cheer for my execution. So easily manipulated. So easily deceived."

"God, I don't know how you can be so calm about this," Doug said. "If someone said that about me, I'd go completely ape-shit."

"But why would they make that up?" Jason asked. "I'm not saying they didn't, but why make up something that's easy to disprove?"

"It either means they think we're already all dead," Doug suggested, "or it means the order has been given to kill anyone they find in here. Who's going to refute their lies if we're all dead? History will remember us as the most despicable villains imaginable." Jason wanted to tell Doug that his claim was absurd, but he knew it wasn't.

"This country will cheer our deaths," David answered quietly. "I guess I should be glad that I at least got my book published. Maybe some people will read it, and at least wonder if the official story is true. If it doesn't get banned, that is."

The words from the radio again caught Jason's attention. "They're doing all the inauguration ceremony stuff. It sounds like Collins is going to be on in an hour," he said. He picked up the radio and turned the handle a few times, to give it a full charge.

"Is it really that late?" Doug asked.

"Yeah, it's inauguration day," David replied. "It slipped my mind, but in just a bit he'll be sworn in."

"Great," Doug said. "Führer Collins is about to accept the crown, and we all know how he feels about us." He scrambled to his feet. "I'm gonna have some beef ravioli before he comes on. Anyone else hungry?"

Jason wasn't. He was in too much pain to eat, though he did feel thirsty. Infection was burning up his shoulder, and he felt generally feverish and weak. But he did his best not to let on. Everyone had enough worries, and what difference would it make now anyway?

"Could I have something hot to drink?" Jessica asked.

After some bustling around with food and heaters and making coffee for six with three cups to drink from, they all settled down again. For a long time there was silence except for the tinny sound of the radio. Jessica sat down next to Jason. "Do you mind if I sit here with you?" she asked softly.

A smile appeared on Jason's sweaty, dirt-smeared face. "I think I could tolerate that." He put his good arm around her shoulders, and pulled her close. Jason never would have imagined that he could feel this peaceful and content while knowing he was almost certainly about to die. Jessica laid her head on his shoulder and he felt her tears soaking into his shirt.

**BETSY** sat off to the side of the stage, out of view of the cameras, ready to hear the inaugural speech she knew almost by heart. Only a few hours earlier the decision had been made, due to fairly severe-sounding weather forecasts, to have the address indoors. Now, after quite a bit of hectic re-planning and rearranging, things were ready to begin. Nearly every member of Congress was in attendance in the giant, grandiose hall, and the gallery beyond them was packed tight with people who had no doubt come from all over the country to witness this historic event.

Grant Collins strode up to the podium. This was the moment of glory they had both worked so hard for. Just a few weeks ago, she had looked forward to this moment with great anticipation. Now she felt the excitement trying to sweep her away, and she resisted it. She knew the truth now. The presidency was everything to Grant. He was willing to throw away truth, justice, and innocent human lives to achieve that goal, as so many others had done before him. She had wanted so much to believe he was different.

Grant gripped the podium, and for a moment just stared into space. All eyes were riveted on him. Then he stepped around the podium and walked up to the very edge of the stage. Betsy saw the cameramen far back in the room suddenly adjust their cameras to follow Grant. She glanced back at him, confused, knowing he couldn't possibly read the teleprompter from there. What was he doing? He folded his hands in front of him, straightened his posture and lifted his head.

"I lied to get elected." There was no shame or apology in the tone of his voice. A murmur began in the room, and for a moment Grant said nothing more. Betsy had been all ready to hear that finely polished inaugural speech, and this certainly wasn't it.

"Of course," Grant continued, holding up his hand to silence the crowd, "lying to get elected doesn't make me any different from anyone else who has acquired a position of power in this government." Betsy scanned the faces of the congressmen, many of whom were now whispering among themselves. There were some looks of anger, some of nervousness, and some of complete bafflement. The words he was saying did not compute. It didn't sound like a joke, nor did it sound like a confession. What was Grant doing?

"I didn't come here to talk to these crooks," Grant said with a dismissive wave of his hand toward the hundreds of senators and representatives before him. Then he pointed up toward the TV cameras and civilian spectators in the back of the room. "I came here with a message for *you*." At this there was much clamor and movement among the congressmen, but given the situation, it seemed that none of them dared to stand up or openly protest.

"All politicians lie," Grant continued. "You know that. But there is something very different about me, and something very different about today." He paused again for a moment, scanning the faces before him. "You see, every other politician lies, and promises to take care of you, and fight for you, and give you goodies, in order to trick you into giving him power. But despite the noble intentions they put on for show, all politicians have only one goal: to be the ones holding the reins of this control machine."

Betsy didn't dare to believe what she was hearing. Was this really happening? Grant was always good at using attention-grabbing tricks, but this didn't seem like a trick. He spoke now, not in the usual pompous, elitist politician tone, but like a man who meant what he was saying.

"Well, not me," he continued. "Unlike everyone else who holds high office here, I didn't climb my way here—with all the usual lies, empty promises, backroom deals, and other scheming—in order to acquire power for myself." For a moment, Betsy thought maybe he would segue into a sermon about "honest government." But then he went on. "No, I didn't come here to seize the power for myself. I came here to *destroy* it."

At this, the entire room broke into a murmur. "Shut up," came Grant's booming but controlled voice, and the noise level in the room dropped to almost nothing. "I have a few things to tell you that you probably aren't going to want to hear. Shut up and listen."

A brief giggle involuntarily burst out of Betsy's mouth. This was unbelievable. Not exactly presidential, she thought, but she was starting to enjoy herself.

"Fourteen years ago," the President continued, "a friend of mine bet me two million dollars that I couldn't become a U.S. senator. And when this guy bet two million dollars, he meant it. We had always talked about whether it was possible to infiltrate this little tyrannical club called the United States government, and strangle the abomination from the inside. He said it wasn't; I said it was. Five years later, I was a state senator in Pennsylvania, running for United States Congress." He paused and looked down at his feet. "That's when I heard that my friend had been murdered." He paused again. "You see, my friend was fighting tyranny from the outside, which is a dangerous thing to do. He was using his connections and his money to expose the political crooks of this town for what they are. Needless to say, the control freaks here didn't take kindly to that. So the FBI made up a false charge, and when they went to get my friend, he wouldn't surrender. So they killed him." His expression was determined and unflinching. "It didn't make the news."

"After that, I kept going with the bet, not for the money anymore, but for my friend. I swore to myself, even if it took the patience of Job, that I would get so deep into the beast that I could reach its heart. And here I am." He held his arms wide, and the murmur began again. This time he ignored it.

"To get right to the point," he went on, letting his arms drop to his sides, "this thing you call government, this god that you pray to, to solve all the problems in your life, this pretended protector and savior, this stinking heap of anti-human oppression that you so eagerly subjugate yourselves to—if anything was ever the epitome of pure evil, this is it. Trouble is, most of you are too stupid to see it. You still worship it, pay tribute to it, and allow it to chain you, shackle you, control you, and monitor you. Instead of thinking for yourselves, you're constantly clamoring for some new leader to save and protect you. Your cowardice and irresponsibility built this monster. It commands, and you obey, like good little slaves. And worst of all, you hold up your unthinking obedience as a virtue; you believe it makes you good people. It doesn't. It makes you stupid robots."

Betsy's attention was on the rows and rows of representatives, many of whom were now looking around the room nervously; a few were trying to be discreet while frantically whispering into their cell phones, and two or three looked as if they were about to walk out.

"Well, I'm here to rudely foist freedom upon you, whether you want it or not. I'm going to tell you things you don't want to hear. I'm going to do things you don't want me to do. You don't have to worry too much, however, because I won't be in office long, and once I'm gone, I'm sure most of you will scramble back into slavery and government-worship as quickly as you possibly can. You'll eagerly flock to the next lying politician who promises to take care of you, throw away your freedom to the next political con man who promises you security. And you will reap the rewards of your own ignorance. I can't save you from your addiction to subservience, and I don't intend to try."

"But there are some of us, however few, who actually *want* freedom, who would rather face an uncertain world as responsible adults than live as slaves in a cage. And now we're going to do it. As for the rest of you, all you have to do is stay out of our way. If you insist on putting shackles on yourselves, be my guest. But you will no longer put them on those of us who choose to be free."

"Now it's time for a little irony. *You* believe that by pushing buttons in voting booths, you give certain people the right to rule you. In reality, I have no more right to rule any of you now than I did yesterday. I'm still only human. Yet, for some reason, you accept it as undeniable gospel that governments have the *right* to rule you, that the Constitution gives moral permission for these liars and thieves to meddle in your lives," he said, gesturing at the congressmen sitting in front of him. "You accept that they own you, and have the right to take what you produce, to tell you what you may and may not do, and to tell you what you *must* do. You refuse to see the truth: that neither constitutions nor voting booths nor legislative rituals can give anyone the right to rule you. You own yourselves, but most of you don't even *want* to. You feel more comfortable being the property of politicians. Well, now I'm going to use your blind faith in this enslavement system against you."

From the expressions she saw in the crowd, Betsy knew that at that point, many of the politicians there would have loved nothing more than to forcibly drag Grant off the stage, and if he was anyone other than the President of the United States, they probably would have done it.

"As newly elected Chief Executive Officer of this bizarre power cult," Grant went on, "my first act will be to sign these pieces of paper." He walked over to the lectern, leaned down behind it, and brought out a bunch of papers and held them above his head. "By the power vested in me by your insane belief in authority," he said, setting the papers on the lectern and writing on them, "I am hereby firing every employee of the IRS, the ATF, the DEA, the TSA, the CIA, the NSA, the ICE, most of the FBI, and a bunch of other federal agencies, some of which you've never even heard of. These executive orders are all perfectly legal, for those of you who believe in that sort of thing." A confused murmur arose again in the crowd. Some faces were openly angry, many were confused, but Betsy noticed, with some surprise, one elderly congressman grinning widely.

"While we're at it," he continued, leaning down and hoisting a huge box from behind the lectern, letting it slam onto the floor in front of him, "here are a million or so presidential pardons, for all those now in federal prison for tax crimes, or on drug charges, or weapons charges—basically, anyone who's been locked up for a victimless crime, which includes most federal inmates. I'll be signing all of these in the coming days." The murmur rose to a dull roar. "Shut up," Grant boomed. "I'm not finished."

**JESSICA** sat in stunned silence as the fading lamplight lit the other five shining, sweaty faces around the damp cellar.

All eyes were wide, mouths open, as the small group listened to the new President addressing the nation.

"It's pathetic how you people still imagine this to be a free country." The voice was slightly distorted, and accompanied by significant white noise, but was easy enough to understand. "There's hardly a single thing or activity left in this country that the parasites haven't gotten their tentacles into. You can't lift a finger without government permission, and without them taking a cut. The kid who sells lemonade in his front yard is breaking half a dozen different laws. You can't produce anything, sell anything, trade anything or build anything, without paying fee after fee, jumping through hoop after hoop, filling out this form and that form, getting this license and that permit, going through all the inspections, groveling before regulators, and then hoping that whatever moronic bureaucrat you end up with decides to give you his holy permission to do what you had the God-given right to do to begin with. And you call yourselves free?"

"God, is this for real?" Doug whispered, and was instantly shushed by everyone else in the room. The voice on the radio continued.

"U.S.A.! We're number one!" came the voice from the radio, in an obviously mocking tone. "Hooray for the pathetic, washed-up, hypocritical, falling-apart slave state that is the United States of America. Exactly what is it about this sheep pasture that you think is still worth celebrating? What the hell do you think that flag represents anymore? What the hell are you proud of? Proud to live in the country with the most intrusive, obnoxious, abusive tax collectors in the world? Proud to live in a country that has a higher percentage of people in prison than any other country in the world? Proud to be ruled by a government that has started and perpetuated more military conflicts in more areas of the world than any other in history? Proud to live in a country where the politicians and bankers have seen to it that you, your children, and your children's children will forever be their indentured servants, to be forever herded and fleeced like sheep? Proud to live in a country where the biggest slimeballs on the planet tell you what you can eat, what you can drink, what you can drive, what you can build, where you can work, what you can produce, and what you can think?"

"Did you know about this, David?" asked Jason.

"No, of course not. Be quiet," came the response. The radio voice went on.

"When July Fourth rolls around, and you're all swigging your beer and waving your flags, does the fact that we are infinitely *less* free than we ever were under British rule ever make its way into what's left of your brains? Hooray, the land of the free, where half of what you earn gets swiped by politicians; where you fall for every crisis the liars in D.C. throw at you. They create problem after problem—war, recession, terrorism, poverty, crime, disease, environmental disaster—and you are such well-trained sheep that time and time again, you demand your own enslavement as the solution. Two hundred years ago, Benjamin Franklin told you that those who would choose temporary security over essential liberty deserve neither. Well, you did, and now you have neither, and it's just what you deserve. You looked to the biggest crooks in the world to be your all-powerful saviors, and now you are paying the price."

"I know first hand how easy you are to deceive and manipulate. You elected me because I pitched the same lies all the parasites in this town do, only I did it more convincingly, and with a slightly slicker presentation. I promised to save you from the economic depression that the government caused. I promised to save you from the wars that the government caused. I promised to save you from the crime that the government caused. I promised to save you from the terrorism that the government caused. I promised you, if you would just accept me as your master and give me control of your lives, that I would save you from all the scary things you could imagine, real or made-up. I used the same lies and deceptions that every politician does; I just did it a little better than the others this time. And while I was duping you, I was also convincing the powers that be, the people who run this whole show behind the scenes, that I would make a good stooge for them, that I would be a good puppet and dance to their tune. Otherwise, I never would have even been on the ballot."

"You voted for me because it comforts you to have someone tell you that if you'll only bow to him and give him unlimited power, he will make all your problems go away. That is the lie you always fall for: that if you just find the right leader, he can make the world a safe, happy place. But that is never their intention, and that is never what they do. They make the world a scary, dangerous place, to ensure that you will forever remain dependent upon them and their so-called solutions. And you keep applauding them as they commit the worst of atrocities based on what they say are the best of motives."

"And what about you, my fellow Americans? What are your motives? You pretend that the things you ask of government, you ask from the best of intentions. You only want to feed the poor, to protect the innocent, to punish the wicked. Or so you say. But if your intentions are indeed so pure and noble, why is it that you fail to notice the damage done by the government's so-called solutions? Haven't you noticed what government welfare has done to the poor, reducing millions of people to stupid, empty shells, without purpose and without hope? Haven't you noticed that the government schools crank out millions of ignorant kids whose one lasting talent is the ability to mindlessly do as they're told? Haven't you noticed that the government's economic solutions, from socialist redistribution to the fraudulent banking system and its fake money, have impoverished this once-prosperous nation? Haven't you noticed that everything the government touches turns to shit? If your motives are pure, why have you not noticed that every time you entrust these challenges to rulers and masters, they end up enslaving the poor, oppressing the innocent, and empowering the wicked? Are you just profoundly unobservant, or is it something worse than that? Could it be that your desire to help others and to fix society is outweighed by your desire to escape the uncertainties and responsibilities of living life as a free human being? Is that why you keep voting for whoever pretends he can save you from reality and magically save you from whatever the future might hold? Why else would you continue to fall for the patently ridiculous lies that all of the politicians keep telling?"

"In your lifetime, every election has been nothing more than that: a contest to choose the better liar. None of them ever meant a word they said. They all had one goal: to rule you. But you never caught on. They kept feeding you a choice between two slimeball crooks, one colored red and one colored blue, and you kept proving that you were too stupid to see through the scam. You kept advocating your own enslavement, unable to comprehend the possibility that you might have the power to do something other than just choosing one of two tyrants to run your lives. Let me make this perfectly clear: if you voted for me—or for my opponent—you're a gullible idiot. You fell for the same tyrant tricks that the megalomaniacs of the world have been using for thousands of years."

"And I'm not expecting to talk you out of your illusions here. These days I'd be more likely to get converts out of a herd of lemmings than out of the American public. No, I'm not here to stop you from enslaving yourselves. I'm here to stop you from enslaving that miniscule minority of Americans who still understand what freedom is, and who still yearn for it. Amazingly, despite the constant authoritarian indoctrination cranked out by the so-called education system and the media in this country, there are still a few people here who value freedom. You've heard of them. They're the people you love to despise and insult. They're the kooks, the extremists, the people who won't get with the program or go with the flow. They're the black sheep, whom you look upon with scorn for wanting to step out of the shearing line. They don't fit in. They're the lunatic fringe. They're not like you."

"No, they're *not* like you. They dare to state the truth. You don't. They can think, and you can't. Every inch of progress in history has been their doing, and they've had to constantly fight upstream against all the insults, condemnation, and outright violence which the dull-witted majority, made up of people like you, has thrown at them. *They* ended slavery, while people like you sat idle. No, it wasn't that fascist, Lincoln.

**315**

*They* put an end to women being treated like animals, while people like you called them names. *They* spoke out against the injustices of regime after regime, while the supposedly good citizens just quietly did as they were told. *They* resisted the war-mongering, of this country and countless others, while people like you either condoned or turned a blind eye to mass murder. *They* put themselves in harm's way for the sake of truth and justice, while people like you quietly avoided making waves. No, they are not like you, those extremists and radicals. *They* have taken on the responsibility of being human beings, while you have remained content to be stupid animals."

In the dimness of the cellar, all eyes had been glued to the radio, as if there was something to see there. Jessica glanced over at David. His head was bowed and his eyes were closed, a smile on his face and tears rolling down his cheeks. For the first time in what seemed like forever, she felt a twinge of hope.

---

**JASON** had just heard the President of the United States fire him, and every other ATF agent. Did this mean they might get out of there alive after all? He tried to picture the other agents out there—how were they reacting to this? Would they all just give up and go away? Or were some of them too juiced-up and bent on revenge to accept the President's order? He wasn't ready to believe that it was safe to come out of hiding, but just then, the possibility that he might live to take Jessica out for lunch or a movie seemed overwhelmingly wonderful. Just minutes before, he hadn't dared to hope for even such a simple thing. But he also hardly dared to believe what he heard coming out of that old radio on its cinderblock stand.

"You glorify people such as Thomas Jefferson and George Washington, Benjamin Franklin and Patrick Henry," the voice on the radio continued. "But have you ever read a word they said? They were all too authoritarian for my liking, but by today's standards they were anti-government extremist terrorists. They advocated breaking the law. They said that when a government infringes on the rights of the individual, the people have a right and a *duty* to do whatever it takes, even if that means bloody revolution, to get rid of that government. Would anyone like to claim that the government we now have is a protector, not a violator, of individual rights? The Founders taught how important it is for the people to remain armed, and to always retain the ability to forcibly overthrow the government if it becomes oppressive. Those kooks, wackos, and extremists that we call our Founding Fathers committed *treason*, advocating violent, illegal resistance against their own government, the British Crown. And over what? A few puny little excise taxes on tea and pieces of paper."

"And what have *you* done with the country they gave you? Today you tolerate a level of oppression and intrusion far beyond King George's wildest dreams, yet you cannot even imagine engaging in passive resistance, much less forcible revolution, in defense of your own freedom. The bravest thing you'll ever do is walk into a booth every few years, where no one can see you, and press a button, to say which of two slave-masters you'd rather be owned by. And when some radical does suggest that it's time to grow a spine and resist this heinous empire, you all rush to be the first to condemn that person. Like well-trained slaves, you take pride in your subservience and obedience, while despising those few who have the will to try to escape the plantation, or worse yet, to overthrow the master. If the Founders could see you today, they'd be ashamed of you for the opportunity you threw away, the freedom they won for you which you have so thoroughly squandered. Samuel Adams might as well have been talking to all of you when he said, 'If ye love wealth better than liberty, the tranquillity of servitude than the animating contest of freedom, go from us in peace; we ask not your counsels or arms; crouch down and lick the hands which feed you. May your chains sit lightly upon you, and may posterity forget that ye were our countrymen'."

Jason looked around the room. In the dim lantern light he saw alert, attentive expressions on all of the faces around him.

"Land of the free and home of the brave?" came the voice from the radio. "Hardly. You are a nation of enslaved cowards, afraid to act, afraid even to think. You keep telling yourselves that you, the American people, are independent, strong, brave, and free. You are none of the above. Again, I don't expect one speech to change your narrow minds, but before you put your heads back in your rear ends—before you switch the channel to some inane trash approved by the Ministry of Truth, guaranteed to keep you distracted and stupid—I have something to say, and you had better listen close."

It still didn't seem real to Jason. The tinny little sound of that radio, compared to the larger-than-life devastation, death and destruction he had seen first hand—it couldn't be real.

"Some of us still love freedom," the President said. "Some of us believe that every person belongs to himself. We don't belong to your stupid collective or to your crooked politicians, and we don't need your permission or legislation from your masters to be free. We don't care what you think. We don't care what this bunch of dishonest jackasses sitting in front of me thinks."

It suddenly occurred to Jason that this rant was happening right in front of Congress, and he tried in vain to imagine how they were reacting to all of this.

"We feel no need to refute the government worship that you imagine to be learned opinions," the President continued. "We're done asking you to let us be free. I'm here to *tell* you, we *will* be free. And if you want to parrot back the rhetoric you've been fed all your lives, about how society can't exist without rulers, about how there would be death, destruction and mayhem if no one was controlling all of us, you go right ahead. Predict doom and gloom until you're blue in the face. Tell us it can't be done all you'd like. And if time proves you right, you can feel smug in your little cages while you say, 'Told ya so.' Or, if time proves us right, as it will, you can watch the *second* great American experiment from a safe distance, and see what humanity could be, without masters and slaves and the false gods you now bow to."

Jason's mind was still a bit on the defensive, suspiciously watching out for the types of cunning propaganda designed to justify lawlessness, the types of rhetoric used by cult leaders to dupe the ignorant. While this renegade president was probably saving Jason's life, that didn't mean he had to agree with him. He felt as if he was floundering in a sea of unfamiliar ideas. Whenever he thought he'd found something solid to stand on, a wave came and washed it away. He'd lost count of the times since he'd been here that he thought one of David's ideas was ridiculous, only to discover, on closer examination, that it made a lot of sense.

He'd heard Grant Collins speak before, and he always sounded good. Jason wasn't much into politics; he just knew that Collins was a big supporter of law enforcement. But Collins sounded different now. He didn't sound like a politician manipulating public opinion, but like a real man honestly expressing deeply held convictions. And, as much as Jason resisted admitting it, even to himself, it felt like the truth—an honest, raw truth he had never heard spoken aloud before.

"You wave your flags and give lip service to freedom, but you wouldn't know freedom if it slapped you in the face. In fact, it *did* slap you in the face, and you called it a terrorist cult, and demanded that it be stamped out. Do you see this symbol? You were told it's the insignia of a terrorist cult, and despite the fact that the truth was one book-read away, most of you just believed what you were told."

"He's talking about your book," Doug said to David in an excited whisper.

"This symbol is nothing more than a way of expressing a very simple, but profoundly important, concept: I, the one displaying this symbol, understand that I own myself, and that you own yourself. It's that simple. My life, and everything I do with my life, belongs to me, as yours does to you. We are free human beings, not domesticated animals. We do not acknowledge anyone's right to own us or to rule us, and likewise, we claim no right to own or rule over anyone else. That's all it means."

"And, contrary to what you were told, this image does not represent some monolithic cult, where everyone believes the same thing about everything. It's about understanding one simple, basic truth of humanity, on top of whatever else someone happens to believe: that it's wrong to start a fight; that it's wrong to be the one to first use force, even if you hide it under the label of 'government.' And that simple belief can be held by all sorts of different people with all sorts of different viewpoints, from goth punks, to hippie flower children, to conservative Christians, or to any average Joe, and to everyone in between. That's the reason for the many colors on the design. Freedom doesn't require us all to be the same. Instead, it allows us all to coexist peacefully *without* being the same. You don't have to agree with everyone else on everything; you don't have to like everyone else. I know I don't. All you must do, to be a piece of the Iron Web, is acknowledge that each person owns himself, and that it is wrong to initiate force or fraud against him, no matter what you think of his religion, his culture, his race, his intelligence, his age, his behavioral choices, his income level, his hairdo, his taste in music, or anything else. We view and treat each other as adult human beings, each responsible for his actions, each obligated to judge right and wrong for himself. We detest the alternative: the giant daycare center that so many of you seem to prefer, where a bunch of whimpering brats whine about their 'needs' and demand preferential treatment based on some twisted, delusional notion of 'fairness,' while at the same time begging the nanny to punish the kids they don't like."

"You evade your responsibility as human beings by hallucinating a false god that relieves you of the duty to think for yourselves. You don't *want* to be free, because being merely obedient requires so much less thought. And so you *demand* to be ruled, you *insist* on being enslaved. Then you beg your masters to please be nice to you. Pathetic. Well, some of us have outgrown such schizophrenic insanity. Some of us realize the self-evident truth that no election, no constitution, no legislation, and no other pseudo-religious political ritual can bestow upon anyone the right to rule another. Nothing can make a man into a rightful master; nothing can make a man into a rightful slave."

Jason turned to look at Jessica's face. She was smiling now, and her eyes were shining with hope. Doug got up and went to the entrance. He went up a couple of steps and pushed the debris away from the entrance hole. The sunlight of a clear day flooded through the gap, lighting up six dirty but hopeful faces.

"Using violence against someone who has committed no force or fraud is wrong," came the voice from the radio. "What could be more self-evident than that? Some people call the concept 'libertarianism.' I have another term for it: stating the bleeding obvious. It's wrong to start a fight. You can call the aggressors 'government,' you can pretend that they represent us all, you can whine about the common good, you can label the bullies 'law enforcers,' and you can call their violence 'law,' or 'regulation,' or 'taxation,' or whatever you like. It's still wrong, and some of us have been trying to explain this to you for centuries. Guess which extremist fringe kook terrorist said this: Quote: *Rightful liberty is unobstructed action according to our will within limits drawn around us by the equal rights of others. I do not add 'within the limits of the law' because law is often but the tyrant's will, and always so when it violates the rights of the individual.* End quote. Imagine that: you can do whatever you want, as long as you let other people do what they want. How extreme. Thomas Jefferson was the radical who said that. He also wrote, in the Declaration of Independence—maybe you've heard of it—that when a government becomes destructive of individual liberty, the people have the right, and the *duty*, to alter or abolish that government. So, how many of you have lifted a finger to resist the federal leviathan? Or are you still telling yourselves that the United States government is pro-freedom? How long will you tell yourselves that lie?"

"Even those of you who consider yourselves rebels, most of you seem to think that acting obnoxious and rude qualifies you as nonconformists, yet you end up as nothing more than useful puppets of the establishment you rail against. From the hippies of the sixties, to the eighties punks with pierced noses and purple hair, to the so-called revolutionaries of today, generation after generation of hip, cool rebels have whined about the status quo, only to turn around and embrace the old, heinous evil of communism, just because it came in a new package. Under the labels of 'social justice' and 'economic equality,' you pitch the same sick, twisted, vicious collectivist oppression implemented by Stalin, Lenin, Mao and Castro. Only you're too ignorant to know it. Even when you can see the evils of a particular regime, you can't escape the mindset of authority worship. Your solution is always to find a new, kinder, wiser master. It never occurs to you that there is no such thing, and *can* be no such thing, as a good slave-master. It never occurs to you to get rid of the tyrannical master of the day and replace him with *nothing*—to yank the despotic king off the throne and to put *no one* in his place—to leave the throne empty. And so, when the people tired of that delusional, god-complex, collectivist, war-mongering lying thief George Bush Sr., they replaced him with Bill Clinton, a delusional, god-complex, collectivist, war-mongering lying thief. And when they got tired of him, after eight years, they put in yet another tyrannical Bush—this one worse than the first—for eight more years. Even the spectacle of having to choose between John McHitler and Barack Ostalin in 2008 wasn't enough to shake the American people out of their blind faith in the cult of democracy."

"A long time ago, Lysander Spooner explained that a man is no less a slave simply because he is allowed to occasionally choose a new master. But you didn't listen. You still believe that your precious right to vote means that you are free. It doesn't. It means only that your masters have found a way to trick you into not resisting, by giving you the illusion that you have some say in what they do."

"H.L. Mencken told you that the urge to save mankind is almost always a front for the urge to rule, but you didn't listen. Time after time, crooks have posed as saviors, and you kept falling for it. Louis Brandeis, when he wasn't rubber-stamping the politicians' socialist agenda, warned that we should be most on guard to protect our liberties when the government's purposes are beneficent. But you weren't listening. Every new goodie, every promise to give something to the needy, to help this or that group, to save the economy—you fall for them all, hook, line and sinker. Two *thousand* years ago, even Plato gave the warning, saying that every tyrant, when he first appears, is a protector. But you weren't listening."

"Alexis de Tocqueville warned that the American Republic would survive until Congress realized it could bribe the people with their own money. But you didn't listen. You still vote for whatever con man promises you the most pork, the best handouts, the most goodies, all of which are paid for with money he stole from you in the first place. Likewise, you weren't listening when Frederic Bastiat warned you that government is the great fiction, through which everyone tries to live at the expense of everyone else."

"Frederick Douglass, a former slave, explained that no man can put a chain around the ankle of his fellow man without eventually finding the other end fastened to his own neck. But you weren't listening. You all clamor to see who can be first to beg government to impose all manner of laws and rules upon your neighbors, and in the process you end up advocating your own enslavement. Mr. Douglass also explained that whatever level of injustice and wrong people will quietly submit to is exactly the level that will be imposed upon them. But you weren't listening."

"Edmund Burke proclaimed that all that is necessary for evil to triumph is for good people to do nothing. You've probably even heard that one, but you still didn't listen. Albert Einstein put it another way, saying that the world is a dangerous place to live, not because of the evil people, but because of the people who don't do anything about it. But you weren't listening. What have *you* done to resist the evils you see in the world, or even in your own country? Hide in a corner to avoid trouble? Keep your head down and try not to make waves? Sophie Scholl, member of the White Rose, an underground group in Germany which spoke out against the Nazis, described the situation quite well. The real damage, she explained, is done by the millions of people who just want to survive, the honest men who just want to be left in peace, who don't want their little lives disturbed by anything bigger than themselves, who don't want to make waves or make enemies. Sophie and her friends had their heads chopped off for daring to say such things, while the hordes of compliant cowards in Germany did nothing. And are you any different from them? You people who live in the land of the free and the home of the brave, when have you lifted a finger to oppose the injustice you see? Or have you even noticed it? Are you so busy getting along and doing what you're told that you can still imagine this to be a free country? Have you not noticed the trillions of dollars the American tyrants steal every year? Have you not noticed the millions of non-violent people who now live as captives behind razor-wire fences? Have you not noticed the hundreds of thousands of people abroad they have exterminated? Have you not noticed their tentacles creeping into every aspect of your lives? Have you been wearing your blinders for so long that you can't see what's going on all around you? As John Hay pointed out, and as millions of people have learned the hard way, the evils of tyranny are rarely seen except by those who resist it. Do you think the fact that you personally haven't gotten into trouble yet, because you're too much of a chicken-shit to even rattle your own cage door, means that you're free?"

"Martin Luther King Jr., when he wasn't falling for collectivist propaganda, explained that true peace is not the absence of violence, but the presence of justice. But you weren't listening. You look around, and you don't see the open strife and violent conflict that exists in many other countries, and you interpret that to mean that we have peace and freedom here. It means nothing of the sort. It means only that most of the victims of oppression here aren't *resisting* it. And that is not a sign that you are strong and free; it is a sign that you are weak and cowardly. When the peasants quietly do as they're told, the violence underlying all government remains hidden. It is only resistance that brings it out into the open. The master doesn't need to whip the obedient slaves, but that doesn't mean those slaves are free."

"For millennia, radicals have been trying to tell you that as a human being, you were born to be free, that your rights do not come from any law or any government, and that it is your right and duty to preserve liberty for yourself, to allow others their freedom, and to never let the schemes and deceptions of would-be tyrants fool you into choosing the predictable, secure life of a caged animal over the uncertain, challenging life of a human being. But you didn't listen. Well, some of us are tired of trying to get you to listen. We're not going to ask you to let us be free anymore. You can continue to choose slavery for yourselves if you wish, but we choose freedom."

By silent agreement, the group had slowly and quietly moved outside into the clearing, still listening to the radio, which David carried out. The ground was still damp, but the sunshine was warm. Doug brought out the M1 Garand and placed it within easy reach; apparently he also had some doubts about all the agents packing up and going home without a fuss.

Jason leaned back against a tree trunk, exhausted. He guessed he was going to need some antibiotics after all.

**BETSY** continued to stare in amazement at Grant. As if it corresponded to his shedding of his official, presidential persona, he had shed his tie and suit jacket while talking. Around thirty congressmen had actually walked out. Those who remained were now sitting, completely dumbfounded, without moving or talking. Grant began to unbutton his dress shirt, as if just for comfort. The audience watched in fascination as he worked his way down to the last button, finally opening the shirt to reveal a black T-shirt beneath bearing the rainbow-colored symbol of the Iron Web.

"Here's the deal," he continued, in a relaxed, down-to-earth tone of voice, "in terms even Joe Six-Pack can understand. So as to not upset your little cages of dependency and delusion, those of us who actually like freedom will be forming small communities across this country. And this symbol will tell you who we are," he said, holding open his dress shirt to display the symbol underneath. "If you believe in the divine right of politicians, stay away from us. If you send your thugs after us, we will not take you to court, and we will not try to vote different people into your 'government' cult. Instead, we will exercise our right of self-defense. Not only will we use whatever force it takes to repel the aggressors you send at us, but we will also hunt down and execute whichever so-called 'legislators' gave them the order to initiate violence against us. Yes, you heard me right. If you leave us alone, we'll leave you alone. Wherever you see this symbol, keep your tax collectors, your regulators, your cops, your inspectors—and every other brand of parasitic bureaucrat your statist machine cranks out—away from us. That's all you have to do. And if you do that, you have nothing to fear from us."

Betsy could hardly believe what was happening. How could she have not known about this, or at least suspected it, when she thought she knew Grant so well? How could he have hidden this from her so well and for so long? Although she felt a hint of hurt at his deception, it was overwhelmed by a feeling of vindication. He really *was* different. In fact, more different than she had ever imagined. Some of what he said made her uneasy, even scared. It was so far outside anything she had ever even thought about that she could hardly even process it. If not for Sandy throwing radical ideas at her for the last year or so—and even *her* ideas seemed moderate compared to this—Betsy wondered whether she would have understood what Grant was saying at all.

"When I leave this stage," he continued, after taking a sip of water from a glass hidden inside the lectern, "and you desperately try to recapture your delusional little worlds of obedience and conformity, I will be heading out to Graveston. And since, by Executive Order, I just fired every employee of the FBI and ATF, I will personally shoot any jackboots who are too stupid to leave before I and my friends get there. As some of you know, I was in the Marines. I have since lost my penchant for blindly following orders, but I have not lost my combat skills, nor have the people who will be coming with me. Whether or not anyone inside is still alive, anyone I see in the area wearing a government uniform I will shoot on sight."

Grant gripped the podium, paused for a moment, looking up into the ceiling lights. Then he lowered and shook his head.

"You cannot begin to imagine in how many ways the world is the opposite of what you have been taught to believe." His voice was very low now, but amplified so everyone could hear it. "You see the guy who sells drugs to willing customers so he can feed his family as the scum of the earth, while you see the hypocrite who gives away stolen money in the name of government as a saint. You see the guy who tries to avoid being robbed by the federal thugs as a crook and a tax cheat, but see as virtuous the politician who gives away the same stolen loot to people to whom it does not belong. You see the cop as a good guy when he drags a man away from his friends and family and throws him in prison for ten years for smoking a leaf, and you see anyone who defends himself from such barbaric fascism as the lowest form of life—a cop-killer. In reality, most drug dealers are more virtuous than any government social worker, and prostitutes have far less to be ashamed of than political whores, because they trade only with what is rightfully theirs, and only with those who want to trade with them. The upstanding, church-going, law-abiding, tax-paying citizen who votes Democrat or Republican is far more despicable, and a bigger threat to humanity, than the most promiscuous, lazy, drug-snorting hippie. Why? Because the hippie is willing to let others be free, and the voter is not. The damage done to society by bad habits and loose morality is nothing compared to the damage done to society by the self-righteous violence committed in the name of the state."

"You imagine yourselves to be charitable and tolerant, when you are nothing of the sort. Even the Nazis had table manners and proper etiquette when they weren't killing people. You think you're good people because you say 'please' and 'thank you'? You think sitting in that big building on Sunday makes you noble and righteous? The difference between you and a common thief is that the thief has the honesty to commit the crime himself, while you whine for government to do your stealing for you. The difference between you and the street thug is that the thug is open about the violence he commits, while you let others forcibly control your neighbors on your behalf. You advocate theft, harassment, assault, and even murder, but accept no responsibility for doing so. You old folks want the government to steal from your kids so you can get your monthly check. You parents want all your neighbors to be robbed to pay for your kids' schooling. You all vote for whichever crook promises to steal money from other people to pay for what *you* want. You demand that those people who engage in behaviors you don't approve of be dragged off and locked up, but feel no guilt for the countless lives your whims have destroyed. You even call the government thugs your 'representatives,' and yet you never take responsibility for the evil they commit. You proudly support the troops as they kill whomever the liars in D.C. tell them to kill, and you feel good about it."

"You call yourselves Christians, or Jews, or claim to follow some other religion, but the truth is, what you call your religion is empty window-dressing. What you truly worship, the god you really bow to, what you really believe in, is the state. 'Thou shalt not steal.' 'Thou shalt not murder.' Unless you can do it by way of government. Then it's just fine, isn't it? If you call it 'taxation' and 'war,' it stops being a sin, right? After all, it was only your *god* that said you shouldn't steal and murder, but the *state* said it was okay. It's pretty obvious which one outranks the other in your minds. Despite all the churches, synagogues, and mosques we see around us, this nation has one god, and only one god, and that god is called 'government'."

"Jesus taught nonviolence, and told you to love your neighbor, but the state encourages you to vote for people who will use the violence of government to butt into every aspect of everyone else's life. Which do you believe? To those about to stone a woman who had committed adultery, Jesus said, 'Let him who is without sin cast the first stone.' But the state says it's perfectly fine to lock someone up if they do something you find distasteful, such as prostitution. Which do you believe? The Christian God says, 'Thou shalt not covet.' But coveting is the lifeblood of the beast that is the state. You are taught to resent, despise, and hate anyone who has anything you don't have. You clamor for the state to tear other people down, steal their property, and give it to you. And you call that 'fairness.' The Bible calls it 'coveting' and 'stealing'."

"You are not Christians. You are not Jews. You are not Muslims. And you certainly aren't atheists. You all have the same god, and its name is 'government.' You're all members of the most evil, insane, destructive cult in history. If there ever was a devil, the state is it. And you worship it with all your heart and soul. You pray to it to solve every problem, to satisfy all your needs, to smite your enemies and to shower its blessings upon you. You worship what Nietzsche called 'the coldest of all cold monsters' and you hate those of us who don't. To you, the greatest sin is disobeying your god—'breaking the law,' you call it—as if anyone could possibly have any moral obligation to obey the arbitrary commands and demands of the corrupt, lying, delusional megalomaniacs who infest this despicable town."

Betsy scanned the faces of the congressmen. Most had their eyes downcast, some seemed to be mumbling to themselves, and a few looked almost comatose with shock.

"Even your ministers, priests and rabbis, more often than not, are traitors to their own religions, teaching that the commands of human 'authority' should supersede adherence to the laws of the gods they say they believe in. Several years ago, I heard one pompous evangelical jackass in particular pontificating on the radio that anyone who disobeys the civil authority, be it a king or any other government, is engaging in rebellion against God—those were the exact words he used. What if the government is doing something wrong? Well, this salesman for Satan opined, that is the business of those in government, and you are still obligated to obey. Everywhere you turn, be it the state or the church, the media or the schools, you are taught one thing above all else: the virtue of subjugating yourselves to mortals who claim to have the right to rule you."

"It is sickening, the reverence with which you speak of the liars and thieves whose feet are so firmly planted on your necks. You call the congressmen and the judges 'honorable,' and you swoon at the magnificence of the grandiose halls they inhabit, like this one," Grant said, raising his arms and looking around the room, "the temples they built to celebrate the domination of mankind. You feel pride at being able to say you once shook a senator's hand, or saw the President in person. Ah, yes, the grand deity himself, His Royal Highness, the President of the United States of America. You speak the title as if you're referring to God Almighty. The vocabulary has changed a bit, but your mindset is no different from that of the groveling peasants of old who bowed low, faces in the dirt, with a feeling of unworthiness and humility, when in the presence of whatever narcissist had declared himself to be their rightful lord and master. The truth of the matter, back then and today, is that these parasites who call themselves 'leaders' are not superior beings, they are not great men and women, they are not honorable, they're not even *average*. The people who earn an honest living, from sophisticated millionaire entrepreneurs to illiterate day laborers doing the most menial tasks you can imagine, *those* people deserve your respect. *Those* people you should treat with courtesy and civility. But the frauds who claim the right to rule you, and demand your subservience and obedience, they deserve only your scorn and contempt. Those who seek so-called high office are the lowest of the low. They may dress better, have larger vocabularies, and do a better job of planning out and executing their schemes, but they are no better than pickpockets, muggers and carjackers. In fact, they are worse, because they don't want to rob you of just your possessions; they want to rob you of your very humanity, deprive you of your free will, by slowly leaching away your ability to think, to judge, to act, reducing you to slaves in both body and mind."

"And still you persist in calling them 'leaders.' Leaders? Where is it that you think you're going, exactly, that would require you to have a leader? If you just live your own life and mind your own damn business, exercising your own talents, pursuing your own dreams, striving to be what you believe you should be, what possible use would you have for a leader? Do you ever actually *think* about the words that you hear, the words that you repeat? You parrot oxymoronic terms such as 'the leader of the free world.' Even pretending for a moment that there is some huge journey or some giant battle that everyone in the entire nation is undertaking together that would require a leader, why would you ever think, even for a moment, that the crooks that infest this town are the sort of people you should listen to, or emulate, or follow anywhere? Somewhere inside your mostly dormant brains, you know full well that politicians are all corrupt liars and thieves, opportunistic con men, exploiters and fear-mongers. You know all this, and yet you still speak as if *you* are the ones who are the stupid, vicious animals, while the politicians are the great, wise role models, teachers, and leaders, without whom civilization could not exist." Grant gestured toward the congressmen. "You think *these* crooks are the ones who make civilization possible? What belief could be more absurd? Yet when they do their pseudo-religious rituals, deciding how to control you this week, you still call it 'law,' and continue to treat their arbitrary demands as if they were moral decrees from the gods, that no decent person would ever consider disobeying."

"You have become so thoroughly indoctrinated into the cult of state-worship that you are truly shocked when the occasional sane person states the bleeding obvious: the mere fact that the political crooks wrote something down and declared their threats to be 'law' does not mean that any human being anywhere has the slightest moral obligation to obey. Every moment of every day, in every location and every situation, you have a moral obligation to do what *you* deem to be right, not what some delusional bloated windbag says is 'legal.' And that requires you to first determine right and wrong for yourself—a responsibility you spend much time and effort trying to dodge."

"You proclaim how proud you are to be 'law-abiding citizens,' and express utter contempt for anyone who considers himself above your so-called 'laws,' laws that are nothing more than the selfish whims of tyrants and thieves. The word 'crime' once meant an act harmful to another person. Now it means disobedience to any one of the myriad of arbitrary commands coming from a parasitical criminal class. To you, the term 'crime' is nearly synonymous with the word 'sin,' implying that the ones whose commands are being disobeyed must be something akin to gods, when in truth they are more akin to leeches. The very phrase, 'taking the law into your own hands,' perfectly expresses what a sacrilege it is, in your eyes, for a mere human being to take upon himself the responsibility to judge right from wrong, and to act accordingly, instead of doing what you do: unthinkingly obeying whatever capricious commands this cesspool of maggots spews forth."

Betsy had to force herself not to laugh out loud. Grant was dead serious, but the absurdity of what she was watching unfold before her very eyes was almost too much for her.

"You glorify this criminal class as 'lawmakers' and believe that no one is lower than a 'lawbreaker'—someone who would dare *disobey* the politicians. Likewise, you speak with pious reverence of 'law enforcers'—those who forcibly impose the politicians' every whim upon the rest of us. When the state uses violence, you imagine it to be inherently righteous and just. And if anyone resists, they are, in your eyes, contemptible lowlifes—lawless, terrorist criminals. Like the lawless, terrorist criminals who helped slaves escape thc plantations; like the lawless, terrorist criminals who helped Jews escape the killing machine of the Third Reich; like the lawless, terrorist criminals who were crushed to death under the tanks of the Red Chinese government in Tiananmen Square; like all the lawless, terrorist criminals in history who had the courage to disobey the never-ending stream of tyrants and oppressors who have called their violence 'authority' and 'law.' And that includes the lawless, terrorist criminals who founded this country."

Grant shook his head again, this time smiling, as if in disbelief.

"Everything you think you know is upside-down, backwards, and inside-out. But what has to take the cake—the height of your insanity—is the fact that you view as violent terrorists the only people on the planet who *oppose* the initiation of violence against their fellow men: anarchists, voluntaryists, and libertarians. We use violence only to defend ourselves against someone who initiates violence against us. We use it for nothing else. Meanwhile, *your* belief system is completely schizophrenic and self-contradictory. On the one hand, you teach the young slaves that violence is never the answer, yet out of the other side of your mouths, you advocate that everyone and everything, everywhere and at all times, be controlled, monitored, taxed, and regulated through the *force* of government. In short, you are teaching your children that the masters may use violence whenever they please, but the slave should never resist. You indoctrinate your children into a life of unthinking, helpless subservience. You are putting the chains around their little necks and fastening the locks tight. And worst of all, you feel good about it."

"Out of one side of your mouths, you condemn the evils of fascism and socialism, and lament the injustices of the regimes of

Hitler, Stalin, and Mao, while out of the other side of your mouths you preach exactly what they did: the worship of the collective, the subjugation of every individual to that evil insanity that wears the deceptive label, 'the common good.' You babble on and on about diversity and open-mindedness, and then beg your masters to regulate and control every aspect of everyone's lives, creating a giant herd of unthinking, conformist drones. You wear different clothes and have different hairstyles, and you think that makes you different, yet all your minds are enslaved to the same club of masters and controllers. You think what they tell you to think, and do what they tell you to do, while imagining yourselves to be progressive, thinking, and enlightened."

"From your position of relative comfort and safety, you now condemn the evils of other lands and other times while turning a blind eye to the injustices happening right in front of you. You tell yourself that, had you lived in those other places in those other times, you would have been among those who stood up against oppression and defended the downtrodden. But that is a lie. You would have been right there with the rest of the flock of well-trained sheep, loudly demanding that the slaves be beaten, that the witches be burned, that the nonconformists and rebels be destroyed. How do I know this? Because that is exactly what you are doing today."

"Today's injustices and oppressions are fashionable and popular, and those who resist them, you tell yourselves, are just malcontents and freaks, people whose rights don't matter, people who *deserve* to be crushed under the boot of authority. Isn't that right? You bunch of spineless, unthinking hypocrites. Look in the mirror, take a good look at what you imagine to be righteous and kind. You are the Devil's plaything. The crowds of thousands wildly applauding the speeches of Adolf Hitler? That was *you*. The mob demanding that Jesus Christ be nailed to the cross? That was *you*. The white invaders who celebrated the wholesale slaughter of those godless redskins? That was you. The throngs filling the Colosseum, applauding as the Christians were fed to the lions? That was you. Throughout history, the perpetual suffering and injustice, occurring on an incomprehensible scale—it was all because of people just like *you*: the well-trained, thoroughly indoctrinated conformists, the people who do as they're told, who proudly bow to their masters, who follow the crowd, believing what everyone else believes and thinking whatever authority tells them to think. That is you."

"And your ignorance is not because the truth is not available to you. There have been radicals preaching it for thousands of years. No, you are ignorant because you shun the truth with all your heart and soul. You close your eyes and run away when a hint of reality lands in front of you. You condemn as extremists and fringe kooks those who try to show you the chains you wear, because you don't *want* to be free; you don't even want to be human. Responsibility and reality scare the hell out of you, so you cling tightly to your own enslavement and lash out at any who seek to free you from it. When someone opens the door to your cage, you cower back in the corner and yell, 'Close it, close it!' "

"Well, some of us are finished with trying to save you. We've wasted enough effort trying to convince you that you should be free. All you ever do is spout back what your masters have taught you: that being free only leads to chaos and destruction, while being obedient and subservient leads to peace and prosperity. There are none so blind as those who will not see. And you, you nation of sheep, would rather die than see the truth."

Grant took a deep breath. "Well, don't worry, because after today, I won't be wasting another breath trying to disentangle you from your deeply ingrained superstitions. After your masters come up with some way to pretend that all of this didn't really happen, and to say that I was never really President, and to put a new master on the throne who will control and rob you like in the good old days, I will be happy to let you cling to whatever self-destructive delusions you wish. You can rebuild your government-god, pray to it again to save you from reality, and suffer the consequences, until you, your children, and your grandchildren are all dust. But what you cannot do—what we will not allow any longer—is to inflict the consequences of your inhuman insanity upon those of us who believe in free will."

"Most of us will even do you the favor of removing ourselves from your pathetic little circus of slaves and masters, and go where you can comfortably pretend that we don't exist. But do not follow us. Do not send the unthinking thugs of your masters after us. Do not seek to punish us for refusing to bow down to your false gods. Unlike the games your masters play, sending pawn to kill pawn, we will not waste our efforts on continually fighting the unthinking robots you call 'law enforcers.' We will go to the top, immediately, and lop the head off of your great god. And we will do it as many times as we must. Leave us alone, and you can keep your gods."

"Likewise, we do not want, and will not accept, the stolen goods with which your false gods so easily buy your loyalty and obedience. We will go out of our way to make sure that we do not benefit at all from the looters' game that you now believe to be the foundation of civilization. We won't be using the indoctrination camps you call schools. We won't be using your phony currency or your fraudulent banking system. We won't be participating in any of the trappings and schemes your masters euphemistically call 'programs' and 'benefits.' We don't want your department of this and bureau of that, your inspectors and regulators, politicians and judges, tax collectors and police, or any of the other crooks and thugs which your gods may spawn. We want nothing from you but to be left alone. And we offer you nothing, except the promise that we will leave you alone if you do the same for us. That is what it means to be a human being. And if any of you ever figure that out, and are ready and willing to give up your chains and embrace true freedom, we will welcome you with open arms. Until then, stay the hell away from us."

Grant took another sip of water and put the glass down on the lectern. For a long time he was still, not saying anything, looking as if he was deep in thought. "I just have one more thing to do today," he finally said, quietly, "and then I'll be finished."

He turned to his right, away from Betsy, and made a gesture to someone she couldn't see. Three men then came up on stage, the one in the middle looking weak and a bit sick, the other two holding his arms. They didn't seem to be holding him so he couldn't escape as much as they were holding him so he wouldn't fall down. At this, a new murmur arose among the remaining congressmen. Betsy recognized the Acting Chief of Staff, the man who had taken over the position just six weeks before, after the former Chief of Staff had a heart attack.

"As you should all know," Grant said, turning back to the audience, "this is Clarence Ferris, the former President's Acting Chief of Staff." He turned to the sick-looking man. "I believe you have something to tell the nation." The man weakly nodded to the others holding his arms, and they let go. He walked unsteadily to the podium, his expression fluctuating between terror and anger.

He swallowed hard, looking down at his notes, which he set on the podium. His hands were shaking, and he accidentally knocked over the glass of water, which rolled off the podium and shattered on the floor. No one moved. A tear rolled down the man's cheek. After an awkward pause, he threw Grant a pitiful look, as if he were pleading to be dismissed. Grant's face showed no emotion. "Do it," he commanded.

"I," the man began, but he could barely speak. It was all he could do to go through the mechanical motions of reading his prepared speech. "I have served my country as best I could. I cannot tell you how much it pains me to do this." He took a deep breath, and looked at Grant again. "When I took the position of Acting Chief of Staff, I made recordings of all my meetings with the President." Now his eyes seemed riveted to his notes. "I made ... I made the following recording of the President—the former President, I mean. This was one of our regular meetings concerning domestic affairs. We were discussing the situation in Graveston. He said some things that I ... things that I ... "

"Just tell them what the tape is, and then play it," Grant instructed, firmly, as if trying to bolster the man's courage. There was another long pause.

The man drew another deep breath. "This is a tape I made, without the President's knowledge, of one of many meetings I had with him. Present were myself, the President, and the Secretary of Defense. This meeting occurred January 9, eleven days ago." His hands trembling and tears streaming from his eyes, he fumbled with a small electronic device, until a hiss could be heard over the loudspeakers on the wall behind him.

"Our intelligence sources aren't giving us much to work with." The voice on the tape matched the voice of the man at the podium.

"We don't need any more damn intelligence," came the familiar voice of the former president. "We need action. Don't you get it?"

"The agent in charge says that if we can show restraint a little longer, he thinks a peaceful resolution might—"

"I'm tired of hearing about caution and restraint. I tried that, and Collins made me look like a damn pussy! So now we're doing something different. After this Flight 422 incident, the public will cheer if we go in and take them all out."

"But how sure are we that members of the group were even to blame? I know what we've been saying to the media, but the intel is still—"

"God, when are you going to grow up?" yelled the former President. "You have no idea what's going on, do you?"

"Sir?"

"Quit being such a Boy Scout! You know what a leader is? It's someone who can do whatever it takes to keep the team strong. You have no idea the pressures, the sacrifices I have to make. History doesn't remember those who show restraint and use caution. It remembers the bold victors. What this country needs most right now is unity, and the best thing for that is a common enemy. I gave them that. I gave them something to rally against."

"I don't follow you, sir."

"What do you think every war is? Conflict is what keeps a people unified, keeps a country together. The sacrifices of war, you need them—you need them to keep a country strong. A people without an enemy is a people without a cause. The damn sheep out there needed something to think about besides their pocketbooks.

Whatever the cost, they needed a common enemy to make them pull together and feel like Americans again. Did you think I was going to sit around until Collins gave them that?"

"What do you mean? Are you saying you *wanted* something like this to happen?"

"Wake up, you jackass!" the former President screamed. "Wanted it to happen? I made damn sure it would happen! I made damn sure that those ungrateful little malcontents down in Graveston wouldn't win any more supporters or sympathizers. And it's working like a charm."

Betsy saw looks of shock on many faces in the crowd.

"Sir? What are you saying?" Ferris' voice demanded. "Are you saying you knew in advance about the plans to hijack the plane, and let it happen?"

"No, you dumb-ass! You still don't get it! Get this through your thick skull! *I gave the order to shoot the fucking plane down!*"

With a loud "click" the tape stopped, and the room fell silent. A single sniffle was heard from the man at the podium, who now wept openly, his head hung low. Grant put a hand on the man's back, and without raising his head, the man turned and walked slowly off the stage and out of sight, the two other men helping to steady him.

"You put him into power," Grant said to the audience, his voice low and calm. "In your quest for a savior, this is the kind of person you put into power, over and over again. These are the people you ask to rule you, to protect you. This one murdered one hundred and seventy-eight people because he thought it might help his image. What makes him different is not that he would do such a thing, or that he *did* such a thing, but only that he got caught. Most of the other so-called 'leaders' have done similar things."

"And you put them here. You made them gods, foolishly hoping that the power you gave them would be used for good. Well, let this reality sink in today. Don't hide behind your delusions. Open your eyes. This is the protector and savior you wanted so badly. This is the monster you worshiped. Take a good, long look, and decide if you want more of the same, or if you're ready to be free."

"All your lives, you've been trained to be subservient and obedient. Through years of authoritarian indoctrination mislabeled as 'education,' one message has been constantly pounded into your heads, by parents, the media, so-called teachers, the entire culture. And that message is this: you cannot find the truth yourself; you cannot be trusted to judge right from wrong; you cannot be trusted to make your own decisions. So if anything comes up that might require you to *think*, or worse yet, might require you to *do* something, to take action, don't worry—just huddle timidly in a corner and let the authorities handle it. And now, having been raised to be perpetually infantile, you are existentially terrified of the idea of having to take care of yourselves, having to protect yourselves, having to effect justice yourselves, having to face an unpredictable world without some all-knowing, all-powerful being holding your hand. And so you appoint an imagined authority to save you from reality. But it doesn't, and it never will. It will betray you and enslave you, keeping you forever powerless and defenseless. It's not a fluke. It's the nature of the beast you worship. It's time for you to open your eyes and grow up."

Betsy was still in shock from what she had just heard. How long had Grant known about this? And what kind of will power must it have taken for him to plan all of this, knowing what he knew?

"In the last couple of days, the media has been theorizing about why the former President would not be attending this inaugural address. It is not because he doesn't like me, or because he is upset, or because he's sick. And he is not vacationing at his winter home, as the media believes. He is dead." Gasps were heard throughout the room. Grant held high a piece of paper. "For those of you who believe in such things, here is a copy of the presidential pardon for the man who killed him. It seems that a few people were not willing to let our so-called justice system decide what to do with one of its former gods. I have been informed that tomorrow the media will be told where to find the body of the man who ordered the murder of one hundred and seventy-eight innocent Americans."

A murmur again arose throughout the room, but Grant ignored it. He reached down and picked up his jacket from the floor, where he had dropped it, and draped it over his shoulder.

"As for me, I'm heading down to Graveston, to shake the hands of some of the few men and women—if any are still alive—who have dared to stand up for truth and freedom in a country that now, for the most part, despises those things."

Grant stepped off the stage, walked over to Betsy, and took her hand, a serious, almost pained expression on his face. He spoke so softly then she could barely understand his words. "Of all the people I had to lie to for all these years, it hurt the most to lie to you." Still in shock, but not unhappy, Betsy could only stare at him in amazement. "Since you're quitting now," Grant continued, "I was wondering if you'd like to be my date on a little trip I have to go on."

A smile slowly crept onto Betsy's face, and she managed to choke out, "I'd love to."

# EPILOGUE

**JESSICA** pushed one last cross piece into the hole of a fence post and straightened herself up, exhausted. She knew she was overdoing it, but she kept thinking she'd stop after the next one, and then the next one. This fence had to be done before Saturday, when five pregnant brood mares were being delivered.

Jessica stepped back, removed her heavy leather gloves, and surveyed her work for a moment. Then she turned and walked back toward the house.

She stopped along the way to check on the chicken tractor; the chickens were still scratching happily in the long grass inside their movable enclosure. Jessica couldn't move it by herself, anyway. To keep coyotes from getting in, they'd had to make it really heavy. Next to the new log house was a large vegetable garden enclosed by a six-foot wire fence. It wasn't attractive, Jessica had to admit, but she did enjoy being able to watch deer and rabbits wander through the yard without wondering if they were about to eat all her food.

Jason came out to meet her, and stopped to give her a kiss. "What, you're giving up already?" he teased. She'd been out there for four hours straight.

"Yes, I'm giving up, and you should too," she replied. "We have to get cleaned up for dinner."

"Yes, I know. Tasha's cooking already. I'll be in in a few minutes."

Jessica watched him head for the barn, and hoped he wouldn't forget himself and stay out there for an hour. Jason loved this place and worked outside constantly.

She remembered back to that January day when their hopeful little group of survivors sat around that old radio, listening to Grant's speech. Their euphoria had quickly turned to anxiety when they realized that Jason was dangerously ill. She remembered sitting in an ambulance, holding Jason's hand as a doctor administered IV antibiotics on the spot.

She remembered her first phone call to her family, when they'd all been too shocked and happy to speak. Jessica had refused to leave while Jason was still in the hospital, so her whole family flew down to Arizona to be reunited with her. Eventually conflicts arose when Jessica said that she was staying there at least until Jason was well, if not permanently. The Graveston area, including the river bend neighborhood, was to be one of the new free communities, and she wanted to be part of it. Her parents could not understand why she would want to stay with these "extremists," even if one of them was the President of the United States. They spoke of Stockholm syndrome, and wanted to take Jessica to a psychiatrist for "deprogramming." But she had insisted, kindly but firmly, that she was old enough to make up her own mind, and that her experience with her new friends *was* the deprogramming.

She was smiling, though her legs ached, as she climbed the front steps of her new home. As she walked in from the bright sunshine and her eyes adjusted to the lower level of light, she could hear the tinny sound of an AM radio playing.

"In yet another of a series of ongoing attacks, seven people were killed when the IRS offices in Ogden—" The sound was cut short as David switched it off.

"I thought you hated listening to the news," commented Jessica, dropping her work gloves on the table.

"I do," David answered, "but I still make myself do it every couple of weeks, just to see what's going on."

"Well, it doesn't sound good," said Jessica, flopping into an old recliner. Her smile faded, and for a moment her own ordeal was all too clear in her memory. "Is it even worth all this? Is it ever going to end? I mean, these days even the ones on *our* side seem to be going too far."

"They're not on *my* side," David declared emphatically.

"Well, you know what I mean."

"You have to understand," David said, "this was bound to happen sooner or later. The parasites have been creating this monster for decades, and now it's broken free."

"You don't approve of all the stuff going on out there, do you?" she asked, pointing at the radio.

"No, certainly not. But it doesn't matter what I think of it. I think it's inevitable. It's like some poor dog that's been beaten since it was a puppy. All its life it cowers and whimpers in fear. Then one day, it snaps and rips its master's throat out."

"Thanks for the pleasant image," Jessica said, making a face. "But the dog isn't only attacking the one who beat it. It sounds like even average bureaucrats are dying out there."

"Remember, those IRS paper-pushers have been emptying bank accounts, taking homes, and ruining lives for years and years. The zoning bureaucrats, the inspectors and regulators—they've all been pushing people around for decades, and it all adds up. As long as the cogs in the machine felt comfortable obeying orders, they went right on doing it, oblivious to the harm they were doing and the suffering they were causing, and oblivious to the resentment and anger they were feeding. Their victims had no recourse back then, so they just put up with it. Well, now all their frustrations are coming out as hatred and a desire for revenge."

"I'm not saying the drones who just follow orders are good, but I don't think they deserve to die," said Jessica, frowning.

"Depending on what you mean by 'deserve,' I agree. But when people are oppressed, humiliated, and tormented for all their lives, even if only a little at a time, and even if they barely notice, it builds up inside them. It's like a poison the body can't get rid of. It builds up and builds up, until something breaks. Now it's the French Revolution all over again. People who have been treated badly all their lives, once they reach the point where their anger outweighs their fear, are capable of some pretty heinous things. Like I said, the tyrants created this monster, and now they're paying the price, whether it's fair and just or not."

"You know," David went on, "all those average agents who sat smugly behind their desks, thinking they could ruin hundreds of people's lives with impunity, they're like ... well, they're like a guy who keeps poking a bull in the face with a stick because he thinks the fence is strong. He deserves a kick in the pants, maybe. But if that fence falls, he's very likely to

**348**

get killed. Human nature is like that. I wish I had some magic power to stop it, but it will just have to work itself out."

"And then what? Utopia and peace on earth?" Jessica asked jokingly, her smile beginning to return.

"Well, in all likelihood, if history is any indication, they'll rebuild the beast called 'authority.' They'll have more wars, more oppression, more suffering and more death. And they'll keep right on doing it for centuries to come."

"What are we supposed to do to stop it?" Jessica asked.

"I know of only one thing we can do: show them, by example, that human beings can live without worshiping monsters. A few might pay attention. Most won't."

"Speaking as a recovering fascist," came Jason's voice from the doorway, "I agree." Jessica hadn't heard him come in. "I know from experience that it takes a lot to change a person's view of reality." He walked to the window and looked out. "It's just so easy to assume that what you were raised to believe is the truth, and that anyone who thinks otherwise should be forced to conform to your viewpoint. Of course, when lots of people with different beliefs do that, the results aren't pretty."

"Wow, you've come a long way, pawn of the oppressor," David chuckled. "Next you'll be saying we should each be true to our own conscience and not bow to any outside authority."

"What do you think I am, some kind of anarchist or something?" Jason said with a smile. "Well, I'd like to stay and repent of my past sins, but I need a shower before dinner." He headed for the back of the house, stopping at the kitchen for a moment to speak to Tasha.

"Why is this so hard to understand?" Jessica said after a moment. David's look said he wasn't sure what she was referring to. "I mean, the idea seemed really weird to me at first, that everyone is just in charge of themselves. I really believed that someone has to make rules and laws to tell the rest of us what we can and can't do. Now that seems so stupid, and what you say seems so obvious."

"This is how it's been for a very long time," David replied. "Even those who have been openly enslaved throughout history were usually completely convinced that they were *meant* to be slaves. Many slaves would actually view running away as stealing from the master, the same way most Americans view not paying taxes as some great sin. Wanting to keep what you earn for yourself, or to spend it or give it away however you choose, instead of giving it to the parasites who claim to own you, is still viewed by many as a crime. It's utterly insane, but billions of people still believe that by being born in a certain place, they somehow acquired an obligation to surrender a portion of their time and effort to a group of people claiming to be their rightful masters. It's the divine right of kings all over again. And yes, once someone has broken free of the delusion, he can see the insanity of it, and he will wonder how he ever could have been tricked into believing something so ridiculous." From outside came the sound of children laughing. "I think back myself, back to when I was a run-of-the-mill conservative, and I wonder how I could ever have clung to such an absurd superstition, and why I tried so hard to cling to it when the truth started making itself known to me."

Jessica got up and looked out the front window. Her next-door neighbor's children were playing catch with Cassie, the golden retriever she and Jason had adopted.

"I'd better get cleaned up too," she said. "I guess we can talk all we want at dinner." She stopped in the doorway, looking back at David. "I just wish the rest of the world would listen."

"Yeah, wouldn't that be neat?" David asked, but his smile looked a little sad.

---

**JASON** stood still, deep in thought, in the middle of the spot where Doug's house had been. A hundred yards away, out back, was a huge black area in the field where they had burned all of the useless debris. They had cleared away everything except for half of the cinderblock foundation, which had survived the onslaught. Nearby was a big pile of what they'd decided was reusable lumber, piping, cinderblocks, and other materials. The new house was still in the designing phase.

Months earlier, Jason had stood in a room, just above where he stood now, and watched a Bradley come through the wall. He had experienced the terror of being on the government's hit list through no fault of his own. He had experienced for himself what hundreds of millions of others had experienced throughout the bloody history of man's oppression of man. He had come face to face with the force of government. Take away the spin, the propaganda, and the euphemisms, and the message is: Comply or we will crush you under our tank treads.

It made Jason shudder to think that he'd once been on the government's side, that he could have killed Halen, or David, or Doug, or Josh. Or even Keith, whose bitterness he understood now, all too well. Suddenly his mind flashed back to a moment he'd forgotten entirely until just then. He was sitting next to his ammo box, loading his rounds one by one, pondering the power of each and every bullet to end a life and asking God to help him make the right decisions. And in the end, he hadn't fired one shot. He touched the tiny silver cross at his throat. "Thank you," he whispered.

Jessica came up behind him and put a hand on his shoulder. "You guys about done here?" she asked.

"Yep," he said. "I think we've got everything usable out of here."

Doug was playing frisbee with Veronica while Sandy sat by a tree, sketching. Sandy was designing a memorial garden where Ben's house and garden had been.

"How do they do it?" Jason asked, still deep in his thoughts. "How do they make people hate each other? How do they make us unwilling to just leave each other alone?"

"They have to keep us from seeing other people as real human beings, like ourselves," Jessica answered. "It's hard enough to comprehend that everyone in this world really matters as much as we do. I think human beings are all too ready to believe that some other group is a bit less human than they are, and that makes it okay to be mean to them or exploit them, or kill them, to make life better for us. And government makes up lies to push us down that path further and faster."

Jason scowled. "How many people are out there having wars, killing each other by the thousands, because some authority keeps telling them to hate each other, and keeps inventing things to divide them and pit one group against another? We're supposed to be so enlightened and informed. Why do we keep falling for it?"

"You're sounding more and more like David every day," Jessica commented with a smile.

"I'm just amazed that I ever believed in all that crap," said Jason. "I was so convinced that making people obey the law was a noble cause. I was so sure, I would have killed people, people who hadn't harmed anyone else. Now that all seems utterly insane to me."

Jessica was surveying the area thoughtfully. "I want to plant a tree over there by the tool shed," she said. "Where we found your friend."

"Red? He wasn't my friend," said Jason. "He was a trigger-happy idiot."

"He was a human being," said Jessica.

**BETSY** felt like the girl on the cover of a corny romance novel as she strolled arm-in-arm with Grant through a field of riotous wildflowers. Bluish mountains loomed in the distance against a clear blue sky. As they approached a group of log cabins, Jessica and Jason came out to meet them.

"Hey, Prez, how's it going?" Jessica asked.

"I told you not to call me that," Grant responded. "Don't make me send the Secret Service after you."

"Yes, sir," Jessica responded with a laugh, standing up straight and saluting.

Betsy was happy to see Jessica looking so well; she'd liked the girl since the moment they met. Grant's inauguration day had been such a blur; it seemed like three days put together. Right after the speech, Grant had whisked her off to Arizona on Air Force One. His first concern had been to find survivors and assure their safety. By the time they landed, Grant had arranged for a hotel suite next door to the hospital so the other survivors could be close to Jason. And he had spoken to David Singh at great length over the phone.

Betsy didn't have much time to talk to him at all, but when he finished talking to David, she had snatched the opportunity to ask him her most burning question: "Why didn't you trust me enough to tell me what you were doing? Did you really think I would give you away?"

"I'm really sorry I had to do that," Grant had said. "It was very hard for me. And when you quit, when you thought I was the most despicable man on the face of the earth, I almost told you then, but I couldn't. It wasn't because I didn't trust you. Not at all. But we were both safer that way. Presidents are not the ultimate power that they pretend to be. They're almost always the puppets of far more powerful people whose names the public wouldn't recognize. And those people like to know who their puppets are. If they didn't have my phones bugged, my office bugged, and my house bugged, I'd be very surprised. Even when I was alone, I had to play the part, day and night. And I can tell you, it wasn't easy." He chuckled. "Someday I'll have to tell you how I got my hands on an 'Iron Web' T-shirt for the speech without anyone knowing. Now *that* was a challenge."

It was unnerving for Betsy to meet David Singh after the way he had been portrayed in the news, and she felt deeply ashamed of her own participation in that portrayal. These people were so astonishingly different from what she had believed they were, she almost felt as if she was in a *Twilight Zone* episode.

The news of the Miracle Girl was all over the country already, with her eye-witness confirmation of the shocking revelations of that morning. When Betsy first met her, she was in the hotel suite hiding from reporters. Betsy could see that the girl's happiness was dampened by her concern for her friend, and she resolved to pamper and distract her as much as possible. Fortunately, Jason turned the corner the next day, and was sitting up eating when the President came in to meet him.

Grant and David, who had become instant friends over the phone, met with the hearty embrace of old comrades. The two men were as different as could be, in looks and personality both. Betsy could hardly imagine a more polite, gentle, considerate man than David. But Grant? He'd always been bold and charismatic, of course, but now it seemed as if a heavy lid had been removed, and his personality was bubbling over. He wasn't faking anymore. He wasn't mincing words. He was laughing louder, and using coarser language. In other words, Betsy thought, he's thoroughly enjoying being himself for the first time in years. And much as she liked this new man, this added to the whole *Twilight Zone* tenor of the day.

Feeling exhausted by the evening, Betsy realized that her day had actually been two hours longer than it should have been, due to her flight west over two time zones. Ever since getting off of Air Force One, Grant had refused to use any government-funded limousines, planes, or anything else. However, a few Secret Service agents, whom Betsy suspected were men that Grant had known from before, had chosen to stay with him, and were constantly on high alert.

"Are those guys ever going to leave us alone?" Betsy had asked, as Grant's bodyguards were carefully surveying every inch of the hotel suite they had reserved near the hospital.

"What would we do if they did?" Grant had asked in return.

"I'm sure I don't know. What would *you* do?"

"Something I've wanted to do for the last three years," he had said. Then he had turned her face toward his and kissed her.

Now, so many months later, the memory of that moment still made tremors run through Betsy's body, and she clung a little tighter to Grant's arm to keep her balance. They were approaching a group of five cabins, three of which looked brand new, with a couple dozen people milling around them. Grant announced loudly, "If anyone wants news of the outside world, I'll be giving my official weekly report in ten minutes."

He led Betsy into a large log building, which had been under construction when Betsy last visited. She expected the inside to be as rustic as the outside, and was surprised to see smooth white walls and a polished floor of pine boards stained to the warm brown of cherry wood. On both sides of the room, she was amazed to see beautifully carved church pews that looked like mahogany. "Where on earth did they get those?" she asked Grant.

"Salvage," he said. "Someone was in the right place at the right time. Lucky find, wasn't it?"

She remembered hearing about the new building from Sandy, who said she was itching to get a real stage built in there, and to get some culture going in this "little podunk town," as she called it. Sandy wouldn't admit it, but Betsy knew that she missed the art and culture of Washington.

"What news from the front?" asked a young man as he came in the front door behind them.

"When the others get here, I'll tell you," Grant answered.

Over the next few minutes, about thirty people filed in, many of them smiling and nodding to Grant and Betsy as they passed, and exchanging warm greetings with each other. Jessica and Jason came in, and Heather, looking tanned and well, and David and Tasha, and Doug with his whole family. And many others she'd never seen before. They all settled into the church pews, still chatting, as Grant walked to the front of the room.

"Okay, I'll try to make this quick," he began. Betsy started to sit down, but Grant beckoned her to him. "The most important thing that has happened in the last month is that I married my secretary, Betsy. Betsy, wave to all the nice wackos." There were chuckles and waves from the audience. Blushing, Betsy looked out at the crowd, and was happy to see Sandy, looking as she always looked, leaning in the doorway, smiling, with Veronica at her side.

"Let me find my list, so I don't forget anything," Grant said, pulling a folded piece of paper out of his pocket. Betsy took her seat. "Okay, here we go. Here are the top stories—from *reliable* sources, *not* the mainstream media—in no particular order. Item number one. In the past few weeks, the governors of California and New Jersey declared martial law." There were murmurs from the crowd. "To make a long story short, it didn't work out well for those in power. Things got bloody, government buildings were burned, lots of civilians and cops shot each other, and then the martial law ended. The reports I've heard say that at this point, some people are considering anyone wearing a police uniform in those states to be fair game. Cops are quitting in droves."

He scribbled a note to himself and continued. "Item number two. So far, forty-seven IRS offices have been burned to the ground." This brought several spontaneous cheers from the audience. "As a result, the bureaucrats stopped showing up to work. As far as I can tell, the IRS is completely out of business, as of one week ago."

At this, applause burst out, almost drowning out one spectator's comment: "Does that mean I don't get my refund check?" Several people close enough to hear him laughed. When the noise had died down a bit, someone else said, "I thought you fired them all anyway."

"Yeah, sorry," Grant said, "I keep forgetting that lots of you still don't know the whole story. You sure wouldn't have gotten it from the loyalist media. The crooks had a bunch of emergency sessions, made up a few new legal principles, and declared my Executive Orders to be invalid. Somewhere around half of the bureaucrats came back for a while, probably just desperate to get a paycheck again. But as I said, the IRS has now ceased to exist."

"Item three. Half of Congress is missing. At least a couple of congressmen have actually been assassinated, but the rest are probably just hiding." There was a murmur, and Betsy could see on the faces in the crowd that some people thought this was a shame, while others seemed to approve. "Either way, Congress has not been in session, at least not publicly, for two weeks now."

"Item four. Oops, I should have done this first, because this is probably why Congress is M.I.A. Several groups, apparently including some active and reserve military folk, forced their way into various offices at the Pentagon, the CIA offices in Langley, and some others, and seized a whole lot of classified documents. They're now all posted on what is left of the internet, and the highlights are being circulated across the country as a pamphlet. As you can probably imagine, the documents expose quite a bit of conspiracy, murder, fraud, and so on, courtesy of the federal government. The conspiracy theorists among you will have a field day with some of the stuff that's been uncovered about 9/11, JFK, Pearl Harbor, Oklahoma City, the Cuban Missile Crisis, the federal income tax hoax, and lots of other stuff—including, of course, that terrorist cult known as the Iron Web." This again brought chuckles from the audience.

"Item five. Washington, D.C., pretty much looks like a war zone now. It seems almost all of the control freaks ran away, and the, uh, less affluent elements of the city decided it was time for some riots and looting." He wrote another note to himself on the paper he was holding. "I haven't been there myself since about a week after my little speech. I did as much damage as I could to the Fourth Reich, before having to flee for my life. You've probably all heard of the three attempts to kill me—well, the three that came close enough to be worth mentioning. Apparently there's still quite a bit of debate over the question of whether I'm still the President or not. They're fishing for some legal excuse to declare VP Conrad the new Prez."

"So he wasn't in on your little charade?" Doug asked.

"No, couldn't risk trying to have another spy," Grant answered. "Conrad was just another political crook like the rest of them. Never saw it coming."

"Item six. You already know about the small patches of freedom sprouting up all over this country. We've already established trade with twenty-seven free communities, at last count. Well, apparently now it's also happening in England, Australia, and Canada."

"Wow, didn't know the Canucks had it in them," came a comment from Doug, who sat in the front row.

"Apparently so," Grant answered. "Good for them. So the Iron Web has gone international." He paused for a moment, looking at his notes. "Oh, and there are now three new free towns consisting entirely of former federal prisoners. Incidentally, those towns seem to have very low crime rates, like all the other free communities."

"Let's see. Item seven. Two more Federal Reserve buildings have been blown up. They were given warning, and no one was inside."

"Pity," came the flippant remark from Doug.

"A few big names in the banking industry and the Federal Reserve have turned up dead recently," Grant continued. "No one has claimed credit yet."

"I wouldn't mind the credit," Doug said.

"Shut up or I'll have you arrested," Grant joked.

"Tyrant," Doug muttered.

"A couple of those deaths may have been suicides," Grant continued. "As you know, the dollar is basically worthless now—not that it was worth much before. Even average Joes are starting to catch on to the idea of trading with silver and gold, or whatever else they happen to have that's portable and valuable. A few states are now beginning to issue their own currencies, but they don't seem to be catching on very well. Much of the economy has screeched to a halt as people try to figure out how to keep the world turning without using Federal Reserve notes."

"Item eight. Something really weird happened up in New Hampshire that I hardly know how to describe. A week ago, in several different municipalities, local governments had their hearings interrupted by groups of armed folk showing up. Here's the weird part: the armed folk brought along a bunch of money, mostly silver and gold, and gave it to the governments, along with a declaration that basically said, if you need money, *ask* us for it. But don't *demand* it from us, and don't try to tax us, or we'll shoot you. And in the following days, a bunch of volunteers—unarmed this time, so as not to intimidate people—went around, door to door, telling all the people in the area that there would be no more property taxes, but asking the people if they wanted to voluntarily contribute for the things the local governments usually handled. Oddly—and this even surprised me—all but one of the towns received more in donations than they had ever collected in taxes."

"But who will build the roads?" Doug asked in a mock whiny voice, bringing chuckles from many. Betsy assumed it was an inside joke of some sort.

"Item nine. When I fired the ICE, it naturally triggered a huge influx from Mexico. That has now died down. In fact, a lot have now gone back home. The ones who wanted free handouts here found out that there aren't any anymore—well, except in a few states, like California, which are still clinging to socialism and going bankrupt because of it. And a lot of the Mexicans who just came here to earn an honest living decided to go back to Mexico and give their own government a well-deserved kick in the pants. The Mexican government is on the brink of collapse."

"Item ten—almost done now. For the third time, what's left of the United States Congress has sent a letter addressed to 'The Iron Web,' whoever that is," Grant said, holding up a piece of paper, "agreeing to meet with us and hear our demands, so that we may begin negotiations."

"Demands? What demands?" asked a solidly built, middle-aged man with a ponytail in the back of the room.

"Does 'Piss off!' count as a demand?" asked Doug, and several people chuckled.

"Apparently they're still having trouble grasping the fact that we don't care what they think, we don't want anything from them, and we don't need their permission to be free. I guess they've been treated like royalty for so long that the concept is incomprehensible to them. Well, there's one for the circular file," Grant said, and crumpled up the letter and dropped it in the waste basket, an action which a dozen or so people applauded.

"Last but not least, item eleven. I don't know the details, but apparently for the last three days there has been heavy fighting at a U.S. Army base in Texas. The fighting seems to be between the Army and itself, or maybe the National Guard against the Army. Again, I don't know the details, but there seems to be a fair amount of mutiny going on, and not just in Texas. There's even a rumor that a former general, in addition to all his other medals, is now wearing an Iron Web lapel pin. I'm not sure if it's true or not." There was a murmur from the crowd.

"Oh, I almost forgot. You already knew that within the last two months, New Hampshire, Wyoming, Texas, Montana, Colorado, and for some reason Florida, all seceded from the union. Well, now you can add Arizona, Nevada and South Dakota to the list."

"Don't forget Maine," came a voice from the back of the room.

"What? When did that happen?" Grant asked.

"I have family up there, and the state legislature—what's left of it, anyway—just passed the bill, and the governor signed it."

"Interesting. And it sounds as if a bunch of states, faced with the very real possibility of violent revolt, have suddenly decided to be libertarian. They're repealing taxes and socialist programs right and left. We'll see how that turns out." Grant folded up his notes and put them in his pocket. "Anyway, that's all I have. While we're all here, does anyone have any more news to report?"

"Yeah. In more important news, Jessica grows the best tomatoes I've ever tasted," said a middle-aged, curly-haired blond woman in the third row.

"And the fish are biting down by the south bend of the river today," added a young boy in the second row.

"If anyone wants to help, tomorrow we're starting on a cabin for Drew and Stacy," Heather added. "They came all the way from Australia, looking for freedom."

"Ya know, I like the news around here a lot more than what the rest of the world is talking about," concluded Grant, folding up his notes and putting them in his pocket. For a moment he had an expression of concern. He looked at Betsy, and the stress in his face evaporated. "Well, my dear, shall we stroll on back to our own little extremist compound?" He offered her his arm. Smiling, she took it.

# Other Books by Larken Rose

## How To Be a Successful Tyrant
*(The Megalomaniac Manifesto)*

The oppression of the masses has evolved into a detailed science, if not an art form. Written as a "how to" manual for aspiring tyrants, the true purpose of this book is to give the people the playbook of the megalomaniacs of the world. Only by understanding how tyrants operate—how they pose as saviors, how they portray their oppressions as necessary or even virtuous, and how they use fear and envy to pit one group against another—can the common folk ever hope to stop falling prey to the schemes and deceptions employed by the power-mongers of the world.

## Kicking the Dragon
*(Confessions of a Tax Heretic)*

Written mostly in prison, this book details the author's eight-year odyssey into the deceptive nature of the "federal income tax." Covering his research into the largest financial fraud in history, his various encounters with the IRS, and the mock trial that put him in prison for a crime he didn't commit—a crime the prosecutors and the judge all *knew* he hadn't committed—this book exposes the ugly truth about what "our" government has become.

**For more information, visit
www.LarkenRose.com**